Irish
Fairy
Tales

General Editor: Jake Jackson

Associate Editor: Catherine Taylor

**FLAME TREE
PUBLISHING**

This is a FLAME TREE Book

FLAME TREE PUBLISHING
6 Melbray Mews
Fulham, London SW6 3NS
United Kingdom
www.flametreepublishing.com

First published 2020
Copyright © 2020 Flame Tree Publishing Ltd

22 24 23 21
3 5 7 9 8 6 4 2

ISBN: 978-1-83964-223-4

Contributors, authors, editors and sources for this series include:
Loren Auerbach, Norman Bancroft-Hunt, George W. Bateman, John D. Batten, James
S. de Benneville, E.M. Berens, Katharine Berry Judson, W.H.I. Bleek and L. C. Lloyd, Laura
Bulbeck, J. F. Campbell, T. Crofton Croker, Jeremiah Curtin, F. Hadland Davis, Elphinstone
Dayrell, O.B. Duane, Dr Ray Dunning, W.W. Gibbings, Alfred Perceval Graves, William
Elliot Griffis, H. A. Guerber, Lafcadio Hearn, Stephen Hodge, James A. Honey M.D., Jake
Jackson, Joseph Jacobs, Judith John, Michael Kerrigan, Andrew Lang, Edmund Leamy, J.W.
Mackail, Alexander Mackenzie, Donald Mackenzie, Chris McNab, D.R. McAnally, Minnie
Martin, A.B. Mitford (Lord Redesdale), Yei Theodora Ozaki, Arthur Rackham, Professor
James Riordan, Sara Robson, Lewis Spence, Henry M. Stanley, Capt. C.H. Stigand, Rachel
Storm, K.E. Sullivan, François-Marie Arouet a.k.a. Voltaire, E.A. Wallis Budge, Dr Roy Willis,
Epiphanius Wilson, Alice Werner, E.T.C. Werner, Morris Meredith Williams, W.B. Yeats.

A copy of the CIP data for this book is available from the British Library.

Printed and bound by Clays Ltd, Elcograf S.p.A

Contents

Foreword

NO EUROPEAN COUNTRY has a richer storytelling heritage than does Ireland. Like their counterparts in other cultures, Irish fairy tales typically represent a half dozen different genres, four of which are included in the current collection: myths, legends, magic tales and literary fairy tales.

In common usage the word 'myth' carries a number of meanings, including the connotation of falsehood, for example: "Politicians' claims are only myths." Folklorists, anthropologists, and historians of culture assign a more dignified meaning to the term, designating with it a body of stories and beliefs that give meaning to some of life's greatest mysteries. The creation of the earth, the nature of good and evil, and the ambiguities of human existence are among the subjects covered by traditional myths. Their characters include deities, demons, superhuman heroes, and treacherous enemies. To the generations that create and disseminate them, myths both define and reflect a value system akin to religion.

Irish myths originated with the Celts, whose ancestors migrated to the British Isles from central Europe, beginning around 700 BC. Ireland's isolation shielded it from Roman colonization and other outside influences, thus helping to preserve Celtic traditions. However, most early Irish myths were not written down until the eighth century or later. The Christian monks who first recorded them undoubtedly removed or altered many of the stories' 'heathen' tenets.

Stories in the current anthology derived from ancient Irish myths include 'The Knighting of Cuculain' and 'The Birth of Oisín'. They feature Ireland's greatest mythological heroes, such as Cú Chulainn (variously spelled), who is often compared to Hercules and Siegfried of Greco-Roman and Germanic traditions.

As used by folklorists, the term 'legend' refers to a narrative that claims to be true. Such accounts often assert credibility by including authentic place names and plausible personal names. For example, the 'Bewitched Butter' tale begins: "Not far from Rathmullen lived, last spring, a family called Hanlon; and in a farm-house, some fields distant, people named Dogherty." Sometimes similar accounts are attributed to different locations and thus are known as migratory legends. For example: 'The Brewery of Eggshells' relates how a fairy changeling is exposed when he expresses surprise at the mother's feigned brewing of eggshells. Comparable tales are told throughout the British Isles, and across continental Europe, always claiming local authenticity.

The aforementioned legends are typical in that they offer supernatural solutions to real-life problems. A family cow ceases to give milk, due to theft by a witch. A human child fails to thrive, because it is actually a fairy changeling. In each instance the ostensible cause is discovered and a magical solution is effected. We no longer believe in witches that steal milk, and in fairies that replace healthy human children with misshapen imps, nor that there are magical charms offering protection against such misfortune. Previous generations found comfort in legends that described such relief, even if these tales were based more on hope than on fact.

The stories known as fairy tales do not necessarily feature fairies and might thus more appropriately be labelled magic tales. Unlike legends, magic tales do not typically claim to be true, but admittedly take place in a realm of make-believe. These stories often provide fantasy solutions to realistic problems. 'Smallhead and the King's Son' offers a good example. The heroine, nicknamed Smallhead by her stepsisters, with magical help survives their persecution and in the end marries a king. This plot resembles the universally loved tale 'Cinderella'. The magic tales of most countries have parallels in other cultures, and Irish stories are no exception. Similarly, 'The Haughty Princess' echoes the basic plot of Shakespeare's The Taming of the Shrew and closely resembles the Grimm brothers' 'King Thrushbeard'.

Our final category is the literary fairy tale. Here the story is not drawn directly from oral tradition, but is instead the invention of a known author, for example Hans Christian Andersen, the famous Danish storyteller. Literary fairy tales, while drawing on traditional motifs and situations, are usually more finely crafted than their orally transmitted counterparts. Examples from the current collection include 'The Enchanted Cave' and 'The Little White Cat', both by Edmund Leamy.

D.L. Ashliman

Introduction to Irish Fairy Tales & Folklore

The Fairy Folk were always there, the Irish said, in a dimension just beyond our own. Sometimes, though, they'd cross over to cast a spell or snatch a child. Mostly they stayed out of sight beneath the earth, in little 'fairy mounds' or *sidhe* – but the way these projected into the air above was a constant reminder of their presence close at hand.

Hence, for the Irish poet Paul Muldoon (*To Ireland, I*, 2008), the 'central tenet of the Irish imagination, that what you see is *never* what you get.' Our earthly order and a more magical and mystic one 'are separated by a cloth, albeit a tattered one. There's a discrepancy between outward appearance and inward reality ... what I'm tempted to call "Eriny".'

Pushed to the Margins

In industrializing Britain – even in the Germany of the Brothers Grimm – Fairy Tales became entertainment at an early date. And entertainment for children at that – even if it isn't necessarily too difficult to find darker anxieties beneath the surface in such stories. (In the English context, indeed, we see Shakespeare shaping the modern idea of fairyhood before our eyes in the cute and winsome spirits of *A Midsummer Night's Dream, c.* 1595.)

Fairyland

Ireland was very different. An agrarian society till very recently, its people were influenced from day to day by factors (seasons, weather, harvests, crop failures ...) that were ceasing to affect more urbanized populations.

The idea of the fairy folk still had a role to play. As the Irish did for the English, who had come to set the cultural terms in the British Isles as a whole and who had started to see the Irish as in some ways fairy-like themselves: fey and dreamy; 'poetic' but essentially simple souls.

A patronizing view, and one with which many in Ireland were to become impatient. Fewer, though – and with less anger – than we might now expect. For as Britain made its way in the world behind the banners of Modernity and Progress, Ireland's other-worldly air became a source of pride. Like modern minority campaigners 'reappropriating' a pejorative term, nineteenth-century nationalists embraced their country's folk traditions.

Far from showing 'backwardness', they felt, the survival of the ancient myths were evidence of integrity; the sign of a nation that had remained true to its origins. Both in Britain and in Ireland, then, Irish fairy tales were seen as revealing the essential identity of the country they had come from in a way that stories from other cultures mostly weren't.

Celtic Currents

The 'Celtic' background of the Irish was to some extent a confection. Certainly, in a complex and often violent history, any direct links to the historical 'Celts' – an Iron Age culture of central European origin – had long since been lost.

But, as raiders and invaders, the Celts had indeed fanned out across Europe in the second half of the first millennium BCE. Or, at least, a warrior elite had expanded across the continent, bringing with them a 'cultural complex' which local populations then adopted, including everything from jewellery and weapon design to religious practices – and myths.

In an Ireland largely left alone by the Romans, these stories had continued to flourish in the oral tradition, until they were written down by medieval monks. These scribes loved the legends, it appears, but for religious reasons demoted gods and goddesses to the status of mortal human heroes, kings and queens. Or, of course, of fairies, their divine powers reframed as fanciful enchantment.

Dusk as Dawn

However tenuous the Celtic connection, it took on immense importance to those who wanted to distinguish the Irish from the Anglo-Saxons they saw as their oppressors. In this context, the great old mythic cycles and the fairy tales they inspired, were seen as much more than a literary resource.

Artists, writers, politicians and, perhaps most famously, the poet William Butler Yeats (1865–1939), made folk culture – and specifically fairy lore – the cornerstone for the great 'Irish Literary Revival'. It is ironic (or, Muldoon might say, 'Erinic') that this 'revival' (which suggests a flaring up into renewed energy and vigour) was also referred to as the 'Celtic Twilight' (which implies a fading out), but this paradox was at the movement's heart.

Britannia's patriots might rule the waves; Ireland's only too clearly didn't. Hence the melancholy, the minor key. The national consciousness they now expressed was underpinned by nostalgia and a sense of loss. In Yeats' poem 'The Stolen Child' (1899), the Fairies may not be benign but they offer an escape from historical realities that cannot be borne:

> *Come away, O human child!*
> *To the waters and the wild,*
> *With a faery, hand in hand,*
> *For the world's more full of weeping than you can understand.*

Poetic Promise

Much of what happens in fairy tales may be unsettling, even sinister, but at the very least it opens up the vision of a different world. Yeats and his friends took the romantic wistfulness and the sense of mystery and of strange possibility that inform the fairy tale, and made these the basis for a new idea of nationhood.

Not that every Irish fairy tale should be read as an allegory of the independence struggle. Most of course long predated modern times. But the nineteenth-century Irish readers who curled up with these stories will have enjoyed them with a special pride, and invested them with significance on that account. Just as, for English readers oppressed by the feeling that modern urban life had been drained of mystery and enchantment, this romantic Ireland represented a 'land of lost content'.

Enchantment and Emotion

Hence the special resonance with which this collection thrills. So much feeling is invested in every story, every character, every image. A love story like 'The Twelve Wild Geese' offers not just empty escapism but the promise of real hope in what seems a situation of despair. A femme fatale and a suffering soul in one, Deirdre speaks to us across the centuries, from the pages of the 'Ulster Cycle', an eternal archetype and a living, loving woman. The stories of Fin, Cuculain and Oisin all spring from the same heroic vein – a tradition fit to stand alongside the Epic of Gilgamesh and the works of Homer and of Virgil.

Then there's the whole gamut of miscellaneous supernatural lore: the mischievous leprechaun (of course); the shape-shifting púca or pooka, bringer of both good and ill; the shrieking bean sí or banshee, bearer of the news of death, and the murúch or merrow, an Irish mermaid. We find all sorts of supernatural forces marshalled here: from the 'evil eye' that bewitches a poor woman's butter to the pudding that spontaneously sets to dancing and the ghosts that haunt some of the other stories here.

Collected with Care

Those who collected these fairy tales and adapted them for publication, did so for a range of different reasons. The Co. Wexford-born bookseller and folklorist Patrick Kennedy (1801–73), for instance, was the son of a well-off peasant who had 'made good'. He had a clear commitment to promoting the education of the poor and to celebrating the cultural heritage of his forebears.

Few Irish Catholics were in a position to devote their lives to studies of this kind, however: most collectors belonged to the Protestant

'Anglo-Irish' landlord class. Hence, as already noted, the ever-present suspicion of condescension. But early collectors like Thomas Crofton Croker (1798–1854), to whose patronizing tone Yeats himself was to take exception, seem nevertheless to have loved their Irish homeland. Despite the sometimes-justified criticisms, moreover, they did their honest best to record a much-admired tradition before it died.

Back from the Brink

There was a real risk of this happening, given the upheavals attendant on the Great Famine of the 1840s. A million died; a million more driven to emigrate. For those who survived, and managed to remain in Ireland, there was still wide-scale dislocation and confusion to be coped with as families and village communities were broken up.

The Famine had hit hardest in the country's poorer, remoter, more westerly regions which had been the heart of the Irish-speaking Gaeltacht till this time. Between death and emigration, Ireland lost a quarter of its people, but it appears to have lost more like half its Irish speakers. In the decades that followed, the language continued to be marginalized by 'modernizing' education. With it went much of a wider Gaelic culture which obviously included a stock of stories.

Hence in part the growing radicalism of collectors like 'Lady Wilde' (1821–96), who recorded the story of 'The Horned Women' here. 'Speranza' ('Hope'), as she called herself, was an outspoken nationalist writer, though to us of course she is more famous as Oscar's mother. Standish Hayes O'Grady (1832–1915) and Letitia McClintock both belonged to the 'Ascendancy' but also to the 'Celtic Twilight' movement of the fin-de-siècle.

Telling Testimony

A fairy tale isn't just a narrative, as diverting and exciting as it might be. It is inevitably a window on another age and frequently a message from somewhere deep within a society's collective psyche, a reflection of its oldest anxieties and discontents. The Irish fairy tale is all these things and more. An oral tradition in the deeper past; written down and reinterpreted in more recent times, it enshrines an entire history; whole centuries of hope and aspiration. It also, as Muldoon says, represents an attitude, a cultural cast of mind for which reality is really never the whole story.

Romance & Tragedy

Fairy tales are often grounded in the pursuit, and perils, of love. Not all of them end in happiness and wedded bliss, as demonstrated by the story, from the Ulster Cycle, of the doomed Deirdre, one of the most famous tragic heroines in Irish legend.

The version of Deirdre's story given here is joined by other stories of adventure and young love. Some are packed with all the elements you could wish for from a fairy tale: magic, royalty, giants, quests and serpents ('The Little White Cat'), while others are moral tales at heart ('The Haughty Princess').

The Enchanted Cave

❧

A LONG, LONG TIME AGO, Prince Cuglas, master of the hounds to the high King of Erin, set out from Tara to the chase. As he was leaving the palace the light mists were drifting away from the hill-tops, and the rays of the morning sun were falling aslant on the grinan or sunny bower of the Princess Ailinn. Glancing towards it the prince doffed his plumed and jewelled hunting-cap, and the princess answered his salute by a wave of her little hand, that was as white as a wild rose in the hedges in June, and leaning from her bower, she watched the huntsman until his tossing plumes were hidden by the green waving branches of the woods.

The Princess Ailinn was over head and ears in love with Cuglas, and Cuglas was over head and ears in love with the Princess Ailinn, and he believed that never was summer morning half as bright, or as sweet, or as fair as she. The glimpse which he had just caught of her filled his heart with delight, and almost put all thought of hunting out of his head, when suddenly the tuneful cries of the hounds, answered by a hundred echoes from the groves, broke upon his ear.

The dogs had started a dappled deer that bounded away through the forest. The prince, spurring his gallant steed, pushed on in eager pursuit.

On through the forest sped the deer, through soft, green, secret ways and flowery dells, then out from the forest, up heathery hills, and over long stretches of moorland, and across brown rushing streams, sometimes in view of the hounds, sometimes lost to sight, but always ahead of them.

All day long the chase continued, and at last, when the sun was sinking, the dogs were close upon the panting deer, and the prince believed he was about to secure his game, when the deer suddenly disappeared through the mouth of a cave which opened before him. The dogs followed at his heels, and the prince endeavoured to rein in his steed, but the impetuous animal bore him on, and soon was clattering over the stony floor of the cave in perfect darkness. Cuglas could hear ahead of him the cries of the hounds growing fainter and fainter, as they increased the distance between them and him. Then the cries ceased altogether, and the only sound the prince heard was the noise of his horse's hoofs sounding in the hollow cave. Once more he endeavoured to check his career, but the reins broke in his hands, and in that instant the prince felt the horse had taken a plunge into a gulf, and was sinking down and down, as a stone cast from the summit of a cliff sinks down to the sea. At last the horse struck the ground again, and the prince was almost thrown out of his saddle, but he succeeded in regaining his seat. Then on through the darkness galloped the steed, and when he came into the light the prince's eyes were for some time unable to bear it. But when he got used to the brightness he saw he was galloping over a grassy plain, and in the distance he perceived the hounds rushing towards a wood faintly visible through a luminous summer haze. The prince galloped on, and as he approached the wood he saw coming towards him a comely champion, wearing a shining brown cloak, fastened by a bright bronze spear-like brooch, and bearing a white hazel wand in one hand, and a single-edged sword with a hilt made from the tooth of a sea-horse in the other; and the prince knew by the dress of the champion, and by his wand and sword, that he was a royal herald. As the herald came close to him the prince's steed stopped of his own accord.

"You are welcome, Cuglas," said the herald, "and I have been sent by the Princess Crede to greet you and to lead you to her court, where you have been so long expected."

"I know not how this may be," said Cuglas.

"How it has come about I shall tell you as we go along," said the herald. "The Princess Crede is the Queen of the Floating Island. And it chanced, once upon a day, when she was visiting her fairy kinsmen, who dwell in one of the pleasant hills that lie near Tara, she saw you with the high king and princes and nobles of Erin following the chase. And seeing you her heart went out to you, and wishing to bring you to her court, she sent one of her nymphs, in the form of a deer, to lure you on through the cave, which is the entrance to this land."

"I am deeply honoured by the preference shown me by the princess," said Cuglas, "but I may not tarry in her court; for above in Erin there is the Lady Ailinn, the loveliest of all the ladies who grace the royal palace, and before the princess and chiefs of Erin she has promised to be my bride."

"Of that I know not," said the herald; "but a true champion, like you, cannot, I know, refuse to come with me to the court of the Princess Crede."

As the herald had said these words the prince and he were on the verge of the wood, and they entered upon a mossy pathway that broadened out as they advanced until it was as wide as one of the great roads of Erin. Before they had gone very far the prince heard the tinkling of silver bells in the distance, and almost as soon as he heard them he saw coming up towards him a troop of warriors on coal black steeds. All the warriors wore helmets of shining silver, and cloaks of blue silk. And on the horses' breasts were crescents of silver, on which were hung tiny silver bells, shaking out music with the motion of the horses. As the prince approached the champions they lowered their spears, and dividing in two lines the prince and the herald passed between the ranks, and the champions, forming again, followed on behind the prince.

At last they passed through the wood, and they found themselves on a green plain, speckled with flowers, and they had not gone far when the prince saw coming towards him a hundred champions on snow-white steeds, and around the breasts of the steeds were crescents of gold, from which were hanging little golden bells. The warriors all wore golden helmets, and the shafts of their shining spears were of gold, and golden sandals on their feet, and yellow silken mantles fell down over their shoulders. And when the prince came near them they lowered their lances, and then they turned their horses' heads around and marched before him. And it was not long until above the pleasant jingle of the bells the prince heard the measured strains of music, and he saw coming towards him a band of harpers, dressed in green and gold, and when the harpers had saluted the prince they marched in front of the cavalcade, playing all the time, and it was not long until they came to a stream that ran like a blue riband around the foot of a green hill, on the top of which was a sparkling palace; the stream was crossed by a golden bridge, so narrow that the horsemen had to go two-by-two. The herald asked the prince to halt and to allow all the champions to go before him; and the cavalcade ascended the hill, the sunlight brightly glancing on helmet and on lance, and when it reached the palace the horsemen filed around the walls.

When at length the prince and herald crossed the bridge and began to climb the hill, the prince thought he felt the ground moving under them, and on looking back he could see no sign of the golden bridge, and the blue stream had already become as wide as a great river, and was becoming wider every second.

"You are on the floating island now," said the herald, "and before you is the palace of the Princess Crede."

At that moment the queen came out through the palace door, and the prince was so dazzled by her beauty, that only for the golden bracelet he wore upon his right arm, under the sleeve of his silken tunic, he might almost have forgotten the Princess Ailinn. This bracelet was made by the dwarfs who dwell in the heart of the Scandinavian Mountains, and was sent with other costly presents by the King of Scandinavia to the King of Erin, and he gave it to the princess, and it was the virtue of this bracelet, that whoever was wearing it could not forget the person who gave it to him, and it could never be loosened from the arm by any art or magic spell; but if the wearer, even for a single moment, liked anyone better than the person who gave it to him, that very moment the bracelet fell off from the arm and could never again be fastened on. And when the princess promised her hand in marriage to the Prince Cuglas, she closed the bracelet on his arm.

The fairy queen knew nothing about the bracelet, and she hoped that before the prince was long in the floating island he would forget all about the princess.

"You are welcome, Cuglas," said the queen, as she held out her hand, and, Cuglas having thanked her for her welcome, they entered the palace together.

"You must be weary after your long journey," said the queen. "My page will lead you to your apartments, where a bath of the cool blue waters of the lake has been made ready for you, and when you have taken your bath the pages will lead you to the banquet hall, where the feast is spread."

At the feast the prince was seated beside the queen, and she talked to him of all the pleasures that were in store for him in fairyland, where pain, and sickness, and sorrow, and old age, are unknown, and where every rosy hour that flies is brighter than the one that has fled before it. And when the feast was ended the queen opened the dance with the prince, and it was not until the moon was high above the floating island that the prince retired to rest.

He was so tired after his journey and the dancing that he fell into a sound sleep. When he awoke the next morning the sun was shining brightly, and he heard outside the palace the jingle of bells and the music of baying hounds, and his heart was stirred by memories of the many pleasant days on which he had led the chase over the plains and through the green woods of Tara.

He looked out through the window, and he saw all the fairy champions mounted on their steeds ready for the chase, and at their head the fairy queen. And at that moment the pages came to say the queen wished to know if he would join them, and the prince went out and found his steed ready saddled and bridled, and they spent the day hunting in the forest that stretched away for miles behind the palace, and the night in feasting and dancing.

When the prince awoke the following morning he was summoned by the pages to the presence of the queen. The prince found the queen on the lawn outside the palace surrounded by her court.

"We shall go on the lake today, Cuglas," said the queen, and taking his arm she led him along the water's edge, all the courtiers following.

When she was close to the water she waved her wand, and in a second a thousand boats, shining like glass, shot up from beneath the lake and set their bows against the bank. The queen and Cuglas stepped into one, and when they were seated two fairy harpers took their places in the prow. All the other boats were soon thronged by fairies, and then the queen waved her wand again, and an awning of purple silk rose over the boat, and silken awning of various colours over the others, and the royal boat moved off from the bank followed by all the rest, and in every boat sat a harper with a golden harp, and when the queen waved her wand for the third time, the harpers struck the trembling chords, and to the sound of the delightful music the boats glided over the sunlit lake. And on they went until they approached the mouth of a gentle river sliding down between banks clad with trees. Up the river, close to the bank and under the drooping trees, they sailed, and when they came to a bend in the river, from which the lake could be no longer seen, they pushed their prows in against the bank, and the queen and Cuglas, and all the party, left the boats and went on under the trees until they came to a mossy glade.

Then the queen waved her wand, and silken couches were spread under the trees, and she and Cuglas sat on one apart from the others, and the courtiers took their places in proper order.

And the queen waved her wand again, and wind shook the trees above them, and the most luscious fruit that was ever tasted fell down into their hands; and when the feast was over there was dancing in the glades to the music of the harps, and when they were tired dancing they set out for the boats, and the moon was rising above the trees as they sailed away over the lake, and it was not long until they reached the bank below the fairy palace.

Well, between hunting in the forest, and sailing over the lake, and dancing in the greenwood glade and in the banquet hall, the days passed, but all the time the prince was thinking of the Princess Ailinn, and one moonlit night, when he was lying awake on his couch thinking of her, a shadow was suddenly cast on the floor.

The prince looked towards the window, and what should he see sitting on the sill outside but a little woman tapping the pane with a golden bodkin.

The prince jumped from his couch and opened the window, and the little woman floated on the moonbeams into the room and sat down on the floor.

"You are thinking of the Princess Ailinn," said the little woman.

"I never think of anyone else," said the prince.

"I know that," said the little woman, "and it's because of your love for each other, and because her mother was a friend to me in the days gone by, that I have come here to try and help you; but there is not much time for talking, the night advances. At the bank below a boat awaits you. Step into it and it will lead you to the mainland, and when you reach it you will find before you a path that will take you to the green fields of Erin and the plains of Tara. I know you will have to face danger. I know not what kind of danger; but whatever it may be do not draw your sword before you tread upon the mainland, for if you do you shall never reach it, and the boat will come back again to the floating island; and now go and may luck go with you;" and saying this the little woman climbed up the moonbeams and disappeared.

The prince left the palace and descended to the lake, and there before him he saw a glistening boat; he stepped into it, and the boat went on and on beneath the moon, and at last he saw the mainland, and he could trace a winding pathway going away from the shore. The sight filled his heart with joy, but suddenly the milk-white moonshine died away, and looking up to the sky he saw the moon turning fiery red, and the waters of the lake, shining like silver a moment before, took a blood-red hue, and a wind arose that stirred the waters, and they leaped up against the little boat, tossing it from side to side. While Cuglas was wondering at the change, he heard a strange, unearthly noise ahead of him, and a bristling monster, lifting its claws above the water, in a moment was beside the boat and stuck one of his claws in the left arm of the prince, and pierced the flesh to the bone. Maddened by the pain the prince drew his sword and chopped off the monster's claw. The monster disappeared beneath the lake, and, as it did so, the colour of the water changed, and the silver moonlight shone down from the sky again, but the boat no longer went on towards the mainland, but sped back towards the floating island, while forth from the island came a fleet of fairy boats to meet it, led by the shallop of the fairy queen. The queen greeted the prince as if she knew not of his attempted flight, and to the music of the harps the fleet returned to the palace.

The next day passed and the night came, and again the prince was lying on the couch, thinking of the Princess Ailinn, and again he saw the shadow on the floor and heard the tapping against the window.

And when he opened it the little woman slid into the room.

"You failed last night," she said, "but I come to give you another chance. Tomorrow the queen must set out on a visit to her fairy kinsmen, who dwell in the green hill near the plain of Tara; she cannot take you with her, for if your feet once touched the green grass that grows in the fruitful fields of Erin, she could never bring you back again. And so, when you find she has left the palace, go at once into the banquet hall and look behind the throne, and you will see a small door let down into the ground. Pull this up and descend the steps which you will see. Where they lead to I cannot tell. What dangers may be before you I do not know; but this I know, if you accept anything, no matter what it is, from anyone you may meet on your way, you shall not set foot on the soil of Erin."

And having said this the little woman, rising from the floor, floated out through the window.

The prince returned to his couch, and the next morning, as soon as he heard the queen had left the palace, he hastened to the banquet hall. He discovered the door and descended the steps, and he found himself in a gloomy and lonesome valley. Jagged mountains, black as night, rose on either side, and huge rocks seemed ready to topple down upon him at every step. Through broken clouds a watery moon shed a faint, fitful light, that came and went as the clouds, driven by a moaning wind, passed over the valley.

Cuglas, nothing daunted, pushed on boldly until a bank of cloud shut out completely the struggling moon, and closing over the valley covered it like a pall, leaving him in perfect darkness. At the same moment the moaning wind died away, and with it died away all sound. The darkness and the death-like silence sent an icy chill to the heart of Cuglas. He held his hand close to his eyes, but he saw it not. He shouted that he might hear the sound of his own voice, but he heard it not. He stamped his foot on the rocky ground, but no sound was returned to him. He rattled his sword in its brazen scabbard, but it gave no answer back to him. His heart grew colder and colder, when suddenly the cloud above him was rent in a dozen places, and lightning flashed through the valley, and the thunder rolled over the echoing mountains. In the lurid glare of the lightning Cuglas saw a hundred ghostly forms sweeping towards him, uttering as they came nearer and nearer shrieks so terrible that the silence of death could more easily be borne. Cuglas turned to escape, but they hemmed him round, and pressed their clammy hands upon his face.

With a yell of horror he drew his sword and slashed about him, and that very moment the forms vanished, the thunder ceased, the dark cloud passed, and the sun shone out as bright as on a summer day, and then Cuglas knew the forms he had seen were those of the wild people of the glen.

With renewed courage he pursued his way through the valley, and after three or four windings it took him out upon a sandy desert. He had no sooner set foot upon the desert than he heard behind him a crashing sound louder than thunder. He looked around, and he saw that the walls of mountain through which he had just passed had fallen into the valley, and filled it up so that he could no longer tell where it had been.

The sun was beating fiercely on the desert, and the sands were almost as hot as burning cinders; and as Cuglas advanced over them his body became dried up, and his tongue clove to the roof of his mouth, and when his thirst was at its height a fountain of sparkling water sprang up in the burning plain a few paces in front of him; but when he came up quite close to it and stretched out his parched hands to cool them in the limped waters, the fountain vanished as suddenly as it appeared. With great pain, and almost choking with heat and thirst, he struggled on, and again the fountain sprang up in front of him and moved before him, almost within his reach. At last he came to the end of the desert, and he saw a green hill up which a pathway climbed; but as he came to the foot of the hill, there, sitting right in his way, was a beautiful fairy holding out towards him a crystal cup, over the rim of which flowed water as clear as crystal. Unable to resist the temptation, the prince seized the cold, bright goblet, and drank the water. When he did so his thirst vanished, but the fairy, and the green hill, and the burning desert disappeared, and he was standing in the forest behind the palace of the fairy queen.

That evening the queen returned, and at the feast she talked as gaily to the prince as if she knew not of his attempt to leave the Floating Island, and the prince spoke as gaily as he could to her, although in his heart there was sadness when he remembered that if he had only dashed away the crystal cup, he would be at that moment in the royal banquet hall of Tara, sitting beside the Princess Ailinn.

And he thought the feast would never end; but it was over at last, and the prince returned to his apartments. And that night, as he lay on his couch, he kept his eyes fixed upon the window; but hours passed, and there was no sign of anyone. At long last, and when he had given up all hope of seeing her, he heard a tapping at the window, and he got up and opened it, and the little woman came in.

"You failed again today," said she – "failed just at the very moment when you were about to step on the green hills of Erin. I can give you only one chance more. It will be your last. The queen will go hunting in the morning. Join the hunt, and when you are separated from the rest of the party in the wood throw your reins upon your horse's neck and he will lead you to the edge of the lake. Then cast this golden bodkin into the lake in the direction of the mainland, and a golden bridge will be thrown across, over which you can pass safely to the fields of Erin; but take care and do not draw your sword, for if you do your steed will bear you back again to the Floating Island, and here you must remain for ever." Then handing the bodkin to the prince, and saying goodbye, the little woman disappeared.

The next morning the queen and the prince and all the court went out to hunt, and a fleet white deer started out before them, and the royal party pressed after him in pursuit. The prince's steed outstripped the others, and when he was alone the prince flung the reins upon his horse's neck, and before long he came to the edge of the lake.

Then the prince cast the bodkin on to the water, and a golden bridge was thrown across to the mainland, and the horse galloped on to it, and when the prince was more than half-way he saw riding towards him a champion wearing a silver helmet, and carrying on his left arm a silver shield, and holding in his right hand a gleaming sword. As he came nearer he struck his shield with his sword and challenged the prince to battle. The prince's sword almost leaped out of its scabbard at the martial sound, and, like a true knight of Tara, he dashed against his foe, and swinging his sword above his head, with one blow he clove the silver helmet, and the strange warrior reeled from his horse and fell upon the golden bridge. The prince, content with this achievement, spurred his horse to pass the fallen champion, but the horse refused to stir, and the bridge broke in two almost at his feet, and the part of it between him and the mainland disappeared beneath the lake, carrying with it the horse and the body of the champion, and before the prince could recover from his surprise, his steed wheeled round and was galloping back, and when he reached the land he rushed through the forest, and the prince was not able to pull him up until he came to the palace door.

All that night the prince lay awake on his couch with his eyes fixed upon the window, but no shadow fell upon the floor, and there was no tapping at the pane, and with a heavy heart he joined the hunting party in the morning. And day followed day, and his heart was sadder and sadder, and found no pleasure in the joys and delights of fairyland. And when all in the palace were at rest he used to roam through the forest, always thinking of the Princess Ailinn, and hoping against hope that the little woman would come again to him, but at last he began to despair of ever seeing her. It chanced one night he rambled so far that he found himself on the verge of the lake, at the very spot from which the golden bridge had been thrown across the waters, and as he gazed wistfully upon them a boat shot up and came swiftly to the bank, and who should he see sitting in the stern but the little woman.

"Ah, Cuglas, Cuglas," she said, "I gave you three chances, and you failed in all of them."

"I should have borne the pain inflicted by the monster's claw," said Cuglas. "I should have borne the thirst on the sandy desert, and dashed the crystal cup untasted from the fairy's hand; but I could never have faced the nobles and chiefs of Erin if I had refused to meet the challenge of the battle champion on the golden bridge."

"And you would have been no true knight of Erin, and you would not have been worthy of the wee girl who loves you, the bonny Princess Ailinn, if you had refused to meet it," said the little woman; "but for all that you can never return to the fair hills of Erin. But cheer up, Cuglas, there are mossy ways and forest paths and nestling bowers in fairyland. Lonely they are, I know, in your eyes now," said the little woman; "but maybe," she added, with a laugh as musical as the ripple on a streamlet when summer is in the air, "maybe you won't always think them so lonely."

"You think I'll forget Ailinn for the fairy queen," said Cuglas, with a sigh.

"I don't think anything of the kind," said she.

"Then what do you mean?" said the prince.

"Oh, I mean what I mean," said the little woman. "But I can't stop here all night talking to you: and, indeed, it is in your bed you ought to be yourself. So now good night; and I have no more to say, except that perhaps, if you happen to be here this night week at this very hour, when the moon will be on the waters, you will see –. But no matter what you will see," said she; "I must be off."

And before the prince could say another word the boat sped away from the bank, and he was alone. He went back to the palace, and he fell asleep that night only to dream of the Princess Ailinn.

As for the princess, she was pining away in the palace of Tara, the colour had fled from her cheeks, and her eyes, which had been once so bright they would have lighted darkness like a star, lost nearly all their lustre, and the king's leeches could do nothing for her, and at last they gave up all hope, and the king and queen of Erin and the ladies of the court watched her couch by night and by day sadly waiting for her last hour.

At length one day, when the sun was shining brightly over Tara's plain, and its light, softened by the intervening curtains, was falling in the sick chamber, the royal watchers noticed a sweet change coming over the face of the princess; the bloom of love and youth were flushing on her cheeks, and from her eyes shone out the old, soft, tender light, and they began to hope she was about to be restored to them, when suddenly the room was in darkness as if the night had swept across the sky, and blotted out the sun. Then they heard the sound of fairy music, and over the couch where the princess lay they beheld a gleam of golden light, but only for a moment; and again there was perfect darkness, and the fairy music ceased. Then, as suddenly as it came the darkness vanished, the softened sunlight once more filled the chamber, and rested upon the couch; but the couch was empty, and the royal watchers, looking at each other, said in whispers: "The fairies have carried away the Princess Ailinn to fairyland."

Well, that very day the prince roamed by himself through the forest, counting the hours until the day would fade in the sky and the moon come climbing up, and at last, when it was shining full above the waters, he went down to the verge of the lake, and he looked out over the gleaming surface watching for the vision promised by the little woman. But he could see nothing, and was about to turn away when he heard the faint sound of fairy music. He listened and listened, and the sound came nearer and clearer, and away in the distance, like drops of glistening water breaking the level of the lake, he saw a fleet of fairy boats, and he thought it was the fairy queen sailing in the moonlight. And it was the fairy queen, and soon he was able to recognise the royal shallop leading the others, and as it came close to the bank he saw the little woman sitting in the prow between the little harpers, and at the stern was the fairy queen, and by her side the lady of his heart, the Princess Ailinn. In a second the boat was against the bank, and the princess in his arms. And he kissed her again and again.

"And have you never a kiss for me," said the little woman, tapping his hand with the little gold bodkin.

"A kiss and a dozen," said Cuglas, as he caught the little fairy up in his arms.

"Oh, fie, Cuglas," said the queen.

"Oh, the princess isn't one bit jealous," said the little woman. "Are you, Ailinn?"

"Indeed I am not," said Ailinn.

"And you should not be," said the fairy queen, "for never lady yet had truer knight than Cuglas. I loved him, and I love him dearly. I lured him here hoping that in the delights of fairyland he might forget you. It was all in vain. I know now that there is one thing no fairy power above or below the stars, or beneath the waters, can ever subdue, and that is love. And here together forever shall you and Cuglas dwell, where old age shall never come upon you, and where pain or sorrow or sickness are unknown."

And Cuglas never returned to the fair hills of Erin, and ages passed away since the morning he followed the hounds into the fatal cave, but his story was remembered by the firesides, and sometimes, even yet, the herdboy watching his cattle in the fields hears the tuneful cry of hounds, and follows it till it leads him to a darksome cave, and as fearfully he listens to the sound becoming fainter and fainter he hears the clatter of hoofs over the stony floor, and to this day the cave bears the name of the prince who entered it never to return.

The Little White Cat

A LONG, LONG TIME AGO, in a valley far away, the giant Trencoss lived in a great castle, surrounded by trees that were always green. The castle had a hundred doors, and every door was guarded by a huge, shaggy hound, with tongue of fire and claws of iron, who tore to pieces anyone who went to the castle without the giant's leave. Trencoss had made war on the King of the Torrents, and, having killed the king, and slain his people, and burned his palace, he carried off his only daughter, the Princess Eileen, to the castle in the valley. Here he provided her with beautiful rooms, and appointed a hundred dwarfs, dressed in blue and yellow satin, to wait upon her, and harpers to play sweet music for her, and he gave her diamonds without number, brighter than the sun; but he would not allow her to go outside the castle, and told her if she went one

step beyond its doors, the hounds, with tongues of fire and claws of iron, would tear her to pieces. A week after her arrival, war broke out between the giant and the king of the islands, and before he set out for battle, the giant sent for the princess, and informed her that on his return he would make her his wife. When the princess heard this she began to cry, for she would rather die than marry the giant who had slain her father.

"Crying will only spoil your bright eyes, my little princess," said Trencoss, "and you will have to marry me whether you like it or no."

He then bade her go back to her room, and he ordered the dwarfs to give her everything she asked for while he was away, and the harpers to play the sweetest music for her. When the princess gained her room she cried as if her heart would break. The long day passed slowly, and the night came, but brought no sleep to Eileen, and in the grey light of the morning she rose and opened the window, and looked about in every direction to see if there were any chance of escape. But the window was ever so high above the ground, and below were the hungry and ever watchful hounds. With a heavy heart she was about to close the window when she thought she saw the branches of the tree that was nearest to it moving. She looked again, and she saw a little white cat creeping along one of the branches.

"Mew!" cried the cat.

"Poor little pussy," said the princess. "Come to me, pussy."

"Stand back from the window," said the cat, "and I will."

The princess stepped back, and the little white cat jumped into the room. The princess took the little cat on her lap and stroked him with her hand, and the cat raised up its back and began to purr.

"Where do you come from, and what is your name?" asked the princess.

"No matter where I come from or what's my name," said the cat, "I am a friend of yours, and I come to help you."

"I never wanted help worse," said the princess.

"I know that," said the cat; "and now listen to me. When the giant comes back from battle and asks you to marry him, say to him you will marry him."

"But I will never marry him," said the princess.

"Do what I tell you," said the cat. "When he asks you to marry him, say to him you will if his dwarfs will wind for you three balls from the fairy dew that lies on the bushes on a misty morning as big as these," said the cat, putting his right forefoot into his ear and taking out three balls – one yellow, one red, and one blue.

"They are very small," said the princess. "They are not much bigger than peas, and the dwarfs will not be long at their work."

"Won't they," said the cat. "It will take them a month and a day to make one, so that it will take three months and three days before the balls are wound; but the giant, like you, will think they can be made in a few days, and so he will readily promise to do what you ask. He will soon find out his mistake, but he will keep his word, and will not press you to marry you until the balls are wound."

"When will the giant come back?" asked Eileen.

"He will return tomorrow afternoon," said the cat.

"Will you stay with me until then?" said the princess. "I am very lonely."

"I cannot stay," said the cat. "I have to go away to my palace on the island on which no man ever placed his foot, and where no man but one shall ever come."

"And where is that island?" asked the princess, "and who is the man?"

"The island is in the far-off seas where vessel never sailed; the man you will see before many days are over; and if all goes well, he will one day slay the giant Trencoss, and free you from his power."

"Ah!" sighed the princess, "that can never be, for no weapon can wound the hundred hounds that guard the castle, and no sword can kill the giant Trencoss."

"There is a sword that will kill him," said the cat; "but I must go now. Remember what you are to say to the giant when he comes home, and every morning watch the tree on which you saw me, and if you see in the branches anyone you like better than yourself," said the cat, winking at the princess, "throw him these three balls and leave the rest to me; but take care not to speak a single word to him, for if you do all will be lost."

"Shall I ever see you again?" asked the princess.

"Time will tell," answered the cat, and, without saying so much as goodbye, he jumped through the window on to the tree, and in a second was out of sight.

The morrow afternoon came, and the giant Trencoss returned from battle. Eileen knew of his coming by the furious barking of the hounds, and her heart sank, for she knew that in a few moments she would be summoned to his presence. Indeed, he had hardly entered the castle when he sent for her, and told her to get ready for the wedding. The princess tried to look cheerful, as she answered:

"I will be ready as soon as you wish; but you must first promise me something."

"Ask anything you like, little princess," said Trencoss.

"Well, then," said Eileen, "before I marry you, you must make your dwarfs wind three balls as big as these from the fairy dew that lies on the bushes on a misty morning in summer."

"Is that all?" said Trencoss, laughing. "I shall give the dwarfs orders at once, and by this time tomorrow the balls will be wound, and our wedding can take place in the evening."

"And will you leave me to myself until then?"

"I will," said Trencoss.

"On your honour as a giant?" said Eileen.

"On my honour as a giant," replied Trencoss.

The princess returned to her rooms, and the giant summoned all his dwarfs, and he ordered them to go forth in the dawning of the morn and to gather all the fairy dew lying on the bushes, and to wind three balls – one yellow, one red, and one blue. The next morning, and the next, and the next, the dwarfs went out into the fields and searched all the hedgerows, but they could gather only as much fairy dew as would make a thread as long as a wee girl's eyelash; and so they had to go out morning after morning, and the giant fumed and threatened, but all to no purpose. He was very angry with the princess, and he was vexed with himself that she was so much cleverer than he was, and, moreover, he saw now that the wedding could not take place as soon as he expected.

When the little white cat went away from the castle he ran as fast as he could up hill and down dale, and never stopped until he came to the Prince of the Silver River. The prince was alone, and very sad and sorrowful he was, for he was thinking of the Princess Eileen, and wondering where she could be.

"Mew," said the cat, as he sprang softly into the room; but the prince did not heed him. "Mew," again said the cat; but again the prince did not heed him.

"Mew," said the cat the third time, and he jumped up on the prince's knee.

"Where do you come from, and what do you want?" asked the prince.

"I come from where you would like to be," said the cat.

"And where is that?" said the prince.

"Oh, where is that, indeed! As if I didn't know what you are thinking of, and of whom you are thinking," said the cat; "and it would be far better for you to try and save her."

"I would give my life a thousand times over for her," said the prince.

"For whom?" said the cat, with a wink. "I named no name, your highness," said he.

"You know very well who she is," said the prince, "if you knew what I was thinking of; but do you know where she is?"

"She is in danger," said the cat. "She is in the castle of the giant Trencoss, in the valley beyond the mountains."

"I will set out there at once," said the prince "and I will challenge the giant to battle, and will slay him."

"Easier said than done," said the cat. "There is no sword made by the hands of man can kill him, and even if you could kill him, his hundred hounds, with tongues of fire and claws of iron, would tear you to pieces."

"Then, what am I to do?" asked the prince.

"Be said by me," said the cat. "Go to the wood that surrounds the giant's castle, and climb the high tree that's nearest to the window that looks towards the sunset, and shake the branches, and you will see what you will see. Then hold out your hat with the silver plumes, and three balls – one yellow, one red, and one blue – will be thrown into it. And then come back here as fast as you can; but speak no word, for if you utter a single word the hounds will hear you, and you shall be torn to pieces."

Well, the prince set off at once, and after two days' journey he came to the wood around the castle, and he climbed the tree that was nearest to the window that looked towards the sunset, and he shook the branches. As soon as he did so, the window opened and he saw the Princess Eileen, looking lovelier than ever. He was going to call out her name, but she placed her fingers on her lips, and he remembered what the cat had told him, that he was to speak no word. In silence he held out the hat with the silver plumes, and the princess threw into it the three balls, one after another, and, blowing him a kiss, she shut the window. And well it was she did so, for at that very moment she heard the voice of the giant, who was coming back from hunting.

The prince waited until the giant had entered the castle before he descended the tree. He set off as fast as he could. He went up hill and down dale, and never stopped until he arrived at his own palace, and there waiting for him was the little white cat.

"Have you brought the three balls?" said he.

"I have," said the prince.

"Then follow me," said the cat.

On they went until they left the palace far behind and came to the edge of the sea.

"Now," said the cat, "unravel a thread of the red ball, hold the thread in your right hand, drop the ball into the water, and you shall see what you shall see."

The prince did as he was told, and the ball floated out to sea, unravelling as it went, and it went on until it was out of sight.

"Pull now," said the cat.

The prince pulled, and, as he did, he saw far away something on the sea shining like silver. It came nearer and nearer, and he saw it was a little silver boat. At last it touched the strand.

"Now," said the cat, "step into this boat and it will bear you to the palace on the island on which no man has ever placed his foot – the island in the unknown seas that were never sailed by vessels made of human hands. In that palace there is a sword with a diamond hilt, and by that sword alone the giant Trencoss can be killed. There also are a hundred cakes, and it is only on eating these the hundred hounds can die. But mind what I say to you: if you eat or drink until you reach the palace of the little cat in the island in the unknown seas, you will forget the Princess Eileen."

"I will forget myself first," said the prince, as he stepped into the silver boat, which floated away so quickly that it was soon out of sight of land.

The day passed and the night fell, and the stars shone down upon the waters, but the boat never stopped. On she went for two whole days and nights, and on the third morning the prince saw an island in the distance, and very glad he was; for he thought it was his journey's end, and he was almost fainting with thirst and hunger. But the day passed and the island was still before him.

At long last, on the following day, he saw by the first light of the morning that he was quite close to it, and that trees laden with fruit of every kind were bending down over the water. The boat sailed round and round the island, going closer and closer every round, until, at last, the drooping branches almost touched it. The sight of the fruit within his reach made the prince hungrier and thirstier than he was before, and forgetting his promise to the little cat – not to eat anything until he entered the palace in the unknown seas – he caught one of the branches, and, in a moment, was in the tree eating the delicious fruit. While he was doing so the boat floated out to sea and soon was lost to sight; but the prince, having eaten, forgot all about it, and, worse still, forgot all about the princess in the giant's castle. When he had eaten enough he descended the tree, and, turning his back on the sea, set out straight before him. He had not gone far when he heard the sound of music, and soon after he saw a number of maidens playing on silver harps coming towards him. When they saw him they ceased playing, and cried out:

"Welcome! Welcome! Prince of the Silver River, welcome to the island of fruits and flowers. Our king and queen saw you coming over the sea, and they sent us to bring you to the palace."

The prince went with them, and at the palace gates the king and queen and their daughter Kathleen received him, and gave him welcome. He hardly saw the king and queen, for his eyes were fixed on the princess Kathleen, who looked more beautiful than a flower. He thought he had never seen anyone so lovely, for, of course, he had forgotten all about poor Eileen pining away in her castle prison in the lonely valley. When the king and queen had given welcome to the prince a great feast was spread, and all the lords and ladies of the court sat down to it, and the prince sat between the queen and the princess Kathleen, and long before the feast was finished he was over head and ears in love with her. When the feast was ended the queen ordered the ballroom to be made ready, and when night fell the dancing began, and was kept up until the morning star, and the prince danced all night with the princess, falling deeper and deeper in love with her every minute. Between dancing by night and feasting by day weeks went by. All the time poor Eileen in the giant's castle was counting the hours, and all this time the dwarfs were winding the balls, and a ball and a half were already wound. At last the prince asked the king and queen for their daughter in marriage, and they were delighted to be able to say yes, and the day was fixed for the wedding. But on the evening before the day on which it was to take place the prince was in his room, getting ready for a dance, when he felt something rubbing against his leg, and, looking down, who should he see but the little white cat. At the sight of him the prince remembered everything, and sad and sorry he was when he thought of Eileen watching and waiting and counting the days until he returned to save her. But he was very fond of the princess Kathleen, and so he did not know what to do.

"You can't do anything tonight," said the cat, for he knew what the prince was thinking of, "but when morning comes go down to the sea, and look not to the right or the left, and let no living thing touch you, for if you do you shall never leave the island. Drop the second ball into the water, as you did the first, and when the boat comes step in at once. Then you may look behind you, and you shall see what you shall see, and you'll know which you love best, the Princess Eileen or the Princess Kathleen, and you can either go or stay."

The prince didn't sleep a wink that night, and at the first glimpse of the morning he stole from the palace. When he reached the sea he threw out the ball, and when it had floated out of sight, he saw the little boat sparkling on the horizon like a newly-risen star. The prince had scarcely passed through the palace doors when he was missed, and the king and queen and the princess, and all the lords and ladies of the court, went in search of him, taking the quickest way to the sea. While the maidens with the silver harps played sweetest music, the princess, whose voice was sweeter than any music, called on the prince by his name, and so moved his heart that he was about to look behind, when he remembered how the cat had told him he should not do so until he was in the boat. Just as it touched the shore the princess put out her hand and almost caught the prince's arm, but he stepped into the boat in time to save himself, and it sped away like a receding wave. A loud scream caused the prince to look round suddenly, and when he did he saw no sign of king or queen, or princess, or lords or ladies, but only big green serpents, with red eyes and tongues, that hissed out fire and poison as they writhed in a hundred horrible coils.

The prince, having escaped from the enchanted island, sailed away for three days and three nights, and every night he hoped the coming morning would show him the island he was in search of. He was faint with hunger and beginning to despair, when on the fourth morning he saw in the distance an island that, in the first rays of the sun, gleamed like fire. On coming closer to it he saw that it was clad with trees, so covered with bright red berries that hardly a leaf was to be seen. Soon the boat was almost within a stone's cast of the island, and it began to sail round and round until it was well under the bending branches. The scent of the berries was so sweet that it sharpened the prince's hunger, and he longed to pluck them; but, remembering what had happened to him on the enchanted island, he was afraid to touch them. But the boat kept on sailing round and round, and at last a great wind rose from the sea and shook the branches, and the bright, sweet berries fell into the boat until it was filled with them, and they fell upon the prince's hands, and he took up some to look at them, and as he looked the desire to eat them grew stronger, and he said to himself it would be no harm to taste one; but when he tasted it the flavour was so delicious he swallowed it, and, of course, at once he forgot all about Eileen, and the boat drifted away from him and left him standing in the water.

He climbed on to the island, and having eaten enough of the berries, he set out to see what might be before him, and it was not long until he heard a great noise, and a huge iron ball knocked down one of the trees in front of him, and before he knew where he was a hundred giants came running after it. When they saw the prince they turned towards him, and one of them caught him up in his hand and held him up that all might see him. The prince was nearly squeezed to death, and seeing this the giant put him on the ground again.

"Who are you, my little man?" asked the giant.

"I am a prince," replied the prince.

"Oh, you are a prince, are you?" said the giant. "And what are you good for?" said he.

The prince did not know, for nobody had asked him that question before.

"I know what he's good for," said an old giantess, with one eye in her forehead and one in her chin. "I know what he's good for. He's good to eat."

When the giants heard this they laughed so loud that the prince was frightened almost to death.

"Why," said one, "he wouldn't make a mouthful."

"Oh, leave him to me," said the giantess, "and I'll fatten him up; and when he is cooked and dressed he will be a nice dainty dish for the king."

The giants, on this, gave the prince into the hands of the old giantess. She took him home with her to the kitchen, and fed him on sugar and spice and all things nice, so that he should be a sweet morsel for the king of the giants when he returned to the island. The poor prince would not eat anything at first, but the giantess held him over the fire until his feet were scorched, and then he said to himself it was better to eat than to be burnt alive.

Well, day after day passed, and the prince grew sadder and sadder, thinking that he would soon be cooked and dressed for the king; but sad as the prince was, he was not half as sad as the Princess Eileen in the giant's castle, watching and waiting for the prince to return and save her.

And the dwarfs had wound two balls, and were winding a third.

At last the prince heard from the old giantess that the king of the giants was to return on the following day, and she said to him:

"As this is the last night you have to live, tell me if you wish for anything, for if you do your wish will be granted."

"I don't wish for anything," said the prince, whose heart was dead within him.

"Well, I'll come back again," said the giantess, and she went away.

The prince sat down in a corner, thinking and thinking, until he heard close to his ear a sound like "purr, purr!" He looked around, and there before him was the little white cat.

"I ought not to come to you," said the cat; "but, indeed, it is not for your sake I come. I come for the sake of the Princess Eileen. Of course, you forgot all about her, and, of course, she is always thinking of you. It's always the way –

"Favoured lovers may forget,
Slighted lovers never yet."

The prince blushed with shame when he heard the name of the princess.

"'Tis you that ought to blush," said the cat; "but listen to me now, and remember, if you don't obey my directions this time you'll never see me again, and you'll never set your eyes on the Princess Eileen. When the old giantess comes back tell her you wish, when the morning comes, to go down to the sea to look at it for the last time. When you reach the sea you will know what to do. But I must go now, as I hear the giantess coming." And the cat jumped out of the window and disappeared.

"Well," said the giantess, when she came in, "is there anything you wish?"

"Is it true I must die tomorrow?" asked the prince.

"It is."

"Then," said he, "I should like to go down to the sea to look at it for the last time."

"You may do that," said the giantess, "if you get up early."

"I'll be up with the lark in the light of the morning," said the prince.

"Very well," said the giantess, and, saying "goodnight", she went away.

The prince thought the night would never pass, but at last it faded away before the grey light of the dawn, and he sped down to the sea. He threw out the third ball, and before long he saw the little boat coming towards him swifter than the wind. He threw himself into it the moment it touched the shore. Swifter than the wind it bore him out to sea, and before he had time to look behind him the island of the giantess was like a faint red speck in the distance. The day passed and the night fell, and the stars looked down, and the boat sailed on, and just as the sun rose above the sea it pushed its silver prow on the golden strand of an island greener than the leaves in summer. The prince jumped out, and went on and on until he entered a pleasant valley, at the head of which he saw a palace white as snow.

As he approached the central door it opened for him. On entering the hall he passed into several rooms without meeting with anyone; but, when he reached the principal apartment, he found himself in a circular room, in which were a thousand pillars, and every pillar was of marble, and on every pillar save one, which stood in the centre of the room, was a little white cat with black eyes. Ranged round the wall, from one door-jamb to the other, were three rows of precious jewels. The first was a row of brooches of gold and silver, with their pins fixed in the wall and their heads outwards; the second a row of torques of gold and silver; and the third a row of great swords, with hilts of gold and silver. And on many tables was food of all kinds, and drinking horns filled with foaming ale.

While the prince was looking about him the cats kept on jumping from pillar to pillar; but seeing that none of them jumped on to the pillar in the centre of the room, he began to wonder why this was so, when, all of a sudden, and before he could guess how it came about, there right before him on the centre pillar was the little white cat.

"Don't you know me?" said he.

"I do," said the prince.

"Ah, but you don't know who I am. This is the palace of the Little White Cat, and I am the King of the Cats. But you must be hungry, and the feast is spread."

Well, when the feast was ended, the king of the cats called for the sword that would kill the giant Trencoss, and the hundred cakes for the hundred watch-dogs.

The cats brought the sword and the cakes and laid them before the king.

"Now," said the king, "take these; you have no time to lose. Tomorrow the dwarfs will wind the last ball, and tomorrow the giant will claim the princess for his bride. So you should go at once; but before you go take this from me to your little girl."

And the king gave him a brooch lovelier than any on the palace walls.

The king and the prince, followed by the cats, went down to the strand, and when the prince stepped into the boat all the cats 'mewed' three times for good luck, and the prince waved his hat three times, and the little boat sped over the waters all through the night as brightly and as swiftly as a shooting star. In the first flush of the morning it touched the strand. The prince jumped out and went on and on, up hill and down dale, until he came to the giant's castle. When the hounds saw him they barked furiously, and bounded towards him to tear him to pieces. The prince flung the cakes to them, and as each hound swallowed his cake he fell dead. The prince then struck his shield three times with the sword which he had brought from the palace of the little white cat.

When the giant heard the sound he cried out: "Who comes to challenge me on my wedding day?"

The dwarfs went out to see, and, returning, told him it was a prince who challenged him to battle.

The giant, foaming with rage, seized his heaviest iron club, and rushed out to the fight. The fight lasted the whole day, and when the sun went down the giant said:

"We have had enough of fighting for the day. We can begin at sunrise tomorrow."

"Not so," said the prince. "Now or never; win or die."

"Then take this," cried the giant, as he aimed a blow with all his force at the prince's head; but the prince, darting forward like a flash of lightning, drove his sword into the giant's heart, and, with a groan, he fell over the bodies of the poisoned hounds.

When the dwarfs saw the giant dead they began to cry and tear their hair. But the prince told them they had nothing to fear, and he bade them go and tell the princess Eileen he wished to speak with her. But the princess had watched the battle from her window, and when she saw the giant fall she rushed out to greet the prince, and that very night he and she and all the dwarfs and harpers set out for the Palace of the Silver River, which they reached the next morning, and from that day to this there never has been a gayer wedding than the wedding of the Prince of the Silver River and the Princess Eileen; and though she had diamonds and pearls to spare, the only jewel she wore on her wedding day was the brooch which the prince had brought her from the Palace of the Little White Cat in the far-off seas.

The Twelve Wild Geese

❧

THERE WAS ONCE a King and Queen that lived very happily together, and they had twelve sons and not a single daughter. We are always wishing for what we haven't, and don't care for what we have, and so it was with the Queen. One day in winter, when the bawn was covered with snow, she was looking out of the

parlour window, and saw there a calf that was just killed by the butcher, and a raven standing near it.

"Oh," says she, "if I had only a daughter with her skin as white as that snow, her cheeks as red as that blood, and her hair as black as that raven, I'd give away every one of my twelve sons for her." The moment she said the word, she got a great fright, and a shiver went through her, and in an instant after, a severe-looking old woman stood before her. "That was a wicked wish you made," said she, "and to punish you it will be granted. You will have such a daughter as you desire, but the very day of her birth you will lose your other children." She vanished the moment she said the words.

And that very way it turned out. When she expected her delivery, she had her children all in a large room of the palace, with guards all round it, but the very hour her daughter came into the world, the guards inside and outside heard a great whirling and whistling, and the twelve princes were seen flying one after another out through the open window, and away like so many arrows over the woods. Well, the king was in great grief for the loss of his sons, and he would be very enraged with his wife if he only knew that she was so much to blame for it.

Everyone called the little princess Snow-white-and-Rose-red on account of her beautiful complexion. She was the most loving and lovable child that could be seen anywhere. When she was twelve years old she began to be very sad and lonely, and to torment her mother, asking her about her brothers that she thought were dead, for none up to that time ever told her the exact thing that happened to them. The secret was weighing very heavy on the Queen's conscience, and as the little girl persevered in her questions, at last she told her. "Well, mother," said she, "it was on my account my poor brothers were changed into wild geese, and are now suffering all sorts of hardship; before the world is a day older, I'll be off to seek them, and try to restore them to their own shapes."

The King and Queen had her well watched, but all was no use. Next night she was getting through the woods that surrounded the palace, and she went on and on that night, and till the evening of next day. She had a few cakes with her, and she got nuts, and *mugoreens* (fruit of the sweet briar), and some sweet crabs, as she went along. At last she came to a nice wooden house just at sunset. There was a fine garden round it, full of the handsomest flowers, and a gate in the hedge. She went in, and saw a table laid out with twelve plates, and twelve knives and forks, and twelve spoons, and there were cakes, and cold wild fowl, and fruit along with the plates, and there was a good fire, and in another long room there were twelve beds. Well, while she was looking about her she heard the gate opening, and footsteps along the walk, and in came twelve young men, and there was great grief and surprise on all their faces when they laid eyes on her. "Oh, what misfortune sent you here?" said the eldest. "For the sake of a girl we were obliged to leave our father's court, and be in the shape of wild geese all day. That's twelve years ago, and we took a solemn oath that we would kill the first young girl that came into our hands. It's a pity to put such an innocent and handsome girl as you are out of the world, but we must keep our oath."

"But," said she, "I'm your only sister, that never knew anything about this till yesterday; and I stole away from our father's and mother's palace last night to find you out and relieve you if I can." Every one of them clasped his hands, and looked down on the floor, and you could hear a pin fall till the eldest cried out, "A curse light on our oath! What shall we do?"

"I'll tell you that," said an old woman that appeared at the instant among them. "Break your wicked oath, which no one should keep. If you attempted to lay an uncivil finger on her I'd change you into twelve *booliaun buis* (stalks of ragweed), but I wish well to you as well as to her. She is appointed to be your deliverer in this way. She must spin and knit twelve shirts for you out of bog-down, to be gathered by her own hands on the moor just outside of the wood. It will take her five years to do it, and if she once speaks, or laughs, or cries the whole time, you will have to remain wild geese by day till you're called out of the world. So take care of your sister; it is worth your while." The fairy then vanished, and it was only a strife with the brothers to see who would be first to kiss and hug their sister.

So for three long years the poor young princess was occupied pulling bog-down, spinning it, and knitting it into shirts, and at the end of the three years she had eight made. During all that time, she never spoke a word, nor laughed, nor cried: the last was the hardest to refrain from. One fine day she was sitting in the garden spinning, when in sprung a fine greyhound and bounded up to her, and laid his paws on her shoulder, and licked her forehead and her hair. The next minute a beautiful young prince rode up to the little garden gate, took off his hat, and asked for leave to come in. She gave him a little nod, and in he walked. He made ever so many apologies for intruding, and asked her ever so many questions, but not a word could he get out of her. He loved her so much from the first moment, that he could not leave her till he told her he was king of a country just bordering on the forest, and he begged her to come home with him, and be his wife. She couldn't help loving him as much as he did her, and though she shook her head very often, and was very sorry to leave her brothers, at last she nodded her head, and put her hand in his. She knew well enough that the good fairy and her brothers would be able to find her out. Before she went she brought out a basket holding all her bog-down, and another holding the eight shirts. The attendants took charge of these, and the prince placed her before him on his horse. The only thing that disturbed him while riding along was the displeasure his stepmother would feel at what he had done. However, he was full master at home, and as soon as he arrived he sent for the bishop, got his bride nicely dressed, and the marriage was celebrated, the bride answering by signs. He knew by her manners she was of high birth, and no two could be fonder of each other.

The wicked stepmother did all she could to make mischief, saying she was sure she was only a woodman's daughter; but nothing could disturb the young king's opinion of his wife. In good time the young queen was delivered of a beautiful boy, and the king was so glad he hardly knew what to do for joy. All the grandeur of the christening and the happiness of the parents tormented the bad woman more than I can tell you, and she determined to put a stop to all their comfort. She got a sleeping posset given to the young mother, and while she was thinking and thinking how she could best make away with the child, she saw a wicked-looking wolf in the garden, looking up at her, and licking his chops. She lost no time, but snatched the child from the arms of the sleeping woman, and pitched it out. The beast caught it in his mouth, and was over the garden fence in a minute. The wicked woman then pricked her own fingers, and dabbled the blood round the mouth of the sleeping mother.

Well, the young king was just then coming into the big bawn from hunting, and as soon as he entered the house, she beckoned to him, shed a few crocodile tears, began to cry and wring her hands, and hurried him along the passage to the bedchamber.

Oh, wasn't the poor king frightened when he saw the queen's mouth bloody, and missed his child? It would take two hours to tell you the devilment of the old queen, the confusion and fright, and grief of the young king and queen, the bad opinion he began to feel of his wife, and the struggle she had to keep down her bitter sorrow, and not give way to it by speaking or lamenting. The young king would not allow anyone to be called, and ordered his stepmother to give out that the child fell from the mother's arms at the window, and that a wild beast ran off with it. The wicked woman pretended to do so, but she told underhand to everybody she spoke to what the king and herself saw in the bedchamber.

The young queen was the most unhappy woman in the three kingdoms for a long time, between sorrow for her child, and her husband's bad opinion; still she neither spoke nor cried, and she gathered bog-down and went on with the shirts. Often the twelve wild geese would be seen lighting on the trees in the park or on the smooth sod, and looking in at her windows. So she worked on to get the shirts finished, but another year was at an end, and she had the twelfth shirt finished except one arm, when she was obliged to take to her bed, and a beautiful girl was born.

Now the king was on his guard, and he would not let the mother and child be left alone for a minute; but the wicked woman bribed some of the attendants, set others asleep, gave the sleepy posset to the queen, and had a person watching to snatch the child away, and kill it. But what should she see but the same wolf in the garden looking up and licking his chops again? Out went the child, and away with it flew the wolf, and she smeared the sleeping mother's mouth and face with blood, and then roared, and bawled, and cried out to the king and to everybody she met, and the room was filled, and everyone was sure the young queen had just devoured her own babe.

The poor mother thought now her life would leave her. She was in such a state she could neither think nor pray, but she sat like a stone, and worked away at the arm of the twelfth shirt.

The king was for taking her to the house in the wood where he found her, but the stepmother, and the lords of the court, and the judges would not hear of it, and she was condemned to be burned in the big bawn at three o'clock the same day. When the hour drew near, the king went to the farthest part of his palace, and there was no more unhappy man in his kingdom at that hour.

When the executioners came and led her off, she took the pile of shirts in her arms. There was still a few stitches wanted, and while they were tying her to the stakes she still worked on. At the last stitch she seemed overcome and dropped a tear on her work, but the moment after she sprang up, and shouted out, "I am innocent; call my husband!" The executioners stayed their hands, except one wicked-disposed creature, who set fire to the faggot next him, and while all were struck in amaze, there was a rushing of wings, and in a moment the twelve wild geese were standing around the pile. Before you could count twelve, she flung a shirt over each bird, and there in the twinkling of an eye were twelve of the finest young men that could be collected out of a thousand. While some were untying their sister, the eldest, taking a strong stake in his hand, struck the busy executioner such a blow that he never needed another.

While they were comforting the young queen, and the king was hurrying to the spot, a fine-looking woman appeared among them holding the babe on one arm and the little prince by the hand. There was nothing but crying for joy, and laughing for joy, and hugging and kissing, and when anyone had time to thank the good fairy, who in the shape of a wolf, carried the child away, she was not to be found. Never was such happiness enjoyed in any palace that ever was built, and if the wicked queen and her helpers were not torn by wild horses, they richly deserved it.

The Haughty Princess

❖

THERE WAS ONCE a very worthy king, whose daughter was the greatest beauty that could be seen far or near, but she was as proud as Lucifer, and no king or prince would she agree to marry. Her father was tired out at last, and invited every king, and prince, and duke, and earl that he knew or didn't know to come to his court to give her one trial more. They all came, and next day

after breakfast they stood in a row in the lawn, and the princess walked along in the front of them to make her choice. One was fat, and says she, "I won't have you, Beer-barrel!" One was tall and thin, and to him she said, "I won't have you, Ramrod!" To a white-faced man she said, "I won't have you, Pale Death"; and to a red-cheeked man she said, "I won't have you, Cockscomb!" She stopped a little before the last of all, for he was a fine man in face and form. She wanted to find some defect in him, but he had nothing remarkable but a ring of brown curling hair under his chin. She admired him a little, and then carried it off with, "I won't have you, Whiskers!"

So all went away, and the king was so vexed, he said to her, "Now to punish your *impudence*, I'll give you to the first beggarman or singing *sthronshuch* that calls"; and, as sure as the hearth-money, a fellow all over-rags, and hair that came to his shoulders, and a bushy red beard all over his face, came next morning, and began to sing before the parlour window.

When the song was over, the hall-door was opened, the singer asked in, the priest brought, and the princess married to Beardy. She roared and she bawled, but her father didn't mind her. "There," says he to the bridegroom, "is five guineas for you. Take your wife out of my sight, and never let me lay eyes on you or her again."

Off he led her, and dismal enough she was. The only thing that gave her relief was the tones of her husband's voice and his genteel manners. "Whose wood is this?" said she, as they were going through one. "It belongs to the king you called Whiskers yesterday." He gave her the same answer about meadows and corn-fields, and at last a fine city. "Ah, what a fool I was!" said she to herself. "He was a fine man, and I might have him for a husband." At last they were coming up to a poor cabin. "Why are you bringing me here?" says the poor lady. "This was my house," said he, "and now it's yours." She began to cry, but she was tired and hungry, and she went in with him.

Ovoch! There was neither a table laid out, nor a fire burning, and she was obliged to help her husband to light it, and boil their dinner, and clean up the place after; and next day he made her put on a stuff gown and a cotton handkerchief. When she had her house readied up, and no business to keep her employed, he brought home *sallies* (willows), peeled them, and showed her how to make baskets. But the hard twigs bruised her delicate fingers, and she began to cry. Well, then he asked her to mend their clothes, but the needle drew blood from her fingers, and she cried again. He couldn't bear to see her tears, so he bought a creel of earthenware, and sent her to the market to sell them. This was the hardest trial of all, but she looked so handsome and sorrowful, and had such a nice air about her, that all her pans, and jugs, and plates, and dishes were gone before noon, and the only mark of her old pride she showed was a slap she gave a buckeen across the face when he *axed* her to go in an' take share of a quart.

Well, her husband was so glad, he sent her with another creel the next day; but faith! Her luck was after deserting her. A drunken huntsman came up riding, and his beast got in among her ware, and made *brishe* of every mother's son of 'em. She went home cryin', and her husband wasn't at all pleased. "I see," said he, "you're not fit for business. Come along, I'll get you a kitchen-maid's place in the palace. I know the cook."

So the poor thing was obliged to stifle her pride once more. She was kept very busy, and the footman and the butler would be very impudent about looking for a kiss, but she let a screech out of her the first attempt was made, and the cook gave the fellow such a lambasting with the besom that he made no second offer. She went home to her husband every night, and she carried broken victuals wrapped in papers in her side pockets.

A week after she got service there was great bustle in the kitchen. The king was going to be married, but no one knew who the bride was to be. Well, in the evening the cook filled the princess's pockets with cold meat and puddings, and, says she, "Before you go, let us have a look at the great doings in the big parlour." So they came near the door to get a peep, and who should come out but the king himself, as handsome as you please, and no other but King Whiskers himself. "Your handsome helper must pay for her peeping," said he to the cook, "and dance a jig with me." Whether she would or no, he held her hand and brought her into the parlour. The fiddlers struck up, and away went *him* with *her*. But they hadn't danced two steps when the meat and the *puddens* flew out of her pockets. Everyone roared out, and she flew to the door, crying piteously. But she was soon caught by the king, and taken into the back parlour. "Don't you know me, my darling?" said he. "I'm both King Whiskers, your husband the ballad-singer, and the drunken huntsman. Your father knew me well enough when he gave you to me, and all was to drive your pride out of you." Well, she didn't know how she was with fright, and shame, and joy. Love was uppermost anyhow, for she laid her head on her husband's breast and cried like a child. The maids-of-honour soon had her away and dressed her as fine as hands and pins could do it; and there were her mother and father, too; and while the company were wondering what end of the handsome girl and the king, he and his queen, *who* they didn't know in her fine clothes, and the other king and queen, came in, and such rejoicings and fine doings as there was, none of us will ever see, any way.

Murtough and the Witch Woman

⬦⬥⬦

IN THE DAYS when Murtough Mac Erca was in the High Kingship of Ireland, the country was divided between the old beliefs of paganism and the new doctrines of the Christian teaching. Part held with the old creed and part with the new, and the thought of the people was troubled between them, for they knew not which way to follow and which to forsake. The faith of their forefathers clung close around them, holding them by many fine and tender threads of memory and custom and tradition; yet still the new faith was making its way, and every day it spread wider and wider through the land.

The family of Murtough had joined itself to the Christian faith, and his three brothers were bishops and abbots of the Church, but Murtough himself remained a pagan, for he was a wild and lawless prince, and the peaceful teachings of the Christian doctrine, with its forgiveness of enemies, pleased him not at all. Fierce and cruel was his life, filled with dark deeds and bloody wars, and savage and tragic was his death, as we shall hear.

Now Murtough was in the sunny summer palace of Cletty, which Cormac, son of Art, had built for a pleasure house on the brink of the slow-flowing Boyne, near the Fairy Brugh of Angus the Ever Young, the God of Youth and Beauty. A day of summer was that day, and the King came forth to hunt on the borders of the Brugh, with all his boon companions around him. But when the high-noon came the sun grew hot, and the King sat down to rest upon the fairy mound, and the hunt passed on beyond him, and he was left alone.

There was a witch woman in that country whose name was 'Sigh, Sough, Storm, Rough Wind, Winter Night, Cry, Wail, and Groan'. Star-bright and beautiful was she in face and form, but inwardly she was cruel as her names. And she hated Murtough because he had scattered and destroyed the Ancient Peoples of the Fairy Tribes of Erin, her country and her fatherland, and because in the battle which he fought at Cerb on the Boyne her father and her mother and her sister had been slain. For in those days women went to battle side by side with men.

She knew, too, that with the coming of the new faith trouble would come upon the fairy folk, and their power and their great majesty would depart from them, and men would call them demons, and would drive them out with psalm-singing and with the saying of prayers, and with the sound of little tinkling bells. So trouble and anger wrought in the witch woman, and she waited the day to be revenged on Murtough, for he being yet a pagan, was still within her power to harm.

So when Sheen (for Sheen or 'Storm' was the name men gave to her) saw the King seated on the fairy mound and all his comrades parted from him, she arose softly, and combed her hair with her comb of silver adorned with little ribs of gold, and she washed her hands in a silver basin wherein were four golden birds sitting on the rim of the bowl, and little bright gems of carbuncle set round about the rim. And she donned her fairy mantle of flowing green, and her cloak, wide and hooded, with silvery fringes, and a brooch of fairest gold. On her head were tresses yellow like to gold, plaited in four locks, with a golden drop at the end of each long tress. The hue of her hair was like the flower of the iris in summer or like red gold after the burnishing thereof. And she wore on her breasts and at her shoulders marvellous clasps of gold, finely worked with the tracery of the skilled craftsman, and a golden twisted torque around her throat. And when she was decked she went softly and sat down beside Murtough on the turfy hunting mound. And after a space Murtough perceived her sitting there, and the sun shining upon her, so that the glittering of the gold and of her golden hair and the bright shining of the green silk of her garments, was like the yellow iris-beds upon the lake on a sunny summer's day. Wonder and terror seized on Murtough at her beauty, and he knew not if he loved her or if he hated her the most; for at one moment all his nature was filled with longing and with love of her, so that it seemed to him that he would give the whole of Ireland for the loan of one hour's space of dalliance with her; but after that he felt a dread of her, because he knew his fate was in her hands, and that she had come to work him ill. But he welcomed her as if she were known to him and he asked her wherefore she was come. "I am come," she said, "because I am beloved of Murtough, son of Erc, King of Erin, and I come to seek him here." Then Murtough was glad, and he said, "Dost thou not know me, maiden?"

"I do," she answered, "for all secret and mysterious things are known to me and thou and all the men of Erin are well known."

After he had conversed with her awhile, she appeared to him so fair that the King was ready to promise her anything in life she wished, so long as she would go with him to Cletty of the Boyne. "My wish," she said, "is that you take me to your house, and that you put out from it your wife and your children because they are of the new faith, and all the clerics that are in your house, and that neither your wife nor any cleric be permitted to enter the house while I am there."

"I will give you," said the King, "a hundred head of every herd of cattle that is within my kingdom, and a hundred drinking horns, and a hundred cups, and a hundred rings of gold, and a feast every other night in the summer palace of Cletty. But I pledge thee my word, oh, maiden, it were easier for me to give thee half of Ireland than to do this thing that thou hast asked." For Murtough feared that when those that were of the Christian faith were put out of his house, she would work her spells upon him, and no power would be left with him to resist those spells.

"I will not take thy gifts," said the damsel, "but only those things that I have asked; moreover, it is thus, that my name must never be uttered by thee, nor must any man or woman learn it."

"What is thy name," said Murtough, "that it may not come upon my lips to utter it?"

And she said, "Sigh, Sough, Storm, Rough Wind, Winter Night, Cry, Wail, Groan, this is my name, but men call me Sheen, for 'Storm' or Sheen is my chief name, and storms are with me where I come."

Nevertheless, Murtough was so fascinated by her that he brought her to his home, and drove out the clerics that were there, with his wife and children along with them, and drove out also the nobles of his own clan, the children of Niall, two great and gallant battalions. And Duivsech, his wife, went crying along the road with her children around her to seek Bishop Cairnech, the half-brother of her husband, and her own soul-friend, that she might obtain help and shelter from him.

But Sheen went gladly and light-heartedly into the House of Cletty, and when she saw the lovely lightsome house and the goodly nobles of the clan of Niall, and the feasting and banqueting and the playing of the minstrels and all the joyous noise of that kingly dwelling, her heart was lifted within her, and "Fair as a fairy palace is this house of Cletty," said she.

"Fair, indeed, it is," replied the King; "for neither the Kings of Leinster nor the Kings of mighty Ulster, nor the lords of the clans of Owen or of Niall, have such a house as this; nay, in Tara of the Kings itself, no house to equal this house of mine is found." And that night the King robed himself in all the splendour of his royal dignity, and on his right hand he seated Sheen, and a great banquet was made before them, and men said that never on earth was to be seen a woman more goodly of appearance than she. And the King was astonished at her, and he began to ask her questions, for it seemed to him that the power of a great goddess of the ancient time was in her; and he asked her whence she came, and what manner was the power that he saw in her. He asked her, too, did she believe in the God of the clerics, or was she herself some goddess of the older world? For he feared her, feeling that his fate was in her hands.

She laughed a careless and a cruel laugh, for she knew that the King was in their power, now that she was there alone with him, and the clerics and the Christian teachers gone.

"Fear me not, O Murtough," she cried; "I am, like thee, a daughter of the race of men of the ancient family of Adam and of Eve; fit and meet my comradeship with thee; therefore, fear not nor regret. And as to that true God of thine, worker of miracles and helper of His people, no miracle in all the world is there that I, by mine own unaided power, cannot work the like. I can create a sun and moon; the heavens I can sprinkle with radiant stars of night. I can call up to life men fiercely fighting in conflict, slaughtering one another. Wine I could make of the cold water of the Boyne, and sheep of lifeless stones, and swine of ferns. In the presence of the hosts I can make gold and silver, plenty and to spare; and hosts of famous fighting men I can produce from naught. Now, tell me, can thy God work the like?"

"Work for us," says the King, "some of these great wonders." Then Sheen went forth out of the house, and she set herself to work spells on Murtough, so that he knew not whether he was in his right mind or no. She took of the water of the Boyne and made a magic wine thereout, and she took ferns and spiked thistles and light puff-balls of the woods, and out of them she fashioned magic swine and sheep and goats, and with these she fed Murtough and the hosts. And when they had eaten, all their strength went from them, and the magic wine sent them into an uneasy sleep and restless slumbers. And out of stones and sods of earth she fashioned three battalions, and one of the battalions she placed at one side of the house, and the other at the further side beyond it, and one encircling the rest southward along the hollow windings of the glen. And thus were these battalions, one of them all made of men stark-naked and their colour blue, and the second with heads of goats with shaggy beards and horned; but the third, more terrible than they, for these were headless men, fighting like human beings, yet finished at the neck; and the sound of heavy shouting as of hosts and multitudes came from the first and the second battalion, but from the third no sound save only that they waved their arms and struck their weapons together, and smote the ground with their feet impatiently. And though terrible was the shout of the blue men and the bleating of the goats with human limbs, more horrible yet was the stamping and the rage of those headless men, finished at the neck.

And Murtough, in his sleep and in his dreams, heard the battle-shout, and he rose impetuously from off his bed, but the wine overcame him, and his strength departed from him, and he fell helplessly upon the floor. Then he heard the challenge a second time, and the stamping of the feet without, and he rose again, and madly, fiercely, he set on them, charging the hosts and scattering them before him, as he thought, as far as the fairy palace of the Brugh. But all his strength was lost in fighting phantoms, for they were but stones and sods and withered leaves of the forest that he took for fighting men.

Now Duivsech, Murtough's wife, knew what was going on. She called upon Cairnech to arise and to gather together the clans of the children of his people, the men of Owen and of Niall, and together they went to the fort; but Sheen guarded it well, so that they could by no means find an entrance. Then Cairnech was angry, and he cursed the place, and he dug a grave before the door, and he stood up upon the mound of the grave, and rang his bells and cursed the King and his house, and prophesied his downfall. But he blessed the clans of Owen and of Niall, and they returned to their own country.

Then Cairnech sent messengers to seek Murtough and to draw him away from the witch woman who sought his destruction, but because she was so lovely the King would believe no evil of her; and whenever he made any sign to go to Cairnech, she threw her spell upon the King, so that he could not break away. When he was so weak and faint that he had no power left, she cast a sleep upon him, and she went round the house, putting everything in readiness. She called upon her magic host of warriors, and set them round the fortress, with their spears and javelins pointed inwards towards the house, so that the King would not dare to go out amongst them. And that night was a night of Samhain-tide, the eve of Wednesday after All Souls' Day.

Then she went everywhere throughout the house, and took lighted brands and burning torches, and scattered them in every part of the dwelling. And she returned into the room wherein Murtough slept, and lay down by his side. And she caused a great wind to spring up, and it came soughing through the house from the north-west; and the King said, "This is the sigh of the winter night." And Sheen smiled, because, unwittingly, the King had spoken her name, for she knew by that that the hour of her revenge had come. "'Tis I myself that am Sigh and Winter Night," she said, "and I am Rough Wind and Storm, a daughter of fair nobles; and I am Cry and Wail, the maid of elfin birth, who brings ill-luck to men."

After that she caused a great snowstorm to come round the house; and like the noise of troops and the rage of battle was the storm, beating and pouring in on every side, so that drifts of deep snow were piled against the walls, blocking the doors and chilling the folk that were feasting within the house. But the King was lying in a heavy, unresting sleep, and Sheen was at his side. Suddenly he screamed out of his sleep and stirred himself, for he heard the crash of falling timbers and the noise of the magic hosts, and he smelled the strong smell of fire in the palace.

He sprang up. "It seems to me," he cried, "that hosts of demons are around the house, and that they are slaughtering my people, and that the house of Cletty is on fire."

"It was but a dream," the witch maiden said. Then he slept again, and he saw a vision, to wit, that he was tossing in a ship at sea, and the ship floundered, and above his head a griffin, with sharp beak and talons, sailed, her wings outspread and covering all the sun, so that it was dark as middle-night; and lo! As she rose on high, her plumes quivered for a moment in the air; then down she swooped and picked him from the waves, carrying him to her eyrie on the dismal cliff outhanging o'er the ocean; and the griffin began to pierce him and to prod him with her talons, and to pick out pieces of his flesh with her beak; and this went on awhile, and then a flame, that came he knew not whence, rose from the nest, and he and the griffin were enveloped in the flame. Then in her beak the griffin picked him up, and together they fell downward over the cliff's edge into the seething ocean; so that, half by fire and half by water, he died a miserable death.

When the King saw that vision, he rose screaming from his sleep, and donned his arms; and he made one plunge forward seeking for the magic hosts, but he found no man to answer him. The damsel went forth from the house, and Murtough made to follow her, but as he turned the flames leaped out, and all between him and the door was one vast sheet of flame.

He saw no way of escape, save the vat of wine that stood in the banqueting hall, and into that he got; but the burning timbers of the roof fell upon his head and the hails of fiery sparks rained on him, so that half of him was burned and half was drowned, as he had seen in his dream.

The next day, amid the embers, the clerics found his corpse, and they took it up and washed it in the Boyne, and carried it to Tuilen to bury it. And they said, "Alas! That Mac Erca, High King of Erin, of the noble race of Conn and of the descendants of Ugaine the Great, should die fighting with sods and stones! Alas! That the Cross of Christ was not signed upon his face that he might have known the witchdoms of the maiden what they were."

As they went thus, bewailing the death of Murtough and bearing him to his grave, Duivsech, wife of Murtough, met them, and when she found her husband dead, she struck her hands together and she made a great and mournful lamentation; and because weakness came upon her she leaned her back against the ancient tree that is in Aenech Reil; and a burst of blood broke from her heart, and there she died, grieving for her husband. And the grave of Murtough was made wide and deep, and there they laid the Queen beside him, two in the one grave, near the north side of the little church that is in Tuilen.

Now, when the burial was finished, and the clerics were reciting over his grave the deeds of the King, and were making prayers for Murtough's soul that it might be brought out of hell, for Cairnech showed great care for this, they saw coming towards them across the sward a lonely woman, star-bright and beautiful, and a kirtle of priceless silk upon her, and a green mantle with its fringes of silver thread flowing to the ground. She reached the place where the clerics were, and saluted them, and they saluted her. And they marvelled at her beauty, but they perceived on her an appearance of sadness and of heavy grief. They asked of her, "Who art thou, maiden, and wherefore art thou come to the house of mourning? For a king lies buried here."

"A king lies buried here, indeed," said she, "and I it was who slew him, Murtough of the many deeds, of the race of Conn and Niall, High King of Ireland and of the West. And though it was I who wrought his death, I myself will die for grief of him."

And they said, "Tell us, maiden, why you brought him to his death, if so be that he was dear to thee?" And she said, "Murtough was dear to me, indeed, dearest of the men of the whole world; for I am Sheen, the daughter of Sige, the son of Dian, from whom Ath Sigi or the 'Ford of Sige' is called today. But Murtough slew my father, and my mother and sister were slain along with him, in the battle of Cerb upon the Boyne, and there was none of my house to avenge their death, save myself alone. Moreover, in his time the Ancient Peoples of the Fairy Tribes of Erin were scattered and destroyed, the folk of the underworld and of my fatherland; and to avenge the wrong and loss he wrought on them I slew the man I loved. I made poison for him; alas! I made for him magic drink and food which took his strength away, and out of the sods of earth and puff-balls that float down the wind, I wrought men and armies of headless, hideous folk, till all his senses were distraught. And, now, take me to thee, O Cairnech, in fervent and true repentance, and sign the Cross of Christ upon my brow, for the time of my death is come." Then she made penitence for the sin that she had sinned, and she died there upon the grave of grief and of sorrow after the King. And they digged a grave lengthways across the foot of the wide grave of Murtough and his spouse, and there they laid the maiden who had wrought them woe. And the clerics wondered at those things, and they wrote them and revised them in a book.

The Story of Deirdre

❧

THERE WAS A MAN in Ireland once who was called Malcolm Harper. The man was a right good man, and he had a goodly share of this world's goods. He had a wife, but no family. What did Malcolm hear but that a soothsayer had come home to the place, and as the man was a right good man, he wished that the soothsayer might come near them. Whether it was that he was invited or that he came of himself, the soothsayer came to the house of Malcolm.

"Are you doing any soothsaying?" says Malcolm. "Yes, I am doing a little. Are you in need of soothsaying?"

"Well, I do not mind taking soothsaying from you, if you had soothsaying for me, and you would be willing to do it."

"Well, I will do soothsaying for you. What kind of soothsaying do you want?"

"Well, the soothsaying I wanted was that you would tell me my lot or what will happen to me, if you can give me knowledge of it."

"Well, I am going out, and when I return, I will tell you." And the soothsayer went forth out of the house and he was not long outside when he returned.

"Well," said the soothsayer, "I saw in my second sight that it is on account of a daughter of yours that the greatest amount of blood shall be shed that has ever been shed in Erin since time and race began. And the three most famous heroes that ever were found will lose their heads on her account."

After a time a daughter was born to Malcolm, he did not allow a living being to come to his house, only himself and the nurse. He asked this woman, "Will you yourself bring up the child to keep her in hiding far away where eye will not see a sight of her nor ear hear a word about her?"

The woman said she would, so Malcolm got three men, and he took them away to a large mountain, distant and far from reach, without the knowledge or notice of anyone. He caused there a hillock, round and green, to be dug out of the middle, and the hole thus made to be covered carefully over so that a little company could dwell there together. This was done.

Deirdre and her foster-mother dwelt in the bothy mid the hills without the knowledge or the suspicion of any living person about them and without anything occurring, until Deirdre was sixteen years of age. Deirdre grew like the white sapling, straight and trim as the rash on the moss. She was the creature of fairest form, of loveliest aspect, and of gentlest nature that existed between earth and heaven in all Ireland – whatever colour of hue she had before, there was nobody that looked into her face but she would blush fiery red over it.

The woman that had charge of her gave Deirdre every information and skill of which she herself had knowledge and skill. There was not a blade of grass growing from root, nor a bird singing in the wood, nor a star shining from heaven but Deirdre had a name for it. But one thing, she did not wish her to have either part or parley with any single living man of the rest of the world. But on a gloomy winter night, with black, scowling clouds, a hunter of game was wearily travelling the hills, and what happened but that he missed the trail of the hunt, and lost his course and companions. A drowsiness came upon the man as he wearily wandered over the hills, and he lay down by the side of the beautiful green knoll in which Deirdre lived, and he slept. The man was faint from hunger and wandering, and benumbed with cold, and a deep sleep fell upon him. When he lay down beside the green hill where Deirdre was, a troubled dream came to the man, and he thought that he enjoyed the warmth of a fairy broch, the fairies being inside playing music. The hunter shouted out in his dream, if there was anyone in the broch, to let him in for the Holy One's sake. Deirdre heard the voice and said to her foster-mother: "O foster-mother, what cry is that?"

"It is nothing at all, Deirdre – merely the birds of the air astray and seeking each other. But let them go past to the bosky glade. There is no shelter or house for them here."

"Oh, foster-mother, the bird asked to get inside for the sake of the God of the Elements, and you yourself tell me that anything that is asked in His name we ought to do. If you will not allow the bird that is being benumbed with cold, and done to death with hunger, to be let in, I do not think much of your language or your faith. But since I give credence to your language and to your faith, which you taught me, I will myself let in the bird." And Deirdre arose and drew the bolt from the leaf of the door, and she let in the hunter. She placed a seat in the place for sitting, food in the place for eating, and drink in the place for drinking for the man who came to the house. "Oh, for this life and raiment, you man that came in, keep restraint on your tongue!" said the old woman. "It is not a great thing for you to keep your mouth shut and your tongue quiet when you get a home and shelter of a hearth on a gloomy winter's night."

"Well," said the hunter, "I may do that – keep my mouth shut and my tongue quiet, since I came to the house and received hospitality from you;

but by the hand of thy father and grandfather, and by your own two hands, if some other of the people of the world saw this beauteous creature you have here hid away, they would not long leave her with you, I swear."

"What men are these you refer to?" said Deirdre.

"Well, I will tell you, young woman," said the hunter. "They are Naois, son of Uisnech, and Allen and Arden his two brothers."

"What like are these men when seen, if we were to see them?" said Deirdre.

"Why, the aspect and form of the men when seen are these," said the hunter: "they have the colour of the raven on their hair, their skin like swan on the wave in whiteness, and their cheeks as the blood of the brindled red calf, and their speed and their leap are those of the salmon of the torrent and the deer of the grey mountain side. And Naois is head and shoulders over the rest of the people of Erin."

However they are," said the nurse, "be you off from here and take another road. And, King of Light and Sun! In good sooth and certainty, little are my thanks for yourself or for her that let you in!"

The hunter went away, and went straight to the palace of King Connachar. He sent word in to the king that he wished to speak to him if he pleased. The king answered the message and came out to speak to the man. "What is the reason of your journey?" said the king to the hunter.

"I have only to tell you, O king," said the hunter, "that I saw the fairest creature that ever was born in Erin, and I came to tell you of it."

"Who is this beauty and where is she to be seen, when she was not seen before till you saw her, if you did see her?"

"Well, I did see her," said the hunter. "But, if I did, no man else can see her unless he get directions from me as to where she is dwelling."

"And will you direct me to where she dwells? And the reward of your directing me will be as good as the reward of your message," said the king.

"Well, I will direct you, O king, although it is likely that this will not be what they want," said the hunter.

Connachar, King of Ulster, sent for his nearest kinsmen, and he told them of his intent. Though early rose the song of the birds mid the rocky caves and the music of the birds in the grove, earlier than that did Connachar, King of Ulster, arise, with his little troop of dear friends, in the delightful twilight of the fresh and gentle May; the dew was heavy on each bush and flower and stem, as they went to bring Deirdre forth from the green knoll where she stayed. Many a youth was there who had a lithe leaping and lissom step when they started whose step was faint, failing, and faltering when they reached the bothy on account of the length of the way and roughness of the road.

"Yonder, now, down in the bottom of the glen is the bothy where the woman dwells, but I will not go nearer than this to the old woman," said the hunter.

Connachar with his band of kinsfolk went down to the green knoll where Deirdre dwelt and he knocked at the door of the bothy. The nurse replied, "No less than a king's command and a king's army could put me out of my bothy tonight. And I should be obliged to you, were you to tell who it is that wants me to open my bothy door."

"It is I, Connachar, King of Ulster." When the poor woman heard who was at the door, she rose with haste and let in the king and all that could get in of his retinue.

When the king saw the woman that was before him that he had been in quest of, he thought he never saw in the course of the day nor in the dream of night a creature so fair as Deirdre and he gave his full heart's weight of love to her. Deirdre was raised on the topmost of the heroes' shoulders and she and her foster-mother were brought to the Court of King Connachar of Ulster.

With the love that Connachar had for her, he wanted to marry Deirdre right off there and then, will she nill she marry him. But she said to him, "I would be obliged to you if you will give me the respite of a year and a day." He said "I will grant you that, hard though it is, if you will give me your unfailing promise that you will marry me at the year's end." And she gave the promise. Connachar got for her a woman-teacher and merry modest maidens fair that would lie down and rise with her, that would play and speak with her. Deirdre was clever in maidenly duties and wifely understanding, and Connachar thought he never saw with bodily eye a creature that pleased him more.

Deirdre and her women companions were one day out on the hillock behind the house enjoying the scene, and drinking in the sun's heat. What did they see coming but three men a-journeying. Deirdre was looking at the men that were coming, and wondering at them. When the men neared them, Deirdre remembered the language of the huntsman, and she said to herself that these were the three sons of Uisnech, and that this was Naois, he having what was above the bend of the two shoulders above the men of Erin all. The three brothers went past without taking any notice of them, without even glancing at the young girls on the hillock. What happened but that love for Naois struck the heart of Deirdre, so that she could not but follow after him. She girded up her raiment and went after the men that went past the base of the knoll, leaving her women attendants there. Allen and Arden had heard of the woman that Connachar, King of Ulster, had with him, and they thought that, if Naois, their brother, saw her, he would have her himself, more especially as she was not married to the King. They perceived the woman coming, and called on one another to hasten their step as they had a long distance to travel, and the dusk of night was coming on. They did so. She cried: "Naois, son of Uisnech, will you leave me?"

"What piercing, shrill cry is that – the most melodious my ear ever heard, and the shrillest that ever struck my heart of all the cries I ever heard?"

"It is anything else but the wail of the wave-swans of Connachar," said his brothers.

"No! Yonder is a woman's cry of distress," said Naois, and he swore he would not go further until he saw from whom the cry came, and Naois turned back. Naois and Deirdre met, and Deirdre kissed Naois three times, and a kiss each to his brothers. With the confusion that she was in, Deirdre went into a crimson blaze of fire, and her colour came and went as rapidly as the movement of the aspen by the stream side. Naois thought he never saw a fairer creature, and Naois gave Deirdre the love that he never gave to thing, to vision, or to creature but to herself. Then Naois placed Deirdre on the topmost height of his shoulder, and told his brothers to keep up their pace, and they kept up their pace. Naois thought that it would not be well for him to remain in Erin on account of the way in which Connachar, King of Ulster, his uncle's son, had gone against him because of the woman, though he had not married her; and he turned back to Alba, that is, Scotland. He reached the side of Loch-Ness and made his habitation there. He could kill the salmon of the torrent from out his own door, and the deer of the grey gorge from out his window. Naois and Deirdre and Allen and Arden dwelt in a tower, and they were happy so long a time as they were there.

By this time the end of the period came at which Deirdre had to marry Connachar, King of Ulster. Connachar made up his mind to take Deirdre away by the sword whether she was married to Naois or not. So he prepared a great and gleeful feast. He sent word far and wide through Erin all to his kinspeople to come to the feast. Connachar thought to himself that Naois would not come though he should bid him; and the scheme that arose in his mind was to send for his father's brother, Ferchar Mac Ro, and to send him on an embassy to Naois. He did so; and Connachar said to Ferchar, "Tell Naois, son of Uisnech, that I am setting forth a great and gleeful feast to my friends and kinspeople throughout the wide extent of Erin all, and that I shall not have rest by day nor sleep by night if he and Allen and Arden be not partakers of the feast."

Ferchar Mac Ro and his three sons went on their journey, and reached the tower where Naois was dwelling by the side of Loch Etive. The sons of Uisnech gave a cordial kindly welcome to Ferchar Mac Ro and his three sons, and asked of him the news of Erin. "The best news that I have for you," said the hardy hero, "is that Connachar, King of Ulster, is setting forth a great sumptuous feast to his friends and kinspeople throughout the wide extent of Erin all, and he has vowed by the earth beneath him, by the high heaven above him, and by the sun that wends to the west, that he will have no rest by day nor sleep by night if the sons of Uisnech, the sons of his own father's brother, will not come back to the land of their home and the soil of their nativity, and to the feast likewise, and he has sent us on embassy to invite you."

"We will go with you," said Naois.

"We will," said his brothers.

But Deirdre did not wish to go with Ferchar Mac Ro, and she tried every prayer to turn Naois from going with him – she said: "I saw a vision, Naois, and do you interpret it to me," – then she sang:

"O Naois, son of Uisnech, hear
What was shown in a dream to me.
There came three white doves out of the South
Flying over the sea,
And drops of honey were in their mouth
From the hive of the honey-bee.
O Naois, son of Uisnech, hear,
What was shown in a dream to me.
I saw three grey hawks out of the south
Come flying over the sea,
And the red red drops they bare in their mouth
They were dearer than life to me."

Said Naois: –

"It is nought but the fear of woman's heart,
And a dream of the night, Deirdre."

"The day that Connachar sent the invitation to his feast will be unlucky for us if we don't go, O Deirdre."

"You will go there," said Ferchar Mac Ro; "and if Connachar show kindness to you, show ye kindness to him; and if he will display wrath towards you display ye wrath towards him, and I and my three sons will be with you."

"We will," said Daring Drop. "We will," said Hardy Holly. "We will," said Fiallan the Fair.

"I have three sons, and they are three heroes, and in any harm or danger that may befall you, they will be with you, and I myself will be along with them." And Ferchar Mac Ro gave his vow and his word in presence of his arms that, in any harm or danger that came in the way of the sons of Uisnech, he and his three sons would not leave head on live body in Erin, despite sword or helmet, spear or shield, blade or mail, be they ever so good.

Deirdre was unwilling to leave Alba, but she went with Naois. Deirdre wept tears in showers and she sang:

"Dear is the land, the land over there,
Alba full of woods and lakes;
Bitter to my heart is leaving thee,
But I go away with Naois."

Ferchar Mac Ro did not stop till he got the sons of Uisnech away with him, despite the suspicion of Deirdre.

The coracle was put to sea,
The sail was hoisted to it;
And the second morrow they arrived
On the white shores of Erin.

As soon as the sons of Uisnech landed in Erin, Ferchar Mac Ro sent word to Connachar, king of Ulster, that the men whom he wanted were come, and let him now show kindness to them. "Well," said Connachar, "I did not expect that the sons of Uisnech would come, though I sent for them, and I am not quite ready to receive them.

But there is a house down yonder where I keep strangers, and let them go down to it today, and my house will be ready before them tomorrow." But he that was up in the palace felt it long that he was not getting word as to how matters were going on for those down in the house of the strangers.

"Go you, Gelban Grednach, son of Lochlin's King, go you down and bring me information as to whether her former hue and complexion are on Deirdre. If they be, I will take her out with edge of blade and point of sword, and if not, let Naois, son of Uisnech, have her for himself," said Connachar.

Gelban, the cheering and charming son of Lochlin's King, went down to the place of the strangers, where the sons of Uisnech and Deirdre were staying. He looked in through the bicker-hole on the door-leaf. Now she that he gazed upon used to go into a crimson blaze of blushes when anyone looked at her. Naois looked at Deirdre and knew that someone was looking at her from the back of the door-leaf. He seized one of the dice on the table before him and fired it through the bicker-hole, and knocked the eye out of Gelban Grednach the Cheerful and Charming, right through the back of his head. Gelban returned back to the palace of King Connachar.

"You were cheerful, charming, going away, but you are cheerless, charmless, returning. What has happened to you, Gelban? But have you seen her, and are Deirdre's hue and complexion as before?" said Connachar.

"Well, I have seen Deirdre, and I saw her also truly, and while I was looking at her through the bicker-hole on the door, Naois, son of Uisnech, knocked out my eye with one of the dice in his hand. But of a truth and verity, although he put out even my eye, it were my desire still to remain looking at her with the other eye, were it not for the hurry you told me to be in," said Gelban.

"That is true," said Connachar; "let three hundred bravo heroes go down to the abode of the strangers, and let them bring hither to me Deirdre, and kill the rest." Connachar ordered three hundred active heroes to go down to the abode of the strangers and to take Deirdre up with them and kill the rest. "The pursuit is coming," said Deirdre.

"Yes, but I will myself go out and stop the pursuit," said Naois.

"It is not you, but we that will go," said Daring Drop, and Hardy Holly, and Fiallan the Fair; "it is to us that our father entrusted your defence from harm and danger when he himself left for home." And the gallant youths, full noble, full manly, full handsome, with beauteous brown locks, went forth girt with battle arms fit for fierce fight and clothed with combat dress for fierce contest fit, which was burnished, bright, brilliant, bladed, blazing, on which were many pictures of beasts and birds and creeping things, lions and lithe-limbed tigers, brown eagle and harrying hawk and adder fierce; and the young heroes laid low three-thirds of the company.

Connachar came out in haste and cried with wrath: "Who is there on the floor of fight, slaughtering my men?"

"We, the three sons of Ferchar Mac Ro."

"Well," said the king, "I will give a free bridge to your grandfather, a free bridge to your father, and a free bridge each to you three brothers, if you come over to my side tonight."

"Well, Connachar, we will not accept that offer from you nor thank you for it. Greater by far do we prefer to go home to our father and tell the deeds of heroism we have done, than accept anything on these terms from you. Naois, son of Uisnech, and Allen and Arden are as nearly related to yourself as they are to us, though you are so keen to shed their blood, and you would shed our blood also, Connachar." And the noble, manly, handsome youths with beauteous, brown locks returned inside. "We are now," said they, "going home to tell our father that you are now safe from the hands of the king." And the youths all fresh and tall and lithe and beautiful, went home to their father to tell that the sons of Uisnech were safe. This happened at the parting of the day and night in the morning twilight time, and Naois said they must go away, leave that house, and return to Alba.

Naois and Deirdre, Allan and Arden started to return to Alba. Word came to the king that the company he was in pursuit of were gone. The king then sent for Duanan Gacha Druid, the best magician he had, and he spoke to him as follows: – "Much wealth have I expended on you, Duanan Gacha Druid, to give schooling and learning and magic mystery to you, if these people get away from me today without care, without consideration or regard for me, without chance of overtaking them, and without power to stop them."

"Well, I will stop them," said the magician, "until the company you send in pursuit return." And the magician placed a wood before them through which no man could go, but the sons of Uisnech marched through the wood without halt or hesitation, and Deirdre held on to Naois's hand. "What is the good of that? That will not do yet," said Connachar. "They are off without bending of their feet or stopping of their step, without heed or respect to me, and I am without power to keep up to them or opportunity to turn them back this night."

"I will try another plan on them," said the druid; and he placed before them a grey sea instead of a green plain. The three heroes stripped and tied their clothes behind their heads, and Naois placed Deirdre on the top of his shoulder.

> They stretched their sides to the stream,
> And sea and land were to them the same,
> The rough grey ocean was the same
> As meadow-land green and plain.

"Though that be good, O Duanan, it will not make the heroes return," said Connachar; "they are gone without regard for me, and without honour to me, and without power on my part to pursue them or to force them to return this night."

"We shall try another method on them, since yon one did not stop them," said the druid. And the druid froze the grey ridged sea into hard rocky knobs, the sharpness of sword being on the one edge and the poison power of adders on the other. Then Arden cried that he was getting tired, and nearly giving over. "Come you, Arden, and sit on my right shoulder," said Naois. Arden came and sat, on Naois's shoulder. Arden was long in this posture when he died; but though he was dead Naois would not let him go.

Allen then cried out that he was getting faint and nigh-well giving up. When Naois heard his prayer, he gave forth the piercing sigh of death, and asked Allen to lay hold of him and he would bring him to land.

Allen was not long when the weakness of death came on him and his hold failed. Naois looked around, and when he saw his two well-beloved brothers dead, he cared not whether he lived or died, and he gave forth the bitter sigh of death, and his heart burst.

"They are gone," said Duanan Gacha Druid to the king, "and I have done what you desired me. The sons of Uisnech are dead and they will trouble you no more; and you have your wife hale and whole to yourself."

"Blessings for that upon you and may the good results accrue to me, Duanan. I count it no loss what I spent in the schooling and teaching of you. Now dry up the flood, and let me see if I can behold Deirdre," said Connachar. And Duanan Gacha Druid dried up the flood from the plain and the three sons of Uisnech were lying together dead, without breath of life, side by side on the green meadow plain and Deirdre bending above showering down her tears.

Then Deirdre said this lament: "Fair one, loved one, flower of beauty; beloved upright and strong; beloved noble and modest warrior. Fair one, blue-eyed, beloved of thy wife; lovely to me at the trysting-place came thy clear voice through the woods of Ireland. I cannot eat or smile henceforth. Break not today, my heart: soon enough shall I lie within my grave. Strong are the waves of sorrow, but stronger is sorrow's self, Connachar."

The people then gathered round the heroes' bodies and asked Connachar what was to be done with the bodies. The order that he gave was that they should dig a pit and put the three brothers in it side by side. Deirdre kept sitting on the brink of the grave, constantly asking the gravediggers to dig the pit wide and free. When the bodies of the brothers were put in the grave, Deirdre said: –

> *"Come over hither, Naois, my love,*
> *Let Arden close to Allen lie;*
> *If the dead had any sense to feel,*
> *Ye would have made a place for Deirdre."*

The men did as she told them. She jumped into the grave and lay down by Naois, and she was dead by his side.

The king ordered the body to be raised from out the grave and to be buried on the other side of the loch. It was done as the king bade, and the pit closed. Thereupon a fir shoot grew out of the grave of Deirdre and a fir shoot from the grave of Naois, and the two shoots united in a knot above the loch. The king ordered the shoots to be cut down, and this was done twice, until, at the third time, the wife whom the king had married caused him to stop this work of evil and his vengeance on the remains of the dead.

Heroes &
Giants

ANCIENT TALES of Celtic warriors and their fearsome opponents exist so strongly in the mind to this day due to the richness of the storytelling tradition. Fionn Mac Cumhail, legendary hero of the Fenian Cycle, features here in the story of 'How Fin went to the Kingdom of the Big Men', while the great Cuchulain of the Ulster cycle is hero of 'The Knighting of Cuculain', told here by Standish O'Grady – note how spellings inevitably vary, revealing again the rich oral development of folklore.

Tales of heroes naturally involve quests and giants. Fionn and Cuchulain encounter giants, as do the protagonists in 'The Giant's Stairs' and 'The Shee An Gannon and the Gruagach Gaire'. Another hero – he of 'The Story of Conn-Eda; or, The Golden Apples of Lough Erne' – embarks on a quest to secure the three golden apples, the black steed and the 'hound of supernatural powers' from the king of the Firbolgs in Lough Erne.

The Knighting of Cuculain

❖

ONE NIGHT in the month of the fires of Bel, Cathvah, the Druid and star-gazer, was observing the heavens through his astrological instruments. Beside him was Cuculain, just then completing his sixteenth year. Since the exile of Fergus MacRoy, Cuculain had attached himself most to the Ard-Druid, and delighted to be along with him in his studies and observations. Suddenly the old man put aside his instruments and meditated a long time in silence.

"Setanta," said he at length, "art thou yet sixteen years of age?"

"No, father," replied the boy.

"It will then be difficult to persuade the king to knight thee and enrol thee among his knights," said Cathvah. "Yet this must be done tomorrow, for it has been revealed to me that he whom Concobar MacNessa shall present with arms tomorrow will be renowned to the most distant ages, and to the ends of the earth. Thou shalt be presented with arms tomorrow, and after that thou mayest retire for a season among thy comrades, nor go out among the warriors until thy strength is mature."

The next day Cathvah procured the king's consent to the knighting of Cuculain. Now on the same morning, one of his grooms came to Concobar MacNessa and said: "O chief of the Red Branch, thou knowest how no horse has eaten barley, or ever occupied the stall where stood the divine steed which, with another of mortal breed, in the days of Kimbay MacFiontann, was accustomed to bear forth to the battle the great war-queen, Macha Monga-Rue; but ever since that stall has been empty, and no mortal steed hath profaned the stall in which the deathless Lia Macha was wont to stand. Yet, O Concobar, as I passed into the great stables on the east side of the courtyard, wherein are the steeds of thy own ambus, and in which is that spot since held sacred, I saw in the empty stall a mare, gray almost to whiteness, and of a size and beauty such as I have never seen, who turned to look upon me as I entered the stable, having very gentle eyes, but such as terrified me, so that I let fall the vessel in which I was bearing curds for the steed of Konaul Clareena; and she approached me, and laid her head upon my shoulder, making a strange noise."

Now as the groom was thus speaking, Cowshra Mend Macha, a younger son of Concobar, came before the king, and said: "Thou knowest, O my father, that house in which is preserved the chariot of Kimbay MacFiontann, wherein he and she, whose name I bear, the great queen that protects our nation, rode forth to the wars in the ancient days, and how it has been preserved ever since, and that it is under my care to keep bright and clean. Now this day at sunrise I approached the house, as is my custom, and approaching, I heard dire voices, clamorous and terrible, that came from within, and noises like the noise of battle, and shouts as of warriors in the agony of the conflict, that raise their voices with short intense cries as they ply their weapons, avoiding or inflicting death. Then I went back terrified, but there met me Minrowar, son of Gerkin, for he came but last night from Moharne, in the east, and he went to look at his own steeds; but together we opened the gate of the chariot-house, and the bronze of the chariot burned like glowing fire, and the voices cried out in acclaim, when we stood in the doorway, and the light streamed into the dark chamber. Doubtless, a great warrior will appear amongst the Red Branch, for men say that not for a hundred years have these voices been heard, and I know not for whom Macha sends these portents, if it be not for the son of Sualtam, though he is not yet of an age to bear arms."

Thus was Concobar prepared for the knighting of Cuculain.

Then in the presence of his court, and his warriors, and the youths who were the comrades and companions of Cuculain, Concobar presented the young hero with his weapons of war, after he had taken the vows of the Red Branch, and having also bound himself by certain gæsa. But Cuculain looked narrowly upon the weapons, and he struck the spears together and clashed the sword upon the shield, and he brake the spears in pieces, and the sword, and made chasms in the shield.

"These are not good weapons, O my King," said the boy.

Then the king presented him with others that were larger and stronger, and these too the boy brake into little pieces.

"These are still worse, O son of Nessa," said the boy, "and it is not seemly, O chief of the Red Branch, that on the day that I am to receive my arms I should be made a laughing-stock before the Clanna Rury, being yet but a boy."

But Concobar MacNessa exulted exceedingly when he beheld the amazing strength and the waywardness of the boy, and beneath delicate brows his eyes glittered like gleaming swords as he glanced rapidly round on the crowd of martial men that surrounded him; but amongst them all he seemed himself a bright torch of valour and war, more pure and clear than polished steel. But he beckoned to one of his knights, who hastened away and returned, bringing Concobar's own shield and spears and the sword out of the Tayta Brac, where they were kept, an equipment in reserve. And Cuculain shook them and bent them, and clashed them together, but they held firm.

"These are good arms, O son of Nessa," said Cuculain.

Then there were led forward a pair of noble steeds and a war-car, and the king conferred them on Cuculain. Then Cuculain sprang into the chariot, and standing with legs apart, he stamped from side to side, and shook and shook, and jolted the car until the axle brake and the car itself was broken in pieces.

"This is not a good chariot, O my King," said the boy.

Then there were led forward three chariots, and all these he brake in succession.

"These are not good chariots, O chief of the Red Branch," said Cuculain. "No brave warrior would enter the battle or fight from such rotten foothold."

Then the king called to his son Cowshra Mead Macha and bade him take Læg, and harness to the war-chariot, of which he had the care, the wondrous gray steed, and that one which had been given him by Kelkar, the son of Uther, and to give Læg a charioteering equipment, to be charioteers of Cuculain. For now it was apparent to all the nobles and to the king that a lion of war had appeared amongst them, and that it was for him Macha had sent these omens.

Then Cuculain's heart leaped in his breast when he heard the thunder of the great war-car and the mad whinnying of the horses that smelt the battle afar. Soon he beheld them with his eyes, and the charioteer with the golden fillet of his office, erect in the car, struggling to subdue their fury. A gray, long-maned steed, whale-bellied, broad-chested, behind one yoke; a black, ugly-maned steed behind the other.

Like a hawk swooping along the face of a cliff when the wind is high, or like the rush of the March wind over the plain, or like the fleetness of the stag roused from his lair by the hounds and covering his first field, was the rush of those steeds when they had broken through the restraint of the charioteer, as though they galloped over fiery flags, so that the earth shook and trembled with the velocity of their motion, and all the time the great car brayed and shrieked as the wheels of solid and glittering bronze went round, for there were demons that had their abode in that car.

The charioteer restrained the steeds before the assembly, but nay-the-less a deep pur, like the pur of a tiger, proceeded from the axle. Then the whole assembly lifted up their voices and shouted for Cuculain, and he himself, Cuculain the son of Sualtam, sprang into his chariot, all armed, with a cry as of a warrior springing into his chariot in the battle, and he stood erect and brandished his spears, and the war-sprites of the Gæil shouted along with them, to the Bocanahs and Bananahs and the Genitii Glindi, the wild people of the glens, and the demons of the air, roared around him, when first the great warrior of the Gæil, his battle-arms in his hands, stood equipped for war in his chariot before all the warriors of his tribe, the kings of the Clanna Rury, and the people of Emain Macha.

How Fin Went to the Kingdom of the Big Men

❈

FIN AND HIS MEN were in the Harbour of the Hill of Howth on a hillock, behind the wind and in front of the sun, where they could see every person, and nobody could see them, when they saw a speck coming from the west. They thought at first it

was the blackness of a shower; but when it came nearer, they saw it was a boat. It did not lower sail till it entered the harbour. There were three men in it; one for guide in the bow, one for steering in the stern, and one for the tackle in the centre. They came ashore, and drew it up seven times its own length in dry grey grass, where the scholars of the city could not make it stock for derision or ridicule.

They then went up to a lovely green spot, and the first lifted a handful of round pebbles or shingle, and commanded them to become a beautiful house, that no better could be found in Ireland; and this was done. The second one lifted a slab of slate, and commanded it to be slate on the top of the house, that there was not better in Ireland; and this was done. The third one caught a bunch of shavings and commanded them to be pine-wood and timber in the house, that there was not in Ireland better; and this was done.

This caused much wonder to Fin, who went down where the men were, and made inquiries of them, and they answered him. He asked whence they were, or whither they were going. They said, "We are three Heroes whom the King of the Big Men has sent to ask combat of the Fians." He then asked, "What was the reason for doing this?" They said they did not know, but they heard that they were strong men, and they came to ask combat of Heroes from them. "Is Fin at Home?"

"He is not." (Great is a man's leaning towards his own life.) Fin then put them under crosses and under enchantments, that they were not to move from the place where they were till they saw him again.

He went away and made ready his coracle, gave its stern to land and prow to sea, hoisted the spotted towering sails against the long, tough, lance-shaped mast, cleaving the billows in the embrace of the wind in whirls, with a soft gentle breeze from the height of the sea-coast, and from the rapid tide of the red rocks, that would take willom from the hill, foliage from the tree, and heather from its stock and roots. Fin was guide in her prow, helm in her stern, and tackle in her middle; and stopping of head or foot he did not make till he reached the Kingdom of the Big Men. He went ashore and drew up his coracle in grey grass. He went up, and a Big Wayfarer met him. Fin asked who he was.

"I am," he said, "the Red-haired Coward of the King of the Big Men; and," said he to Fin, "you are the one I am in quest of. Great is my esteem and respect towards you; you are the best maiden I have ever seen; you will yourself make a dwarf for the King, and your dog (this was Bran) a lapdog. It is long since the King has been in want of a dwarf and a lapdog." He took with him Fin; but another Big Man came, and was going to take Fin from him. The two fought; but when they had torn each other's clothes, they left it to Fin to judge. He chose the first one. He took Fin with him to the palace of the King, whose worthies and high nobles assembled to see the little man. The king lifted him upon the palm of his hand, and went three times round the town with Fin upon one palm and Bran upon the other. He made a sleeping-place for him at the end of his own bed. Fin was waiting, watching, and observing everything that was going on about the house. He observed that the King, as soon as night came, rose and went out, and returned no more till morning. This caused him much wonder, and at last he asked the King why he went away every night and left the Queen by herself. "Why," said the King, "do you ask?"

"For satisfaction to myself," said Fin; "for it is causing me much wonder." Now the King had a great liking for Fin; he never saw anything that gave him more pleasure than he did; and at last he told him. "There is," he said, "a great Monster who wants my daughter in marriage, and to have half my kingdom to himself; and there is not another man in the kingdom who can meet him but myself; and I must go every night to hold combat with him."

"Is there," said Fin, "no man to combat with him but yourself?"

"There is not," said the King, "one who will war with him for a single night."

"It is a pity," said Fin, "that this should be called the Kingdom of the Big Men. Is he bigger than yourself?"

"Never you mind," said the King.

"I will mind," said Fin; "take your rest and sleep tonight, and I shall go to meet him."

"Is it you?" said the King; "you would not keep half a stroke against him."

When night came, and all men went to rest, the King was for going away as usual; but Fin at last prevailed upon him to allow himself to go. "I shall combat him," said he, "or else he knows a trick."

"I think much," said the King, "of allowing you to go, seeing he gives myself enough to do."

"Sleep you soundly tonight," said Fin, "and let me go; if he comes too violently upon me, I shall hasten home."

Fin went and reached the place where the combat was to be. He saw no one before him, and he began to pace backwards and forwards. At last he saw the sea coming in kilns of fire and as a darting serpent, till it came down below where he was. A Huge Monster came up and looked towards him, and from him. "What little speck do I see there?" he said.

"It is I," said Fin. "What are you doing here?"

"I am a messenger from the King of the Big Men; he is under much sorrow and distress; the Queen has just died, and I have come to ask if you will be so good as to go home tonight without giving trouble to the kingdom."

"I shall do that," said he; and he went away with the rough humming of a song in his mouth.

Fin went home when the time came, and lay down in his own bed, at the foot of the King's bed. When the King awoke, he cried out in great anxiety, "My kingdom is lost, and my dwarf and my lapdog are killed!"

"They are not," said Fin; "I am here yet; and you have got your sleep, a thing you were saying it was rare for you to get."

"How," said the King, "did you escape, when you are so little, while he is enough for myself, though I am so big."

"Though you," said Fin, "are so big and strong, I am quick and active."

Next night the King was for going; but Fin told him to take his sleep tonight again. "I shall stand myself in your place, or else a better hero than yonder one must come."

"He will kill you," said the King. "I shall take my chance," said Fin.

He went, and as happened the night before, he saw no one; and he began to pace backwards and forwards. He saw the sea coming in fiery kilns and as a darting serpent; and that Huge Man came up. "Are you here tonight again?" said he. "I am, and this is my errand: when the Queen was being put in the coffin, and the King heard the coffin being nailed, and the joiner's stroke, he broke his heart with pain and grief; and the Parliament has sent me to ask you to go home tonight till they get the

King buried." The Monster went this night also, roughly humming a song; and Fin went home when the time came.

In the morning the King awoke in great anxiety, and called out, "My kingdom is lost, and my dwarf and my lapdog are killed!" and he greatly rejoiced that Fin and Bran were alive, and that he himself got rest, after being so long without sleep.

Fin went the third night, and things happened as before. There was no one before him, and he took to pacing to and fro. He saw the sea coming till it came down below him: the Big Monster came up; he saw the little black speck, and asked who was there, and what he wanted. "I have come to combat you," said Fin.

Fin and Bran began the combat. Fin was going backwards, and the Huge Man was following. Fin called to Bran, "Are you going to let him kill me?" Bran had a venomous shoe; and he leaped and struck the Huge Man with the venomous shoe on the breast-bone, and took the heart and lungs out of him. Fin drew his sword, Mac-a-Luin, cut off his head, put it on a hempen rope, and went with it to the Palace of the King. He took it into the Kitchen, and put it behind the door. In the morning the servant could not turn it, nor open the door. The King went down; he saw the Huge Mass, caught it by the top of the head, and lifted it, and knew it was the head of the Man who was for so long a time asking combat from him, and keeping him from sleep. "How at all," said he, "has this head come here? Surely it is not my dwarf that has done it."

"Why," said Fin, "should he not?"

Next night the King wanted to go himself to the place of combat; "because," said he, "a bigger one than the former will come tonight, and the kingdom will be destroyed, and you yourself killed; and I shall lose the pleasure I take in having you with me." But Fin went, and that Big Man came, asking vengeance for his son, and to have the kingdom for himself, or equal combat. He and Fin fought; and Fin was going backwards. He spoke to Bran, "Are you going to allow him to kill me?" Bran whined, and went and sat down on the beach. Fin was ever being driven back, and he called out again to Bran. Then Bran jumped and struck the Big Man with the venomous shoe, and took the heart and the lungs out of him. Fin cut the head off, and took it with him, and left it in front of the house. The

King awoke in great terror, and cried out, "My kingdom is lost, and my dwarf and my lapdog are killed!" Fin raised himself up and said, "They are not"; and the King's joy was not small when he went out and saw the head that was in front of the house.

The next night a Big Hag came ashore, and the tooth in the door of her mouth would make a distaff. She sounded a challenge on her shield: "You killed," she said, "my husband and my son."

"I did kill them," said Fin. They fought; and it was worse for Fin to guard himself from the tooth than from the hand of the Big Hag. When she had nearly done for him Bran struck her with the venomous shoe, and killed her as he had done to the rest. Fin took with him the head, and left it in front of the house. The King awoke in great anxiety, and called out, "My kingdom is lost, and my dwarf and my lapdog are killed!"

"They are not," said Fin, answering him; and when they went out and saw the head, the King said, "I and my kingdom will have peace ever after this. The mother herself of the brood is killed; but tell me who you are. It was foretold for me that it would be Fin-mac-Coul that would give me relief, and he is only now eighteen years of age. Who are you, then, or what is your name?"

"There never stood," said Fin, "on hide of cow or horse, one to whom I would deny my name. I am Fin, the Son of Coul, son of Looach, son of Trein, son of Fin, son of Art, son of the young High King of Erin; and it is time for me now to go home. It has been with much wandering out of my way that I have come to your kingdom; and this is the reason why I have come, that I might find out what injury I have done to you, or the reason why you sent the three heroes to ask combat from me, and bring destruction on my Men."

"You never did any injury to me," said the King; "and I ask a thousand pardons. I did not send the heroes to you. It is not the truth they told. They were three men who were courting three fairy women, and these gave them their shirts; and when they have on their shirts, the combat of a hundred men is upon the hand of every one of them. But they must put off the shirts every night, and put them on the backs of chairs; and if the shirts were taken from them they would be next day as weak as other people."

Fin got every honour, and all that the King could give him, and when he went away, the King and the Queen and the people went down to the shore to give him their blessing.

Fin now went away in his coracle, and was sailing close by the side of the shore, when he saw a young man running and calling out to him. Fin came in close to land with his coracle, and asked what he wanted.

"I am," said the young man, "a good servant wanting a master."

"What work can you do?" said Fin.

"I am," said he, "the best soothsayer that there is."

"Jump into the boat then." The soothsayer jumped in, and they went forward.

They did not go far when another youth came running. "I am," he said, "a good servant wanting a master."

"What work can you do?" said Fin.

"I am as good a thief as there is."

"Jump into the boat, then"; and Fin took with him this one also. They saw then a third young man running and calling out. They came close to land. "What man are you?" said Fin.

"I am," said he, "the best climber that there is. I will take up a hundred pounds on my back in a place where a fly could not stand on a calm summer day."

"Jump in"; and this one came in also. "I have my pick of servants now," said Fin; "it cannot be but these will suffice."

They went; and stop of head or foot they did not make till they reached the Harbour of the Hill of Howth. He asked the soothsayer what the three Big Men were doing. "They are," he said, "after their supper, and making ready for going to bed."

He asked a second time. "They are," he said, "after going to bed; and their shirts are spread on the back of chairs."

After a while, Fin asked him again, "What are the Big Men doing now?"

"They are," said the soothsayer, "sound asleep."

"It would be a good thing if there was now a thief to go and steal the shirts."

"I would do that," said the thief, "but the doors are locked, and I cannot get in."

"Come," said the climber, "on my back, and I shall put you in." He took him up upon his back to the top of the chimney, and let him down, and he stole the shirts.

Fin went where the Fian band was; and in the morning they came to the house where the three Big Men were. They sounded a challenge upon their shields, and asked them to come out to combat.

They came out. "Many a day," said they, "have we been better for combat than we are today," and they confessed to Fin everything as it was. "You were," said Fin, "impertinent, but I will forgive you"; and he made them swear that they would be faithful to himself ever after, and ready in every enterprise he would place before them.

The Birth of Oisín

ONE DAY as Finn and his companions and dogs were returning from the chase to their Dún on the Hill of Allen, a beautiful fawn started up on their path and the chase swept after her, she taking the way which led to their home. Soon, all the pursuers were left far behind save only Finn himself and his two hounds Bran and Sceolaun. Now these hounds were of strange breed, for Tyren, sister to Murna, the mother of Finn, had been changed into a hound by the enchantment of a woman of the Fairy Folk, who loved Tyren's husband Ullan; and the two hounds of Finn were the children of Tyren, born to her in that shape. Of all hounds in Ireland they were the best, and Finn loved them much, so that it was said he wept but twice in his life, and once was for the death of Bran.

At last, as the chase went on down a valley side, Finn saw the fawn stop and lie down, while the two hounds began to play round her and to lick her face and limbs. So he gave commandment that none should hurt her, and she followed them to the Dún of Allen, playing with the hounds as she went.

The same night Finn awoke and saw standing by his bed the fairest woman his eyes had ever beheld.

"I am Saba, O Finn," she said, "and I was the fawn ye chased today. Because I would not give my love to the Druid of the Fairy Folk, who is named the Dark, he put that shape upon me by his sorceries, and I have borne it these three years. But a slave of his, pitying me, once revealed to me that if I could win to thy great Dún of Allen, O Finn, I should be safe from all enchantments and my natural shape would come to me again. But I feared to be torn in pieces by thy dogs, or wounded by thy hunters, till at last I let myself be overtaken by thee alone and by Bran and Sceolaun, who have the nature of man and would do me no hurt."

"Have no fear, maiden," said Finn, "we the Fianna, are free and our guest-friends are free; there is none who shall put compulsion on you here."

So Saba dwelt with Finn, and he made her his wife; and so deep was his love for her that neither the battle nor the chase had any delight for him, and for months he never left her side. She also loved him as deeply, and their joy in each other was like that of the Immortals in the Land of Youth. But at last word came to Finn that the warships of the Northmen were in the bay of Dublin, and he summoned his heroes to the fight, "for," said he to Saba, "the men of Erinn give us tribute and hospitality to defend them from the foreigner, and it were shame to take it from them and not to give that to which we, on our side, are pledged." And he called to mind that great saying of Goll mac Morna when they were once sore bested by a mighty host – "a man," said Goll, "lives after his life but not after his honour."

Seven days was Finn absent, and he drove the Northmen from the shores of Erinn. But on the eighth day he returned, and when he entered his Dún he saw trouble in the eyes of his men and of their fair womenfolk, and Saba was not on the rampart expecting his return. So he bade them tell him what had chanced, and they said –

"Whilst thou, our father and lord, wert afar off smiting the foreigner, and Saba looking ever down the pass for thy return, we saw one day as it were the likeness of thee approaching, and Bran and Sceolaun at thy heels. And we seemed also to hear the notes of the Fian hunting call blown on the wind. Then Saba hastened to the great gate, and we could not stay her, so eager was she to rush to the phantom. But when she came near, she halted and gave a loud and bitter cry, and the shape of thee smote her with a hazel wand, and lo, there was no woman there anymore, but a deer. Then those hounds chased it, and ever as it strove to reach again the gate of the Dún they turned it back. We all now seized what arms we could and ran out to drive away the enchanter, but when we reached the place there was nothing to be seen, only still we heard the rushing of flying feet and the baying of dogs, and one thought it came from here, and another from there, till at last the uproar died away and all was still. What we could do, O Finn, we did; Saba is gone."

Finn then struck his hand on his breast but spoke no word, and he went to his own chamber. No man saw him for the rest of that day, nor for the day after. Then he came forth, and ordered the matters of the Fianna as of old, but for seven years thereafter he went searching for Saba through every remote glen and dark forest and cavern of Ireland, and he would take no hounds with him save Bran and Sceolaun. But at last he renounced all hope of finding her again, and went hunting as of old. One day as he was following the chase on Ben Gulban in Sligo, he heard the musical bay of the dogs change of a sudden to a fierce growling and yelping as though they were in combat with some beast, and running hastily up he and his men beheld, under a great tree, a naked boy with long hair, and around him the hounds struggling to seize him, but Bran and Sceolaun fighting with them and keeping them off. And the lad was tall and shapely, and as the heroes gathered round he gazed undauntedly on them, never heeding the rout of dogs at his feet. The Fians beat off the dogs and brought the lad home with them, and Finn was very silent and continually searched the lad's countenance with his eyes. In time, the use of speech came to him, and the story that he told was this:

He had known no father, and no mother save a gentle hind with whom he lived in a most green and pleasant valley shut in on every side by towering cliffs that could not be scaled, or by deep chasms in the earth. In the summer he lived on fruits and such-like, and in the winter, store of provisions was laid for him in a cave. And there came to them sometimes a tall dark-visaged man, who spoke to his mother, now tenderly, and now in loud menace, but she always shrunk away in fear, and the man departed in anger. At last there came a day when the Dark Man spoke very long with his mother in all tones of entreaty and of tenderness and of rage, but she would still keep aloof and give no sign save of fear and abhorrence. Then at length the Dark Man drew near and smote her with a hazel wand; and with that he turned and went his way, but she, this time, followed him, still looking back at her son and piteously complaining. And he, when he strove to follow, found himself unable to move a limb; and crying out with rage and desolation he fell to the earth and his senses left him. When he came to himself he was on the mountain side, on Ben Gulban, where he remained some days, searching for that green and hidden valley, which he never found again. And after a while the dogs found him; but of the hind his mother and of the Dark Druid, there is no man knows the end.

Finn called his name Oisín, and he became a warrior of fame, but far more famous for the songs and tales that he made; so that of all things to this day that are told of the Fianna of Erinn, men are wont to say, "So sang the bard, Oisín, son of Finn."

The Lad with the Goat-Skin

❧

LONG AGO, a poor widow woman lived down near the iron forge, by Enniscorth, and she was so poor she had no clothes to put on her son; so she used to fix him in the ash-hole, near the fire, and pile the warm ashes about him; and according as he grew up, she sunk the pit deeper. At last, by hook or by crook, she got a goat-skin, and fastened it round his waist, and he felt quite grand, and took a walk down the street. So says she to him next morning, "Tom, you thief, you never done any good yet, and you six foot high, and past nineteen – take that rope and bring me a faggot from the wood."

"Never say't twice, mother," says Tom – "here goes."

When he had it gathered and tied, what should come up but a big giant, nine foot high, and made a lick of a club at him. Well become Tom, he jumped a-one side, and picked up a ram-pike; and the first crack he gave the big fellow, he made him kiss the clod.

"If you have e'er a prayer," says Tom, "now's the time to say it, before I make fragments of you."

"I have no prayers," says the giant; "but if you spare my life I'll give you that club; and as long as you keep from sin, you'll win every battle you ever fight with it."

Tom made no bones about letting him off; and as soon as he got the club in his hands, he sat down on the bresna, and gave it a tap with the kippeen, and says, "Faggot, I had great trouble gathering you, and run the risk of my life for you, the least you can do is to carry me home." And sure enough, the wind o' the word was all it wanted. It went off through the wood, groaning and crackling, till it came to the widow's door.

Well, when the sticks were all burned, Tom was sent off again to pick more; and this time he had to fight with a giant that had two heads on him. Tom had a little more trouble with him – that's all; and the prayers he said, was to give Tom a fife; that nobody could help dancing when he was playing it. Begonies, he made the big faggot dance home, with himself sitting on it. The next giant was a beautiful boy with three heads on him. He had neither prayers nor catechism no more nor the others; and so he gave Tom a bottle of green ointment, that wouldn't let you be burned, nor scalded, nor wounded. "And now," says he, "there's no more of us. You may come and gather sticks here till little Lunacy Day in Harvest, without giant or fairy-man to disturb you."

Well, now, Tom was prouder nor ten paycocks, and used to take a walk down street in the heel of the evening; but some o' the little boys had no more manners than if they were Dublin jackeens, and put out their tongues at Tom's club and Tom's goat-skin. He didn't like that at all, and it would be mean to give one of them a clout. At last, what should come through the town but a kind of a bellman, only it's a big bugle he had, and a huntsman's cap on his head, and a kind of a painted shirt. So this – he wasn't a bellman, and I don't know what to call him – bugleman, maybe, proclaimed that the King of Dublin's daughter was so melancholy that she didn't give a laugh for seven years, and that her father would grant her in marriage to whoever could make her laugh three times.

"That's the very thing for me to try," says Tom; and so, without burning any more daylight, he kissed his mother, curled his club at the little boys, and off he set along the yalla highroad to the town of Dublin.

At last Tom came to one of the city gates, and the guards laughed and cursed at him instead of letting him in. Tom stood it all for a little time, but at last one of them – out of fun, as he said – drove his bayonet half an inch or so into his side. Tom done nothing but take the fellow by the scruff o' the neck and the waistband of his corduroys, and fling him into the canal. Some run to pull the fellow out, and others to let manners into the vulgarian with their swords and daggers; but a tap from his club sent them headlong into the moat or down on the stones, and they were soon begging him to stay his hands.

So at last one of them was glad enough to show Tom the way to the palace-yard; and there was the king, and the queen, and the princess, in a gallery, looking at all sorts of wrestling, and sword-playing, and long-dances, and mumming, all to please the princess; but not a smile came over her handsome face.

Well, they all stopped when they seen the young giant, with his boy's face, and long black hair, and his short curly beard – for his poor mother couldn't afford to buy razors – and his great strong arms, and bare legs, and no covering but the goat-skin that reached from his waist to his knees. But an envious wizened bit of a fellow, with a red head, that wished to be married to the princess, and didn't like how she opened her eyes at Tom, came forward, and asked his business very snappishly.

"My business," says Tom, says he, "is to make the beautiful princess, God bless her, laugh three times."

"Do you see all them merry fellows and skilful swordsmen," says the other, "that could eat you up with a grain of salt, and not a mother's soul of 'em ever got a laugh from her these seven years?"

So the fellows gathered round Tom, and the bad man aggravated him till he told them he didn't care a pinch o' snuff for the whole bilin' of 'em; let 'em come on, six at a time, and try what they could do.

The king, who was too far off to hear what they were saying, asked what did the stranger want.

"He wants," says the red-headed fellow, "to make hares of your best men."

"Oh!" says the king, "if that's the way, let one of 'em turn out and try his mettle."

So one stood forward, with sword and pot-lid, and made a cut at Tom. He struck the fellow's elbow with the club, and up over their heads flew the sword, and down went the owner of it on the gravel from a thump he got on the helmet. Another took his place, and another, and another, and then half a dozen at once, and Tom sent swords, helmets, shields, and bodies, rolling over and over, and themselves bawling out that they were kilt, and disabled, and damaged, and rubbing their poor elbows and hips, and limping away. Tom contrived not to kill anyone; and the princess was so amused, that she let a great sweet laugh out of her that was heard over all the yard.

"King of Dublin," says Tom, "I've quarter your daughter."

And the king didn't know whether he was glad or sorry, and all the blood in the princess's heart run into her cheeks.

So there was no more fighting that day, and Tom was invited to dine with the royal family. Next day, Redhead told Tom of a wolf, the size of a yearling heifer, that used to be serenading about the walls, and eating people and cattle; and said what a pleasure it would give the king to have it killed.

"With all my heart," says Tom; "send a jackeen to show me where he lives, and we'll see how he behaves to a stranger."

The princess was not well pleased, for Tom looked a different person with fine clothes and a nice green birredh over his long curly hair; and besides, he'd got one laugh out of her. However, the king gave his consent; and in an hour and a half the horrible wolf was walking into the palace-yard, and Tom a step or two behind, with his club on his shoulder, just as a shepherd would be walking after a pet lamb.

The king and queen and princess were safe up in their gallery, but the officers and people of the court that wor padrowling about the great bawn, when they saw the big baste coming in, gave themselves up, and began to make for doors and gates; and the wolf licked his chops, as if he was saying, "Wouldn't I enjoy a breakfast off a couple of yez!"

The king shouted out, "O Tom with the Goat-skin, take away that terrible wolf, and you must have all my daughter."

But Tom didn't mind him a bit. He pulled out his flute and began to play like vengeance; and dickens a man or boy in the yard but began shovelling away heel and toe, and the wolf himself was obliged to get on his hind legs and dance 'Tatther Jack Walsh', along with the rest. A good deal of the people got inside, and shut the doors, the way the hairy fellow wouldn't pin them; but Tom kept playing, and the outsiders kept dancing and shouting, and the wolf kept dancing and roaring with the pain his legs were giving him; and all the time he had his eyes on Redhead, who was shut out along with the rest. Wherever Redhead went, the wolf followed, and kept one eye on him and the other on Tom, to see if he would give him leave to eat him. But Tom shook his head, and never stopped the tune, and Redhead never stopped dancing and bawling, and the wolf dancing and roaring, one leg up and the other down, and he ready to drop out of his standing from fair tiresomeness.

When the princess seen that there was no fear of anyone being kilt, she was so diverted by the stew that Redhead was in, that she gave another great laugh; and well become Tom, out he cried, "King of Dublin, I have two halves of your daughter."

"Oh, halves or alls," says the king, "put away that divel of a wolf, and we'll see about it."

So Tom put his flute in his pocket, and says he to the baste that was sittin' on his currabingo ready to faint, "Walk off to your mountain, my fine fellow, and live like a respectable baste; and if ever I find you come within seven miles of any town, I'll –"

He said no more, but spit in his fist, and gave a flourish of his club. It was all the poor divel of a wolf wanted: he put his tail between his legs, and took to his pumps without looking at man or mortal, and neither sun, moon, or stars ever saw him in sight of Dublin again.

At dinner everyone laughed but the foxy fellow; and sure enough he was laying out how he'd settle poor Tom next day.

"Well, to be sure!" says he, "King of Dublin, you are in luck. There's the Danes moidhering us to no end. Deuce run to Lusk wid 'em! and if anyone can save us from 'em, it is this gentleman with the goat-skin. There is a flail hangin' on the collar-beam, in hell, and neither Dane nor devil can stand before it."

"So," says Tom to the king, "will you let me have the other half of the princess if I bring you the flail?"

"No, no," says the princess; "I'd rather never be your wife than see you in that danger."

But Redhead whispered and nudged Tom about how shabby it would look to reneague the adventure. So he asked which way he was to go, and Redhead directed him.

Well, he travelled and travelled, till he came in sight of the walls of hell; and, bedad, before he knocked at the gates, he rubbed himself over with the greenish ointment. When he knocked, a hundred little imps popped their heads out through the bars, and axed him what he wanted.

"I want to speak to the big divel of all," says Tom: "open the gate."

It wasn't long till the gate was thrune open, and the Ould Boy received Tom with bows and scrapes, and axed his business.

"My business isn't much," says Tom. "I only came for the loan of that flail that I see hanging on the collar-beam, for the king of Dublin to give a thrashing to the Danes."

"Well," says the other, "the Danes is much better customers to me; but since you walked so far I won't refuse. Hand that flail," says he to a young imp; and he winked the far-off eye at the same time. So, while some were barring the gates, the young devil climbed up, and took down the flail that had the handstaff and booltheen both made out of red-hot iron. The little vagabond was grinning to think how it would burn the hands o' Tom, but the dickens a burn it made on him, no more nor if it was a good oak sapling.

"Thankee," says Tom. "Now would you open the gate for a body, and I'll give you no more trouble."

"Oh, tramp!" says Ould Nick; "is that the way? It is easier getting inside them gates than getting out again. Take that tool from him, and give him a dose of the oil of stirrup."

So one fellow put out his claws to seize on the flail, but Tom gave him such a welt of it on the side of the head that he broke off one of his horns, and made him roar like a devil as he was. Well, they rushed at Tom, but he gave them, little and big, such a thrashing as they didn't forget for a while. At last says the ould thief of all, rubbing his elbow, "Let the fool out; and woe to whoever lets him in again, great or small."

So out marched Tom, and away with him, without minding the shouting and cursing they kept up at him from the tops of the walls; and when he got home to the big bawn of the palace, there never was such running and racing as to see himself and the flail. When he had his story told, he laid down the flail on the stone steps, and bid no one for their lives to touch it. If the king, and queen, and princess, made much of him before, they made ten times more of him now; but Redhead, the mean scruff-hound, stole over, and thought to catch hold of the flail to make an end of him. His fingers hardly touched it, when he let a roar out of him as if heaven and earth were coming together, and kept flinging his arms about and dancing, that it was pitiful to look at him. Tom run at him as soon as he could rise, caught his hands in his own two, and rubbed them this way and that, and the burning pain left them before you could reckon one. Well the poor fellow, between the pain that was only just gone, and the comfort he was in, had the comicalest face that you ever see, it was such a mixtherum-gatherum of laughing and crying. Everybody burst out a laughing – the princess could not stop no more than the rest; and then says Tom, "Now, ma'am, if there were fifty halves of you, I hope you'll give me them all."

Well, the princess looked at her father, and by my word, she came over to Tom, and put her two delicate hands into his two rough ones, and I wish it was myself was in his shoes that day!

Tom would not bring the flail into the palace. You may be sure no other body went near it; and when the early risers were passing next morning, they found two long clefts in the stone, where it was after burning itself an opening downwards, nobody could tell how far. But a messenger came in at noon, and said that the Danes were so frightened when they heard of the flail coming into Dublin, that they got into their ships, and sailed away.

Well, I suppose, before they were married, Tom got some man, like Pat Mara of Tomenine, to learn him the 'principles of politeness', fluxions, gunnery, and fortification, decimal fractions, practice, and the rule of three direct, the way he'd be able to keep up a conversation with the royal family. Whether he ever lost his time learning them sciences, I'm not sure, but it's as sure as fate that his mother never more saw any want till the end of her days.

The Story of Conn-Eda
or, The Golden Apples of Lough Erne

⬥

IT WAS LONG BEFORE the time the western districts of *Innis Fodhla* had any settled name, but were indiscriminately called after the person who took possession of them, and whose name they retained only as long as his sway lasted, that a powerful king reigned over this part of the sacred island. He was a puissant warrior, and no individual was found able to compete with him either on land or sea, or question his right to his conquest. The great king of the west held uncontrolled sway from the island of Rathlin to the mouth of the Shannon by sea, and far as the glittering length by land. The ancient king of the west, whose name was Conn, was good as well as great, and passionately loved by his people. His queen was a *Breaton* (British) princess, and was equally beloved and esteemed, because she was the great counterpart of the king in every respect; for whatever good qualification was wanting in the one, the other was certain to indemnify the omission. It was plainly manifest that heaven approved of the career in life of the virtuous couple; for during their reign the earth produced exuberant crops, the trees fruit ninefold commensurate with their usual bearing, the rivers, lakes, and surrounding sea teemed with abundance of choice fish, while herds and flocks were unusually prolific, and kine and sheep yielded such abundance of rich milk that they shed it in torrents upon the pastures; and furrows and cavities were always filled with the pure lacteal produce of the dairy. All these

were blessings heaped by heaven upon the western districts of
***Innis Fodhla*, over which the benignant and just Conn swayed**
his sceptre, in approbation of the course of government he had
marked out for his own guidance.

It is needless to state that the people who owned the authority of this great
and good sovereign were the happiest on the face of the wide expanse
of earth. It was during his reign, and that of his son and successor, that
Ireland acquired the title of the 'happy isle of the west' among foreign
nations. Con Mór and his good Queen Eda reigned in great glory during
many years; they were blessed with an only son, whom they named Conn-
eda, after both his parents, because the Druids foretold at his birth that he
would inherit the good qualities of both. According as the young prince
grew in years, his amiable and benignant qualities of mind, as well as his
great strength of body and manly bearing, became more manifest. He was
the idol of his parents, and the boast of his people; he was beloved and
respected to that degree that neither prince, lord, nor plebeian swore an
oath by the sun, moon, stars, or elements, except by the head of Conn-
eda. This career of glory, however, was doomed to meet a powerful but
temporary impediment, for the good Queen Eda took a sudden and severe
illness, of which she died in a few days, thus plunging her spouse, her son,
and all her people into a depth of grief and sorrow from which it was found
difficult to relieve them.

The good king and his subjects mourned the loss of Queen Eda for a year
and a day, and at the expiration of that time Conn Mór reluctantly yielded
to the advice of his Druids and counsellors, and took to wife the daughter
of his Arch-Druid. The new queen appeared to walk in the footsteps of
the good Eda for several years, and gave great satisfaction to her subjects.
But, in course of time, having had several children, and perceiving that
Conn-eda was the favourite son of the king and the darling of the people,
she clearly foresaw that he would become successor to the throne after
the demise of his father, and that her son would certainly be excluded.
This excited the hatred and inflamed the jealousy of the Druid's daughter
against her step-son to such an extent, that she resolved in her own mind
to leave nothing in her power undone to secure his death, or even exile

from the kingdom. She began by circulating evil reports of the prince; but, as he was above suspicion, the king only laughed at the weakness of the queen; and the great princes and chieftains, supported by the people in general, gave an unqualified contradiction; while the prince himself bore all his trials with the utmost patience, and always repaid her bad and malicious acts towards him with good and benevolent ones. The enmity of the queen towards Conn-eda knew no bounds when she saw that the false reports she circulated could not injure him. As a last resource, to carry out her wicked projects, she determined to consult her *Cailleach-chearc* (hen-wife), who was a reputed enchantress.

Pursuant to her resolution, by the early dawn of morning she hied to the cabin of the *Cailleach-chearc*, and divulged to her the cause of her trouble.

"I cannot render you any help," said the *Cailleach*, "until you name the *duais*" (reward).

"What *duais* do you require?" asked the queen, impatiently.

"My *duais*," replied the enchantress, "is to fill the cavity of my arm with wool, and the hole I shall bore with my distaff with red wheat."

"Your *duais* is granted, and shall be immediately given you," said the queen. The enchantress thereupon stood in the door of her hut, and bending her arm into a circle with her side, directed the royal attendants to thrust the wool into her house through her arm, and she never permitted them to cease until all the available space within was filled with wool. She then got on the roof of her brother's house, and, having made a hole through it with her distaff, caused red wheat to be spilled through it, until that was filled up to the roof with red wheat, so that there was no room for another grain within. "Now," said the queen, "since you have received your *duais*, tell me how I can accomplish my purpose."

"Take this chess-board and chess, and invite the prince to play with you; you shall win the first game. The condition you shall make is, that whoever wins a game shall be at liberty to impose whatever *geasa* (conditions) the winner pleases on the loser. When you win, you must bid the prince, under the penalty either to go into *ionarbadh* (exile), or procure for you, within the space of a year and a day, the three golden apples that grew in the garden, the *each dubh* (black steed), and *coileen con na mbuadh* (hound of supernatural powers), called Samer, which are in the possession of the king of the Firbolg race, who resides in Lough Erne. Those two things are so precious, and so well guarded, that he can never attain them by his own power; and, if he would rashly attempt to seek them, he should lose his life."

The queen was greatly pleased at the advice, and lost no time in inviting Conn-eda to play a game at chess, under the conditions she had been instructed to arrange by the enchantress. The queen won the game, as the enchantress foretold, but so great was her anxiety to have the prince completely in her power, that she was tempted to challenge him to play a second game, which Conn-eda, to her astonishment, and no less mortification, easily won.

"Now," said the prince, "since you won the first game, it is your duty to impose your *geis* first."

"My *geis*" said the queen, "which I impose upon you, is to procure me the three golden apples that grow in the garden, the *each dubh* (black steed), and *cuileen con na mbuadh* (hound of supernatural powers), which are in the keeping of the king of the Firbolgs, in Lough Erne, within the space of a year and a day; or, in case you fail, to go into *ionarbadh* (exile), and never return, except you surrender yourself to lose your head and *comhead beatha* (preservation of life)."

"Well, then," said the prince, "the *geis* which I bind you by, is to sit upon the pinnacle of yonder tower until my return, and to take neither food nor nourishment of any description, except what red-wheat you can pick up with the point of your bodkin; but if I do not return, you are at perfect liberty to come down at the expiration of the year and a day."

In consequence of the severe *geis* imposed upon him, Conn-eda was very much troubled in mind; and, well knowing he had a long journey to make before he would reach his destination, immediately prepared to set out on his way, not, however, before he had the satisfaction of witnessing the ascent of the queen to the place where she was obliged to remain exposed to the scorching sun of the summer and the blasting storms of winter, for the space of one year and a day, at least. Conn-eda being ignorant of what steps he should take to procure the *each dubh* and *cuileen con na mbuadh*, though he was well aware that human energy would prove unavailing, thought proper to consult the great Druid, Fionn Dadhna, of Sleabh Badhna, who was a friend of his before he ventured to proceed to Lough Erne. When he arrived at the bruighean of the Druid, he was received with cordial friendship, and the *failte* (welcome), as usual, was poured out before him, and when he was seated, warm water was fetched, and his feet bathed, so that the fatigue he felt after his journey was greatly relieved. The Druid, after he had partaken of refreshments, consisting of the newest of food and oldest of liquors, asked him the reason for paying the visit, and more particularly the cause of his sorrow; for the prince appeared exceedingly depressed in spirit. Conn-eda told his friend the whole history of the transaction with his stepmother from the beginning to end.

"Can you not assist me?" asked the Prince, with downcast countenance.

"I cannot, indeed, assist you at present," replied the Druid; "but I will retire to my *grianan* (green place) at sun-rising on the morrow, and learn by virtue of my Druidism what can be done to assist you."

The Druid, accordingly, as the sun rose on the following morning, retired to his *grianan*, and consulted the god he adored, through the power of his *draoidheacht*. When he returned, he called Conn-eda aside on the plain, and addressed him thus:

"My dear son, I find you have been under a severe – an almost impossible – *geis* intended for your destruction; no person on earth could have advised the queen to impose it except the Cailleach of Lough Corrib, who is the greatest Druidess now in Ireland, and sister to the Firbolg, King of Lough Erne. It is not in my power, nor in that of the Deity I adore, to interfere in your behalf; but go directly to Sliabh Mis, and consult *Eánchinn-duine* (the bird of the human head), and if there be any possibility of relieving you, that bird can do it, for there is not a bird in the western world so celebrated as that bird, because it knows all things that are past, all things that are present and exist, and all things that shall hereafter exist. It is difficult to find access to his place of concealment, and more difficult still to obtain an answer from him; but I will endeavour to regulate that matter for you; and that is all I can do for you at present."

The Arch-Druid then instructed him thus: – "Take," said he, "yonder little shaggy steed, and mount him immediately, for in three days the bird will make himself visible, and the little shaggy steed will conduct you to his place of abode. But lest the bird should refuse to reply to your queries, take this precious stone (*leag lorgmhar*), and present it to him, and then little danger and doubt exist but that he will give you a ready answer." The prince returned heartfelt thanks to the Druid, and, having saddled and mounted the little shaggy horse without much delay, received the precious stone from the Druid, and, after having taken his leave of him, set out on his journey. He suffered the reins to fall loose upon the neck of the horse according as he had been instructed, so that the animal took whatever road he chose.

It would be tedious to relate the numerous adventures he had with the little shaggy horse, which had the extraordinary gift of speech, and was a *draoidheacht* horse during his journey.

The Prince having reached the hiding-place of the strange bird at the appointed time, and having presented him with the *leag lorgmhar*, according to Fionn Badhna's instructions, and proposed his questions relative to the manner he could best arrange for the fulfilment of his *geis*, the bird took up in his mouth the jewel from the stone on which it was placed, and flew to an inaccessible rock at some distance, and, when there perched, he thus addressed the prince, "Conn-eda, son of the King of Cruachan," said he, in a loud, croaking human voice, "remove the stone just under your right foot, and take the ball of iron and *corna* (cup) you shall find under it; then mount your horse, cast the ball before you, and having so done, your horse will tell you all the other things necessary to be done." The bird, having said this, immediately flew out of sight.

Conn-eda took great care to do everything according to the instructions of the bird. He found the iron ball and *corna* in the place which had been pointed out. He took them up, mounted his horse, and cast the ball before him. The ball rolled on at a regular gait, while the little shaggy horse followed on the way it led until they reached the margin of Lough Erne. Here the ball rolled in the water and became invisible.

"Alight now," said the *draoidheacht* pony, "and put your hand into mine ear; take from thence the small bottle of *ice* (all-heal) and the little wicker basket which you will find there, and remount with speed, for just now your great dangers and difficulties commence."

Conn-eda, ever faithful to the kind advice of his *draoidheacht* pony, did what he had been advised. Having taken the basket and bottle of *ice* from the animal's ear, he remounted and proceeded on his journey, while the water of the lake appeared only like an atmosphere above his head. When he entered the lake the ball again appeared, and rolled along until it came to the margin, across which was a causeway, guarded by three frightful serpents; the hissings of the monsters was heard at a great distance, while, on a nearer approach, their yawning mouths and formidable fangs were quite sufficient to terrify the stoutest heart.

"Now," said the horse, "open the basket and cast a piece of the meat you find in it into the mouth of each serpent; when you have done this, secure yourself in your seat in the best manner you can, so that we may make all due arrangements to pass those *draoidheacht peists*. If you cast the pieces of meat into the mouth of each *peist* unerringly, we shall pass them safely, otherwise we are lost." Conn-eda flung the pieces of meat into the jaws of the serpents with unerring aim.

"Bare a benison and victory," said the *draoidheacht* steed, "for you are a youth that will win and prosper." And, on saying these words, he sprang aloft, and cleared in his leap the river and ford, guarded by the serpents, seven measures beyond the margin.

"Are you still mounted, prince Conn-eda?" said the steed.

"It has taken only half my exertion to remain so," replied Conn-eda.

"I find," said the pony, "that you are a young prince that deserves to succeed; one danger is now over, but two others remain."

They proceeded onwards after the ball until they came in view of a great mountain flaming with fire. "Hold yourself in readiness for another dangerous leap," said the horse. The trembling prince had no answer to make, but seated himself as securely as the magnitude of the danger before him would permit. The horse in the next instant sprang from the earth, and flew like an arrow over the burning mountain.

"Are you still alive, Conn-eda, son of Conn-mór?" inquired the faithful horse.

"I'm just alive, and no more, for I'm greatly scorched," answered the prince.

"Since you are yet alive, I feel assured that you are a young man destined to meet supernatural success and benisons," said the Druidic steed. "Our greatest dangers are over," added he, "and there is hope that we shall overcome the next and last danger."

After they had proceeded a short distance, his faithful steed, addressing Conn-eda, said, "Alight, now, and apply a portion of the little bottle of *ice* to your wounds." The prince immediately followed the advice of his monitor, and, as soon as he rubbed the *ice* (all-heal) to his wounds, he became as whole and fresh as ever he had been before. After having done this, Conn-eda remounted, and following the track of the ball, soon came in sight of a great city surrounded by high walls. The only gate that was visible was not defended by armed men, but by two great towers that emitted flames that could be seen at a great distance.

"Alight on this plain," said the steed, "and take a small knife from my other ear; and with this knife you shall kill and flay me. When you have done this, envelop yourself in my hide, and you can pass the gate unscathed and unmolested. When you get inside you can come out at pleasure; because when once you enter there is no danger, and you can pass and repass whenever you wish; and let me tell you that all I have to ask of you in return is that you, when once inside the gates, will immediately return and drive away the birds of prey that may be fluttering round to feed on my carcass; and more, that you will pour any drop of that powerful *ice*, if such still remain in the bottle, upon my flesh, to preserve it from corruption. When you do this in memory of me, if it be not too troublesome, dig a pit, and cast my remains into it."

"Well," said Conn-eda, "my noblest steed, because you have been so faithful to me hitherto, and because you still would have rendered me further service, I consider such a proposal insulting to my feelings as a man, and totally in variance with the spirit which can feel the value of gratitude, not to speak of my feelings as a prince. But as a prince I am able to say, come what may – come death itself in its most hideous forms and terrors – I never will sacrifice private friendship to personal interest. Hence, I am, I swear by my arms of valour, prepared to meet the worst – even death itself – sooner than violate the principles of humanity, honour, and friendship! What a sacrifice do you propose!"

"Pshaw, man! Heed not that; do what I advise you, and prosper."

"Never! never!" exclaimed the prince.

"Well, then, son of the great western monarch," said the horse, with a tone of sorrow, "if you do not follow my advice on this occasion, I tell you that both you and I shall perish, and shall never meet again; but, if you act as I have instructed you, matters shall assume a happier and more pleasing aspect than you may imagine. I have not misled you heretofore, and, if I have not, what need have you to doubt the most important portion of my counsel? Do exactly as I have directed you, else you will cause a worse fate than death to befall me. And, moreover, I can tell you that, if you persist in your resolution, I have done with you for ever."

When the prince found that his noble steed could not be persuaded from his purpose, he took the knife out of his ear with reluctance, and with a faltering and trembling hand essayed experimentally to point the weapon at his throat. Conn-eda's eyes were bathed in tears; but no sooner had he pointed the Druidic *scian* to the throat of his good steed, than the dagger, as if impelled by some Druidic power, stuck in his neck, and in an instant the work of death was done, and the noble animal fell dead at his feet. When the prince saw his noble steed fall dead by his hand, he cast himself on the ground, and cried aloud until his consciousness was gone. When he recovered, he perceived that the steed was quite dead; and, as he thought there was no hope of resuscitating him, he considered it the most prudent course he could adopt to act according to the advice he had given him. After many misgivings of mind and abundant showers of tears, he essayed the task of flaying him, which was only that of a few minutes. When he found he had the hide separated from the body, he, in the derangement of the moment, enveloped himself in it, and proceeding towards the magnificent city in rather a demented state of mind, entered it without any molestation or opposition. It was a surprisingly populous city, and an extremely wealthy place; but its beauty, magnificence, and wealth had no charms for Conneda, because the thoughts of the loss he sustained in his dear steed were paramount to those of all other earthly considerations.

He had scarcely proceeded more than fifty paces from the gate, when the last request of his beloved *draoidheacht* steed forced itself upon his mind, and compelled him to return to perform the last solemn injunctions upon him. When he came to the spot upon which the remains of his beloved *draoidheacht* steed lay, an appalling sight presented itself; ravens and other carnivorous birds of prey were tearing and devouring the flesh of his dear steed. It was but short work to put them to flight; and having uncorked his little jar of *ice*, he deemed it a labour of love to embalm the now mangled remains with the precious ointment. The potent *ice* had scarcely touched the inanimate flesh, when, to the surprise of Conn-eda, it commenced to undergo some strange change, and in a few minutes, to his unspeakable astonishment and joy, it assumed the form of one of the handsomest and noblest young men imaginable, and in the twinkling of an eye the prince was locked in his embrace, smothering him with kisses, and drowning him with tears of joy. When one recovered from his ecstasy of joy, the other from his surprise, the strange youth thus addressed the prince:

"Most noble and puissant prince, you are the best sight I ever saw with my eyes, and I am the most fortunate being in existence for having met you! Behold in my person, changed to the natural shape, your little shaggy *draoidheacht* steed! I am brother of the king of the city; and it was the wicked Druid, Fionn Badhna, who kept me so long in bondage; but he was forced to give me up when you came to *consult* him, for my *geis* was then broken; yet I could not recover my pristine shape and appearance unless you had acted as you have kindly done. It was my own sister that urged the queen, your stepmother, to send you in quest of the steed and powerful puppy hound, which my brother has now in keeping. My sister, rest assured, had no thought of doing you the least injury, but much good, as you will find hereafter; because, if she were maliciously inclined towards you, she could have accomplished her end without any trouble. In short, she only wanted to free you from all future danger and disaster, and recover me from my relentless enemies through your instrumentality. Come with me, my friend and deliverer, and the steed and the puppy-hound of extraordinary powers, and the golden apples, shall be yours, and a cordial welcome shall greet you in my brother's abode; for you will deserve all this and much more."

The exciting joy felt on the occasion was mutual, and they lost no time in idle congratulations, but proceeded on to the royal residence of the King of Lough Erne. Here they were both received with demonstrations of joy by the king and his chieftains; and, when the purpose of Conn-eda's visit became known to the king, he gave a free consent to bestow on Conn-eda the black steed, the *coileen con-na-mbuadh*, called Samer, and the three apples of health that were growing in his garden, under the special condition, however, that he would consent to remain as his guest until he could set out on his journey in proper time, to fulfil his *geis*. Conn-eda, at the earnest solicitation of his friends, consented, and remained in the royal residence of the Firbolg, King of Lough Erne, in the enjoyment of the most delicious and fascinating pleasures during that period.

When the time of his departure came, the three golden apples were plucked from the crystal tree in the midst of the pleasure-garden, and deposited in his bosom; the puppy-hound, Samer, was leashed, and the leash put into his hand; and the black steed, richly harnessed, was got in readiness for him to mount. The king himself helped him on horseback, and both he and his brother assured him that he might not fear burning mountains or hissing serpents, because none would impede him, as his steed was always a passport to and from his subaqueous kingdom. And both he and his brother extorted a promise from Conn-eda, that he would visit them once every year at least.

Conn-eda took leave of his dear friend, and the king his brother. The parting was a tender one, soured by regret on both sides. He proceeded on his way without meeting anything to obstruct him, and in due time came in sight of the *dún* of his father, where the queen had been placed on the pinnacle of the tower, in full hope that, as it was the last day of her imprisonment there, the prince would not make his appearance, and thereby forfeit all pretensions and right to the crown of his father for ever. But her hopes were doomed to meet a disappointment, for when it had been announced to her by her couriers, who had been posted to watch the arrival of the prince, that he approached, she was incredulous; but when she saw him mounted on a foaming black steed, richly harnessed, and leading a strange kind of animal by a silver chain, she at once knew he was returning in triumph, and that her schemes laid for his destruction were frustrated. In the excess of grief at her disappointment, she cast herself from the top of the tower, and was instantly dashed to pieces. Conn-eda met a welcome reception from his father, who mourned him as lost to him for ever, during his absence; and, when the base conduct of the queen became known, the king and his chieftains ordered her remains to be consumed to ashes for her perfidy and wickedness.

Conn-eda planted the three golden apples in his garden, and instantly a great tree, bearing similar fruit, sprang up. This tree caused all the district to produce an exuberance of crops and fruits, so that it became as fertile and plentiful as the dominions of the Firbolgs, in consequence of the extraordinary powers possessed by the golden fruit. The hound Samer and the steed were of the utmost utility to him; and his reign was long and prosperous, and celebrated among the old people for the great abundance of corn, fruit, milk, fowl, and fish that prevailed during this happy reign. It was after the name Conn-eda the province of Connaucht, or *Conneda*, or *Connacht*, was so called.

The Shee An Gannon and the Gruagach Gaire

◈

THE SHEE AN GANNON was born in the morning, named at noon, and went in the evening to ask his daughter of the king of Erin.

"I will give you my daughter in marriage," said the king of Erin; "you won't get her, though, unless you go and bring me back the tidings that I want, and tell me what it is that put a stop to the laughing of the Gruagach Gaire, who before this laughed always, and laughed so loud that the whole world heard him. There are twelve iron spikes out here in the garden behind my castle. On eleven of the spikes are the heads of kings' sons who came seeking my daughter in marriage, and all of them went away to get the knowledge I wanted. Not one was able to get it and tell me what stopped the Gruagach Gaire from laughing. I took the heads off them all when they came back without the tidings for which they went, and I'm greatly in dread that your head'll be on the twelfth spike, for I'll do the same to you that I did to the eleven kings' sons unless you tell what put a stop to the laughing of the Gruagach."

The Shee an Gannon made no answer, but left the king and pushed away to know could he find why the Gruagach was silent.

He took a glen at a step, a hill at a leap, and travelled all day till evening. Then he came to a house. The master of the house asked him what sort was he, and he said: "A young man looking for hire."

"Well," said the master of the house, "I was going tomorrow to look for a man to mind my cows. If you'll work for me, you'll have a good place, the best food a man could have to eat in this world, and a soft bed to lie on."

The Shee an Gannon took service, and ate his supper. Then the master of the house said: "I am the Gruagach Gaire; now that you are my man and have eaten your supper, you'll have a bed of silk to sleep on."

Next morning after breakfast the Gruagach said to the Shee an Gannon: "Go out now and loosen my five golden cows and my bull without horns, and drive them to pasture; but when you have them out on the grass, be careful you don't let them go near the land of the giant."

The new cowboy drove the cattle to pasture, and when near the land of the giant, he saw it was covered with woods and surrounded by a high wall. He went up, put his back against the wall, and threw in a great stretch of it; then he went inside and threw out another great stretch of the wall, and put the five golden cows and the bull without horns on the land of the giant.

Then he climbed a tree, ate the sweet apples himself, and threw the sour ones down to the cattle of the Gruagach Gaire.

Soon a great crashing was heard in the woods, – the noise of young trees bending, and old trees breaking. The cowboy looked around and saw a five-headed giant pushing through the trees; and soon he was before him.

"Poor miserable creature!" said the giant; "but weren't you impudent to come to my land and trouble me in this way? You're too big for one bite, and too small for two. I don't know what to do but tear you to pieces."

"You nasty brute," said the cowboy, coming down to him from the tree, "'tis little I care for you"; and then they went at each other. So great was the noise between them that there was nothing in the world but what was looking on and listening to the combat.

They fought till late in the afternoon, when the giant was getting the upper hand; and then the cowboy thought that if the giant should kill him, his father and mother would never find him or set eyes on him again, and he would never get the daughter of the king of Erin. The heart in his body grew strong at this thought. He sprang on the giant, and with the first squeeze and thrust he put him to his knees in the hard ground, with the second thrust to his waist, and with the third to his shoulders.

"I have you at last; you're done for now!", said the cowboy. Then he took out his knife, cut the five heads off the giant, and when he had them off he cut out the tongues and threw the heads over the wall.

Then he put the tongues in his pocket and drove home the cattle. That evening the Gruagach couldn't find vessels enough in all his place to hold the milk of the five golden cows.

But when the cowboy was on the way home with the cattle, the son of the king of Tisean came and took the giant's heads and claimed the princess in marriage when the Gruagach Gaire should laugh.

After supper the cowboy would give no talk to his master, but kept his mind to himself, and went to the bed of silk to sleep.

On the morning the cowboy rose before his master, and the first words he said to the Gruagach were:

"What keeps you from laughing, you who used to laugh so loud that the whole world heard you?"

"I'm sorry," said the Gruagach, "that the daughter of the king of Erin sent you here."

"If you don't tell me of your own will, I'll make you tell me," said the cowboy; and he put a face on himself that was terrible to look at, and running through the house like a madman, could find nothing that would give pain enough to the Gruagach but some ropes made of untanned sheepskin hanging on the wall.

He took these down, caught the Gruagach, fastened him by the three smalls, and tied him so that his little toes were whispering to his ears. When he was in this state the Gruagach said: "I'll tell you what stopped my laughing if you set me free."

So the cowboy unbound him, the two sat down together, and the Gruagach said:

"I lived in this castle here with my twelve sons. We ate, drank, played cards, and enjoyed ourselves, till one day when my sons and I were playing, a slender brown hare came rushing in, jumped on to the hearth, tossed up the ashes to the rafters and ran away.

"On another day he came again; but if he did, we were ready for him, my twelve sons and myself. As soon as he tossed up the ashes and ran off, we made after him, and followed him till nightfall, when he went into a glen. We saw a light before us. I ran on, and came to a house with a great apartment, where there was a man named Yellow Face with twelve daughters, and the hare was tied to the side of the room near the women.

"There was a large pot over the fire in the room, and a great stork boiling in the pot. The man of the house said to me: 'There are bundles of rushes at the end of the room, go there and sit down with your men!'

"He went into the next room and brought out two pikes, one of wood, the other of iron, and asked me which of the pikes would I take. I said, 'I'll take the iron one'; for I thought in my heart that if an attack should come on me, I could defend myself better with the iron than the wooden pike.

"Yellow Face gave me the iron pike, and the first chance of taking what I could out of the pot on the point of the pike. I got but a small piece of the stork, and the man of the house took all the rest on his wooden pike. We had to fast that night; and when the man and his twelve daughters ate the flesh of the stork, they hurled the bare bones in the faces of my sons and myself. We had to stop all night that way, beaten on the faces by the bones of the stork.

"Next morning, when we were going away, the man of the house asked me to stay a while; and going into the next room, he brought out twelve loops of iron and one of wood, and said to me: 'Put the heads of your twelve sons into the iron loops, or your own head into the wooden one'; and I said: 'I'll put the twelve heads of my sons in the iron loops, and keep my own out of the wooden one.'

"He put the iron loops on the necks of my twelve sons, and put the wooden one on his own neck. Then he snapped the loops one after another, till he took the heads off my twelve sons and threw the heads and bodies out of the house; but he did nothing to hurt his own neck.

"When he had killed my sons he took hold of me and stripped the skin and flesh from the small of my back down, and when he had done that he took the skin of a black sheep that had been hanging on the wall for seven years and clapped it on my body in place of my own flesh and skin; and the sheepskin grew on me, and every year since then I shear myself, and every bit of wool I use for the stockings that I wear I clip off my own back."

When he had said this, the Gruagach showed the cowboy his back covered with thick black wool.

After what he had seen and heard, the cowboy said: "I know now why you don't laugh, and small blame to you. But does that hare come here still?"

"He does indeed," said the Gruagach.

Both went to the table to play, and they were not long playing cards when the hare ran in; and before they could stop him he was out again.

But the cowboy made after the hare, and the Gruagach after the cowboy, and they ran as fast as ever their legs could carry them till nightfall; and when the hare was entering the castle where the twelve sons of the Gruagach were killed, the cowboy caught him by the two hind legs and dashed out his brains against the wall; and the skull of the hare was knocked into the chief room of the castle, and fell at the feet of the master of the place.

"Who has dared to interfere with my fighting pet?" screamed Yellow Face.

"I," said the cowboy; "and if your pet had had manners, he might be alive now."

The cowboy and the Gruagach stood by the fire. A stork was boiling in the pot, as when the Gruagach came the first time. The master of the house went into the next room and brought out an iron and a wooden pike, and asked the cowboy which would he choose.

"I'll take the wooden one," said the cowboy; "and you may keep the iron one for yourself."

So he took the wooden one; and going to the pot, brought out on the pike all the stork except a small bite, and he and the Gruagach fell to eating, and they were eating the flesh of the stork all night. The cowboy and the Gruagach were at home in the place that time.

In the morning the master of the house went into the next room, took down the twelve iron loops with a wooden one, brought them out, and asked the cowboy which would he take, the twelve iron or the one wooden loop.

"What could I do with the twelve iron ones for myself or my master? I'll take the wooden one."

He put it on, and taking the twelve iron loops, put them on the necks of the twelve daughters of the house, then snapped the twelve heads off them, and turning to their father, said: "I'll do the same thing to you unless you bring the twelve sons of my master to life, and make them as well and strong as when you took their heads."

The master of the house went out and brought the twelve to life again; and when the Gruagach saw all his sons alive and as well as ever, he let a laugh out of himself, and all the Eastern world heard the laugh.

Then the cowboy said to the Gruagach: "It's a bad thing you have done to me, for the daughter of the king of Erin will be married the day after your laugh is heard."

"Oh! Then we must be there in time," said the Gruagach; and they all made away from the place as fast as ever they could, the cowboy, the Gruagach, and his twelve sons.

They hurried on; and when within three miles of the king's castle there was such a throng of people that no one could go a step ahead. "We must clear a road through this," said the cowboy.

"We must indeed," said the Gruagach; and at it they went, threw the people some on one side and some on the other, and soon they had an opening for themselves to the king's castle.

As they went in, the daughter of the king of Erin and the son of the king of Tisean were on their knees just going to be married. The cowboy drew his hand on the bride-groom, and gave a blow that sent him spinning till he stopped under a table at the other side of the room.

"What scoundrel struck that blow?" asked the king of Erin.

"It was I," said the cowboy.

"What reason had you to strike the man who won my daughter?"

"It was I who won your daughter, not he; and if you don't believe me, the Gruagach Gaire is here himself. He'll tell you the whole story from beginning to end, and show you the tongues of the giant."

So the Gruagach came up and told the king the whole story, how the Shee an Gannon had become his cowboy, had guarded the five golden cows and the bull without horns, cut off the heads of the five-headed giant, killed the wizard hare, and brought his own twelve sons to life. "And then," said the Gruagach, "he is the only man in the whole world I have ever told why I stopped laughing, and the only one who has ever seen my fleece of wool."

When the king of Erin heard what the Gruagach said, and saw the tongues of the giant fitted in the head, he made the Shee an Gannon kneel down by his daughter, and they were married on the spot.

Then the son of the king of Tisean was thrown into prison, and the next day they put down a great fire, and the deceiver was burned to ashes.

The wedding lasted nine days, and the last day was better than the first.

Lawn Dyarrig and the Knight of Terrible Valley

❖

THERE WAS A KING in his own time in Erin, and he went hunting one day. The King met a man whose head was out through his cap, whose elbows and knees were out through his clothing, and whose toes were out through his shoes. The man went up to the King, gave him a blow on the face, and drove three teeth from his mouth. The same blow put the King's head in the dirt. When he rose from the earth, the King went back to his castle, and lay down sick and sorrowful.

The King had three sons, and their names were Ur, Arthur, and Lawn Dyarrig. The three were at school that day, and came home in the evening. The father sighed when the sons were coming in.

"What is wrong with our father?" asked the eldest.

"Your father is sick on his bed," said the mother.

109

The three sons went to their father and asked what was on him.

"A strong man that I met today gave me a blow in the face, put my head in the dirt, and knocked three teeth from my mouth. What would you do to him if you met him?" asked the father of the eldest son.

"If I met that man," replied Ur, "I would make four parts of him between four horses."

You are my son," said the King. "What would you do if you met him?" asked he then as he turned to the second son.

"If I had a grip on that man I would burn him between four fires."

"You, too, are my son. What would you do?" asked the King of Lawn Dyarrig.

"If I met that man, I would do my best against him, and he might not stand long before me."

"You are not my son. I would not lose lands or property on you," said the father. "You must go from me, and leave this tomorrow."

On the following morning the three brothers rose with the dawn; the order was given Lawn Dyarrig to leave the castle and make his own way for himself. The other two brothers were going to travel the world to know could they find the man who had injured their father. Lawn Dyarrig lingered outside till he saw the two, and they going off by themselves.

"It is a strange thing," said he, "for two men of high degree to go travelling without a servant."

"We need no one," said Ur.

"Company wouldn't harm us," said Arthur.

The two let Lawn Dyarrig go with them as a serving-boy, and set out to find the man who had struck down their father. They spent all that day walking, and came late to a house where one woman was living. She shook hands with Ur and Arthur, and greeted them. Lawn Dyarrig she kissed and welcomed; called him son of the King of Erin.

"It is a strange thing to shake hands with the elder, and kiss the younger," said Ur.

"This is a story to tell," said the woman, "the same as if your death were in it."

They made three parts of that night. The first part they spent in conversation, the second in telling tales, the third in eating and drinking, with sound sleep and sweet slumber. As early as the day dawned next morning the old woman was up, and had food for the young men. When the three had eaten, she spoke to Ur, and this is what she asked of him: "What was it that drove you from home, and what brought you to this place?"

"A champion met my father, and took three teeth from him and put his head in the dirt. I am looking for that man, to find him alive or dead."

"That was the Green Knight from Terrible Valley. He is the man who took the three teeth from your father. I am three hundred years living in this place, and there is not a year of the three hundred in which three hundred heroes, fresh, young, and noble, have not passed on the way to Terrible Valley, and never have I seen one coming back, and each of them had the look of a man better than you. And now where are you going, Arthur?"

"I am on the same journey with my brother."

"Where are you going, Lawn Dyarrig?"

"I am going with these as a servant," said Lawn Dyarrig.

God's help to you, it's bad clothing that's on your body," said the woman. "And now I will speak to Ur. A day and a year since a champion passed this way. He wore a suit as good as was ever above ground. I had a daughter sewing there in the open window. He came outside, put a finger under her girdle, and took her with him. Her father followed straightway to save her, but I have never seen daughter nor father from that day to this. That man was the Green Knight of Terrible Valley. He is better than all the men that could stand on a field a mile in length and a mile in breadth. If you take my advice you'll turn back and go home to your father."

'Tis how she vexed Ur with this talk, and he made a vow to himself to go on. When Ur did not agree to turn home, the woman said to Lawn Dyarrig, "Go back to my chamber; you'll find in it the apparel of a hero."

He went back, and there was not a bit of the apparel he did not go into with a spring.

"You may be able to do something now," said the woman, when Lawn Dyarrig came to the front. "Go back to my chamber and search through all the old swords. You will find one at the bottom. Take that."

He found the old sword, and at the first shake that he gave he knocked seven barrels of rust out of it; after the second shake it was as bright as when made.

"You may be able to do well with that," said the woman. "Go out, now, to that stable abroad, and take the slim white steed that is in it. That one will never stop nor halt in any place till he brings you to the Eastern World. If you like, take these two men behind you; if not, let them walk. But I think it is useless for you to have them at all with you."

Lawn Dyarrig went out to the stable, took the slim white steed, mounted, rode to the front, and catching the two brothers, planted them on the horse behind him.

"Now, Lawn Dyarrig," said the woman, "this horse will never stop till he stands on the little white meadow in the Eastern World. When he stops, you'll come down, and cut the turf under his beautiful right front foot."

The horse started from the door, and at every leap he crossed seven hills and valleys, seven castles with villages, acres, roods, and odd perches. He could overtake the whirlwind before him seven hundred times before the whirlwind behind him could overtake him once. Early in the afternoon of the next day he was in the Eastern World.

When he dismounted, Lawn Dyarrig cut the sod from under the foot of the slim white steed, in the name of the Father, Son, and Holy Ghost, and Terrible Valley was down under him there. What he did next was to tighten the reins on the neck of the steed and let him go home.

"Now," said Lawn Dyarrig to his brothers, "which would you rather be doing – making a basket or twisting gads (withes)?"

"We would rather be making a basket; our help is among ourselves," answered they.

Ur and Arthur went at the basket and Lawn Dyarrig at twisting the gads. When Lawn Dyarrig came to the opening with the gads all twisted and made into one, they hadn't the ribs of the basket in the ground yet.

"Oh, then, haven't ye anything done but that?"

"Stop your mouth," said Ur, "or we'll make a mortar of your head on the next stone."

"To be kind to one another is the best for us," said Lawn Dyarrig. "I'll make the basket."

While they'd be putting one rod in the basket he had the basket finished.

"Oh, brother," said they, "you are a quick workman."

They had not called him brother since they left home till that moment.

"Who will go in the basket now?" said Lawn Dyarrig when it was finished and the gad tied to it.

"Who but me?" said Ur. "I am sure, brothers, if I see anything to frighten me you'll draw me up."

"We will," said the other two.

He went in, but had not gone far when he cried to pull him up again.

"By my father, and the tooth of my father, and by all that is in Erin, dead or alive, I would not give one other sight on Terrible Valley!" he cried, when he stepped out of the basket.

"Who will go now?" said Lawn Dyarrig.

"Who will go but me?" answered Arthur.

Whatever length Ur went, Arthur didn't go the half of it.

"By my father, and the tooth of my father, I wouldn't give another look at Terrible Valley for all that's in Erin, dead or alive!"

"I will go now," said Lawn Dyarrig, "and as I put no foul play on you, I hope ye'll not put foul play on me."

"We will not, indeed," said they.

Whatever length the other two went, Lawn Dyarrig didn't go the half of it, till he stepped out of the basket and went down on his own feet. It was not far he had travelled in Terrible Valley when he met seven hundred heroes guarding the country.

"In what place here has the Green King his castle?" asked he of the seven hundred.

"What sort of a sprisawn goat or sheep from Erin are you?" asked they.

"If we had a hold of you, the two arms of me, that's a question you would not put a second time; but if we haven't you, we'll not be so long."

They faced Lawn Dyarrig then and attacked him; but he went through them like a hawk or a raven through small birds. He made a heap of their feet, a heap of their heads, and a castle of their arms.

After that he went his way walking, and had not gone far when he came to a spring. "I'll have a drink before I go further," thought he. With that he stooped down and took a drink of the water. When he had drunk he lay on the ground and fell asleep.

Now, there wasn't a morning that the lady in the Green Knight's castle didn't wash in the water of that spring, and she sent a maid for the water each time. Whatever part of the day it was when Lawn Dyarrig fell asleep, he was sleeping in the morning when the girl came. She thought it was dead the man was, and she was so in dread of him that she would not come near the spring for a long time. At last she saw he was asleep, and then she took the water. Her mistress was complaining of her for being so long.

"Do not blame me," said the maid.

"I am sure that if it was yourself that was in my place you'd not come back so soon."

"How so?" asked the lady.

"The finest hero that ever a woman laid eyes on is sleeping at the spring."

"That's a thing that cannot be till Lawn Dyarrig comes to the age of a hero. When that time comes he'll be sleeping at the spring."

"He is in it now," said the girl.

The lady did not stop to get any drop of the water on herself, but ran quickly from the castle. When she came to the spring she roused Lawn Dyarrig. If she found him lying, she left him standing. She smothered him with kisses, drowned him with tears, dried him with garments of fine silk and with her own hair. Herself and himself locked arms and walked into the castle of the Green Knight. After that they were inviting each other with the best food and entertainment till the middle of the following day. Then the lady said:

"When the Green Knight bore me away from my father and mother he brought me straight to this castle, but I put him under bonds not to marry me for seven years and a day, and he cannot; still, I must serve him. When he goes fowling he spends three days away and the next three days at home. This is the day for him to come back, and for me to prepare his dinner. There is no stir that you or I have made here today but that brass head beyond there will tell of it."

"It is equal to you what it tells," said Lawn Dyarrig, "only make ready a clean long chamber for me."

She did so, and he went back into it. Herself rose up then to prepare dinner for the Green Knight. When he came, she welcomed him as every day. She left down his food before him, and he sat to take his dinner. He was sitting with knife and fork in hand when the brass head spoke. "I thought when I saw you taking food and drink with your wife that you had the blood of a man in you. If you could see that sprisawn of a goat or sheep out of Erin taking meat and drink with her all day, what would you do?"

"Oh, my suffering and sorrow!" cried the knight. "I'll never take another bite or sup till I eat some of his liver and heart. Let three hundred heroes, fresh and young, go back and bring his heart to me, with the liver and lights, till I eat them."

The three hundred heroes went, and hardly were they behind in the chamber when Lawn Dyarrig had them all dead in one heap.

"He must have some exercise to delay my men, they are so long away," said the knight. "Let three hundred more heroes go for his heart, with the liver and lights, and bring them here to me."

The second three hundred went, and as they were entering the chamber Lawn Dyarrig was making a heap of them, till the last one was inside, where there were two heaps.

"He has some way of coaxing my men to delay," said the knight. "Do you go now, three hundred of my savage hirelings, and bring him." The three hundred savage hirelings went, and Lawn Dyarrig let every man of them enter before he raised a hand, then he caught the bulkiest of them all by the two ankles, and began to wallop the others with him, and he walloped them till he drove the life out of the two hundred and ninety-nine. The bulkiest one was worn to the shin-bones that Lawn Dyarrig held in his two hands. The Green Knight, who thought Lawn Dyarrig was coaxing the men, called out then, "Come down, my men, and take dinner."

"I'll be with you," said Lawn Dyarrig, "and have the best food in the house, and I'll have the best bed in the house. God not be good to you for it, either."

He went down to the Green Knight, and took the food from before him and put it before himself. Then he took the lady, set her on his own knee, and he and she went on eating. After dinner he put his finger under her girdle, took her to the best chamber in the castle, and stood on guard upon it till morning. Before dawn the lady said to Lawn Dyarrig:

"If the Green Knight strikes the pole of combat first, he'll win the day; if you strike first, you'll win if you do what I tell you. The Green Knight has so much enchantment that if he sees it is going against him the battle is, he'll rise like a fog in the air, come down in the same form, strike you, and make a green stone of you. When yourself and himself are going out to fight in the morning, cut a sod a perch long, in the name of the Father, Son, and Holy Ghost; you'll leave the sod on the next little hillock you meet. When the Green Knight is coming down and is ready to strike, give him a blow with the sod. You'll make a green stone of him."

As early as the dawn Lawn Dyarrig rose and struck the pole of combat. The blow that he gave did not leave calf, foal, lamb, kid, or child waiting for birth, without turning them five times to the left and five times to the right.

"What do you want?" asked the knight.

"All that's in your kingdom to be against me the first quarter of the day, and yourself the second quarter.

"You have not left in the kingdom now but myself, and it is early enough for you that I'll be at you."

The knight faced him, and they went at each other, and fought till late in the day. The battle was strong against Lawn Dyarrig, when the lady stood in the door of the castle.

"Increase on your blows and increase on your courage," cried she. "There is no woman here but myself to wail over you, or to stretch you before burial."

When the knight heard the voice he rose in the air like a lump of fog. As he was coming down Lawn Dyarrig struck him with the sod on the right side of his breast, and made a green stone of him.

The lady rushed out then, and whatever welcome she had for Lawn Dyarrig the first time, she had twice as much now. Herself and himself went into the castle, and spent that night very comfortably. In the morning they rose early, and collected all the gold, utensils, and treasures. Lawn Dyarrig found the three teeth of his father in a pocket of the Green

Knight, and took them. He and the lady brought all the riches to where the basket was. "If I send up this beautiful lady," thought Lawn Dyarrig, "she may be taken from me by my brothers; if I remain below with her, she may be taken from me by people here." He put her in the basket, and she gave him a ring so that they might know each other if they met. He shook the gad, and she rose in the basket.

When Ur saw the basket, he thought, "What's above let it be above, and what's below let it stay where it is."

"I'll have you as wife for ever for myself," said he to the lady.

"I put you under bonds," says she, "not to lay a hand on me for a day and three years."

"That itself would not be long even if twice the time," said Ur.

The two brothers started home with the lady; on the way Ur found the head of an old horse with teeth in it, and took them, saying, "These will be my father's three teeth."

They travelled on, and reached home at last. Ur would not have left a tooth in his father's mouth, trying to put in the three that he had brought; but the father stopped him.

Lawn Dyarrig, left in Terrible Valley, began to walk around for himself. He had been walking but one day when whom should he meet but the lad Short-clothes, and he saluted him. "By what way can I leave Terrible Valley?" asked Lawn Dyarrig.

"If I had a grip on you that's what you wouldn't ask me a second time," said Short-clothes.

"If you haven't touched me, you will before you are much older."

"If you do, you will not treat me as you did all my people and my master."

"I'll do worse to you than I did to them," said Lawn Dyarrig.

They caught each other then, one grip under the arm and one on the shoulder. 'Tis not long they were wrestling when Lawn Dyarrig had Short-clothes on the earth, and he gave him the five thin tyings dear and tight.

"You are the best hero I have ever met," said Short-clothes; "give me quarter for my soul – spare me. When I did not tell you of my own will, I must tell in spite of myself."

"It is as easy for me to loosen you as to tie you," said Lawn Dyarrig, and he freed him.

"Since you are not dead now," said Short-clothes, "there is no death allotted to you. I'll find a way for you to leave Terrible Valley. Go and take that old bridle hanging there beyond and shake it; whatever beast comes and puts its head into the bridle will carry you."

Lawn Dyarrig shook the bridle, and a dirty, shaggy little foal came and put its head in the bridle. Lawn Dyarrig mounted, dropped the reins on the foal's neck, and let him take his own choice of roads. The foal brought Lawn Dyarrig out by another way to the upper world, and took him to Erin. Lawn Dyarrig stopped some distance from his father's castle, and knocked at the house of an old weaver.

"Who are you?" asked the old man.

"I am a weaver," said Lawn Dyarrig.

"What can you do?"

"I can spin for twelve and twist for twelve."

"This is a very good man," said the old weaver to his sons, "let us try him."

The work they had been doing for a year he had done in one hour. When dinner was over the old man began to wash and shave, and his two sons began to do the same.

"Why is this?" asked Lawn Dyarrig.

"Haven't you heard that Ur, son of the King, is to marry tonight the woman that he took from the Green Knight of Terrible Valley?"

"I have not," said Lawn Dyarrig; "as all are going to the wedding, I suppose I may go without offence?"

"Oh, you may," said the weaver; "there will be a hundred thousand welcomes before you."

"Are there any linen sheets within?"

"There are," said the weaver.

"It is well to have bags ready for yourself and two sons."

The weaver made bags for the three very quickly. They went to the wedding. Lawn Dyarrig put what dinner was on the first table into the weaver's bag, and sent the old man home with it. The food of the second table he put in the eldest son's bag, filled the second son's bag from the third table, and sent the two home.

The complaint went to Ur that an impudent stranger was taking all the food.

"It is not right to turn any man away," said the bridegroom, "but if that stranger does not mind he will be thrown out of the castle."

"Let me look at the face of the disturber," said the bride.

"Go and bring the fellow who is troubling the guests," said Ur to the servants.

Lawn Dyarrig was brought right away, and stood before the bride, who filled a glass with wine and gave it to him. Lawn Dyarrig drank half the wine, and dropped in the ring which the lady had given him in Terrible Valley.

When the bride took the glass again the ring went of itself with one leap on to her finger. She knew then who was standing before her.

"This is the man who conquered the Green Knight and saved me from Terrible Valley," said she to the King of Erin; "this is Lawn Dyarrig, your son."

Lawn Dyarrig took out the three teeth and put them in his father's mouth. They fitted there perfectly, and grew into their old place. The King was satisfied, and as the lady would marry no man but Lawn Dyarrig, he was the bridegroom.

"I must give you a present," said the bride to the Queen. "Here is a beautiful scarf which you are to wear as a girdle this evening."

The Queen put the scarf round her waist.

"Tell me now," said the bride to the Queen, "who was Ur's father."

"What father could he have but his own father, the King of Erin?"

"Tighten, scarf," said the bride.

That moment the Queen thought that her head was in the sky and the lower half of her body down deep in the earth.

"Oh, my grief and my woe!" cried the Queen.

"Answer my question in truth, and the scarf will stop squeezing you. Who was Ur's father?"

"The gardener," said the Queen.

"Whose son is Arthur?"

"The King's son."

"Tighten, scarf," said the bride.

If the Queen suffered before, she suffered twice as much this time, and screamed for help.

"Answer me truly, and you'll be without pain; if not, death will be on you this minute. Whose son is Arthur?"

"The swineherd's."

"Who is the King's son?"

"The King has no son but Lawn Dyarrig."

"Tighten, scarf."

The scarf did not tighten, and if the Queen had been commanding it a day and a year it would not have tightened, for the Queen told the truth that time. When the wedding was over, the King gave Lawn Dyarrig half his kingdom, and made Ur and Arthur his servants.

Fairies &
Sea-Folk

N HIS BOOKS on fairies, Yeats tell us that the Irish word for fairy is sheehogue (*sidheóg*), a diminutive of 'shee' in banshee, and that fairies are deenee shee (*daoine sidh* – fairy people). This section covers both of what Yeats defines as 'trooping fairies' and 'solitary fairies', along with their often mischievous and fickle ways.

Towards the end of the chapter we also turn to the watery depths of the sea, with classic Irish stories of sea-people, mermaids and merrow – the latter being an Irish type of mermaid whose enchanted cap enables it to swim down deep in the sea.

The Golden Spears

❧❧❧

ONCE UPON A TIME there lived in a little house under a hill a little old woman and her two children, whose names were Connla and Nora. Right in front of the door of the little house lay a pleasant meadow, and beyond the meadow rose up to the skies a mountain whose top was sharp-pointed like a spear. For more than half-way up it was clad with heather, and when the heather was in bloom it looked like a purple robe falling from the shoulders of the mountain down to its feet. Above the heather it was bare and grey, but when the sun was sinking in the sea, its last rays rested on the bare mountain top and made it gleam like a spear of gold, and so the children always called it the 'Golden Spear'.

In summer days they gambolled in the meadow, plucking the sweet wild grasses – and often and often they clambered up the mountain side, knee deep in the heather, searching for frechans and wild honey, and sometimes they found a bird's nest – but they only peeped into it, they never touched the eggs or allowed their breath to fall upon them, for next to their little mother they loved the mountain, and next to the mountain they loved the wild birds who made the spring and summer weather musical with their songs.

Sometimes the soft white mist would steal through the glen, and creeping up the mountain would cover it with a veil so dense that the children could not see it, and then they would say to each other: "Our mountain is gone away from us." But when the mist would lift and float off into the skies, the children would clap their hands, and say: "Oh, there's our mountain back again."

In the long nights of winter they babbled of the spring and summertime to come, when the birds would once more sing for them, and never a day passed that they didn't fling crumbs outside their door, and on the borders of the wood that stretched away towards the glen.

When the spring days came they awoke with the first light of the morning, and they knew the very minute when the lark would begin to sing, and when the thrush and the blackbird would pour out their liquid notes, and when the robin would make the soft, green, tender leaves tremulous at his song.

It chanced one day that when they were resting in the noontide heat, under the perfumed shade of a hawthorn in bloom, they saw on the edge of the meadow, spread out before them, a speckled thrush cowering in the grass.

"Oh, Connla! Connla! Look at the thrush – and, look, look up in the sky, there is a hawk!" cried Nora.

Connla looked up, and he saw the hawk with quivering wings, and he knew that in a second it would pounce down on the frightened thrush. He jumped to his feet, fixed a stone in his sling, and before the whirr of the stone shooting through the air was silent, the stricken hawk tumbled headlong in the grass.

The thrush, shaking its wings, rose joyously in the air, and perching upon an elm-tree in sight of the children, he sang a song so sweet that they left the hawthorn shade and walked along together until they stood under the branches of the elm; and they listened and listened to the thrush's song, and at last Nora said:

"Oh, Connla! Did you ever hear a song so sweet as this?"

"No," said Connla, "and I do believe sweeter music was never heard before."

"Ah," said the thrush, "that's because you never heard the nine little pipers playing. And now, Connla and Nora, you saved my life today."

"It was Nora saved it," said Connla, "for she pointed you out to me, and also pointed out the hawk which was about to pounce on you."

"It was Connla saved you," said Nora, "for he slew the hawk with his sling."

"I owe my life to both of you," said the thrush. "You like my song, and you say you have never heard anything so sweet; but wait till you hear the nine little pipers playing."

"And when shall we hear them?" said the children.

"Well," said the thrush, "sit outside your door tomorrow evening, and wait and watch until the shadows have crept up the heather, and then, when the mountain top is gleaming like a golden spear, look at the line where the shadow on the heather meets the sunshine, and you shall see what you shall see."

And having said this, the thrush sang another song sweeter than the first, and then saying "goodbye", he flew away into the woods.

The children went home, and all night long they were dreaming of the thrush and the nine little pipers; and when the birds sang in the morning, they got up and went out into the meadow to watch the mountain.

The sun was shining in a cloudless sky, and no shadows lay on the mountain, and all day long they watched and waited, and at last, when the birds were singing their farewell song to the evening star, the children saw the shadows marching from the glen, trooping up the mountainside and dimming the purple of the heather.

And when the mountain top gleamed like a golden spear, they fixed their eyes on the line between the shadow and the sunshine.

"Now," said Connla, "the time has come."

"Oh, look! Look!" said Nora, and as she spoke, just above the line of shadow a door opened out, and through its portals came a little piper dressed in green and gold. He stepped down, followed by another and another, until they were nine in all, and then the door slung back again. Down through the heather marched the pipers in single file, and all the time they played a music so sweet that the birds, who had gone to sleep in their nests, came out upon the branches to listen to them and then they crossed the meadow, and they went on and on until they disappeared in the leafy woods.

While they were passing the children were spell-bound, and couldn't speak, but when the music had died away in the woods, they said:

"The thrush is right, that is the sweetest music that was ever heard in all the world."

And when the children went to bed that night the fairy music came to them in their dreams. But when the morning broke, and they looked out upon their mountain and could see no trace of the door above the heather, they asked each other whether they had really seen the little pipers, or only dreamt of them.

That day they went out into the woods, and they sat beside a stream that pattered along beneath the trees, and through the leaves tossing in the breeze the sun flashed down upon the streamlet, and shadow and sunshine danced upon it. As the children watched the water sparkling where the sunlight fell, Nora said:

"Oh, Connla, did you ever see anything so bright and clear and glancing as that?"

"No," said Connla, "I never did."

"That's because you never saw the crystal hall of the fairy of the mountains," said a voice above the heads of the children.

And when they looked up, who should they see perched on a branch but the thrush.

"And where is the crystal hall of the fairy?" said Connla.

"Oh, it is where it always was, and where it always will be," said the thrush. "And you can see it if you like."

"We would like to see it," said the children.

"Well, then," said the thrush, "if you would, all you have to do is to follow the nine little pipers when they come down through the heather, and cross the meadow tomorrow evening."

And the thrush having said this, flew away.

Connla and Nora went home, and that night they fell asleep talking of the thrush and the fairy and the crystal hall.

All the next day they counted the minutes, until they saw the shadows thronging from the glen and scaling the mountain side. And, at last, they saw the door springing open, and the nine little pipers marching down.

They waited until the pipers had crossed the meadow and were about to enter the wood. And then they followed them, the pipers marching on before them and playing all the time. It was not long until they had passed through the wood, and then, what should the children see rising up before them but another mountain, smaller than their own, but, like their own, clad more than half-way up with purple heather, and whose top was bare and sharp-pointed, and gleaming like a golden spear.

Up through the heather climbed the pipers, up through the heather the children clambered after them, and the moment the pipers passed the heather a door opened and they marched in, the children following, and the door closed behind them.

Connla and Nora were so dazzled by the light that hit their eyes, when they had crossed the threshold, that they had to shade them with their hands; but, after a moment or two, they became able to bear the splendour, and when they looked around they saw that they were in a noble hall, whose crystal roof was supported by two rows of crystal pillars rising from a crystal floor; and the walls were of crystal, and along the walls were crystal couches, with coverings and cushions of sapphire silk with silver tassels.

Over the crystal floor the little pipers marched; over the crystal floor the children followed, and when a door at the end of the hall was opened to let the pipers pass, a crowd of colours came rushing in, and floor, and ceiling, and stately pillars, and glancing couches, and shining walls, were stained with a thousand dazzling hues.

Out through the door the pipers marched; out through the door the children followed, and when they crossed the threshold they were treading on clouds of amber, of purple, and of gold.

"Oh, Connla," said Nora, "we have walked into the sunset!"

And around and about them everywhere were soft, fleecy clouds, and over their heads was the glowing sky, and the stars were shining through it, as a lady's eyes shine through a veil of gossamer. And the sky and stars seemed so near that Connla thought he could almost touch them with his hand.

When they had gone some distance, the pipers disappeared, and when Connla and Nora came up to the spot where they had seen the last of them, they found themselves at the head of a ladder, all the steps of which were formed of purple and amber clouds that descended to what appeared to be a vast and shining plain, streaked with purple and gold. In the spaces between the streaks of gold and purple they saw soft, milk-white stars. And the children thought that the great plain, so far below them, also belonged to cloudland.

They could not see the little pipers, but up the steps was borne by the cool, sweet air the fairy music; and lured on by it step by step they travelled down the fleecy stairway. When they were little more than half-way down there came mingled with the music a sound almost as sweet – the sound of waters toying in the still air with pebbles on a shelving beach, and with the sound came the odorous brine of the ocean. And then the children knew that what they thought was a plain in the realms of cloudland was the sleeping sea unstirred by wind or tide, dreaming of the purple clouds and stars of the sunset sky above it.

When Connla and Nora reached the strand they saw the nine little pipers marching out towards the sea, and they wondered where they were going to. And they could hardly believe their eyes when they saw them stepping out upon the level ocean as if they were walking upon the land; and away the nine little pipers marched, treading the golden line cast upon the waters by the setting sun. And as the music became fainter and fainter as the pipers passed into the glowing distance, the children began to wonder what was to become of themselves. Just at that very moment they saw coming towards them from the sinking sun a little white horse, with flowing mane and tail and golden hoofs. On the horse's back was a little man dressed in shining green silk. When the horse galloped on to the strand the little man doffed his hat, and said to the children:

"Would you like to follow the nine little pipers?" The children said, "Yes."

"Well, then," said the little man, "come up here behind me; you, Nora, first, and Connla after."

Connla helped up Nora, and then climbed on to the little steed himself; and as soon as they were properly seated the little man said "swish", and away went the steed, galloping over the sea without wetting hair or hoof. But fast as he galloped the nine little pipers were always ahead of him, although they seemed to be going only at a walking pace. When at last he came up rather close to the hindmost of them the nine little pipers disappeared, but the children heard the music playing beneath the waters. The white steed pulled up suddenly, and wouldn't move a step further.

"Now," said the little man to the children, "clasp me tight, Nora, and do you, Connla, cling on to Nora, and both of you shut your eyes."

The children did as they were bidden, and the little man cried:

"Swish! Swash!"

And the steed went down and down until at last his feet struck the bottom.

"Now open your eyes," said the little man.

And when the children did so they saw beneath the horse's feet a golden strand, and above their heads the sea like a transparent cloud between them and the sky. And once more they heard the fairy music, and marching on the strand before them were the nine little pipers.

"You must get off now," said the little man, "I can go no farther with you."

The children scrambled down, and the little man cried "swish", and himself and the steed shot up through the sea, and they saw him no more. Then they set out after the nine little pipers, and it wasn't long until they saw rising up from the golden strand and pushing their heads up into the sea above, a mass of dark grey rocks. And as they were gazing at them they saw the rocks opening, and the nine little pipers disappearing through them.

The children hurried on, and when they came up close to the rocks they saw sitting on a flat and polished stone a mermaid combing her golden hair, and singing a strange sweet song that brought the tears to their eyes, and by the mermaid's side was a little sleek brown otter.

When the mermaid saw them she flung her golden tresses back over her snow-white shoulders, and she beckoned the children to her. Her large eyes were full of sadness; but there was a look so tender upon her face that the children moved towards her without any fear.

"Come to me, little one," she said to Nora, "come and kiss me," and in a second her arms were around the child. The mermaid kissed her again and again, as the tears rushed to her eyes, she said:

"Oh, Nora, avourneen, your breath is as sweet as the wild rose that blooms in the green fields of Erin, and happy are you, my children, who have come so lately from the pleasant land. Oh, Connla! Connla! I get the scent of the dew of the Irish grasses and of the purple heather from your feet. And you both can soon return to Erin of the Streams, but I shall not see it till three hundred years have passed away, for I am Liban the Mermaid, daughter of a line of kings. But I may not keep you here. The Fairy Queen is waiting for you in her snow-white palace and her fragrant bowers. And now kiss me once more, Nora, and kiss me, Connla. May luck and joy go with you, and all gentleness be upon you both."

Then the children said good-bye to the mermaid, and the rocks opened for them and they passed through, and soon they found themselves in a meadow starred with flowers, and through the meadow sped a sunlit stream. They followed the stream until it led them into a garden of roses, and beyond the garden, standing on a gentle hill, was a palace white as snow. Before the palace was a crowd of fairy maidens pelting each other with rose-leaves. But when they saw the children they gave over their play, and came trooping towards them.

"Our queen is waiting for you," they said; and then they led the children to the palace door. The children entered, and after passing through a long corridor they found themselves in a crystal hall so like the one they had seen in the mountain of the golden spear that they thought it was the same. But on all the crystal couches fairies, dressed in silken robes of many colours, were sitting, and at the end of the hall, on a crystal throne, was seated the fairy queen, looking lovelier than the evening star. The queen descended from her throne to meet the children, and taking them by the hands, she led them up the shining steps. Then, sitting down, she made them sit beside her, Connla on her right hand and Nora on her left.

Then she ordered the nine little pipers to come before her, and she said to them:

"So far you have done your duty faithfully, and now play one more sweet air and your task is done."

And the little pipers played, and from the couches at the first sound of the music all the fairies rose, and forming partners, they danced over the crystal floor as lightly as the young leaves dancing in the wind.

Listening to the fairy music, and watching the wavy motion of the dancing fairies, the children fell asleep. When they awoke next morning and rose from their silken beds they were no longer children. Nora was a graceful and stately maiden, and Connla a handsome and gallant youth. They looked at each other for a moment in surprise, and then Connla said:

"Oh, Nora, how tall and beautiful you are!"

"Oh, not so tall and handsome as you are, Connla," said Nora, as she flung her white arms round his neck and kissed her brother's lips.

Then they drew back to get a better look of each other, and who should step between them but the fairy queen.

"Oh, Nora, Nora," said she, "I am not as high as your knee, and as for you, Connla, you look as straight and as tall as one of the round towers of Erin."

"And how did we grow so tall in one night?" said Connla.

"In one night!" said the fairy queen. "One night, indeed! Why, you have been fast asleep, the two of you, for the last seven years!"

"And where was the little mother all that time?" said Connla and Nora together.

"Oh, the little mother was all right. She knew where you were; but she is expecting you today, and so you must go off to see her, although I would like to keep you – if I had my way – all to myself here in the fairyland under the sea. And you will see her today; but before you go here is a necklace for you, Nora; it is formed out of the drops of the ocean spray, sparkling in the sunshine. They were caught by my fairy nymph, for you, as they skimmed the sunlit billows under the shape of sea-birds, and no queen or princess in the world can match their lustre with the diamonds won with toil from the caves of earth. As for you, Connla, see here's a helmet of shining gold fit for a king of Erin – and a king of Erin you will be yet; and here's a spear that will pierce any shield, and here's a shield that no spear can pierce and no sword can cleave as long as you fasten your warrior cloak with this brooch of gold."

And as she spoke she flung round Connla's shoulders a flowing mantle of yellow silk, and pinned it at his neck with a red gold brooch.

"And now, my children, you must go away from me. You, Nora, will be a warrior's bride in Erin of the Streams. And you, Connla, will be king yet over the loveliest province in all the land of Erin; but you will have to fight for your crown, and days of battle are before you. They will not come for a long time after you have left the fairyland under the sea, and until they come lay aside your helmet, shield, and spear, and warrior's cloak and golden brooch. But when the time comes when you will be called to battle, enter not upon it without the golden brooch I give you fastened in your cloak, for if you do harm will come to you. Now, kiss me, children; your little mother is waiting for you at the foot of the golden spear, but do not forget to say goodbye to Liban the Mermaid, exiled from the land she loves, and pining in sadness beneath the sea."

Connla and Nora kissed the fairy queen, and Connla, wearing his golden helmet and silken cloak, and carrying his shield and spear, led Nora with him. They passed from the palace through the garden of roses, through the flowery meadow, through the dark grey rocks, until they reached the golden strand; and there, sitting and singing the strange, sweet song, was Liban the Mermaid.

"And so you are going up to Erin," she said, "up through the covering waters. Kiss me, children, once again; and when you are in Erin of the Streams, sometimes think of the exile from Erin beneath the sea."

And the children kissed the mermaid, and with sad hearts, bidding her goodbye, they walked along the golden strand. When they had gone what seemed to them a long way, they began to feel weary; and just then they saw coming towards them a little man in a red jacket leading a coal-black steed.

When they met the little man, he said: "Connla, put Nora up on this steed; then jump up before her."

Connla did as he was told, and when both of them were mounted –

"Now, Connla," said the little man, "catch the bridle in your hands, and you, Nora, clasp Connla round the waist, and close your eyes."

They did as they were bidden, and then the little man said, "Swash, swish!" and the steed shot up from the strand like a lark from the grass, and pierced the covering sea, and went bounding on over the level waters; and when his hoofs struck the hard ground, Connla and Nora opened their eyes, and they saw that they were galloping towards a shady wood.

On went the steed, and soon he was galloping beneath the branches that almost touched Connla's head. And on they went until they had passed through the wood, and then they saw rising up before them the 'Golden Spear'.

"Oh, Connla," said Nora, "we are at home at last."

"Yes," said Connla, "but where is the little house under the hill?"

And no little house was there; but in its stead was standing a lime-white mansion.

"What can this mean?" said Nora.

But before Connla could reply, the steed had galloped up to the door of the mansion, and, in the twinkling of an eye, Connla and Nora were standing on the ground outside the door, and the steed had vanished.

Before they could recover from their surprise the little mother came rushing out to them, and flung her arms around their necks, and kissed them both again and again.

"Oh, children! Children! You are welcome home to me; for though I knew it was all for the best, my heart was lonely without you."

And Connla and Nora caught up the little mother in their arms, and they carried her into the hall and set her down on the floor.

"Oh, Nora!" said the little mother, "you are a head over me; and as for you, Connla, you look almost as tall as one of the round towers of Erin."

"That's what the fairy queen said, mother," said Nora.

"Blessings on the fairy queen," said the little mother. "Turn round, Connla, till I look at you."

Connla turned round, and the little mother said:

"Oh, Connla, with your golden helmet and your spear, and your glancing shield, and your silken cloak, you look like a king. But take them off, my boy, beautiful as they are. Your little mother would like to see you, her own brave boy, without any fairy finery."

And Connla laid aside his spear and shield, and took off his golden helmet and his silken cloak. Then he caught the little mother and kissed her, and lifted her up until she was as high as his head. And said he:

"Don't you know, little mother, I'd rather have you than all the world."

And that night, when they were sitting down by the fire together, you may be sure that in the whole world no people were half as happy as Nora, Connla, and the little mother.

The Brewery of Egg-Shells

MRS. SULLIVAN fancied that her youngest child had been exchanged by 'fairies theft', and certainly appearances warranted such a conclusion; for in one night her healthy, blue-eyed boy had become shrivelled up into almost nothing, and never ceased squalling and crying. This naturally made poor Mrs. Sullivan very unhappy; and all the neighbours, by way of comforting her, said that her own child was, beyond any kind of doubt, with the good people, and that one of themselves was put in his place.

Mrs. Sullivan of course could not disbelieve what every one told her, but she did not wish to hurt the thing; for although its face was so withered, and its body wasted away to a mere skeleton, it had still a strong resemblance to her own boy. She, therefore, could not find it in her heart to roast it alive on the griddle, or to burn its nose off with the red-hot tongs, or to throw it out in the snow on the road-side, notwithstanding these, and several like proceedings, were strongly recommended to her for the recovery of her child.

One day who should Mrs. Sullivan meet but a cunning woman, well known about the country by the name of Ellen Leah (or Grey Ellen). She had the gift, however she got it, of telling where the dead were, and what was good for the rest of their souls; and could charm away warts and wens, and do a great many wonderful things of the same nature.

"You're in grief this morning, Mrs. Sullivan," were the first words of Ellen Leah to her.

"You may say that, Ellen," said Mrs. Sullivan, "and good cause I have to be in grief, for there was my own fine child whipped of from me out of his cradle, without as much as 'by your leave' or 'ask your pardon', and an ugly dony bit of a shrivelled-up fairy put in his place; no wonder, then, that you see me in grief, Ellen."

"Small blame to you, Mrs. Sullivan," said Ellen Leah, "but are you sure 'tis a fairy?"

"Sure!" echoed Mrs. Sullivan, "sure enough I am to my sorrow, and can I doubt my own two eyes? Every mother's soul must feel for me!"

"Will you take an old woman's advice?" said Ellen Leah, fixing her wild and mysterious gaze upon the unhappy mother; and, after a pause, she added, "but maybe you'll call it foolish?"

"Can you get me back my child, my own child, Ellen?" said Mrs. Sullivan with great energy.

"If you do as I bid you," returned Ellen Leah, "you'll know." Mrs. Sullivan was silent in expectation, and Ellen continued, "Put down the big pot, full of water, on the fire, and make it boil like mad; then get a dozen new-laid eggs, break them, and keep the shells, but throw away the rest; when that is done, put the shells in the pot of boiling water, and you will soon know whether it is your own boy or a fairy. If you find that it is a fairy in the cradle, take the red-hot poker and cram it down his ugly throat, and you will not have much trouble with him after that, I promise you."

Home went Mrs. Sullivan, and did as Ellen Leah desired. She put the pot on the fire, and plenty of turf under it, and set the water boiling at such a rate, that if ever water was red-hot, it surely was.

The child was lying, for a wonder, quite easy and quiet in the cradle, every now and then cocking his eye, that would twinkle as keen as a star in a frosty night, over at the great fire, and the big pot upon it; and he looked on with great attention at Mrs. Sullivan breaking the eggs and putting down the egg-shells to boil. At last he asked, with the voice of a very old man, "What are you doing, mammy?"

Mrs. Sullivan's heart, as she said herself, was up in her mouth ready to choke her, at hearing the child speak. But she contrived to put the poker in the fire, and to answer, without making any wonder at the words, "I'm brewing, *a vick* (my son)".

"And what are you brewing, mammy?" said the little imp, whose supernatural gift of speech now proved beyond question that he was a fairy substitute.

"I wish the poker was red," thought Mrs. Sullivan; but it was a large one, and took a long time heating; so she determined to keep him in talk until the poker was in a proper state to thrust down his throat, and therefore repeated the question.

"Is it what I'm brewing, *a vick*," said she, "you want to know?"

"Yes, mammy: what are you brewing?" returned the fairy.

"Egg-shells, *a vick*," said Mrs. Sullivan.

"Oh!" shrieked the imp, starting up in the cradle, and clapping his hands together, "I'm fifteen hundred years in the world, and I never saw a brewery of egg-shells before!" The poker was by this time quite red, and Mrs. Sullivan, seizing it, ran furiously towards the cradle; but somehow or other her foot slipped, and she fell flat on the floor, and the poker flew out of her hand to the other end of the house. However, she got up without much loss of time and went to the cradle, intending to pitch the wicked thing that was in it into the pot of boiling water, when there she saw her own child in a sweet sleep, one of his soft round arms rested upon the pillow – his features were as placid as if their repose had never been disturbed, save the rosy mouth, which moved with a gentle and regular breathing.

The Fairy Nurse

<><><>

THERE WAS ONCE a little farmer and his wife living near **Coolgarrow. They had three children, and my story happened while the youngest was a baby. The wife was a good wife enough, but her mind was all on her family and her farm, and she hardly ever went to her knees without falling asleep, and she thought the time spent in the chapel was twice as long as it need be. So, friends,**

she let her man and her two children go before her one day to Mass, while she called to consult a fairy man about a disorder one of her cows had. She was late at the chapel, and was sorry all the day after, for her husband was in grief about it, and she was very fond of him.

Late that night he was wakened up by the cries of his children calling out "Mother! Mother!" When he sat up and rubbed his eyes, there was no wife by his side, and when he asked the little ones what was become of their mother, they said they saw the room full of nice little men and women, dressed in white and red and green, and their mother in the middle of them, going out by the door as if she was walking in her sleep. Out he ran, and searched everywhere round the house but, neither tale nor tidings did he get of her for many a day.

Well, the poor man was miserable enough, for he was as fond of his woman as she was of him. It used to bring the salt tears down his cheeks to see his poor children neglected and dirty, as they often were, and they'd be bad enough only for a kind neighbour that used to look in whenever she could spare time. The infant was away with a nurse.

About six weeks after – just as he was going out to his work one morning – a neighbour, that used to mind women when they were ill, came up to him, and kept step by step with him to the field, and this is what she told him.

"Just as I was falling asleep last night, I heard a horse's tramp on the grass and a knock at the door, and there, when I came out, was a fine-looking dark man, mounted on a black horse, and he told me to get ready in all haste, for a lady was in great want of me. As soon as I put on my cloak and things, he took me by the hand, and I was sitting behind him before I felt myself stirring. "Where are we going, sir?" says I. "You'll soon know," says he; and he drew his fingers across my eyes, and not a ray could I see. I kept a tight grip of him, and I little knew whether he was going backwards or forwards, or how long we were about it, till my hand was taken again, and I felt the ground under me. The fingers went the other way across my eyes, and there we were before a castle door, and in we went through a big hall and great rooms all painted in fine green colours, with red and gold bands and ornaments, and the finest carpets and chairs and tables and window curtains, and grand ladies and gentlemen walking about. At last we came to a bedroom, with a beautiful lady in bed, with a fine bouncing boy beside her. The lady clapped her hands, and in came the Dark Man and kissed her and the baby, and praised me, and gave me a bottle of green ointment to rub the child all over.

"Well, the child I rubbed, sure enough; but my right eye began to smart, and I put up my finger and gave it a rub, and then stared, for never in all my life was I so frightened. The beautiful room was a big, rough cave, with water oozing over the edges of the stones and through the clay; and the lady, and the lord, and the child weazened, poverty-bitten creatures – nothing but skin and bone – and the rich dresses were old rags. I didn't let on that I found any difference, and after a bit says the Dark Man, 'Go before me to the hall door, and I will be with you in a few moments, and see you safe home.' Well, just as I turned into the outside cave, who should I see watching near the door but poor Molly. She looked round all terrified, and says she to me in a whisper, 'I'm brought here to nurse the child of the king and queen of the fairies; but there is one chance of saving me. All the court will pass the cross near Templeshambo next Friday night, on a visit to the fairies of Old Ross. If John can catch me by the hand or cloak when I ride by, and has courage not to let go his grip, I'll be safe. Here's the king. Don't open your mouth to answer. I saw what happened with the ointment.'

"The Dark Man didn't once cast his eye towards Molly, and he seemed to have no suspicion of me. When we came out I looked about me, and where do you think we were but in the dyke of the Rath of Cromogue. I was on the horse again, which was nothing but a big rag-weed, and I was in dread every minute I'd fall off; but nothing happened till I found myself in my own cabin. The king slipped five guineas into my hand as soon as I was on the ground, and thanked me, and bade me good night. I hope I'll never see his face again. I got into bed, and couldn't sleep for a long time; and when I examined my five guineas this morning, that I left in the table drawer the last thing, I found five withered leaves of oak – bad luck to the giver!"

Well, you may all think the fright, and the joy, and the grief the poor man was in when the woman finished her story. They talked and they talked, but we needn't mind what they said till Friday night came, when both were standing where the mountain road crosses the one going to Ross.

There they stood, looking towards the bridge of Thuar, in the dead of the night, with a little moonlight shining from over Kilachdiarmid. At last she gave a start, and "By this and by that," says she, "here they come, bridles jingling and feathers tossing!" He looked, but could see nothing; and she stood trembling and her eyes wide open, looking down the way to the ford of Ballinacoola. "I see your wife," says she, "riding on the outside just so as to rub against us. We'll walk on quietly, as if we suspected nothing, and when we are passing I'll give you a shove. If you don't do *your* duty then, woe be with you!"

Well, they walked on easy, and the poor hearts beating in both their breasts; and though he could see nothing, he heard a faint jingle and trampling and rustling, and at last he got the push that she promised. He spread out his arms, and there was his wife's waist within them, and he could see her plain; but such a hullabulloo rose as if there was an earthquake, and he found himself surrounded by horrible-looking things, roaring at him and striving to pull his wife away. But he made the sign of the cross and bid them begone in God's name, and held his wife as if it was iron his arms were made of. Bedad, in one moment everything was as silent as the grave, and the poor woman lying in a faint in the arms of her husband and her good neighbour.

Well, all in good time she was minding her family and her business again; and I'll go bail, after the fright she got, she spent more time on her knees, and avoided fairy men all the days of the week, and particularly on Sunday.

It is hard to have anything to do with the good people without getting a mark from them. My brave nurse didn't escape no more than another. She was one Thursday at the market of Enniscorthy, when what did she see walking among the tubs of butter but the Dark Man, very hungry-looking, and taking a scoop out of one tub and out of another. "Oh, sir," says she, very foolish, "I hope your lady is well, and the baby."

"Pretty well, thank you," says he, rather frightened like. "How do I look in this new suit?" says he, getting to one side of her.

"I can't see you plain at all, sir," says she.

"Well, now?" says he, getting round her back to the other side.

"Musha, indeed, sir, your coat looks no better than a withered dock-leaf."

"Maybe, then," says he, "it will be different now," and he struck the eye next him with a switch. Friends, she never saw a glimmer after with that one till the day of her death.

Connla and the Fairy Maiden

❖

CONNLA OF THE FIERY HAIR was son of Conn of the Hundred Fights. One day as he stood by the side of his father on the height of Usna, he saw a maiden clad in strange attire coming towards him.

"Whence comest thou, maiden?" said Connla.

"I come from the Plains of the Ever Living," she said, "there where there is neither death nor sin. There we keep holiday always, nor need we help from any in our joy. And in all our pleasure we have no strife. And because we have our homes in the round green hills, men call us the Hill Folk."

The king and all with him wondered much to hear a voice when they saw no one. For save Connla alone, none saw the Fairy Maiden.

"To whom art thou talking, my son?" said Conn the king.

Then the maiden answered, "Connla speaks to a young, fair maid, whom neither death nor old age awaits. I love Connla, and now I call him away to the Plain of Pleasure, Moy Mell, where Boadag is king for aye, nor has there been complaint or sorrow in that land since he has held the kingship. Oh, come with me, Connla of the Fiery Hair, ruddy as the dawn with thy tawny skin. A fairy crown awaits thee to grace thy comely face and royal form. Come, and never shall thy comeliness fade, nor thy youth, till the last awful day of judgment."

The king in fear at what the maiden said, which he heard though he could not see her, called aloud to his Druid, Coran by name.

"Oh, Coran of the many spells," he said, "and of the cunning magic, I call upon thy aid. A task is upon me too great for all my skill and wit, greater than any laid upon me since I seized the kingship. A maiden unseen has met us, and by her power would take from me my dear, my comely son. If thou help not, he will be taken from thy king by woman's wiles and witchery."

Then Coran the Druid stood forth and chanted his spells towards the spot where the maiden's voice had been heard. And none heard her voice again, nor could Connla see her longer. Only as she vanished before the Druid's mighty spell, she threw an apple to Connla.

For a whole month from that day Connla would take nothing, either to eat or to drink, save only from that apple. But as he ate it grew again and always kept whole. And all the while there grew within him a mighty yearning and longing after the maiden he had seen.

But when the last day of the month of waiting came, Connla stood by the side of the king his father on the Plain of Arcomin, and again he saw the maiden come towards him, and again she spoke to him.

"'Tis a glorious place, forsooth, that Connla holds among short-lived mortals awaiting the day of death. But now the folk of life, the ever-living ones, beg and bid thee come to Moy Mell, the Plain of Pleasure, for they have learnt to know thee, seeing thee in thy home among thy dear ones."

When Conn the king heard the maiden's voice he called to his men aloud and said:

"Summon swift my Druid Coran, for I see she has again this day the power of speech."

Then the maiden said: "Oh, mighty Conn, fighter of a hundred fights, the Druid's power is little loved; it has little honour in the mighty land, peopled with so many of the upright. When the Law will come, it will do away with the Druid's magic spells that come from the lips of the false black demon."

Then Conn the king observed that since the maiden came, Connla his son spoke to none that spake to him. So Conn of the hundred fights said to him, "Is it to thy mind what the woman says, my son?"

"'Tis hard upon me," then said Connla; "I love my own folk above all things; but yet, but yet a longing seizes me for the maiden."

When the maiden heard this, she answered and said "The ocean is not so strong as the waves of thy longing. Come with me in my curragh, the gleaming, straight-gliding crystal canoe. Soon we can reach Boadag's realm. I see the bright sun sink, yet far as it is, we can reach it before dark. There is, too, another land worthy of thy journey, a land joyous to all that seek it. Only wives and maidens dwell there. If thou wilt, we can seek it and live there alone together in joy."

When the maiden ceased to speak, Connla of the Fiery Hair rushed away from them and sprang into the curragh, the gleaming, straight-gliding crystal canoe. And then they all, king and court, saw it glide away over the bright sea towards the setting sun. Away and away, till eye could see it no longer, and Connla and the Fairy Maiden went their way on the sea, and were no more seen, nor did any know where they came.

How Cormac Mac Art Went to Faery

CORMAC, SON OF ART, son of Conn of the Hundred Battles, was high King of Ireland, and held his Court at Tara. One day he saw a youth upon the green having in his hand a glittering fairy branch with nine apples of red. And whensoever the branch was shaken, wounded men and women enfeebled by illness would be lulled to sleep by the sound of the very sweet fairy music which those apples uttered, nor could anyone upon earth bear in mind any want, woe, or weariness of soul when that branch was shaken for him.

"Is that branch thy own?" said Cormac.

"It is indeed mine."

"Wouldst thou sell it? And what wouldst thou require for it?"

"Will you give me what I ask?" said the youth.

The king promised, and the youth then claimed his wife, his daughter, and his son. Sorrowful of heart was the king, heaviness of heart filled his wife and children when they learned that they must part from him. But Cormac shook the branch amongst them, and when they heard the soft sweet music of the branch they forgot all care and sorrow and went forth to meet the youth, and he and they took their departure and were seen no more. Loud cries of weeping and mourning were made throughout Erin when this was known: but Cormac shook the branch so that there was no longer any grief or heaviness of heart upon anyone.

After a year Cormac said: "It is a year today since my wife, my son, and my daughter were taken from me. I will follow them by the same path that they took."

Cormac went off, and a dark magical mist rose about him, and he chanced to come upon a wonderful marvellous plain. Many horsemen were there, busy thatching a house with the feathers of foreign birds; when one side was thatched they would go and seek more, and when they returned not a feather was on the roof. Cormac gazed at them for a while and then went forward.

Again, he saw a youth dragging up trees to make a fire; but before he could find a second tree the first one would be burnt, and it seemed to Cormac that his labour would never end.

Cormac journeyed onwards until he saw three immense wells on the border of the plain, and on each well was a head. From out the mouth of the first head there flowed two streams, into it there flowed one; the second head had a stream flowing out of and another stream into its mouth, whilst three streams were flowing from the mouth of the third head. Great wonder seized Cormac, and he said: "I will stay and gaze upon these wells, for I should find no man to tell me your story." With that he set onwards till he came to a house in the middle of a field. He entered and greeted the inmates.

There sat within a tall couple clad in many-hued garments, and they greeted the king, and bade him welcome for the night.

Then the wife bade her husband seek food, and he arose and returned with a huge wild boar upon his back and a log in his hand. He cast down the swine and the log upon the floor, and said: "There is meat; cook it for yourselves."

"How can I do that?" said Cormac.

"I will teach you," said the youth. "Split this great log, make four pieces of it, and make four quarters of the hog; put a log under each quarter; tell a true story, and the meat will be cooked."

"Tell the first story yourself," said Cormac.

"Seven pigs I have of the same kind as the one I brought, and I could feed the world with them. For if a pig is killed I have but to put its bones into the stye again, and it will be found alive the next morning."

The story was true, and a quarter of the pig was cooked.

Then Cormac begged the woman of the house to tell a story.

"I have seven white cows, and they fill seven cauldrons with milk every day, and I give my word that they yield as much milk as would satisfy the men of the whole world if they were out on yonder plain drinking it."

That story was true, and a second quarter of the pig was cooked.

Cormac was bidden now to tell a story for his quarter, and he told how he was upon a search for his wife, his son and his daughter that had been borne away from him a year before by a youth with a fairy branch.

"If what thou sayest be true," said the man of the house, "thou art indeed Cormac, son of Art, son of Conn of the Hundred Battles."

"Truly I am," quoth Cormac.

That story was true, and a quarter of the pig was cooked.

"Eat thy meal now," said the man of the house.

"I never ate before," said Cormac, "having only two people in my company."

"Wouldst thou eat it with three others?"

"If they were dear to me, I would," said Cormac.

Then the door opened, and there entered the wife and children of Cormac: great was his joy and his exultation.

Then Manannan mac Lir, lord of the fairy Cavalcade, appeared before him in his own true form, and said thus:

"I it was, Cormac, who bore away these three from thee. I it was who gave thee this branch, all that I might bring thee here. Eat now and drink."

"I would do so," said Cormac, "could I learn the meaning of the wonders I saw today."

"Thou shalt learn them," said Manannan. "The horsemen thatching the roof with feathers are a likeness of people who go forth into the world to seek riches and fortune; when they return their houses are bare, and so they go on for ever. The young man dragging up the trees to make a fire is a likeness of those who labour for others: much trouble they have, but they never warm themselves at the fire. The three heads in the wells are three kinds of men. Some there are who give freely when they get freely; some who give freely though they get little; some who get much and give little, and they are the worst of the three, Cormac," said Manannan.

After that Cormac and his wife and his children sat down, and a table-cloth was spread before them.

"That is a very precious thing before thee," said Manannan, "there is no food however delicate that shall be asked of it but it shall be had without doubt."

"That is well," quoth Cormac.

After that Manannan thrust his hand into his girdle and brought out a goblet and set it upon his palm. "This cup has this virtue," said he, "that when a false story is told before it, it makes four pieces of it, and when a true story is related it is made whole again."

"Those are very precious things you have, Manannan," said the king.

"They shall all be thine," said Manannan, "the goblet, the branch and the tablecloth."

Then they ate their meal, and that meal was good, for they could not think of any meat but they got it upon the table-cloth, nor of any drink but they got it in the cup. Great thanks did they give to Manannan.

When they had eaten their meal a couch was prepared for them and they laid down to slumber and sweet sleep.

Where they rose on the morrow morn was in Tara of the kings, and by their side were tablecloth, cup, and branch.

Thus did Cormac fare at the Court of Manannan, and this is how he got the fairy branch.

The Legend of Knockgrafton

<><

THERE WAS ONCE a poor man who lived in the fertile glen of Aherlow, at the foot of the gloomy Galtee mountains, and he had a great hump on his back: he looked just as if his body had been rolled up and placed upon his shoulders; and his head was pressed down with the weight so much that his chin, when he was sitting, used to rest upon his knees for support. The country people were rather shy of meeting him in any lonesome place, for though, poor creature, he was as harmless and as inoffensive as a new-born infant, yet his deformity was so great that he scarcely appeared to be a human creature, and some ill-minded persons had set strange stories about him afloat. He was said to have a great knowledge of herbs and charms; but certain it was that he had a mighty skilful hand in plaiting straw and rushes into hats and baskets, which was the way he made his livelihood.

Lusmore, for that was the nickname put upon him by reason of his always wearing a sprig of the fairy cap, or lusmore (the foxglove), in his little straw hat, would ever get a higher penny for his plaited work than anyone else, and perhaps that was the reason why someone, out of envy, had circulated the strange stories about him.

Be that as it may, it happened that he was returning one evening from the pretty town of Cahir towards Cappagh, and as little Lusmore walked very slowly, on account of the great hump upon his back, it was quite dark when he came to the old moat of Knockgrafton, which stood on the right-hand side of his road. Tired and weary was he, and noways comfortable in his own mind at thinking how much farther he had to travel, and that he should be walking all the night; so he sat down under the moat to rest himself, and began looking mournfully enough upon the moon.

Presently there rose a wild strain of unearthly melody upon the ear of little Lusmore; he listened, and he thought that he had never heard such ravishing music before. It was like the sound of many voices, each mingling and blending with the other so strangely that they seemed to be one, though all singing different strains, and the words of the song were these – *Da Luan, Da Mort, Da Luan, Da Mort, Da Luan, Da Mort*; when there would be a moment's pause, and then the round of melody went on again.

Lusmore listened attentively, scarcely drawing his breath lest he might lose the slightest note. He now plainly perceived that the singing was within the moat; and though at first it had charmed him so much, he began to get tired of hearing the same round sung over and over so often without any change; so availing himself of the pause when the *Da Luan, Da Mort*, had been sung three times, he took up the tune, and raised it with the words *augus Da Cadine*, and then went on singing with the voices inside of the moat, *Da Luan, Da Mort*, finishing the melody, when the pause again came, with *augus Da Cadine*.

The fairies within Knockgrafton, for the song was a fairy melody, when they heard this addition to the tune, were so much delighted that, with instant resolve, it was determined to bring the mortal among them, whose musical skill so far exceeded theirs, and little Lusmore was conveyed into their company with the eddying speed of a whirlwind.

Glorious to behold was the sight that burst upon him as he came down through the moat, twirling round and round, with the lightness of a straw, to the sweetest music that kept time to his motion. The greatest honour was then paid him, for he was put above all the musicians, and he had servants tending upon him, and everything to his heart's content, and a hearty welcome to all; and, in short, he was made as much of as if he had been the first man in the land.

Presently Lusmore saw a great consultation going forward among the fairies, and, notwithstanding all their civility, he felt very much frightened, until one stepping out from the rest came up to him and said –

> *"Lusmore! Lusmore!*
> *Doubt not, nor deplore,*
> *For the hump which you bore*
> *On your back is no more;*
> *Look down on the floor,*
> *And view it, Lusmore!"*

When these words were said, poor little Lusmore felt himself so light, and so happy, that he thought he could have bounded at one jump over the moon, like the cow in the history of the cat and the fiddle; and he saw, with inexpressible pleasure, his hump tumble down upon the ground from his shoulders. He then tried to lift up his head, and he did so with becoming caution, fearing that he might knock it against the ceiling of the grand hall, where he was; he looked round and round again with greatest wonder and delight upon everything, which appeared more and more beautiful; and, overpowered at beholding such a resplendent scene, his head grew dizzy, and his eyesight became dim. At last he fell into a sound sleep, and when he awoke he found that it was broad daylight, the sun shining brightly, and the birds singing sweetly; and that he was lying just at the foot of the moat of Knockgrafton, with the cows and sheep grazing peacefully round about him. The first thing Lusmore did, after saying his prayers, was to put his hand behind to feel for his hump, but no sign of one was there on his back, and he looked at himself with great pride, for he had now become a well-shaped dapper little fellow, and more than that, found himself in a full suit of new clothes, which he concluded the fairies had made for him.

Towards Cappagh he went, stepping out as lightly, and springing up at every step as if he had been all his life a dancing-master. Not a creature who met Lusmore knew him without his hump, and he had a great work to persuade everyone that he was the same man – in truth he was not, so far as outward appearance went.

Of course it was not long before the story of Lusmore's hump got about, and a great wonder was made of it. Through the country, for miles round, it was the talk of every one, high and low.

One morning, as Lusmore was sitting contented enough, at his cabin door, up came an old woman to him, and asked him if he could direct her to Cappagh.

"I need give you no directions, my good woman," said Lusmore, "for this is Cappagh; and whom may you want here?"

"I have come," said the woman, "out of Decie's country, in the county of Waterford looking after one Lusmore, who, I have heard tell, had his hump taken off by the fairies; for there is a son of a gossip of mine who has got a hump on him that will be his death; and maybe if he could use the same charm as Lusmore, the hump may be taken off him. And now I have told you the reason of my coming so far: 'tis to find out about this charm, if I can."

Lusmore, who was ever a good-natured little fellow, told the woman all the particulars, how he had raised the tune for the fairies at Knockgrafton, how his hump had been removed from his shoulders, and how he had got a new suit of clothes into the bargain.

The woman thanked him very much, and then went away quite happy and easy in her own mind. When she came back to her gossip's house, in the county of Waterford, she told her everything that Lusmore had said, and they put the little hump-backed man, who was a peevish and cunning creature from his birth, upon a car, and took him all the way across the country. It was a long journey, but they did not care for that, so the hump was taken from off him; and they brought him, just at nightfall, and left him under the old moat of Knockgrafton.

Jack Madden, for that was the humpy man's name, had not been sitting there long when he heard the tune going on within the moat much sweeter than before; for the fairies were singing it the way Lusmore had settled their music for them, and the song was going on; *Da Luan, Da Mort, Da Luan,*

Da Mort, Da Luan, Da Mort, augus Da Cadine, without ever stopping. Jack Madden, who was in a great hurry to get quit of his hump, never thought of waiting until the fairies had done, or watching for a fit opportunity to raise the tune higher again than Lusmore had; so having heard them sing it over seven times without stopping, out he bawls, never minding the time or the humour of the tune, or how he could bring his words in properly, *augus Da Cadine, augus Da Hena*, thinking that if one day was good, two were better; and that if Lusmore had one new suit of clothes given him, he should have two.

No sooner had the words passed his lips than he was taken up and whisked into the moat with prodigious force; and the fairies came crowding round about him with great anger, screeching, and screaming, and roaring out, "Who spoiled our tune? Who spoiled our tune?" and one stepped up to him, above all the rest and said:

> *"Jack Madden! Jack Madden!*
> *Your words came so bad in*
> *The tune we felt glad in; –*
> *This castle you're had in,*
> *That your life we may sadden;*
> *Here's two humps for Jack Madden!"*

And twenty of the strongest fairies brought Lusmore's hump and put it down upon poor Jack's back, over his own, where it became fixed as firmly as if it was nailed on with twelve-penny nails, by the best carpenter that ever drove one. Out of their castle they then kicked him; and, in the morning, when Jack Madden's mother and her gossip came to look after their little man, they found him half dead, lying at the foot of the moat, with the other hump upon his back. Well to be sure, how they did look at each other! But they were afraid to say anything, lest a hump might be put upon their own shoulders. Home they brought the unlucky Jack Madden with them, as downcast in their hearts and their looks as ever two gossips were; and what through the weight of his other hump, and the long journey, he died soon after, leaving they say his heavy curse to anyone who would go to listen to fairy tunes again.

The Field of Boliauns

❖

ONE FINE DAY IN HARVEST – it was indeed Lady-day in harvest, that everybody knows to be one of the greatest holidays in the year – Tom Fitzpatrick was taking a ramble through the ground, and went along the sunny side of a hedge; when all of a sudden he heard a clacking sort of noise a little before him in the hedge. "Dear me," said Tom, "but isn't it surprising to hear the stonechatters singing so late in the season?" So Tom stole on, going on the tops of his toes to try if he could get a sight of what was making the noise, to see if he was right in his guess. The noise stopped; but as Tom looked sharply through the bushes, what should he see in a nook of the hedge but a brown pitcher, that might hold about a gallon and a half of liquor; and by-and-by a little wee teeny tiny bit of an old man, with a little motty of a cocked hat stuck upon the top of his head, a deeshy daushy leather apron hanging before him, pulled out a little wooden stool, and stood up upon it, and dipped a little piggin into the pitcher, and took out the full of it, and put it beside the stool, and then sat down under the pitcher, and began to work at putting a heel-piece on a bit of a brogue just fit for himself. "Well, by the powers," said Tom to himself, "I often heard tell of the Leprechauns, and, to tell God's truth, I never rightly believed in them – but here's one of them in real earnest. If I go knowingly to work, I'm a made man. They say a body must never take their eyes off them, or they'll escape."

Tom now stole on a little further, with his eye fixed on the little man just as a cat does with a mouse. So when he got up quite close to him, "God bless your work, neighbour," said Tom.

The little man raised up his head, and "Thank you kindly," said he.

"I wonder you'd be working on the holiday!" said Tom.

"That's my own business, not yours," was the reply.

"Well, maybe you'd be civil enough to tell us what you've got in the pitcher there?" said Tom.

"That I will, with pleasure," said he; "it's good beer."

"Beer!" said Tom. "Thunder and fire! Where did you get it?"

"Where did I get it, is it? Why, I made it. And what do you think I made it of?"

"Devil a one of me knows," said Tom; "but of malt, I suppose, what else?"

"There you're out. I made it of heath."

"Of heath!" said Tom, bursting out laughing; "sure you don't think me to be such a fool as to believe that?"

"Do as you please," said he, "but what I tell you is the truth. Did you never hear tell of the Danes?"

"Well, what about *them*?" said Tom.

"Why, all the about them there is, is that when they were here they taught us to make beer out of the heath, and the secret's in my family ever since."

"Will you give a body a taste of your beer?" said Tom.

"I'll tell you what it is, young man, it would be fitter for you to be looking after your father's property than to be bothering decent quiet people with your foolish questions. There now, while you're idling away your time here, there's the cows have broke into the oats, and are knocking the corn all about."

Tom was taken so by surprise with this that he was just on the very point of turning round when he recollected himself; so, afraid that the like might happen again, he made a grab at the Leprechaun, and caught him up in his hand; but in his hurry he overset the pitcher, and spilt all the beer, so that he could not get a taste of it to tell what sort it was. He then swore that he would kill him if he did not show him where his money was. Tom looked so wicked and so bloody-minded that the little man was quite frightened; so says he, "Come along with me a couple of fields off, and I'll show you a crock of gold."

So they went, and Tom held the Leprechaun fast in his hand, and never took his eyes from off him, though they had to cross hedges and ditches, and a crooked bit of bog, till at last they came to a great field all full of boliauns, and the Leprechaun pointed to a big boliaun, and says he, "Dig under that boliaun, and you'll get the great crock all full of guineas."

Tom in his hurry had never thought of bringing a spade with him, so he made up his mind to run home and fetch one; and that he might know the place again he took off one of his red garters, and tied it round the boliaun.

Then he said to the Leprechaun, "Swear ye'll not take that garter away from that boliaun." And the Leprechaun swore right away not to touch it.

"I suppose," said the Leprechaun, very civilly, "you have no further occasion for me?"

"No," says Tom; "you may go away now, if you please, and God speed you, and may good luck attend you wherever you go."

"Well, goodbye to you, Tom Fitzpatrick," said the Leprechaun; "and much good may it do you when you get it."

So Tom ran for dear life, till he came home and got a spade, and then away with him, as hard as he could go, back to the field of boliauns; but when he got there, lo and behold! Not a boliaun in the field but had a red garter, the very model of his own, tied about it; and as to digging up the whole field, that was all nonsense, for there were more than forty good Irish acres in it. So Tom came home again with his spade on his shoulder, a little cooler than he went, and many's the hearty curse he gave the Leprechaun every time he thought of the neat turn he had served him.

Taming the Pooka

❧

THE WEST AND NORTHWEST coast of Ireland shows many remarkable geological formations, but, excepting the Giant's Causeway, no more striking spectacle is presented than that to the south of Galway Bay. From the sea, the mountains rise in terraces like gigantic stairs, the layers of stone being apparently harder and denser on the upper surfaces than beneath, so the lower portion of each layer, disintegrating first, is washed away by the rains and a clearly defined step is formed. These terraces are generally about twenty feet high, and of a breadth, varying with the situation and exposure, of from ten to fifty feet.

The highway from Ennis to Ballyvaughn, a fishing village opposite Galway, winds, by a circuitous course, through these freaks of nature, and, on the long descent from the high land to the sea level, passes the most conspicuous of the neighboring mountains, the Corkscrew Hill. The general shape of the mountain is conical, the terraces composing it are of wonderful regularity from the base to the peak, and the strata being sharply upturned from the horizontal, the impression given is that of a broad road carved out of the sides of the mountain and winding by an easy ascent to the summit.

"'Tis the Pooka's Path they call it," said the car-man. "Phat's the Pooka? Well, that's not aisy to say. It's an avil sper't that does be always in mischief, but sure it niver does sarious harrum axceptin' to thim that desarves it, or thim that shpakes av it disrespictful. I never seen it, Glory be to God, but there's thim that has, and be the same token, they do say that it looks like the finest black horse that iver wore shoes. But it isn't a horse at all at all, for no horse 'ud have eyes av fire, or be breathin' flames av blue wid a shmell o' sulfur, savin' yer presince, or a shnort like thunder, and no mortial horse 'ud take the lapes it does, or go as fur widout gettin' tired. Sure when it give Tim O'Bryan the ride it give him, it wint from Gort to Athlone wid wan jump, an' the next it tuk he was in Mullingyar, and the next was in Dublin, and back agin be way av Kilkenny an' Limerick, an' niver turned a hair. How far is that? Faith I dunno, but it's a power av distance, an' clane acrost Ireland an' back. He knew it was the Pooka bekase it shpake to him like a Christian mortial, only it isn't agrayble in its language an' 'ull niver give ye a dacint word afther ye're on its back, an' sometimes not before aither.

"Sure Dennis O'Rourke was afther comin' home wan night, it was only a boy I was, but I mind him tellin' the shtory, an' it was at a fair in Galway he'd been. He'd been havin' a sup, some says more, but whin he come to the rath, and jist beyant where the fairies dance and ferninst the wall where the polisman was shot last winther, he fell in the ditch, quite spint and tired complately. It wasn't the length as much as the wideness av the road was in it, fur he was goin' from wan side to the other an' it was too much fur him entirely. So he laid shtill fur a bit and thin thried fur to get up, but his legs wor light and his head was heavy, an' whin he attimpted to get his feet an the road 'twas his head that was an it, bekase his legs cudn't balance it. Well, he laid there and was bet entirely, an' while he was studyin' how he'd raise, he heard the throttin' av a horse on the road. "'Tis meself 'ull get the lift now,' says he, and laid waitin', and up comes the Pooka. Whin Dennis seen him, begob, he kivered his face wid his hands and turned on the breast av him, and roared wid fright like a bull.

"'Arrah thin, ye snakin' blaggârd,' says the Pooka, mighty short, 'lave aff yer bawlin' or I'll kick ye to the ind av next week,' says he to him.

"But Dennis was scairt, an' bellered louder than afore, so the Pooka, wid his hoof, give him a crack on the back that knocked the wind out av him.

"'Will ye lave aff,' says the Pooka, 'or will I give ye another, ye roarin' dough-face?'

"Dennis left aff blubberin' so the Pooka got his timper back.

"'Shtand up, ye guzzlin' sarpint,' says the Pooka, 'I'll give ye a ride.'

"'Plaze yer Honor,' says Dennis, 'I can't. Sure I've not been afther drinkin' at all, but shmokin' too much an' atin', an' it's sick I am, and not ontoxicated.'

"'Och, ye dhrunken buzzard,' says the Pooka, 'Don't offer fur to desave me,' liftin' up his hoof agin, an' givin' his tail a swish that sounded like the noise av a catheract, 'Didn't I thrack ye for two miles be yer breath,' says he, 'An' you shmellin' like a potheen fact'ry,' says he, 'An' the nose on yer face as red as a turkey-cock's. Get up, or I'll lift ye,' says he, jumpin' up an' cracking his hind fut like he was doin' a jig.

"Dennis did his best, an' the Pooka helped him wid a grip o' the teeth on his collar.

"'Pick up yer caubeen,' says the Pooka, 'an' climb up. I'll give ye such a ride as ye niver dhramed av.'

"'Ef it's plazin' to yer Honor,' says Dennis, 'I'd laver walk. Ridin' makes me dizzy,' says he.

"''Tis not plazin',' says the Pooka, 'will ye get up or will I kick the shtuffin' out av yer cowardly carkidge,' says he, turnin' round an' flourishin' his heels in Dennis' face.

"Poor Dennis thried, but he cudn't, so the Pooka tuk him to the wall an' give him a lift an it, an' whin Dennis was mounted, an' had a tight howld on the mane, the first lep he give was down the rock there, a thousand feet into the field ye see, thin up agin, an' over the mountain, an' into the say, an' out agin, from the top av the waves to the top av the mountain, an' afther the poor soggarth av a ditcher was nigh onto dead, the Pooka come back here wid him an' dhropped him in the ditch where he found him, an' blowed in his face to put him to slape, so lavin' him. An' they found Dennis in the mornin' an' carried him home, no more cud he walk for a fortnight be razon av the wakeness av his bones fur the ride he'd had.

"But sure, the Pooka's a different baste entirely to phat he was afore King Bryan-Boru tamed him. Niver heard av him? Well, he was the king av Munster an' all Ireland an' tamed the Pooka wanst fur all on the Corkschrew Hill ferninst ye.

"Ye see, in the owld days, the counthry was full av avil sper'ts, an' fairies an' witches, an' divils entirely, and the harrum they done was onsaycin', for they wor always comin' an' goin', like Mulligan's blanket, an' widout so much as sayin', by yer lave. The fairies 'ud be dancin' on the grass every night be the light av the moon, an' stalin' away the childhre, an' many's the wan they tuk that niver come back. The owld rath on the hill beyant was full av the dead, an' afther nightfall they'd come from their graves an' walk in a long line wan afther another to the owld church in the valley where they'd go in an' stay till cock-crow, thin they'd come out agin an' back to the rath. Sorra a parish widout a witch, an' some nights they'd have a great enthertainmint on the Corkschrew Hill, an' you'd see thim, wid shnakes on their arrums an' necks an' ears, be way av jewels, an' the eyes av dead men in their hair, comin' for miles an' miles, some ridin' through the air on shticks an' bats an' owls, an' some walkin', an' more on Pookas an' horses wid wings that 'ud come up in line to the top av the hill, like the cabs at the dure o' the theayter, an' lave thim there an' hurry aff to bring more.

"Sometimes the Owld Inimy, Satan himself, 'ud be there at the enthertainmint, comin' an a monsthrous draggin, wid grane shcales an' eyes like the lightnin' in the heavens, an' a roarin' fiery mouth like a lime-kiln. It was the great day thin, for they do say all the witches brought their rayports at thim saysons fur to show him phat they done.

"Some 'ud tell how they shtopped the wather in a spring, an' inconvanienced the nabers, more 'ud show how they dhried the cow's milk, an' made her kick the pail, an' they'd all laugh like to shplit. Some had blighted the corn, more had brought the rains on the harvest. Some towld how their enchantmints made the childhre fall ill, some said how they set the thatch on fire, more towld how they shtole the eggs, or spiled the crame in the churn, or bewitched the butther so it 'udn't come, or led the shape into the bog. But that wasn't all.

"Wan 'ud have the head av a man murthered be her manes, an' wid it the hand av him hung fur the murther; wan 'ud bring the knife she'd scuttled a boat wid an' pint in the say to where the corpses laid av the fishermen she'd dhrownded; wan 'ud carry on her breast the child she'd shtolen an' meant to bring up in avil, an' another wan 'ud show the little white body av a babby she'd smothered in its slape. And the corpse-candles 'ud tell how they desaved the thraveller, bringin' him to the river, an' the avil sper'ts 'ud say how they dhrew him in an' down to the bottom in his sins an' thin to the pit wid him. An' owld Belzebub 'ud listen to all av thim, wid a rayporther, like thim that's afther takin' down the spaches at a Lague meetin', be his side, a-writing phat they said, so as whin they come to be paid, it 'udn't be forgotten.

"Thim wor the times fur the Pookas too, fur they had power over thim that wint forth afther night, axceptin' it was on an arriant av marcy they were. But sorra a sinner that hadn't been to his juty reglar 'ud iver see the light av day agin afther meetin' a Pooka thin, for the baste 'ud aither kick him to shmithereens where he stud, or lift him on his back wid his teeth an' jump into the say wid him, thin dive, lavin' him to dhrownd, or shpring over a clift wid him an' tumble him to the bottom a bleedin' corpse. But wasn't there the howls av joy whin a Pooka 'ud catch a sinner unbeknownst, an' fetch him on the Corkscrew wan o' the nights Satan was there. Och, God defind us, phat a sight it was. They made a ring wid the corpse-candles, while the witches tore him limb from limb, an' the fiends drunk his blood in red-hot iron noggins wid shrieks o' laughter to smother his schreams, an' the Pookas jumped on his body an' thrampled it into the ground, an' the timpest 'ud whishle a chune, an' the mountains about 'ud kape time, an' the Pookas, an' witches, an' sper'ts av avil, an' corpse-candles, an' bodies o' the dead, an' divils, 'ud all jig together round the rock where owld Belzebub 'ud set shmilin', as fur to say he'd ax no betther divarshun. God's presince be wid us, it makes me crape to think av it.

"Well, as I was afther sayin', in the time av King Bryan, the Pookas done a dale o' harrum, but as thim that they murthered wor dhrunken bastes that wor in the shebeens in the day an' in the ditch be night, an' wasn't missed whin the Pookas tuk them, the King paid no attintion, an' small blame to him that 's.

"But wan night, the queen's babby fell ill, an' the king says to his man, says he, 'Here, Riley, get you up an' on the white mare an' go fur the docther.'

"'Musha thin,' says Riley, an' the king's counthry house was in the break o' the hills, so Riley 'ud pass the rath an' the Corkschrew on the way afther the docther; 'Musha thin,' says he, aisey and on the quiet, 'it's mesilf that doesn't want that same job.'

"So he says to the king, 'Won't it do in the mornin'?'

"'It will not,' says the king to him. 'Up, ye lazy beggar, atin' me bread, an' the life lavin' me child.'

"So he wint, wid great shlowness, tuk the white mare, an' aff, an' that was the last seen o' him or the mare aither, fur the Pooka tuk 'em. Sorra a taste av a lie's in it, fur thim that said they seen him in Cork two days afther, thrading aff the white mare, was desaved be the sper'ts, that made it seem to be him whin it wasn't that they've a thrick o' doin'.

"Well, the babby got well agin, bekase the docther didn't get there, so the king left botherin' afther it and begun to wondher about Riley an' the white mare, and sarched fur thim but didn't find thim. An' thin he knewn that they was gone entirely, bekase, ye see, the Pooka didn't lave as much as a hair o' the mare's tail.

"'Wurra thin,' says he, 'is it horses that the Pooka 'ull be stalin'? Bad cess to its impidince! This 'ull niver do. Sure we'll be ruinated entirely,' says he.

"Mind ye now, it's my consate from phat he said, that the king wasn't consarned much about Riley, fur he knewn that he cud get more Irishmen whin he wanted thim, but phat he meant to say was that if the Pooka tuk to horse-stalin', he'd be ruinated entirely, so he would, for where 'ud he get another white mare? So it was a mighty sarious question an' he retired widin himself in the coort wid a big book that he had that towld saycrets. He'd a sight av larnin', had the king, aquel to a school-masther, an' a head that 'ud sarcumvint a fox.

"So he read an' read as fast as he cud, an' afther readin' widout shtoppin', barrin' fur the bit an' sup, fur siven days an' nights, he come out, an' whin they axed him cud he bate the Pooka now, he said niver a word, axceptin' a wink wid his eye, as fur to say he had him.

"So that day he was in the fields an' along be the hedges an' ditches from sunrise to sunset, collectin' the matarials av a dose fur the Pooka, but phat he got, faith, I dunno, no more does anywan, fur he never said, but kep the saycret to himself an' didn't say it aven to the quane, fur he knewn that saycrets run through a woman like wather in a ditch. But there was wan thing about it that he cudn't help tellin', fur he wanted it but cudn't get it widout help, an' that was three hairs from the Pooka's tail, axceptin' which the charm 'udn't work. So he towld a man he had, he'd give him no end av goold if he'd get thim fur him, but the felly pulled aff his caubeen an' scrotched his head an' says, 'Faix, yer Honor, I dunno phat'll be the good to me av the goold if the Pooka gets a crack at me carkidge wid his hind heels,' an' he wudn't undhertake the job on no wages, so the king begun to be afeared that his loaf was dough.

"But it happen'd av the Friday, this bein' av a Chewsday, that the Pooka caught a sailor that hadn't been on land only long enough to get bilin' dhrunk, an' got him on his back, so jumped over the clift wid him lavin' him dead enough, I go bail. Whin they come to sarch the sailor to see phat he had in his pockets, they found three long hairs round the third button av his top-coat. So they tuk thim to the king tellin' him where they got thim, an' he was greatly rejiced, bekase now he belaved he had the Pooka sure enough, so he ended his inchantmint.

"But as the avenin' come, he riz a doubt in the mind av him thish-a-way. Ev the three hairs wor out av the Pooka's tail, the charm 'ud be good enough, but if they wasn't, an' was from his mane inshtead, or from a horse inshtead av a Pooka, the charm 'udn't work an' the Pooka 'ud get atop av him wid all the feet he had at wanst an' be the death av him immejitly. So this nate and outprobrious argymint shtruck the king wid great force an' fur a bit, he was onaisey. But wid a little sarcumvintion, he got round it, for he confist an' had absolution so as he'd be ready, thin he towld wan av the sarvints to come in an' tell him afther supper, that there was a poor widdy in the boreen beyant the Corkschrew that wanted help that night, that it 'ud be an arriant av marcy he'd be on, an' so safe agin the Pooka if the charm didn't howld.

"'Sure, phat'll be the good o' that?' says the man, 'It 'ull be a lie, an' won't work.'

"'Do you be aisey in yer mind,' says the king to him agin, 'do as yer towld an' don't argy, for that's a pint av mettyfisics,' says he, faix it was a dale av deep larnin' he had, 'that's a pint av mettyfisics an' the more ye argy on thim subjics, the less ye know,' says he, an' it's thrue fur him. 'Besides, aven if it's a lie, it'll desave the Pooka, that's no mettyfishian, an' it's my belafe that the end is good enough for the manes,' says he, a-thinking av the white mare.

"So, afther supper, as the king was settin' afore the fire, an' had the charm in his pocket, the sarvint come in and towld him about the widdy.

"'Begob,' says the king, like he was surprised, so as to desave the Pooka complately, 'Ev that's thrue, I must go relave her at wanst.' So he riz an' put on sojer boots, wid shpurs on 'em a fut acrost, an' tuk a long whip in his hand, for fear, he said, the widdy 'ud have dogs, thin wint to his chist an' tuk his owld stockin' an' got a suv'rin out av it, – Och, 'twas the shly wan he was, to do everything so well – an' wint out wid his right fut first, an' the shpurs a-rattlin' as he walked.

"He come acrost the yard, an' up the hill beyant yon an' round the corner, but seen nothin' at all. Thin up the fut path round the Corkscrew an' met niver a sowl but a dog that he cast a shtone at. But he didn't go out av the road to the widdy's, for he was afeared that if he met the Pooka an' he caught him in a lie, not bein' in the road to where he said he was goin', it 'ud be all over wid him. So he walked up an' down bechuxt the owld church below there an' the rath on the hill, an' jist as the clock was shtrikin' fur twelve, he heard a horse in front av him, as he was walkin' down, so he turned an' wint the other way, gettin' his charm ready, an' the Pooka come up afther him.

"'The top o' the mornin' to yer Honor,' says the Pooka, as perlite as a Frinchman, for he seen be his close that the king wasn't a common blaggård like us, but was wan o' the rale quolity.

"'Me sarvice to ye,' says the king to him agin, as bowld as a ram, an' whin the Pooka heard him shpake, he got perliter than iver, an' made a low bow an' shcrape wid his fut, thin they wint on together an' fell into discoorse.

"''Tis a black night for thravelin',' says the Pooka.

"'Indade it is,' says the king, 'it's not me that 'ud be out in it, if it wasn't a case o' needcessity. I'm on an arriant av charity,' says he.

"'That's rale good o' ye,' says the Pooka to him, 'and if I may make bowld to ax, phat's the needcessity?'

"''Tis to relave a widdy-woman,' says the king.

"'Oho,' says the Pooka, a-throwin' back his head laughin' wid great plazin'ness an' nudgin' the king wid his leg on the arrum, beways that it was a joke it was bekase the king said it was to relave a widdy he was goin'. 'Oho,' says the Pooka, ''tis mesilf that's glad to be in the comp'ny av an iligint jintleman that's on so plazin' an arriant av marcy,' says he. 'An' how owld is the widdy-woman?' says he, bustin' wid the horrid laugh he had.

"'Musha thin,' says the king, gettin' red in the face an' not likin' the joke the laste bit, for jist betune us, they do say that afore he married the quane, he was the laddy-buck wid the wimmin, an' the quane's maid towld the cook, that towld the footman, that said to the gârdener, that towld the nabers that many's the night the poor king was as wide awake as a hare from sun to sun wid the quane a-gostherin' at him about that same. More betoken, there was a widdy in it, that was as sharp as a rat-thrap an' surrounded him whin he was young an' hadn't as much sinse as a goose, an' was like to marry him at wanst in shpite av all his relations, as widdys undhershtand how to do. So it's my consate that it wasn't dacint for the Pooka to be afther laughin' that-a-way, an' shows that avil sper'ts is dirthy blaggârds that can't talk wid jintlemin. 'Musha,' thin, says the king, bekase the Pooka's laughin' wasn't agrayble to listen to, 'I don't know that same, fur I niver seen her, but, be jagers, I belave she's a hundherd, an' as ugly as Belzebub, an' whin her owld man was alive, they tell me she had a timper like a gandher, an' was as aisey to manage as an armful o' cats,' says he. 'But she's in want, an' I'm afther bringin' her a suv'rin,' says he.

"Well, the Pooka sayced his laughin', fur he seen the king was very vexed, an' says to him, 'And if it's plazin', where does she live?'

"'At the ind o' the boreen beyant the Corkschrew,' says the king, very short.

"'Begob, that's a good bit,' says the Pooka.

"'Faix, it's thrue for ye,' says the king, 'more betoken, it's up hill ivery fut o' the way, an' me back is bruk entirely wid the stapeness,' says he, be way av a hint he'd like a ride.

"'Will yer Honor get upon me back,' says the Pooka. 'Sure I'm afther goin' that-a-way, an' you don't mind gettin' a lift?' says he, a-fallin' like the stupid baste he was, into the thrap the king had made fur him.

"'Thanks,' says the king, 'I b'lave not. I've no bridle nor saddle,' says he, 'besides, it's the shpring o' the year, an' I'm afeared ye're sheddin', an' yer hair 'ull come aff an' spile me new britches,' says he, lettin' on to make axcuse.

"'Have no fear,' says the Pooka. 'Sure I niver drop me hair. It's no ordhinary garron av a horse I am, but a most oncommon baste that's used to the quolity,' says he.

"'Yer spache shows that,' says the king, the clever man that he was, to be perlite that-a-way to a Pooka, that's known to be a divil out-en-out, 'but ye must exqueeze me this avenin', bekase, d'ye mind, the road's full o' shtones an' monsthrous stape, an' ye look so young, I'm afeared ye'll shtumble an' give me a fall,' says he.

"'Arrah thin,' says the Pooka, 'it's thrue fur yer Honor, I do look young,' an' he begun to prance on the road givin' himself airs like an owld widdy man afther wantin' a young woman, 'but me age is owlder than ye'd suppoge. How owld 'ud ye say I was,' says he, shmilin'.

"'Begorra, divil a bit know I,' says the king, 'but if it's agrayble to ye, I'll look in yer mouth an' give ye an answer,' says he.

"So the Pooka come up to him fair an' soft an' stratched his mouth like as he thought the king was wantin' fur to climb in, an' the king put his hand on his jaw like as he was goin' to see the teeth he had: and thin, that minnit he shlipped the three hairs round the Pooka's jaw, an' whin he done that, he dhrew thim tight, an' said the charm crossin' himself the while, an' immejitly the hairs wor cords av stale, an' held the Pooka tight, be way av a bridle.

"'Arra-a-a-h, now, ye bloody baste av a murtherin' divil ye,' says the king, pullin' out his big whip that he had consaled in his top-coat, an' giving the Pooka a crack wid it undher his stummick, 'I'll give ye a ride ye won't forgit in a hurry,' says he, 'ye black Turk av a four-legged nagur an' you shtaling me white mare,' says he, hittin' him agin.

"'Oh my,' says the Pooka, as he felt the grip av the iron on his jaw an' knewn he was undher an inchantmint, 'Oh my, phat's this at all,' rubbin' his breast wid his hind heel, where the whip had hit him, an' thin jumpin' wid his fore feet out to cotch the air an' thryin' fur to break away. 'Sure I'm ruined, I am, so I am,' says he.

"'It's thrue fur ye,' says the king, 'begob it's the wan thrue thing ye iver said,' says he, a-jumpin' on his back, an' givin' him the whip an' the two shpurs wid all his might.

"Now I forgot to tell ye that whin the king made his inchantmint, it was good fur siven miles round, and the Pooka knewn that same as well as the king an' so he shtarted like a cunshtable was afther him, but the king was afeared to let him go far, thinkin' he'd do the siven miles in a jiffy, an' the inchantmint 'ud be broken like a rotten shtring, so he turned him up the Corkschrew.

"'I'll give ye all the axercise ye want,' says he, 'in thravellin' round this hill,' an' round an' round they wint, the king shtickin' the big shpurs in him every jump an' crackin' him wid the whip till his sides run blood in shtrames like a mill race, an' his schreams av pain wor heard all over the worruld so that the king av France opened his windy and axed the polisman why he didn't shtop the fightin' in the shtrate. Round an' round an' about the Corkschrew wint the king, a-lashin' the Pooka, till his feet made the path ye see on the hill bekase he wint so often.

"And whin mornin' come, the Pooka axed the king phat he'd let him go fur, an' the king was gettin' tired an' towld him that he must niver shtale another horse, an' never kill another man, barrin' furrin blaggârds that wasn't Irish, an' whin he give a man a ride, he must bring him back to the shpot where he got him an' lave him there. So the Pooka consinted, Glory be to God, an' got aff, an' that's the way he was tamed, an' axplains how it was that Dennis O'Rourke was left be the Pooka in the ditch jist where he found him."

"More betoken, the Pooka's an althered baste every way, fur now he dhrops his hair like a common horse, and it's often found shtickin' to the hedges where he jumped over, an' they do say he doesn't shmell half as shtrong o' sulfur as he used, nor the fire out o' his nose isn't so bright. But all the king did fur him 'ud n't taiche him to be civil in his spache, an' whin he meets ye in the way, he spakes just as much like a blaggârd as ever. An' it's out av divilmint entirely he does it, bekase he can be perlite as ye know be phat I towld ye av him sayin' to the king, an' that proves phat I said to ye that avil sper'ts can't larn rale good manners, no matther how hard they thry.

"But the fright he got never left him, an' so he kapes out av the highways an' thravels be the futpaths, an' so isn't often seen. An' it's my belafe that he can do no harrum at all to thim that fears God, an' there's thim that says he niver shows himself nor meddles wid man nor mortial barrin' they're in dhrink, an' mebbe there's something in that too, fur it doesn't take much dhrink to make a man see a good dale."

The Kildare Pooka

❖

MR. H— R—, when he was alive, used to live a good deal in Dublin, and he was once a great while out of the country on account of the 'ninety-eight' business. But the servants kept on in the big house at Rath— all the same as if the family was at home. Well, they used to be frightened out of their lives after going to their beds with the banging of the kitchen-door, and the clattering of fire-irons, and the pots and plates and dishes. One evening they sat up ever so long, keeping one another in heart with telling stories about ghosts and fetches, and that when – what would you have of it? – the little scullery boy that used to be sleeping over the horses, and could not get room at the fire, crept into the hot hearth, and when he got tired listening to the stories, sorra fear him, but he fell dead asleep.

Well and good, after they were all gone and the kitchen fire raked up, he was woke with the noise of the kitchen door opening, and the trampling of an ass on the kitchen floor. He peeped out, and what should he see but a big ass, sure enough, sitting on his curabingo and yawning before the fire. After a little he looked about him, and began scratching his ears as if he was quite tired, and says he, "I may as well begin first as last." The poor boy's teeth began to chatter in his head, for says he, "Now he's goin' to ate me"; but the fellow with the long ears and tail on him had something else to do. He stirred the fire, and then he brought in a pail of water from the pump, and filled a big pot that he put on the fire before he went out. He then put in his hand – foot, I mean – into the hot hearth, and pulled out the little boy. He let a roar out of him with the fright, but the pooka only looked at him, and thrust out his lower lip to show how little he valued him, and then he pitched him into his pew again.

Well, he then lay down before the fire till he heard the boil coming on the water, and maybe there wasn't a plate, or a dish, or a spoon on the dresser that he didn't fetch and put into the pot, and wash and dry the whole bilin' of 'em as well as e'er a kitchen-maid from that to Dublin town. He then put all of them up on their places on the shelves; and if he didn't give a good sweepin' to the kitchen, leave it till again. Then he comes and sits foment the boy, let down one of his ears, and cocked up the other, and gave a grin. The poor fellow strove to roar out, but not a dheeg 'ud come out of his throat. The last thing the pooka done was to rake up the fire, and walk out, giving such a slap o' the door, that the boy thought the house couldn't help tumbling down.

Well, to be sure if there wasn't a hullabullo next morning when the poor fellow told his story! They could talk of nothing else the whole day. One said one thing, another said another, but a fat, lazy scullery girl said the wittiest thing of all. "Musha!" says she, "if the pooka does be cleaning up everything that way when we are asleep, what should we be slaving ourselves for doing his work?"

"*Shu gu dheine*," says another; "them's the wisest words you ever said, Kauth; it's meeself won't contradict you."

So said, so done. Not a bit of a plate or dish saw a drop of water that evening, and not a besom was laid on the floor, and everyone went to bed soon after sundown. Next morning everything was as fine as fine in the kitchen, and the lord mayor might eat his dinner off the flags. It was great ease to the lazy servants, you may depend, and everything went on well till a foolhardy gag of a boy said he would stay up one night and have a chat with the pooka.

He was a little daunted when the door was thrown open and the ass marched up to the fire.

"An then, sir," says he, at last, picking up courage, "if it isn't taking a liberty, might I ax who you are, and why you are so kind as to do half of the day's work for the girls every night?"

"No liberty at all," says the pooka, says he: "I'll tell you, and welcome. I was a servant in the time of Squire R.'s father, and was the laziest rogue that ever was clothed and fed, and done nothing for it. When my time came for the other world, this is the punishment was laid on me – to come here and do all this labour every night, and then go out in the cold. It isn't so bad in the fine weather; but if you only knew what it is to stand with your head between your legs, facing the storm, from midnight to sunrise, on a bleak winter night."

"And could we do anything for your comfort, my poor fellow?" says the boy.

"Musha, I don't know," says the pooka; "but I think a good quilted frieze coat would help to keep the life in me them long nights."

"Why then, in troth, we'd be the ungratefullest of people if we didn't feel for you."

To make a long story short, the next night but two the boy was there again; and if he didn't delight the poor pooka, holding up a fine warm coat before him, it's no mather! Betune the pooka and the man, his legs was got into the four arms of it, and it was buttoned down the breast and the belly, and he was so pleazed he walked up to the glass to see how he looked. "Well," says he, "it's a long lane that has no turning. I am much obliged to you and your fellow-servants. You have made me happy at last. Good-night to you."

So he was walking out, but the other cried, "Och! Sure your going too soon. What about the washing and sweeping?"

"Ah, you may tell the girls that they must now get their turn. My punishment was to last till I was thought worthy of a reward for the way I done my duty. You'll see me no more." And no more they did, and right sorry they were for having been in such a hurry to reward the ungrateful pooka.

The Huntsman's Son

ALONG, LONG TIME AGO there lived in a little hut on the borders of a great forest a huntsman and his wife and son. From his earliest years the boy, whose name was Fergus, used to hunt with his father in the forest, and he grew up strong and active, sure and swift-footed as a deer, and as free and fearless as the wind. He was tall and handsome; as supple as a mountain ash, his lips were as red as its berries; his eyes were as blue as the skies in spring; and his hair fell down over his shoulders like a shower of gold. His heart was as light as a bird's, and no bird was fonder of green woods and waving branches. He had lived since his birth in the hut in the forest, and had never wished to leave it, until one winter night a wandering minstrel sought shelter there, and paid for his night's lodging with songs of love and battle. Ever since that night Fergus pined for another life. He no longer found joy in the music of the hounds or in the cries of the huntsmen in forest glades. He yearned for the chance of battle, and the clang of shields, and the fierce shouts of fighting warriors, and he spent all his spare hours practising on the harp and learning the use of arms, for in those days the bravest warriors were also bards. In this way the spring and summer and autumn passed; and when the winter came again it chanced that on a stormy night, when thunder was rattling through the forest, smiting the huge oaks and hurling them crashing to the earth, Fergus lay awake thinking of his present lot, and wondering what the future might have in store for him. The lightning was playing around the hut, and every now and then a flash brightened up the interior.

After a peal, louder than any which had preceded it, Fergus heard three loud knocks at the door. He called out to his parents that someone was knocking.

"If that is so," said his father, "open at once; this is no night to keep a poor wanderer outside our door."

Fergus did as he was bidden, and as he opened the door a flash of lightning showed him, standing at the threshold, a little wizened old man with a small harp under his arm.

"Come in, and welcome," said Fergus, and the little man stepped into the room.

"It is a wild night, neighbours," said he.

"It is, indeed, a wild night," said the huntsman and his wife, who had got up and dressed themselves; "and sorry we are we have no better shelter or better fare to offer you, but we give you the best we have."

"A king cannot do more than his best," said the little man.

The huntsman's wife lit the fire, and soon the pine logs flashed up into a blaze, and made the hut bright and warm. She then brought forth a peggin of milk and a cake of barley-bread.

"You must be hungry, sir," she said.

"Hungry I am," said he; "but I wouldn't ask for better fare than this if I were in the king's palace."

"Thank you kindly, sir," said she, "and I hope you will eat enough, and that it will do you good."

"And while you are eating your supper," said the huntsman, "I'll make you a bed of fresh rushes."

"Don't put yourself to that trouble," said the little man. "When I have done my supper I'll lie down here by the fire, if it is pleasing to you, and I'll sleep like a top until morning. And now go back to your beds and leave me to myself, and maybe some time when you won't be expecting it I'll do a good turn for your kindness to the poor wayfarer."

"Oh, it's no kindness at all," said the huntsman's wife. "It would be a queer thing if an Irish cabin would not give shelter and welcome in a wild night like this. So goodnight, now, and we hope you will sleep well."

"Goodnight," said the little man, "and may you and yours never sup sorrow until your dying day."

The huntsman and his wife and Fergus then went back to their beds, and the little man, having finished his supper, curled himself up by the fire, and was soon fast asleep.

About an hour after a loud clap of thunder awakened Fergus, and before it had died away he heard three knocks at the door. He aroused his parents and told them.

"Get up at once," said his mother, "this is no night to keep a stranger outside our door."

Fergus rose and opened the door, and a flash of lightning showed him a little old woman, with a shuttle in her hand, standing outside.

"Come in, and welcome," said he, and the little old woman stepped into the room.

"Blessings be on them who give welcome to a wanderer on a wild night like this," said the old woman.

"And who wouldn't give welcome on a night like this?" said the huntsman's wife, coming forward with a peggin of milk and a barley cake in her hand, "and sorry we are we have not better fare to offer you."

"Enough is as good as a feast," said the little woman, "and now go back to your beds and leave me to myself."

"Not till I shake down a bed of rushes for you," said the huntsman's wife.

"Don't mind the rushes," said the little woman; "go back to your beds. I'll sleep here by the fire."

The huntsman's wife went to bed, and the little old woman, having eaten her supper, lay down by the fire, and was soon fast asleep.

About an hour later another clap of thunder startled Fergus. Again he heard three knocks at the door. He roused his parents, but he did not wait for orders from them. He opened the door, and a flash of lightning showed him outside the threshold a low-sized, shaggy, wild-looking horse. And Fergus knew it was the Pooka, the wild horse of the mountains. Bold as Fergus was, his heart beat quickly as he saw fire issuing from the Pooka's nostrils. But, banishing fear, he cried out:

"Come in, and welcome."

"Welcome you are," said the huntsman, "and sorry we are that we have not better shelter or fare to offer you."

"I couldn't wish a better welcome," said the Pooka, as he came over near the fire and sat down on his haunches.

"Maybe you would like a little bit of this, Master Pooka," said the huntsman's wife, as she offered him a barley cake.

"I never tasted anything sweeter in my life," said the Pooka, crunching it between his teeth, "and now if you can give me a sup of milk, I'll want for nothing."

The huntsman's wife brought him a peggin of milk. When he had drunk it, "Now," says the Pooka, "go back to your beds, and I'll curl myself up by the fire and sleep like a top till morning."

And soon everybody in the hut was fast asleep.

When the morning came the storm had gone, and the sun was shining through the windows of the hut. At the song of the lark Fergus got up, and no one in the world was ever more surprised than he when he saw no sign of the little old man, or the little old woman, or the wild horse of the mountains. His parents were also surprised, and they all thought that they must have been dreaming until they saw the empty peggins around the fire and some pieces of broken bread; and they did not know what to think of it all.

From that day forward the desire grew stronger in the heart of Fergus for a change of life; and one day he told his parents that he was resolved to seek his fortune. He said he wished to be a soldier, and that he would set out for the king's palace, and try to join the ranks of the Feni.

About a week afterwards he took leave of his parents, and having received their blessing he struck out for the road that led to the palace of the High King of Erin. He arrived there just at the time when the great captain of the Fenian host was recruiting his battalions, which had been thinned in recent battle.

The manly figure of Fergus, his gallant bearing, and handsome face, all told in his favour. But before he could be received into the Fenian ranks he had to prove that he could play the harp like a bard, that he could contend with staff and shield against nine Fenian warriors, that he could run with plaited hair through the tangled forest without loosening a single hair, and that in his course he could jump over trees as high as his head, and stoop under trees as low as his knee, and that he could run so lightly that the rotten twigs should not break under his feet. Fergus proved equal to all the tests, thanks to the wandering minstrel who taught him the use of the harp, to his own brave heart, and to his forest training. He was enrolled in the second battalion of the Feni, and before long he was its bravest and ablest champion.

At that very time it happened that the niece of the High King of Erin was staying with the king and queen in their palace at Tara. The princess was the loveliest lady in all the land. She was as proud as she was beautiful. The princes and chieftains of Erin in vain sought her hand in marriage. From Alba and Spain, and the far-off isles of Greece, kings came to woo her. From the northern lands came vikings in stately galleys with brazen prows, whose oarsmen tore the white foam from the emerald seas as they swept towards the Irish coasts. But the lady had vowed she would wed with no one except a battle champion who could excel in music the chief bard of the High King of Erin; who could outstrip on his steed in the great race of Tara the white steed of the plains; and who could give her as a wedding robe a garment of all the colours of the rainbow, so finely spun that when folded up it would fit in the palm of her small white hand. To fulfil these three conditions was impossible for all her suitors, and it seemed as if the loveliest lady of the land should go unmarried to her grave.

It chanced that once, on a day when the Fenian battalions were engaged in a hurling-match, Fergus beheld the lady watching the match from her sunny bower. He no sooner saw her than he fell over head and ears in love with her, and he thought of her by night, and he thought of her by day, and believing that his love was hopeless, he often wished he had never left his forest-home.

The great fair of Tara was coming on, and all the Feni were busy from morning till night practising feats of arms and games, in order to take part in the contests to be held during the fair. And Fergus, knowing that the princess would be present, determined to do his best to win the prizes which were to be contended for before the ladies' eyes.

The fair began on the 1st of August, but for a whole week before the five great roads of Erin were thronged with people of all sorts. Princes and warriors on their steeds, battle champions in their chariots, harpers in hundreds, smiths with gleaming spears and shields and harness for battle steeds and chariots; troops of men and boys leading racehorses; jewellers with gold drinking-horns, and brooches, and pins, and earrings, and costly gems of all kinds, and chess-boards of silver and gold, and golden and silver chessmen in bags of woven brass; dyers with their many-coloured fabrics; bands of jugglers; drovers goading on herds of cattle; shepherds driving their sheep; huntsmen with spoils of the chase; dwellers in the lakes or by the fish-abounding rivers with salmon and speckled trout; and countless numbers of peasants on horseback and on foot, all wending their way to the great meeting-place by the mound, which a thousand years before had been raised over the grave of the great queen. For there the fair was to be held.

On the opening day the High King, attended by the four kings of Erin, set out from the palace, and with them went the queen and the ladies of the court in sparkling chariots. The princess rode in the chariot with the high queen, under an awning made of the wings of birds, to protect them from the rays of the sun. Following the queen were the court ladies in other chariots, under awnings of purple or of yellow silk. Then came the brehons, the great judges of the land, and the chief bards of the high court of Tara, and the Druids, crowned with oak leaves, and carrying wands of divination in their hands.

When the royal party reached the ground it took its place in enclosures right up against the monumental mound. The High King sat with the four kings of Erin, all wearing their golden helmets, for they wore their diadems in battle only. In an enclosure next to the king's sat the queen and the princess and all the ladies of the court. At either side of the royal pavilions were others for the dames and ladies and nobles and chiefs of different degrees, forming part of a circle on the plain, and the stands and benches for the people were so arranged as to complete the circle, and in the round green space within it, so that all might hear and see, the contests were to take place.

At a signal from the king, who was greeted with a thunderous cheer, the heralds rode round the circle, and having struck their sounding shields three times with their swords, they made a solemn proclamation of peace. Then was sung by all the assembled bards, to the accompaniment of their harps, the chant in honour of the mighty dead. When this was ended, again the heralds struck their shields, and the contests began. The first contest was the contest of spear-throwing between the champions of the seven battalions of the Feni. When the seven champions took their places in front of the royal enclosure, everyone, even the proud princess, was struck by the manly beauty and noble bearing of Fergus.

The champions poised their spears, and at a stroke from the heralds upon their shields the seven spears sped flashing through the air. They all struck the ground, shafts up, and it was seen that two were standing side by side in advance of the rest, one belonged to Fergus, the other to the great chief, Oscar. The contest for the prize then lay between Oscar and Fergus, and when they stood in front of the king, holding their spears aloft, every heart was throbbing with excitement. Once more the heralds struck their shields, and, swifter than the lightning's flash, forth went the spears, and when Fergus's spear was seen shivering in the ground a full length ahead of the great chief Oscar's, the air was shaken by a wild cheer that was heard far beyond the plains of Tara. And as Fergus approached the high king to receive the prize the cheers were renewed. But Fergus thought more of the winsome glance of the princess than he did of the prize or the sounding cheers. And Princess Maureen was almost sorry for her vow, for her heart was touched by the beauty of the Fenian champion.

Other contests followed, and the day passed, and the night fell, and while the Fenian warriors were revelling in their camps the heart of Fergus, victor as he was, was sad and low. He escaped from his companions, and stole away to his native forest, for –

> *"When the heart is sick and sorest,*
> *There is balsam in the forest –*
> *There is balsam in the forest*
> *For its pain."*

And as he lay under the spreading branches, watching the stars glancing through the leaves, and listening to the slumb'rous murmur of the waters, a strange peace came over him.

But in the camp which he had left, and in the vast multitude on the plains of Tara, there was stir and revelry, and babbling speculation as to the contest of tomorrow – the contest which was to decide whether the chief bard of Erin was to hold his own against all comers, or yield the palm. For rumour said that a great Skald had come from the northern lands to compete with the Irish bard.

At last, over the Fenian camp, and over the great plain and the multitude that thronged it, sleep fell, clothing them with a silence as deep as that which dwelt in the forest, where, dreaming of the princess, Fergus lay. He awoke at the first notes of the birds, but though he felt he ought to go back to his companions and be witness of the contest which might determine whether the princess was to be another's bride, his great love and his utter despair of winning her so oppressed him that he lay as motionless as a broken reed. He scarcely heard the music of the birds, and paid no heed to the murmur of the brook rushing by his feet. The crackling of branches near him barely disturbed him, but when a shadow fell across his eyes he looked up gloomily, and saw, or thought he saw, someone standing before him. He started up, and who should he see but the little wizened old man who found shelter in his father's hut on the stormy night.

"This is a nice place for a battle champion to be. This is a nice place for *you* to be on the day which is to decide who will be the successful suitor of the princess."

"What is it to me," said Fergus, "who is to win her since I cannot."

"I told you," said the little man, "the night you opened the door for me, that the time might come when I might be able to do a good turn for you and yours. The time has come. Take this harp, and my luck go with you, and in the contest of the bards today you'll reap the reward of the kindness you did when you opened your door to the poor old wayfarer in the midnight storm."

The little man handed his harp to Fergus and disappeared as swiftly as the wind that passes through the leaves.

Fergus, concealing the harp under his silken cloak, reached the camp before his comrades had aroused themselves from sleep.

At length the hour arrived when the great contest was to take place.

The king gave the signal, and as the chief bard of Erin was seen ascending the mound in front of the royal enclosures he was greeted with a roar of cheers, but at the first note of his harp silence like that of night fell on the mighty gathering.

As he moved his fingers softly over the strings every heart was hushed, filled with a sense of balmy rest. The lark soaring and singing above his head paused mute and motionless in the still air, and no sound was heard over the spacious plain save the dreamy music. Then the bard struck another key, and a gentle sorrow possessed the hearts of his hearers, and unbidden tears gathered to their eyes. Then, with bolder hand, he swept his fingers across his lyre, and all hearts were moved to joy and pleasant laughter, and eyes that had been dimmed by tears sparkled as brightly as running waters dancing in the sun. When the last notes had died away a cheer arose, loud as the voice of the storm in the glen when the live thunder is revelling on the mountain tops. As soon as the bard had descended the mound the Skald from the northern lands took his place, greeted by cries of welcome from a hundred thousand throats. He touched his harp, and in the perfect silence was heard the strains of the mermaid's song, and through it the pleasant ripple of summer waters on the pebbly beach. Then the theme was changed, and on the air was borne the measured sweep of countless oars and the swish of waters around the prows of contending galleys, and the breezy voices of the sailors and the sea-bird's cry. Then his theme was changed to the mirth and laughter of the banquet-hall, the clang of meeting drinking-horns, and songs of battle. When the last strain ended, from the mighty host a great shout went up, loud as the roar of winter billows breaking in the hollows of the shore; and men knew not whom to declare the victor, the chief bard of Erin or the Skald of the northern lands.

In the height of the debate the cry arose that another competitor had ascended the mound, and there standing in view of all was Fergus, the huntsman's son. All eyes were fastened upon him, but no one looked so eagerly as the princess.

He touched his harp with gentle fingers, and a sound low and soft as a faint summer breeze passing through forest trees stole out, and then was heard the rustle of birds through the branches, and the dreamy murmur of waters lost in deepest woods, and all the fairy echoes whispering when the leaves are motionless in the noonday heat; then followed notes cool and soft as the drip of summer showers on the parched grass, and then the song of the blackbird, sounding as clearly as it sounds in long silent spaces of the evening, and then in one sweet jocund burst the multitudinous voices that hail the breaking of the morn. And the lark, singing and soaring above the minstrel, sank mute and motionless upon his shoulder, and from all the leafy woods the birds came thronging out and formed a fluttering canopy above his head.

When the bard ceased playing no shout arose from the mighty multitude, for the strains of his harp, long after its chords were stilled, held their hearts spell-bound.

And when he had passed away from the mound of contest all knew there was no need to declare the victor. And all were glad the comely Fenian champion had maintained the supremacy of the bards of Erin. But there was one heart sad, the heart of the princess; and now she wished more than ever that she had never made her hateful vow.

Other contests went on, but Fergus took no interest in them; and once more he stole away to the forest glade. His heart was sorrowful, for he thought of the great race of the morning, and he knew that he could not hope to compete with the rider of the white steed of the plains. And as he lay beneath the spreading branches during the whole night long his thoughts were not of the victory he had won, but of the princess, who was as far away from him as ever. He passed the night without sleep, and when the morning came he rose and walked aimlessly through the woods.

A deer starting from a thicket reminded him of the happy days of his boyhood, and once more the wish came back to him that he had never left his forest home. As his eyes followed the deer wistfully, suddenly he started in amazement. The deer vanished from view, and in his stead was the wild horse of the mountains.

"I told you I'd do you a good turn," said the Pooka, "for the kindness you and yours did me on that wild winter's night. The day is passing. You have no time to lose. The white steed of the plains is coming to the starting-post. Jump on my back, and remember, 'Faint heart never won fair lady.'"

In half a second Fergus was bestride the Pooka, whose coat of shaggy hair became at once as glossy as silk, and just at the very moment when the king was about to declare there was no steed to compete with the white steed of the plains, the Pooka with Fergus upon his back, galloped up in front of the royal enclosure. When the people saw the champion a thunderous shout rose up that startled the birds in the skies, and sent them flying to the groves.

And in the ladies' enclosure was a rustle of many-coloured scarves waving in the air. At the striking of the shields the contending steeds rushed from the post with the swiftness of a swallow's flight. But before the white steed of the plains had gone half-way round, Fergus and the wild horse of the mountains had passed the winning post, greeted by such cheers as had never before been heard on the plains of Tara.

Fergus heard the cheers, but scarcely heeded them, for his heart went out through his eyes that were fastened on the princess, and a wild hope stirred him that his glance was not ungrateful to the loveliest lady of the land.

And the princess was sad and sorry for her vow, for she believed that it was beyond the power of Fergus to bring her a robe of all the colours of the rainbow, so subtly woven as to fit in the palm of her soft, white hand.

That night also Fergus went to the forest, not too sad, because there was a vague hope in his heart that had never been there before. He lay down under the branches, with his feet towards the rustling waters, and the smiles of the princess gilded his slumbers, as the rays of the rising sun gild the glades of the forest; and when the morning came he was scarcely surprised when before him appeared the little old woman with the shuttle he had welcomed on the winter's night.

"You think you have won her already," said the little woman. "And so you have, too; her heart is all your own, and I'm half inclined to think that my trouble will be thrown away, for if you had never a wedding robe to give her, she'd rather have you this minute than all the kings of Erin, or than all the other princes and kings and chieftains in the whole world. But you and your father and mother were kind to me on a wild winter's night, and I'd never see your mother's son without a wedding robe fit for the greatest princess that ever set nations to battle for her beauty. So go and pluck me a handful of wild forest flowers, and I'll weave out of them a wedding robe with all the colours of the rainbow, and one that will be as sweet and as fragrant as the ripe, red lips of the princess herself."

Fergus, with joyous heart, culled the flowers, and brought them to the little old woman.

In the twinkling of an eye she wove with her little shuttle a wedding robe, with all the colours of the rainbow, as light as the fairy dew, as soft as the hand of the princess, as fragrant as her little red mouth, and so small that it would pass through the eye of a needle.

"Go now, Fergus," said she, "and may luck go with you; but, in the days of your greatness and of the glory which will come to you when you are wedded to the princess, be as kind, and have as open a heart and as open a door for the poor as you had when you were only a poor huntsman's son."

Fergus took the robe and went towards Tara. It was the last day of the fair, and all the contests were over, and the bards were about to chant the farewell strains to the memory of the great queen. But before the chief bard could ascend the mound, Fergus, attended by a troop of Fenian warriors on their steeds, galloped into the enclosure, and rode up in front of the queen's pavilion. Holding up the glancing and many-coloured robe, he said:

"O Queen and King of Erin! I claim the princess for my bride. You, O king, have decided that I have won the prize in the contest of the bards; that I have won the prize in the race against the white steed of the plains; it is for the princess to say if the robe which I give her will fit in the hollow of her small white hand."

"Yes," said the king. "You are victor in the contests; let the princess declare if you have fulfilled the last condition."

The princess took the robe from Fergus, closed her fingers over it, so that no vestige of it was seen.

"Yes, O king!" said she, "he has fulfilled the last condition; but before ever he had fulfilled a single one of them, my heart went out to the comely champion of the Feni. I was willing then, I am ready now, to become the bride of the huntsman's son."

How Thomas Connolly
Met the Banshee

❖

"AW, THE BANSHEE, sir? Well, sir, as I was striving to tell ye, I was going home from work one day, from Mr. Cassidy's that I tould ye of, in the dusk o' the evening. I had more nor a mile – aye, it was nearer two mile – to thrack to, where I was lodgin' with a dacent widdy woman I knew, Biddy Maguire be name, so as to be near me work.

"It was the first week in November, an' a lonesome road I had to travel, an' dark enough, wid threes above it; an' about half-ways there was a bit of a brudge I had to cross, over one o' them little sthrames that runs into the Doddher. I walked on in the middle iv the road, for there was no toe-path at that time, Misther Harry, nor for many a long day afther that; but, as I was sayin', I walked along till I come nigh upon the brudge, where the road was a bit open, an' there, right enough, I seen the hog's back o' the ould-fashioned brudge that used to be there till it was pulled down, an' a white mist steamin' up out o' the wather all around it.

"Well, now, Misther Harry, often as I'd passed by the place before, that night it seemed sthrange to me, an' like a place ye might see in a dhrame; an' as I come up to it I began to feel a could wind blowin' through the hollow o' me heart. 'Musha Thomas,' sez I to meself, 'is it yerself that's in it?' sez I; 'or, if it is, what's the matter wid ye at all, at all?' sez I; so I put a bould face on it, an' I made a sthruggle to set one leg afore the other, ontil I came to the rise o' the brudge. And there, God be good to us! In a cantle o' the wall I seen an ould woman, as I thought, sittin' on her hunkers, all crouched together, an' her head bowed down, seemin'ly in the greatest affliction.

"Well, sir, I pitied the ould craythur, an' thought I wasn't worth a thraneen, for the mortial fright I was in, I up an' sez to her, 'That's a cowld lodgin' for ye, ma'am.' Well, the sorra ha'porth she sez to that, nor tuk no more notice o' me than if I hadn't let a word out o' me, but kep' rockin' herself to an' fro, as if her heart was breakin'; so I sez to her again, 'Eh, ma'am, is there anythin' the matther wid ye?' An' I made for to touch her on the shouldher, on'y somethin' stopt me, for as I looked closer at her I saw she was no more an ould woman nor she was an ould cat. The first thing I tuk notice to, Misther Harry, was her hair, that was sthreelin' down over his showldhers, an' a good yard on the ground on aich side of her. O, be the hoky farmer, but that was the hair! The likes of it I never seen on mortial woman, young or ould, before nor sense. It grew as sthrong out of her as out of e'er a young slip of a girl ye could see; but the colour of it was a misthery to describe. The first squint I got of it I thought it was silvery grey, like an ould crone's; but when I got up beside her I saw, be the glance o' the sky, it was a soart iv an Iscariot colour, an' a shine out of it like floss silk. It ran over her showldhers and the two shapely arms she was lanin' her head on, for all the world like Mary Magdalen's in a picther; and then I persaved that the grey cloak and the green gownd undhernaith it was made of no earthly matarial I ever laid eyes on. Now, I needn't tell ye, sir, that I seen all this in the twinkle of a bed-post – long as I take to make the narration of it. So I made a step back from her, an' 'The Lord be betune us an' harm!' sez I, out loud, an' wid that I blessed meself. Well, Misther Harry, the word wasn't out o' me mouth afore she turned her face on me. Aw, Misther Harry, but 'twas that was the awfullest apparation ever I seen, the face of her as she looked up at me! God forgive me for sayin' it, but 'twas more like the face of the 'Axy Homo' beyand in Marlboro' Sthreet Chapel nor like any face I could mintion – as pale as a corpse, an' a most o' freckles on it, like the freckles on a turkey's egg; an' the two eyes sewn in wid red thread, from the terrible power o' crying the' had to do; an' such a pair iv eyes as the' wor, Misther Harry, as blue as two forget-me-nots, an' as cowld as the moon in a bog-hole of a frosty night, an' a dead-an'-live look in them that sent a cowld shiver through the marra o' me bones. Be the mortial! Ye could ha' rung a tay cupful o' cowld paspiration out o' the hair o' me head that minute, so ye could. Well, I thought the life 'ud lave me intirely when she riz up from her hunkers, till, bedad! She looked mostly as tall as Nelson's Pillar; an' wid the two eyes gazin' back at me, an' her two arms stretched out before hor, an' a keine out of her that riz the hair o' me scalp till it was as stiff as the hog's bristles in a new hearth broom, away she glides – glides round the angle o' the brudge, an' down with her into the sthrame that ran undhernaith it. 'Twas then I began to suspect what she was. 'Wisha, Thomas!' says I to meself, sez I; an' I made a great struggle to get me two legs into a throt, in spite o' the spavin o' fright the pair o' them wor in; an' how I brought meself home that same night the Lord in heaven only knows, for I never could tell; but I must ha' tumbled agin the door, and shot in head foremost into the middle o' the flure, where I lay in a dead swoon for mostly an hour; and the first I knew was Mrs. Maguire stannin' over me with a jorum o' punch she was pourin' down me throath (throat), to bring back the life into me, an' me head in a pool of cowld wather she dashed over me in her first fright. 'Arrah, Mister Connolly,' shashee, 'what ails ye?' shashee, 'to put the scare on a lone woman like that?' shashee. 'Am I in this world or the next?' sez I. 'Musha! Where else would ye be on'y here in my kitchen?' shashee. 'O, glory be to God!' sez I, 'but I thought I was in Purgathory at the laste, not to mintion an uglier place,' sez I, 'only it's too cowld I find meself, an' not too hot,' sez I. 'Faix, an' maybe ye wor more nor half-ways there, on'y for me,' shashee; 'but what's come to you at all, at all? Is it your fetch ye seen, Mister Connolly?' – 'Aw, naboclish!' sez I. 'Never mind what I seen,' sez I. So be degrees I began to come to a little; an' that's the way I met the banshee, Misther Harry!"

"But how did you know it really was the banshee after all, Thomas?"

"Begor, sir, I knew the apparation of her well enough; but 'twas confirmed by a sarcumstance that occurred the same time. There was a Misther O'Nales was come on a visit, ye must know, to a place in the neighbourhood – one o' the ould O'Nales iv the county Tyrone, a rale ould Irish family – an' the banshee was heard keening round the house that same night, be more then one that was in it; an' sure enough, Misther

Harry, he was found dead in his bed the next mornin'. So if it wasn't the banshee I seen that time, I'd like to know what else it could a' been."

The Wonderful Tune

❖

MAURICE CONNOR was the king, and that's no small word, of all the pipers in Munster. He could play jig and planxty without end, and Ollistrum's March, and the Eagle's Whistle, and the Hen's Concert, and odd tunes of every sort and kind. But he knew one, far more surprising than the rest, which had in it the power to set everything dead or alive dancing.

In what way he learned it is beyond my knowledge, for he was mighty cautious about telling how he came by so wonderful a tune. At the very first note of that tune, the brogues began shaking upon the feet of all who heard it – old or young it mattered not – just as if their brogues had the ague; then the feet began going – going – going from under them, and at last up and away with them, dancing like mad! – Whisking here, there, and everywhere, like a straw in a storm – there was no halting while the music lasted!

Not a fair, nor a wedding, nor a patron in the seven parishes round, was counted worth the speaking of without "blind Maurice and his pipes". His mother, poor woman, used to lead him about from one place to another, just like a dog.

Down through Iveragh – a place that ought to be proud of itself, for 'tis Daniel O'Connell's country – Maurice Connor and his mother were taking their rounds. Beyond all other places Iveragh is the place for stormy coast and steep mountains: as proper a spot it is as any in Ireland to get yourself drowned, or your neck broken on the land, should you prefer that. But, notwithstanding, in Ballinskellig bay there is a neat bit of ground, well fitted for diversion, and down from it towards the water, is a clean smooth piece of strand – the dead image of a calm summer's sea on a moonlight night, with just the curl of the small waves upon it.

Here it was that Maurice's music had brought from all parts a great gathering of the young men and the young women – O *the darlints!* – for 'twas not every day the strand of Trafraska was stirred up by the voice of a bagpipe. The dance began; and as pretty a rinkafadda it was as ever was danced. "Brave music," said every body, "and well done," when Maurice stopped.

"More power to your elbow, Maurice, and a fair wind in the bellows," cried Paddy Dorman, a hump-backed dancing-master, who was there to keep order. "'Tis a pity," said he, "if we'd let the piper run dry after such music; 'twould be a disgrace to Iveragh, that didn't come on it since the week of the three Sundays." So, as well became him, for he was always a decent man, says he: "Did you drink, piper?"

"I will, sir," says Maurice, answering the question on the safe side, for you never yet knew piper or schoolmaster who refused his drink.

"What will you drink, Maurice?" says Paddy.

"I'm no ways particular," says Maurice; "I drink anything, and give God thanks, barring *raw* water; but if 'tis all the same to you, mister Dorman, maybe you wouldn't lend me the loan of a glass of whiskey."

"I've no glass, Maurice," said Paddy; "I've only the bottle."

"Let that be no hindrance," answered Maurice; "my mouth just holds a glass to the drop; often I've tried it, sure."

So Paddy Dorman trusted him with the bottle – more fool was he; and, to his cost, he found that though Maurice's mouth might not hold more than the glass at one time, yet, owing to the hole in his throat, it took many a filling.

"That was no bad whisky neither," says Maurice, handing back the empty bottle.

"By the holy frost, then!" says Paddy, "'tis but *cowld* comfort there's in that bottle now; and 'tis your word we must take for the strength of the whisky, for you've left us no sample to judge by": and to be sure Maurice had not.

Now I need not tell any gentleman or lady with common understanding, that if he or she was to drink an honest bottle of whiskey at one pull, it is not at all the same thing as drinking a bottle of water; and in the whole course of my life, I never knew more than five men who could do so without being overtaken by the liquor. Of these Maurice Connor was not one, though he had a stiff head enough of his own – he was fairly tipsy. Don't think I blame him for it; 'tis often a good man's case; but true is the word that says, "when liquor's in, sense is out"; and puff, at a breath, before you could say "Lord save us!" out he blasted his wonderful tune.

'Twas really then beyond all belief or telling the dancing Maurice himself could not keep quiet; staggering now on one leg, now on the other, and rolling about like a ship in a cross sea, trying to humour the tune. There was his mother too, moving her old bones as light as the youngest girl of them all; but her dancing, no, nor the dancing of all the rest, is not worthy the speaking about to the work that was going on down on the strand. Every inch of it covered with all manner of fish jumping and plunging about to the music, and every moment more and more would tumble in out of the water, charmed by the wonderful tune. Crabs of monstrous size spun round and round on one claw with the nimbleness of a dancing-master, and twirled and tossed their other claws about like limbs that did not belong to them. It was a sight surprising to behold. But perhaps you may have heard of father Florence Conry, a Franciscan Friar, and a great Irish poet; *bolg an dana*, as they used to call him – a wallet of poems. If you have not he was as pleasant a man as one would wish to drink with of a hot summer's day; and he has rhymed out all about the dancing fishes so neatly, that it would be a thousand pities not to give you his verses; so here's my hand at an upset of them into English:

> *The big seals in motion,*
> *Like waves of the ocean,*
> *Or gouty feet prancing,*
> *Came heading the gay fish,*
> *Crabs, lobsters, and cray fish,*
> *Determined on dancing.*
> *The sweet sounds they follow'd,*
> *The gasping cod swallow'd;*
> *'Twas wonderful, really!*
> *And turbot and flounder,*
> *'Mid fish that were rounder,*
> *Just caper'd as gaily.*
> *John-dories came tripping;*
> *Dull hake, by their skipping*

To frisk it seem'd given;
Bright mackerel went springing,
Like small rainbows winging
Their flight up to heaven.
The whiting and haddock
Left salt-water paddock,
This dance to be put in:
Where skate with flat faces
Edged out some odd plaices;
But soles kept their footing.
Sprats and herrings in powers
Of silvery showers
All number out-number'd;
And great ling so lengthy
Were there in such plenty,
The shore was encumber'd.
The scollop and oyster
Their two shells did roister,
Like castanets fitting;
While limpets moved clearly,
And rocks very nearly
With laughter were splitting.

Never was such an ullabulloo in this world, before or since; 'twas as if heaven and earth were coming together; and all out of Maurice Connor's wonderful tune!

In the height of all these doings, what should there be dancing among the outlandish set of fishes but a beautiful young woman – as beautiful as the dawn of day! She had a cocked hat upon her head; from under it her long green hair – just the colour of the sea – fell down behind, without hinderance to her dancing. Her teeth were like rows of pearl; her lips for all the world looked like red coral; and she had an elegant gown, as white as the foam of the wave, with little rows of purple and red sea-weeds settled out upon it; for you never yet saw a lady, under the water or over the water, who had not a good notion of dressing herself out.

Up she danced at last to Maurice, who was flinging his feet from under him as fast as hops – for nothing in this world could keep still while that tune of his was going on – and says she to him, chaunting it out with a voice as sweet as honey –

> *"I'm a lady of honour*
> *Who live in the sea;*
> *Come down, Maurice Connor,*
> *And be married to me.*

> *"Silver plates and gold dishes*
> *You shall have, and shall be*
> *The king of the fishes,*
> *When you're married to me."*

Drink was strong in Maurice's head, and out he chaunted in return for her great civility. It is not every lady, maybe, that would be after making such an offer to a blind piper; therefore 'twas only right in him to give her as good as she gave herself – so says Maurice,

> *"I'm obliged to you, madam:*
> *Off a gold dish or plate,*
> *If a king, and I had 'em,*
> *I could dine in great state.*

> *"With your own father's daughter*
> *I'd be sure to agree;*
> *But to drink the salt water*
> *Wouldn't do so with me!"*

The lady looked at him quite amazed, and swinging her head from side to side like a great scholar, "Well," says she, "Maurice, if you're not a poet, where is poetry to be found?"

In this way they kept on at it, framing high compliments; one answering the other, and their feet going with the music as fast as their tongues. All the fish kept dancing too: Maurice heard the clatter, and was afraid to stop playing lest it might be displeasing to the fish, and not knowing what so many of them may take it into their heads to do to him if they got vexed.

Well, the lady with the green hair kept on coaxing of Maurice with soft speeches, till at last she overpersuaded him to promise to marry her, and be king over the fishes, great and small. Maurice was well fitted to be their king, if they wanted one that could make them dance; and he surely would drink, barring the salt water, with any fish of them all.

When Maurice's mother saw him, with that unnatural thing in the form of a green-haired lady as his guide, and he and she dancing down together so lovingly to the water's edge through the thick of the fishes, she called out after him to stop and come back. "Oh then," says she, "as if I was not widow enough before, there he is going away from me to be married to that scaly woman. And who knows but 'tis grandmother I may be to a hake or a cod – Lord help and pity me, but 'tis a mighty unnatural thing! – and maybe 'tis boiling and eating my own grandchild I'll be, with a bit of salt butter, and I not knowing it! – Oh Maurice, Maurice, if there's any love or nature left in you, come back to your own *ould* mother, who reared you like a decent Christian!"

Then the poor woman began to cry and ullagoane so finely that it would do anyone good to hear her.

Maurice was not long getting to the rim of the water; there he kept playing and dancing on as if nothing was the matter, and a great thundering wave coming in towards him ready to swallow him up alive; but as he could not see it, he did not fear it. His mother it was who saw it plainly through the big tears that were rolling down her cheeks; and though she saw it, and her heart was aching as much as ever mother's heart ached for a son, she kept dancing, dancing, all the time for the bare life of her. Certain it was she could not help it, for Maurice never stopped playing that wonderful tune of his.

He only turned the bothered ear to the sound of his mother's voice, fearing it might put him out in his steps, and all the answer he made back was –

"Whisht with you, mother – sure I'm going to be king over the fishes down in the sea, and for a token of luck, and a sign that I am alive and well, I'll send you in, every twelvemonth on this day, a piece of burned wood to Trafraska." Maurice had not the power to say a word more, for the strange lady with the green hair, seeing the wave just upon them, covered him up with herself in a thing like a cloak with a big hood to it, and the wave curling over twice as high as their heads, burst upon the strand, with a rush and a roar that might be heard as far as Cape Clear.

That day twelvemonth the piece of burned wood came ashore in Trafraska. It was a queer thing for Maurice to think of sending all the way from the bottom of the sea. A gown or a pair of shoes would have been something like a present for his poor mother; but he had said it, and he kept his word. The bit of burned wood regularly came ashore on the appointed day for as good, ay, and better than a hundred years. The day is now forgotten, and may be that is the reason why people say how Maurice Connor has stopped sending the luck-token to his mother. Poor woman, she did not live to get as much as one of them; for what through the loss of Maurice, and the fear of eating her own grandchildren, she died in three weeks after the dance – some say it was the fatigue that killed her, but whichever it was, Mrs. Connor was decently buried with her own people.

Seafaring men have often heard off the coast of Kerry, on a still night, the sound of music coming up from the water; and some, who have had good ears, could plainly distinguish Maurice Connor's voice singing these words to his pipes:

> *"Beautiful shore, with thy spreading strand,*
> *Thy crystal water, and diamond sand;*
> *Never would I have parted from thee*
> *But for the sake of my fair ladie."*

The Lady of Gollerus

❖

ON THE SHORE of Smerwick harbour, one fine summer's morning, just at daybreak, stood Dick Fitzgerald 'shoghing the dudeen', which may be translated, smoking his pipe. The sun was gradually rising behind the lofty Brandon, the dark sea was getting green in the light, and the mists clearing away out of the

valleys went rolling and curling like the smoke from the corner of Dick's mouth.

"'Tis just the pattern of a pretty morning," said Dick, taking the pipe from between his lips, and looking towards the distant ocean, which lay as still and tranquil as a tomb of polished marble. "Well, to be sure," continued he, after a pause, "'tis mighty lonesome to be talking to one's self by way of company, and not to have another soul to answer one – nothing but the child of one's own voice, the echo! I know this, that if I had the luck, or may be the misfortune," said Dick, with a melancholy smile, "to have the woman, it would not be this way with me! And what in the wide world is a man without a wife? He's no more surely than a bottle without a drop of drink in it, or dancing without music, or the left leg of a scissors, or a fishing-line without a hook, or any other matter that is no ways complete. Is it not so?" said Dick Fitzgerald, casting his eyes towards a rock upon the strand, which, though it could not speak, stood up as firm and looked as bold as ever Kerry witness did.

But what was his astonishment at beholding, just at the foot of that rock, a beautiful young creature combing her hair, which was of a sea-green colour; and now the salt water shining on it appeared, in the morning light, like melted butter upon cabbage.

Dick guessed at once that she was a Merrow, although he had never seen one before, for he spied the *cohuleen driuth*, or little enchanted cap, which the sea people use for diving down into the ocean, lying upon the strand near her; and he had heard that, if once he could possess himself of the cap she would lose the power of going away into the water: so he seized it with all speed, and she, hearing the noise, turned her head about as natural as any Christian.

When the Merrow saw that her little diving-cap was gone, the salt tears – doubly salt, no doubt, from her – came trickling down her cheeks, and she began a low mournful cry with just the tender voice of a new-born infant. Dick, although he knew well enough what she was crying for, determined to keep the *cohuleen driuth*, let her cry never so much, to see what luck would come out of it. Yet he could not help pitying her; and when the dumb thing looked up in his face, with her cheeks all moist with tears, 'twas enough to make anyone feel, let alone Dick, who had ever and always, like most of his countrymen, a mighty tender heart of his own.

"Don't cry, my darling," said Dick Fitzgerald; but the Merrow, like any bold child, only cried the more for that.

Dick sat himself down by her side, and took hold of her hand by way of comforting her. 'Twas in no particular an ugly hand, only there was a small web between the fingers, as there is in a duck's foot; but 'twas as thin and as white as the skin between egg and shell.

"What's your name, my darling?" says Dick, thinking to make her conversant with him; but he got no answer; and he was certain sure now, either that she could not speak, or did not understand him: he therefore squeezed her hand in his, as the only way he had of talking to her. It's the universal language; and there's not a woman in the world, be she fish or lady, that does not understand it.

The Merrow did not seem much displeased at this mode of conversation; and making an end of her whining all at once, "Man," says she, looking up in Dick Fitzgerald's face; "man, will you eat me?"

"By all the red petticoats and check aprons between Dingle and Tralee," cried Dick, jumping up in amazement, "I'd as soon eat myself, my jewel! Is it I eat you, my pet? Now, 'twas some ugly ill-looking thief of a fish put that notion into your own pretty head, with the nice green hair down upon it, that is so cleanly combed out this morning!"

"Man," said the Merrow, "what will you do with me if you won't eat me?"

Dick's thoughts were running on a wife: he saw, at the first glimpse, that she was handsome; but since she spoke, and spoke too like any real woman, he was fairly in love with her. 'Twas the neat way she called him man that settled the matter entirely.

"Fish," says Dick, trying to speak to her after her own short fashion; "fish," says he, "here's my word, fresh and fasting, for you this blessed morning, that I'll make you Mistress Fitzgerald before all the world, and that's what I'll do."

"Never say the word twice," says she; "I'm ready and willing to be yours, Mister Fitzgerald; but stop, if you please, till I twist up my hair." It was some time before she had settled it entirely to her liking; for she guessed,

I suppose, that she was going among strangers, where she would be looked at. When that was done, the Merrow put the comb in her pocket, and then bent down her head and whispered some words to the water that was close to the foot of the rock.

Dick saw the murmur of the words upon the top of the sea, going out towards the wide ocean, just like a breath of wind rippling along, and, says he, in the greatest wonder, "Is it speaking you are, my darling, to the salt water?"

"It's nothing else," says she, quite carelessly; "I'm just sending word home to my father not to be waiting breakfast for me; just to keep him from being uneasy in his mind."

"And who's your father, my duck?" said Dick.

"What!" said the Merrow, "did you never hear of my father? He's the king of the waves to be sure!"

"And yourself, then, is a real king's daughter?" said Dick, opening his two eyes to take a full and true survey of his wife that was to be. "Oh, I'm nothing else but a made man with you, and a king your father; to be sure he has all the money that's down at the bottom of the sea!"

"Money," repeated the Merrow, "what's money?"

"'Tis no bad thing to have when one wants it," replied Dick; "and maybe now the fishes have the understanding to bring up whatever you bid them?"

"Oh yes," said the Merrow, "they bring me what I want."

"To speak the truth then," said Dick, "'tis a straw bed I have at home before you, and that, I'm thinking, is no ways fitting for a king's daughter; so if 'twould not be displeasing to you, just to mention a nice feather bed, with a pair of new blankets – but what am I talking about? Maybe you have not such things as beds down under the water?"

"By all means," said she, "Mr. Fitzgerald – plenty of beds at your service. I've fourteen oyster-beds of my own, not to mention one just planting for the rearing of young ones."

"You have?" says Dick, scratching his head and looking a little puzzled. "'Tis a feather bed I was speaking of; but, clearly, yours is the very cut of a decent plan to have bed and supper so handy to each other, that a person when they'd have the one need never ask for the other."

However, bed or no bed, money or no money, Dick Fitzgerald determined to marry the Merrow, and the Merrow had given her consent. Away they went, therefore, across the strand, from Gollerus to Ballinrunnig, where Father Fitzgibbon happened to be that morning.

"There are two words to this bargain, Dick Fitzgerald," said his Reverence, looking mighty glum. "And is it a fishy woman you'd marry? The Lord preserve us! Send the scaly creature home to her own people; that's my advice to you, wherever she came from."

Dick had the *cohuleen driuth* in his hand, and was about to give it back to the Merrow, who looked covetously at it, but he thought for a moment, and then says he, "Please your Reverence, she's a king's daughter."

"If she was the daughter of fifty kings," said Father Fitzgibbon, "I tell you, you can't marry her, she being a fish."

"Please your Reverence," said Dick again, in an undertone, "she is as mild and as beautiful as the moon."

"If she was as mild and as beautiful as the sun, moon, and stars, all put together, I tell you, Dick Fitzgerald," said the Priest, stamping his right foot, "you can't marry her, she being a fish."

"But she has all the gold that's down in the sea only for the asking, and I'm a made man if I marry her; and," said Dick, looking up slily, "I can make it worth anyone's while to do the job."

"Oh! That alters the case entirely," replied the Priest; "why there's some reason now in what you say: why didn't you tell me this before? Marry her by all means, if she was ten times a fish. Money, you know, is not to be refused in these bad times, and I may as well have the hansel of it as another, that maybe would not take half the pains in counselling you that I have done."

So Father Fitzgibbon married Dick Fitzgerald to the Merrow, and like any loving couple, they returned to Gollerus well pleased with each other. Everything prospered with Dick – he was at the sunny side of the world; the Merrow made the best of wives, and they lived together in the greatest contentment.

It was wonderful to see, considering where she had been brought up, how she would busy herself about the house, and how well she nursed the children; for, at the end of three years there were as many young Fitzgeralds – two boys and a girl.

In short, Dick was a happy man, and so he might have been to the end of his days if he had only had the sense to take care of what he had got; many another man, however, beside Dick, has not had wit enough to do that.

One day, when Dick was obliged to go to Tralee, he left the wife minding the children at home after him, and thinking she had plenty to do without disturbing his fishing-tackle.

Dick was no sooner gone than Mrs. Fitzgerald set about cleaning up the house, and chancing to pull down a fishing-net, what should she find behind it in a hole in the wall but her own *cohuleen driuth*. She took it out and looked at it, and then she thought of her father the king, and her mother the queen, and her brothers and sisters, and she felt a longing to go back to them.

She sat down on a little stool and thought over the happy days she had spent under the sea; then she looked at her children, and thought on the love and affection of poor Dick, and how it would break his heart to lose her. "But," says she, "he won't lose me entirely, for I'll come back to him again, and who can blame me for going to see my father and my mother after being so long away from them?"

She got up and went towards the door, but came back again to look once more at the child that was sleeping in the cradle. She kissed it gently, and as she kissed it a tear trembled for an instant in her eye and then fell on its rosy cheek. She wiped away the tear, and turning to the eldest little girl, told her to take good care of her brothers, and to be a good child herself until she came back. The Merrow then went down to the strand. The sea was lying calm and smooth, just heaving and glittering in the sun, and she thought she heard a faint sweet singing, inviting her to come down. All her old ideas and feelings came flooding over her mind, Dick and her children were at the instant forgotten, and placing the *cohuleen driuth* on her head she plunged in.

Dick came home in the evening, and missing his wife he asked Kathleen, his little girl, what had become of her mother, but she could not tell him. He then inquired of the neighbours, and he learned that she was seen going towards the strand with a strange-looking thing like a cocked hat in her hand. He returned to his cabin to search for the *cohuleen driuth*. It was gone, and the truth now flashed upon him.

Year after year did Dick Fitzgerald wait expecting the return of his wife, but he never saw her more. Dick never married again, always thinking that the Merrow would sooner or later return to him, and nothing could ever persuade him but that her father the king kept her below by main force; "for," said Dick, "she surely would not of herself give up her husband and her children."

While she was with him she was so good a wife in every respect that to this day she is spoken of in the tradition of the country as the pattern for one, under the name of The Lady of Gollerus.

Supernatural Forces

reland has a long folkloric history involving witches, ghosts and enchantment. Whether it's bewitched domestic items (such as the dancing pudding in 'The Pudding Bewitched'), people being transformed into animals or objects (see 'Morraha'), or spooky visitations from beyond the grave ('The Fate of Frank M'Kenna', 'The Beresford Ghost'), the idea of supernatural help or hindrance is a common theme in fairy tale storytelling.

Often the purposes or morality of such interference is beyond our control or understanding, making the stories sometimes frightening and often entertaining – as in the memorable examples gathered here.

Bewitched Butter

❖

NOT FAR from Rathmullen lived, last spring, a family called Hanlon; and in a farm-house, some fields distant, people named Dogherty. Both families had good cows, but the Hanlons were fortunate in possessing a Kerry cow that gave more milk and yellower butter than the others.

Grace Dogherty, a young girl, who was more admired than loved in the neighbourhood, took much interest in the Kerry cow, and appeared one night at Mrs. Hanlon's door with the modest request –

"Will you let me milk your Moiley cow?"

"An' why wad you wish to milk wee Moiley, Grace, dear?" inquired Mrs. Hanlon.

"Oh, just becase you're sae throng at the present time."

"Thank you kindly, Grace, but I'm no too throng to do my ain work. I'll no trouble you to milk."

The girl turned away with a discontented air; but the next evening, and the next, found her at the cow-house door with the same request.

At length Mrs. Hanlon, not knowing well how to persist in her refusal, yielded, and permitted Grace to milk the Kerry cow.

She soon had reason to regret her want of firmness. Moiley gave no more milk to her owner.

When this melancholy state of things lasted for three days, the Hanlons applied to a certain Mark McCarrion, who lived near Binion.

"That cow has been milked by someone with an evil eye," said he. "Will she give you a wee drop, do you think? The full of a pint measure wad do."

"Oh, ay, Mark, dear; I'll get that much milk frae her, any way."

"Weel, Mrs. Hanlon, lock the door, an' get nine new pins that was never used in clothes, an' put them into a saucepan wi' the pint o' milk. Set them on the fire, an' let them come to the boil."

The nine pins soon began to simmer in Moiley's milk.

Rapid steps were heard approaching the door, agitated knocks followed, and Grace Dogherty's high-toned voice was raised in eager entreaty.

"Let me in, Mrs. Hanlon!" she cried. "Tak off that cruel pot! Tak out them pins, for they're pricking holes in my heart, an' I'll never offer to touch milk of yours again."

The Horned Women

❖

A RICH WOMAN sat up late one night carding and preparing wool while all the family and servants were asleep. Suddenly a knock was given at the door, and a voice called out, "Open! Open!"

"Who is there?" said the woman of the house.

"I am the Witch of the One Horn," was answered.

The mistress, supposing that one of her neighbours had called and required assistance, opened the door, and a woman entered, having in her hand a pair of wool carders, and bearing a horn on her forehead, as if growing there. She sat down by the fire in silence, and began to card the wool with violent haste. Suddenly she paused, and said aloud, "Where are the women; they delay too long?"

Then a second knock came to the door, and a voice called as before, "Open! Open!"

The mistress felt herself constrained to rise and open to the call, and immediately a second witch entered, having two horns on her forehead, and in her hand a wheel for spinning wool.

"Give me place," she said; "I am the Witch of the Two Horns"; and she began to spin as quick as lightning.

And so the knocks went on, and the call was heard and the witches entered, until at last twelve women sat round the fire – the first with one horn, the last with twelve horns.

And they carded the thread and turned their spinning-wheels, and wound and wove.

All singing together an ancient rhyme, but no word did they speak to the mistress of the house. Strange to hear and frightful to look upon were these twelve women, with their horns and their wheels; and the mistress felt near to death, and she tried to rise that she might call for help, but she could not move, nor could she utter a word or a cry, for the spell of the witches was upon her.

Then one of them called to her in Irish, and said, "Rise, woman, and make us a cake." Then the mistress searched for a vessel to bring water from the well that she might mix the meal and make the cake, but she could find none.

And they said to her, "Take a sieve, and bring water in it." And she took the sieve, and went to the well; but the water poured from it, and she could fetch none for the cake, and she sat down by the well and wept.

Then came a voice by her, and said, "Take yellow clay and moss and bind them together, and plaster the sieve so that it will hold."

This she did, and the sieve held the water for the cake; and the voice said again:

"Return, and when thou comest to the north angle of the house cry aloud three times, and say, 'The mountain of the Fenian women and the sky over it is all on fire.'"

And she did so.

When the witches inside heard the call, a great and terrible cry broke from their lips, and they rushed forth with wild lamentations and shrieks, and fled away to Slievenamon, where was their chief abode. But the Spirit of the Well bade the mistress of the house to enter and prepare her home against the enchantments of the witches, if they returned again.

And first, to break their spells, she sprinkled the water in which she had washed her child's feet (the feet-water) outside the door on the threshold; secondly, she took the cake which the witches had made in her absence, of meal mixed with the blood drawn from the sleeping family, and she broke the cake in bits, and placed a bit in the mouth of each sleeper, and they were restored; and she took the cloth they had woven, and placed it half in and half out of the chest with the padlock; and, lastly, she secured the door with a great crossbeam fastened in the jambs, so that they could not enter, and having done these things she waited.

Not long were the witches in coming, and they raged and called for vengeance.

"Open! Open!" they screamed. "Open, feet-water!"

"I cannot," said the feet-water; "I am scattered on the ground, and my path is down to the Lough."

"Open, open, wood and trees and beam!" they cried to the door.

"I cannot," said the door, "for the beam is fixed in the jambs, and I have no power to move."

"Open, open, cake that we have made and mingled with blood!" they cried again.

"I cannot," said the cake, "for I am broken and bruised, and my blood is on the lips of the sleeping children."

Then the witches rushed through the air with great cries, and fled back to Slievenamon, uttering strange curses on the Spirit of the Well, who had wished their ruin. But the woman and the house were left in peace, and a mantle dropped by one of the witches was kept hung up by the mistress as a sign of the night's awful contest; and this mantle was in possession of the same family from generation to generation for five hundred years after.

The Witches' Excursion

❖

SHEMUS (RED JAMES) awakened from his sleep one night by noises in his kitchen. Stealing to the door, he saw half-a-dozen old women sitting round the fire, jesting and laughing, his old housekeeper, Madge, quite frisky and gay, helping her sister crones to cheering glasses of punch. He began to admire the impudence and imprudence of Madge, displayed in the invitation and the riot, but recollected on the instant her officiousness in urging him to take a comfortable posset, which she had brought to his bedside just before he fell asleep. Had he drunk it, he would have been just now deaf to the witches' glee. He heard and saw them drink his

health in such a mocking style as nearly to tempt him to charge them, besom in hand, but he restrained himself.

The jug being emptied, one of them cried out, "Is it time to be gone?" and at the same moment, putting on a red cap, she added –

> *"By yarrow and rue,*
> *And my red cap too,*
> *Hie over to England."*

Making use of a twig which she held in her hand as a steed, she gracefully soared up the chimney, and was rapidly followed by the rest. But when it came to the housekeeper, Shemus interposed. "By your leave, ma'am," said he, snatching twig and cap. "Ah, you desateful ould crocodile! If I find you here on my return, there'll be wigs on the green –

> *'By yarrow and rue,*
> *And my red cap too,*
> *Hie over to England.'"*

The words were not out of his mouth when he was soaring above the ridge pole, and swiftly ploughing the air. He was careful to speak no word (being somewhat conversant with witch-lore), as the result would be a tumble, and the immediate return of the expedition.

In a very short time they had crossed the Wicklow hills, the Irish Sea, and the Welsh mountains, and were charging, at whirlwind speed, the hall door of a castle. Shemus, only for the company in which he found himself, would have cried out for pardon, expecting to be *mummy* against the hard oak door in a moment; but, all bewildered, he found himself passing through the key-hole, along a passage, down a flight of steps, and through a cellar-door key-hole before he could form any clear idea of his situation.

Waking to the full consciousness of his position, he found himself sitting on a stillion, plenty of lights glimmering round, and he and his companions, with full tumblers of frothing wine in hand, hob-nobbing and drinking healths as jovially and recklessly as if the liquor was honestly come by, and they were sitting in *Shemus's* own kitchen. The red birredh had assimilated *Shemus's* nature for the time being to that of his unholy companions. The heady liquors soon got into their brains, and a period of unconsciousness succeeded the ecstasy, the head-ache, the turning round of the barrels, and the 'scattered sight' of poor Shemus. He woke up under the impression of being roughly seized, and shaken, and dragged upstairs, and subjected to a disagreeable examination by the lord of the castle, in his state parlour. There was much derision among the whole company, gentle and simple, on hearing Shemus's explanation, and, as the thing occurred in the dark ages, the unlucky Leinster man was sentenced to be hung as soon as the gallows could be prepared for the occasion.

The poor Hibernian was in the cart proceeding on his last journey, with a label on his back, and another on his breast, announcing him as the remorseless villain who for the last month had been draining the casks in my lord's vault every night. He was surprised to hear himself addressed by his name, and in his native tongue, by an old woman in the crowd.

"Ach, Shemus, alanna! Is it going to die you are in a strange place without your *cappeen d'yarrag*?" These words infused hope and courage into the poor victim's heart. He turned to the lord and humbly asked leave to die in his red cap, which he supposed had dropped from his head in the vault. A servant was sent for the head-piece, and Shemus felt lively hope warming his heart while placing it on his head. On the platform he was graciously allowed to address the spectators, which he proceeded to do in the usual formula composed for the benefit of flying stationers –

"Good people all, a warning take by me"; but when he had finished the line, "My parents reared me tenderly," he unexpectedly added – "By yarrow and rue," etc., and the disappointed spectators saw him shoot up obliquely through the air in the style of a sky-rocket that had missed its aim. It is said that the lord took the circumstance much to heart, and never afterwards hung a man for twenty-four hours after his offence.

Smallhead and the King's Sons

❖

LONG AGO THERE LIVED in Erin a woman who married a man of high degree and had one daughter. Soon after the birth of the daughter the husband died.

The woman was not long a widow when she married a second time, and had two daughters. These two daughters hated their half-sister, thought she was not so wise as another, and nicknamed her Smallhead. When the elder of the two sisters was fourteen years old their father died. The mother was in great grief then, and began to pine away. She used to sit at home in the corner and never left the house. Smallhead was kind to her mother, and the mother was fonder of her eldest daughter than of the other two, who were ashamed of her.

At last the two sisters made up in their minds to kill their mother. One day, while their half-sister was gone, they put the mother in a pot, boiled her, and threw the bones outside. When Smallhead came home there was no sign of the mother.

"Where is my mother?" asked she of the other two.

"She went out somewhere. How should we know where she is?"

"Oh, wicked girls! You have killed my mother," said Smallhead.

Smallhead wouldn't leave the house now at all, and the sisters were very angry.

"No man will marry either one of us," said they, "if he sees our fool of a sister."

Since they could not drive Smallhead from the house they made up their minds to go away themselves. One fine morning they left home unknown to their half-sister and travelled on many miles. When Smallhead discovered that her sisters were gone she hurried after them and never stopped till she came up with the two. They had to go home with her that day, but they scolded her bitterly.

The two settled then to kill Smallhead, so one day they took twenty needles and scattered them outside in a pile of straw. "We are going to that

198

hill beyond," said they, "to stay till evening, and if you have not all the needles that are in that straw outside gathered and on the tables before us, we'll have your life."

Away they went to the hill. Smallhead sat down, and was crying bitterly when a short grey cat walked in and spoke to her.

"Why do you cry and lament so?" asked the cat.

"My sisters abuse me and beat me," answered Smallhead. "This morning they said they would kill me in the evening unless I had all the needles in the straw outside gathered before them."

"Sit down here," said the cat, "and dry your tears."

The cat soon found the twenty needles and brought them to Smallhead. "Stop there now," said the cat, "and listen to what I tell you. I am your mother; your sisters killed me and destroyed my body, but don't harm them; do them good, do the best you can for them, save them: obey my words and it will be better for you in the end."

The cat went away for herself, and the sisters came home in the evening. The needles were on the table before them. Oh, but they were vexed and angry when they saw the twenty needles, and they said someone was helping their sister!

One night when Smallhead was in bed and asleep they started away again, resolved this time never to return. Smallhead slept till morning. When she saw that the sisters were gone she followed, traced them from place to place, inquired here and there day after day, till one evening some person told her that they were in the house of an old hag, a terrible enchantress, who had one son and three daughters: that the house was a bad place to be in, for the old hag had more power of witchcraft than anyone and was very wicked.

Smallhead hurried away to save her sisters, and facing the house knocked at the door, and asked lodgings for God's sake.

"Oh, then," said the hag, "it is hard to refuse anyone lodgings, and besides on such a wild, stormy night. I wonder if you are anything to the young ladies who came the way this evening?"

The two sisters heard this and were angry enough that Smallhead was in it, but they said nothing, not wishing the old hag to know their relationship. After supper the hag told the three strangers to sleep in a room on the right side of the house. When her own daughters were going to bed Smallhead saw her tie a ribbon around the neck of each one of them, and heard her say: "Do you sleep in the left-hand bed." Smallhead hurried and said to her sisters: "Come quickly, or I'll tell the woman who you are."

They took the bed in the left-hand room and were in it before the hag's daughters came.

"Oh," said the daughters, "the other bed is as good." So they took the bed in the right-hand room. When Smallhead knew that the hag's daughters were asleep she rose, took the ribbons off their necks, and put them on her sister's necks and on her own. She lay awake and watched them. After a while she heard the hag say to her son:

"Go, now, and kill the three girls; they have the clothes and money."

"You have killed enough in your life and so let these go," said the son.

But the old woman would not listen. The boy rose up, fearing his mother, and taking a long knife, went to the right-hand room and cut the throats of the three girls without ribbons. He went to bed then for himself, and when Smallhead found that the old hag was asleep she roused her sisters, told what had happened, made them dress quickly and follow her. Believe me, they were willing and glad to follow her this time.

The three travelled briskly and came soon to a bridge, called at that time 'The Bridge of Blood'. Whoever had killed a person could not cross the bridge. When the three girls came to the bridge the two sisters stopped: they could not go a step further. Smallhead ran across and went back again.

"If I did not know that you killed our mother," said she, "I might know it now, for this is the Bridge of Blood."

She carried one sister over the bridge on her back and then the other. Hardly was this done when the hag was at the bridge.

"Bad luck to you, Smallhead!" said she, "I did not know that it was you that was in it last evening. You have killed my three daughters."

"It wasn't I that killed them, but yourself," said Smallhead.

The old hag could not cross the bridge, so she began to curse, and she put every curse on Smallhead that she could remember. The sisters travelled on till they came to a King's castle. They heard that two servants were needed in the castle.

"Go now," said Smallhead to the two sisters, "and ask for service. Be faithful and do well. You can never go back by the road you came."

The two found employment at the King's castle. Smallhead took lodgings in the house of a blacksmith near by.

"I should be glad to find a place as kitchen-maid in the castle," said Smallhead to the blacksmith's wife.

"I will go to the castle and find a place for you if I can," said the woman.

The blacksmith's wife found a place for Smallhead as kitchen-maid in the castle, and she went there next day.

"I must be careful," thought Smallhead, "and do my best. I am in a strange place. My two sisters are here in the King's castle. Who knows, we may have great fortune yet."

She dressed neatly and was cheerful. Everyone liked her, liked her better than her sisters, though they were beautiful. The King had two sons, one at home and the other abroad. Smallhead thought to herself one day: "It is time for the son who is here in the castle to marry. I will speak to him the first time I can." One day she saw him alone in the garden, went up to him, and said:

"Why are you not getting married, it is high time for you?"

He only laughed and thought she was too bold, but then thinking that she was a simple-minded girl who wished to be pleasant, he said:

"I will tell you the reason: My grandfather bound my father by an oath never to let his oldest son marry until he could get the Sword of Light, and I am afraid that I shall be long without marrying."

"Do you know where the Sword of Light is, or who has it?" asked Smallhead.

"I do," said the King's son, "an old hag who has great power and enchantment, and she lives a long distance from this, beyond the Bridge of Blood. I cannot go there myself, I cannot cross the bridge, for I have killed men in battle. Even if I could cross the bridge I would not go, for many is the King's son that hag has destroyed or enchanted."

"Suppose some person were to bring the Sword of Light, and that person a woman, would you marry her?"

"I would, indeed," said the King's son.

"If you promise to marry my elder sister I will strive to bring the Sword of Light."

"I will promise most willingly," said the King's son.

Next morning early, Smallhead set out on her journey. Calling at the first shop she bought a stone weight of salt, and went on her way, never stopping or resting till she reached the hag's house at nightfall. She climbed to the gable, looked down, and saw the son making a great pot of stirabout for his mother, and she hurrying him. "I am as hungry as a hawk!" cried she.

Whenever the boy looked away, Smallhead dropped salt down, dropped it when he was not looking, dropped it till she had the whole stone of salt in the stirabout. The old hag waited and waited till at last she cried out: "Bring the stirabout. I am starving! Bring the pot. I will eat from the pot. Give the milk here as well."

The boy brought the stirabout and the milk, the old woman began to eat, but the first taste she got she spat out and screamed: "You put salt in the pot in place of meal!"

"I did not, mother."

"You did, and it's a mean trick that you played on me. Throw this stirabout to the pig outside and go for water to the well in the field."

"I cannot go," said the boy, "the night is too dark; I might fall into the well."

"You must go and bring the water; I cannot live till morning without eating."

"I am as hungry as yourself," said the boy, "but how can I go to the well without a light? I will not go unless you give me a light."

"If I give you the Sword of Light there is no knowing who may follow you; maybe that devil of a Smallhead is outside."

But sooner than fast till morning the old hag gave the Sword of Light to her son, warning him to take good care of it. He took the Sword of Light and went out. As he saw no one when he came to the well he left the sword on the top of the steps going down to the water, so as to have good light. He had not gone down many steps when Smallhead had the sword, and away she ran over hills, dales, and valleys towards the Bridge of Blood.

The boy shouted and screamed with all his might. Out ran the hag. "Where is the sword?" cried she.

"Someone took it from the step."

Off rushed the hag, following the light, but she didn't come near Smallhead till she was over the bridge.

"Give me the Sword of Light, or bad luck to you," cried the hag.

"Indeed, then, I will not; I will keep it, and bad luck to yourself," answered Smallhead.

On the following morning she walked up to the King's son and said:

"I have the Sword of Light; now will you marry my sister?"

"I will," said he.

The King's son married Smallhead's sister and got the Sword of Light. Smallhead stayed no longer in the kitchen – the sister didn't care to have her in kitchen or parlour.

The King's second son came home. He was not long in the castle when Smallhead said to herself, "Maybe he will marry my second sister."

She saw him one day in the garden, went toward him; he said something, she answered, then asked: "Is it not time for you to be getting married like your brother?"

"When my grandfather was dying," said the young man, "he bound my father not to let his second son marry till he had the Black Book. This book used to shine and give brighter light than ever the Sword of Light did, and I suppose it does yet. The old hag beyond the Bridge of Blood has the book, and no one dares to go near her, for many is the King's son killed or enchanted by that woman."

"Would you marry my second sister if you were to get the Black Book?"

"I would, indeed; I would marry any woman if I got the Black Book with her. The Sword of Light and the Black Book were in our family till my grandfather's time, then they were stolen by that cursed old hag."

"I will have the book," said Smallhead, "or die in the trial to get it."

Knowing that stirabout was the main food of the hag, Smallhead settled in her mind to play another trick. Taking a bag she scraped the chimney, gathered about a stone of soot, and took it with her. The night was dark and rainy. When she reached the hag's house, she climbed up the gable to the chimney and found that the son was making stirabout for his mother. She dropped the soot down by degrees till at last the whole stone of soot was in the pot; then she scraped around the top of the chimney till a lump of soot fell on the boy's hand.

"Oh, mother," said he, "the night is wet and soft, the soot is falling."

"Cover the pot," said the hag. "Be quick with that stirabout, I am starving."

The boy took the pot to his mother.

"Bad luck to you," cried the hag the moment she tasted the stirabout, "this is full of soot; throw it out to the pig."

"If I throw it out there is no water inside to make more, and I'll not go in the dark and rain to the well."

"You must go!" screamed she.

"I'll not stir a foot out of this unless I get a light," said the boy.

"Is it the book you are thinking of, you fool, to take it and lose it as you did the sword? Smallhead is watching you."

"How could Smallhead, the creature, be outside all the time? If you have no use for the water you can do without it."

Sooner than stop fasting till morning, the hag gave her son the book, saying: "Do not put this down or let it from your hand till you come in, or I'll have your life."

The boy took the book and went to the well. Smallhead followed him carefully. He took the book down into the well with him, and when he was stooping to dip water she snatched the book and pushed him into the well, where he came very near drowning.

Smallhead was far away when the boy recovered, and began to scream and shout to his mother. She came in a hurry, and finding that the book was gone, fell into such a rage that she thrust a knife into her son's heart and ran after Smallhead, who had crossed the bridge before the hag could come up with her.

When the old woman saw Smallhead on the other side of the bridge facing her and dancing with delight, she screamed:

"You took the Sword of Light and the Black Book, and your two sisters are married. Oh, then, bad luck to you. I will put my curse on you wherever you go. You have all my children killed, and I a poor, feeble, old woman."

"Bad luck to yourself," said Smallhead. "I am not afraid of a curse from the like of you. If you had lived an honest life you wouldn't be as you are today."

"Now, Smallhead," said the old hag, "you have me robbed of everything, and my children destroyed. Your two sisters are well married. Your fortune began with my ruin. Come, now, and take care of me in my old age. I'll take my curse from you, and you will have good luck. I bind myself never to harm a hair of your head."

Smallhead thought awhile, promised to do this, and said: "If you harm me, or try to harm me, it will be the worse for yourself."

The old hag was satisfied and went home. Smallhead went to the castle and was received with great joy. Next morning she found the King's son in the garden, and said: "If you marry my sister tomorrow, you will have the Black Book."

"I will marry her gladly," said the King's son.

Next day the marriage was celebrated and the King's son got the book. Smallhead remained in the castle about a week, then she left good health with her sisters and went to the hag's house. The old woman was glad to see her and showed the girl her work. All Smallhead had to do was to wait on the hag and feed a large pig that she had.

"I am fatting that pig," said the hag; "he is seven years old now, and the longer you keep a pig the harder his meat is: we'll keep this pig a while longer, and then we'll kill and eat him."

Smallhead did her work; the old hag taught her some things, and Smallhead learned herself far more than the hag dreamt of. The girl fed the pig three times a day, never thinking that he could be anything but a pig. The hag had sent word to a sister that she had in the Eastern World, bidding her come and they would kill the pig and have a great feast. The sister came, and one day when the hag was going to walk with her sister she said to Smallhead:

"Give the pig plenty of meal today; this is the last food he'll have; give him his fill."

The pig had his own mind and knew what was coming. He put his nose under the pot and threw it on Smallhead's toes, and she barefoot. With that she ran into the house for a stick, and seeing a rod on the edge of the loft, snatched it and hit the pig.

That moment the pig was a splendid young man.

Smallhead was amazed.

"Never fear," said the young man, "I am the son of a King that the old hag hated, the King of Munster. She stole me from my father seven years ago and enchanted me – made a pig of me."

Smallhead told the King's son, then, how the hag had treated her. "I must make a pig of you again," said she, "for the hag is coming. Be patient and I'll save you, if you promise to marry me."

"I promise you," said the King's son.

With that she struck him, and he was a pig again. She put the switch in its place and was at her work when the two sisters came. The pig ate his meal now with a good heart, for he felt sure of rescue.

"Who is that girl you have in the house, and where did you find her?" asked the sister.

"All my children died of the plague, and I took this girl to help me. She is a very good servant."

At night the hag slept in one room, her sister in another, and Smallhead in a third. When the two sisters were sleeping soundly Smallhead rose, stole the hag's magic book, and then took the rod. She went next to where the pig was, and with one blow of the rod made a man of him.

With the help of the magic book Smallhead made two doves of herself and the King's son, and they took flight through the air and flew on without stopping. Next morning the hag called Smallhead, but she did not come. She hurried out to see the pig. The pig was gone. She ran to her book. Not a sign of it.

"Oh!" cried she, "that villain of a Smallhead has robbed me. She has stolen my book, made a man of the pig, and taken him away with her."

What could she do but tell her whole story to the sister. "Go you," said she, "and follow them. You have more enchantment than Smallhead has."

"How am I to know them?" asked the sister.

"Bring the first two strange things that you find; they will turn themselves into something wonderful."

The sister then made a hawk of herself and flew away as swiftly as any March wind.

"Look behind," said Smallhead to the King's son some hours later; "see what is coming."

"I see nothing," said he, "but a hawk coming swiftly."

"That is the hag's sister. She has three times more enchantment than the hag herself. But fly down on the ditch and be picking yourself as doves do in rainy weather, and maybe she'll pass without seeing us."

The hawk saw the doves, but thinking them nothing wonderful, flew on till evening, and then went back to her sister.

"Did you see anything wonderful?"

"I did not; I saw only two doves, and they picking themselves."

"You fool, those doves were Smallhead and the King's son. Off with you in the morning and don't let me see you again without the two with you."

Away went the hawk a second time, and swiftly as Smallhead and the King's son flew, the hawk was gaining on them. Seeing this Smallhead and the King's son dropped down into a large village, and, it being market-day, they made two heather brooms of themselves. The two brooms began to sweep the road without anyone holding them, and swept toward each other. This was a great wonder. Crowds gathered at once around the two brooms.

The old hag flying over in the form of a hawk saw this and thinking that it must be Smallhead and the King's son were in it, came down, turned into a woman, and said to herself:

"I'll have those two brooms."

She pushed forward so quickly through the crowd that she came near knocking down a man standing before her. The man was vexed.

"You cursed old hag!" cried he, "do you want to knock us down?" With that he gave her a blow and drove her against another man, that man gave her a push that sent her spinning against a third man, and so on till between them all they came near putting the life out of her, and pushed her away from the brooms. A woman in the crowd called out then:

"It would be nothing but right to knock the head off that old hag, and she trying to push us away from the mercy of God, for it was God who sent the brooms to sweep the road for us."

"True for you," said another woman. With that the people were as angry as angry could be, and were ready to kill the hag. They were going to take the head off the hag when she made a hawk of herself and flew away, vowing never to do another stroke of work for her sister. She might do her own work or let it alone.

When the hawk disappeared the two heather brooms rose and turned into doves. The people felt sure when they saw the doves that the brooms were a blessing from heaven, and it was the old hag that drove them away.

On the following day Smallhead and the King's son saw his father's castle, and the two came down not too far from it in their own forms. Smallhead was a very beautiful woman now, and why not? She had the magic and didn't spare it. She made herself as beautiful as ever she could: the like of her was not to be seen in that kingdom or the next one.

The King's son was in love with her that minute, and did not wish to part with her, but she would not go with him.

"When you are at your father's castle," said Smallhead, "all will be overjoyed to see you, and the king will give a great feast in your honour. If you kiss anyone or let any living thing kiss you, you'll forget me for ever."

"I will not let even my own mother kiss me," said he.

The King's son went to the castle. All were overjoyed; they had thought him dead, had not seen him for seven years. He would let no one come near to kiss him. "I am bound by oath to kiss no one," said he to his mother. At that moment an old grey hound came in, and with one spring was on his shoulder licking his face: all that the King's son had gone through in seven years was forgotten in one moment.

Smallhead went toward a forge near the castle. The smith had a wife far younger than himself, and a stepdaughter. They were no beauties. In the rear of the forge was a well and a tree growing over it. "I will go up in that tree," thought Smallhead, "and spend the night in it." She went up and sat just over the well. She was not long in the tree when the moon came out high above the hill tops and shone on the well. The blacksmith's stepdaughter, coming for water, looked down in the well, saw the face of the woman above in the tree, thought it her own face, and cried:

"Oh, then, to have me bringing water to a smith, and I such a beauty. I'll never bring another drop to him." With that she cast the pail in the ditch and ran off to find a king's son to marry.

When she was not coming with the water, and the blacksmith waiting to wash after his day's work in the forge, he sent the mother. The mother had nothing but a pot to get the water in, so off she went with that, and coming to the well saw the beautiful face in the water.

"Oh, you black, swarthy villain of a smith," cried she, "bad luck to the hour that I met you, and I such a beauty. I'll never draw another drop of water for the life of you!"

She threw the pot down, broke it, and hurried away to find some king's son.

When neither mother nor daughter came back with water the smith himself went to see what was keeping them. He saw the pail in the ditch, and, catching it, went to the well; looking down, he saw the beautiful face of a woman in the water. Being a man, he knew that it was not his own face that was in it, so he looked up, and there in the tree saw a woman. He spoke to her and said:

"I know now why my wife and her daughter did not bring water. They saw your face in the well, and, thinking themselves too good for me, ran away. You must come now and keep the house till I find them."

"I will help you," said Smallhead. She came down, went to the smith's house, and showed the road that the women took. The smith hurried after them, and found the two in a village ten miles away. He explained their own folly to them, and they came home.

The mother and daughter washed fine linen for the castle. Smallhead saw them ironing one day, and said:

"Sit down: I will iron for you."

She caught the iron, and in an hour had the work of the day done.

The women were delighted. In the evening the daughter took the linen to the housekeeper at the castle.

"Who ironed this linen?" asked the housekeeper.

"My mother and I."

"Indeed, then, you did not. You can't do the like of that work, and tell me who did it."

The girl was in dread now and answered:

"It is a woman who is stopping with us who did the ironing."

The housekeeper went to the Queen and showed her the linen.

"Send that woman to the castle," said the Queen.

Smallhead went: the Queen welcomed her, wondered at her beauty; put her over all the maids in the castle. Smallhead could do anything; everybody was fond of her. The King's son never knew that he had seen her before, and she lived in the castle a year; what the Queen told her she did.

The King had made a match for his son with the daughter of the King of Ulster. There was a great feast in the castle in honour of the young couple, the marriage was to be a week later. The bride's father brought many of his people who were versed in all kinds of tricks and enchantment.

The King knew that Smallhead could do many things, for neither the Queen nor himself had asked her to do a thing that she did not do in a twinkle.

"Now," said the King to the Queen, "I think she can do something that his people cannot do." He summoned Smallhead and asked:

"Can you amuse the strangers?"

"I can if you wish me to do so."

When the time came and the Ulster men had shown their best tricks, Smallhead came forward and raised the window, which was forty feet from the ground. She had a small ball of thread in her hand; she tied one end of the thread to the window, threw the ball out and over a wall near the castle; then she passed out the window, walked on the thread and kept time to music from players that no man could see. She came in; all cheered her and were greatly delighted.

"I can do that," said the King of Ulster's daughter, and sprang out on the string; but if she did she fell and broke her neck on the stones below. There were cries, there was lamentation, and, in place of a marriage, a funeral.

The King's son was angry and grieved and wanted to drive Smallhead from the castle in some way.

"She is not to blame," said the King of Munster, who did nothing but praise her.

Another year passed: the King got the daughter of the King of Connacht for his son. There was a great feast before the wedding day, and as the Connacht people are full of enchantment and witchcraft, the King of Munster called Smallhead and said:

"Now show the best trick of any."

"I will," said Smallhead.

When the feast was over and the Connacht men had shown their tricks the King of Munster called Smallhead.

She stood before the company, threw two grains of wheat on the floor, and spoke some magic words. There was a hen and a cock there before her of beautiful plumage; she threw a grain of wheat between them; the hen sprang to eat the wheat, the cock gave her a blow of his bill, the hen drew back, looked at him, and said:

"Bad luck to you, you wouldn't do the like of that when I was serving the old hag and you her pig, and I made a man of you and gave you back your own form."

The King's son looked at her and thought, "There must be something in this."

Smallhead threw a second grain. The cock pecked the hen again. "Oh," said the hen, "you would not do that the day the hag's sister was hunting us, and we two doves."

The King's son was still more astonished.

She threw a third grain. The cock struck the hen, and she said, "You would not do that to me the day I made two heather brooms out of you and myself." She threw a fourth grain. The cock pecked the hen a fourth time. "You would not do that the day you promised not to let any living thing kiss you or kiss anyone yourself but me – you let the hound kiss you and you forgot me."

The King's son made one bound forward, embraced and kissed Smallhead, and told the King his whole story from beginning to end.

"This is my wife," said he; "I'll marry no other woman."

"Whose wife will my daughter be?" asked the King of Connacht.

"Oh, she will be the wife of the man who will marry her," said the King of Munster, "my son gave his word to this woman before he saw your daughter, and he must keep it."

So Smallhead married the King of Munster's son.

The Pudding Bewitched

❖

"MOLL ROE RAFFERTY was the son – daughter I mane – of ould Jack Rafferty, who was remarkable for a habit he had of always wearing his head undher his hat; but indeed the same family was a quare one, as everybody knew that was acquainted wid them. It was said of them – but whether it was thrue or not I won't undhertake to say, for 'fraid I'd tell a lie – that whenever they didn't wear shoes or boots they always went barefooted; but I heard afthcrwards that this was disputed, so rather than say anything to injure their character, I'll let that pass. Now, ould Jack Rafferty had two sons, Paddy and Molly – hut! what are you all laughing at? – I mane a son and daughter, and it was generally believed among the neighbours that they were brother and sisther, which you know might be thrue or it might not: but that's a thing that, wid the help o' goodness, we have nothing to say to. Troth there was many ugly things put out on them that I don't wish to repate, such as that neither Jack nor his son Paddy ever walked a perch widout puttin' one foot afore the other like a salmon; an' I know it was whispered about, that whinever Moll Roe slep', she had an out-of-the-way custom of keepin' her eyes shut. If she did, however, for that matther the loss was her own; for sure we all know that when one comes to shut their eyes they can't see as far before them as another.

"Moll Roe was a fine young bouncin' girl, large and lavish, wid a purty head o' hair on her like scarlet, that bein' one of the raisons why she was called *Roe*, or red; her arms an' cheeks were much the colour of the hair, an' her saddle nose was the purtiest thing of its kind that ever was on a face. Her fists – for, thank goodness, she was well sarved wid them too – had a strong simularity to two thumpin' turnips, reddened by the sun; an' to keep all right and tight, she had a temper as fiery as her head – for, indeed, it was well known that all the Raffertys were *warm*-hearted. Howandiver, it appears that God gives nothing in vain, and of coorse the same fists, big and red as they were, if all that is said about them is thrue, were not so much given to her for ornament as use. At laist, takin' them in connection wid her lively temper, we have it upon good authority, that there was no danger of their getting blue-moulded for want of practice. She had a twist, too, in one of her eyes that was very becomin' in its way, and made her poor husband, when she got him, take it into his head that she could see round a corner. She found him out in many quare things, widout doubt; but whether it was owin' to that or not, I wouldn't undertake to say *for fraid I'd tell a lie*.

"Well, begad, anyhow it was Moll Roe that was the *dilsy*. It happened that there was a nate vagabone in the neighbourhood, just as much overburdened wid beauty as herself, and he was named Gusty Gillespie. Gusty, the Lord guard us, was what they call a black-mouth Prosbytarian, and wouldn't keep Christmas-day, the blagard, except what they call 'ould style'. Gusty was rather good-lookin' when seen in the dark, as well as Moll herself; and, indeed, it was purty well known that – accordin' as the talk went – it was in nightly meetings that they had an opportunity of becomin' detached to one another. The quensequence was, that in due time both families began to talk very seriously as to what was to be done. Moll's brother, Pawdien O'Rafferty, gave Gusty the best of two choices. What they were it's not worth spakin' about; but at any rate *one* of them was a poser, an' as Gusty knew his man, he soon came to his senses. Accordianly everything was deranged for their marriage, and it was appointed that they should be spliced by the Rev. Samuel M'Shuttle, the Prosbytarian parson, on the following Sunday.

"Now this was the first marriage that had happened for a long time in the neighbourhood betune a black-mouth an' a Catholic, an' of coorse there was strong objections on both sides aginst it; an' begad, only for one thing, it would never 'a tuck place at all. At any rate, faix, there was one of the bride's uncles, ould Harry Connolly, a fairy-man, who could cure all complaints wid a secret he had, and as he didn't wish to see his niece married upon sich a fellow, he fought bittherly against the match. All Moll's friends, however, stood up for the marriage barrin' him, an' of coorse the Sunday was appointed, as I said, that they were to be dove-tailed together.

"Well, the day arrived, and Moll, as became her, went to mass, and Gusty to meeting, afther which they were to join one another in Jack Rafferty's, where the priest, Father M'Sorley, was to slip up afther mass to take his dinner wid them, and to keep Misther M'Shuttle, who was to marry them, company. Nobody remained at home but ould Jack Rafferty an' his wife, who stopped to dress the dinner, for, to tell the truth, it was to be a great let-out entirely. Maybe, if all was known, too, that Father M'Sorley was to give them a cast of his office over an' above the ministher, in regard that Moll's friends were not altogether satisfied at the kind of marriage which M'Shuttle could give them. The sorrow may care about that – splice here – splice there – all I can say is, that when Mrs. Rafferty was goin' to tie up a big bag pudden, in walks Harry Connolly, the fairy-man, in a rage, and shouts out – 'Blood and blunderbushes, what are yez here for?'

"'Arrah why, Harry? Why, avick?'

"'Why, the sun's in the suds and the moon in the high Horicks; there's a clipstick comin' an, an' there you're both as unconsarned as if it was about to rain mether. Go out and cross yourselves three times in the name o' the four Mandromarvins, for as prophecy says: – Fill the pot, Eddy, supernaculum – a blazing star's a rare spectaculum. Go out both of you and look at the sun, I say, an' ye'll see the condition he's in – off!'

"Begad, sure enough, Jack gave a bounce to the door, and his wife leaped like a two-year-ould, till they were both got on a stile beside the house to see what was wrong in the sky.

"'Arrah, what is it, Jack,' said she; 'can you see anything?'

"'No,' says he, 'sorra the full o' my eye of anything I can spy, barrin' the sun himself, that's not visible in regard of the clouds. God guard us! I doubt there's something to happen.'

"'If there wasn't, Jack, what 'ud put Harry, that knows so much, in the state he's in?'

"'I doubt it's this marriage,' said Jack: 'betune ourselves, it's not over an' above religious for Moll to marry a black-mouth, an' only for –; but it can't be helped now, though you see not a taste o' the sun is willin' to show his face upon it.'

"'As to that,' says the wife, winkin' wid both her eyes, 'if Gusty's satisfied wid Moll, it's enough. I know who'll carry the whip hand, anyhow; but in the manetime let us ax Harry 'ithin what ails the sun.'

"Well, they accordianly went in an' put the question to him:

"'Harry, what's wrong, ahagur? What is it now, for if anybody alive knows, 'tis yourself?'

"'Ah!' said Harry, screwin' his mouth wid a kind of a dhry smile, 'the sun has a hard twist o' the cholic; but never mind that, I tell you you'll have a merrier weddin' than you think, that's all'; and havin' said this, he put on his hat and left the house.

"Now, Harry's answer relieved them very much, and so, afther calling to him to be back for the dinner, Jack sat down to take a shough o' the pipe, and the wife lost no time in tying up the pudden and puttin' it in the pot to be boiled.

"In this way things went on well enough for a while, Jack smokin' away, an' the wife cookin' and dhressin' at the rate of a hunt. At last, Jack, while sittin', as I said, contentedly at the fire, thought he could persave an odd dancin' kind of motion in the pot that puzzled him a good deal.

"'Katty,' said he, 'what the dickens is in this pot on the fire?'

"'Nerra thing but the big pudden. Why do you ax?' says she.

"'Why,' said he, 'if ever a pot tuck it into its head to dance a jig, and this did. Thundher and sparbles, look at it!'

"Begad, it was thrue enough; there was the pot bobbin' up an' down and from side to side, jiggin' away as merry as a grig; an' it was quite aisy to see that it wasn't the pot itself, but what was inside of it, that brought about the hornpipe.

"'Be the hole o' my coat,' shouted Jack, 'there's something alive in it, or it would never cut sich capers!'

"'Be gorra, there is, Jack; something sthrange entirely has got into it. Wirra, man alive, what's to be done?'

"Jist as she spoke, the pot seemed to cut the buckle in prime style, and afther a spring that 'ud shame a dancin'-masther, off flew the lid, and out bounced the pudden itself, hoppin', as nimble as a pea on a drum-head, about the floor. Jack blessed himself, and Katty crossed herself. Jack shouted, and Katty screamed. 'In the name of goodness, keep your distance; no one here injured you!'

"The pudden, however, made a set at him, and Jack lepped first on a chair and then on the kitchen table to avoid it. It then danced towards Kitty, who was now repatin' her prayers at the top of her voice, while the cunnin' thief of a pudden was hoppin' and jiggin' it round her, as if it was amused at her distress.

"'If I could get the pitchfork,' said Jack, 'I'd dale wid it – by goxty I'd thry its mettle.'

"'No, no,' shouted Katty, thinkin' there was a fairy in it; 'let us spake it fair. Who knows what harm it might do? Aisy now,' said she to the pudden, 'aisy, dear; don't harm honest people that never meant to offend you. It wasn't us – no, in troth, it was ould Harry Connolly that bewitched you; pursue *him* if you wish, but spare a woman like me; for, whisper, dear, I'm not in a condition to be frightened – troth I'm not.'

"The pudden, bedad, seemed to take her at her word, and danced away from her towards Jack, who, like the wife, believin' there was a fairy in it, an' that spakin' it fair was the best plan, thought he would give it a soft word as well as her.

"'Plase your honour,' said Jack, 'she only spaiks the truth; an', upon my voracity, we both feels much oblaiged to your honour for your quietness. Faith, it's quite clear that if you weren't a gentlemanly pudden all out, you'd act otherwise. Ould Harry, the rogue, is your mark; he's jist gone down the road there, and if you go fast you'll overtake him. Be me song, your dancin' masther did his duty, anyhow. Thank your honour! God speed you, an' may you never meet wid a parson or alderman in your thravels!'

"Jist as Jack spoke the pudden appeared to take the hint, for it quietly hopped out, and as the house was directly on the road-side, turned down towards the bridge, the very way that ould Harry went. It was very natural, of coorse, that Jack and Katty should go out to see how it intended to thravel; and, as the day was Sunday, it was but natural, too, that a greater number of people than usual were passin' the road. This was a fact; and when Jack and his wife were seen followin' the pudden, the whole neighbourhood was soon up and afther it.

"'Jack Rafferty, what is it? Katty, ahagur, will you tell us what it manes?'

"'Why,' replied Katty, 'it's my big pudden that's bewitched, an' it's now hot foot pursuin' –'; here she stopped, not wishin' to mention her brother's name – 'someone or other that surely put pishrogues an it.'

"This was enough; Jack, now seein' that he had assistance, found his courage comin' back to him; so says he to Katty, 'Go home,' says he, 'an' lose no time in makin' another pudden as good, an' here's Paddy Scanlan's wife, Bridget, says she'll let you boil it on her fire, as you'll want our own to dress the rest o' the dinner: and Paddy himself will lend me a pitchfork, for purshuin to the morsel of that same pudden will escape till I let the wind out of it, now that I've the neighbours to back an' support me,' says Jack.

"This was agreed to, and Katty went back to prepare a fresh pudden, while Jack an' half the townland pursued the other wid spades, graips, pitchforks, scythes, flails, and all possible description of instruments. On the pudden went, however, at the rate of about six Irish miles an hour, an' sich a chase never was seen. Catholics, Prodestants, an' Prosbytarians, were all afther it, armed, as I said, an' bad end to the thing but its own activity could save it. Here it made a hop, and there a prod was made at it; but off it went, an' someone, as eager to get a slice at it on the other side, got the prod instead of the pudden. Big Frank Farrell, the miller of Ballyboulteen, got a prod backwards that brought a hullabaloo out of him you might hear at the other end of the parish. One got a slice of a scythe, another a whack of a flail, a third a rap of a spade that made him look nine ways at wanst.

"'Where is it goin'?' asked one. 'My life for you, it's on its way to Meeting. Three cheers for it if it turns to Carntaul.' 'Prod the sowl out of it, if it's a Prodestan',' shouted the others; 'if it turns to the left, slice it into pancakes. We'll have no Prodestan' puddens here.'

"Begad, by this time the people were on the point of beginnin' to have a regular fight about it, when, very fortunately, it took a short turn down a little by-lane that led towards the Methodist praichin-house, an' in an instant all parties were in an uproar against it as a Methodist pudden. 'It's a Wesleyan,' shouted several voices; 'an' by this an' by that, into a Methodist chapel it won't put a foot today, or we'll lose a fall. Let the wind out of it. Come, boys, where's your pitchforks?'

"The divle purshuin to the one of them, however, ever could touch the pudden, an' jist when they thought they had it up against the gavel of the Methodist chapel, begad it gave them the slip, and hops over to the left, clane into the river, and sails away before all their eyes as light as an egg-shell.

"Now, it so happened that a little below this place, the demesne-wall of Colonel Bragshaw was built up to the very edge of the river on each side of its banks; and so findin' there was a stop put to their pursuit of it, they went home again, every man, woman, and child of them, puzzled to think what the pudden was at all, what it meant, or where it was goin'! Had Jack Rafferty an' his wife been willin' to let out the opinion they held about Harry Connolly bewitchin' it, there is no doubt of it but poor Harry might be badly trated by the crowd, when their blood was up. They had sense enough, howandiver, to keep that to themselves, for Harry bein' an' ould bachelor, was a kind friend to the Raffertys. So, of coorse, there was all kinds of talk about it – some guessin' this, and some guessin' that –one party sayin' the pudden was of there side, another party denyin' it, an' insistin' it belonged to them, an' so on.

"In the manetime, Katty Rafferty, for 'fraid the dinner might come short, went home and made another pudden much about the same size as the one that had escaped, and bringin' it over to their next neighbour, Paddy Scanlan's, it was put into a pot and placed on the fire to boil, hopin' that it might be done in time, espishilly as they were to have the ministher, who loved a warm slice of a good pudden as well as e'er a gintleman in Europe.

"Anyhow, the day passed; Moll and Gusty were made man an' wife, an' no two could be more lovin'. Their friends that had been asked to the weddin' were saunterin' about in pleasant little groups till dinner-time, chattin' an' laughin'; but, above all things, sthrivin' to account for the figaries of the pudden; for, to tell the truth, its adventures had now gone through the whole parish.

"Well, at any rate, dinner-time was dhrawin' near, and Paddy Scanlan was sittin' comfortably wid his wife at the fire, the pudden boilen before their eyes, when in walks Harry Connolly, in a flutter, shoutin' – 'Blood an' blunderbushes, what are yez here for?'

"'Arra, why, Harry – why, avick?' said Mrs. Scanlan.

"'Why,' said Harry, 'the sun's in the suds an' the moon in the high Horicks! Here's a clipstick comin' an, an' there you sit as unconsarned as if it was about to rain mether! Go out both of you, an' look at the sun, I say, and ye'll see the condition he's in – off!'

"'Ay, but, Harry, what's that rowled up in the tail of your *cothamore* (big coat)?'

"'Out wid yez,' said Harry, 'an' pray aginst the clipstick – the sky's fallin'!'

"Begad, it was hard to say whether Paddy or the wife got out first, they were so much alarmed by Harry's wild thin face an' piercin' eyes; so out they went to see what was wondherful in the sky, an' kep' lookin' an' lookin' in every direction, but not a thing was to be seen, barrin' the sun shinin' down wid great good-humour, an' not a single cloud in the sky.

"Paddy an' the wife now came in laughin', to scould Harry, who, no doubt, was a great wag in his way when he wished. 'Musha, bad scran to you, Harry –.' They had time to say no more, howandiver, for, as they were goin' into the door, they met him comin' out of it wid a reek of smoke out of his tail like a lime-kiln.

"'Harry,' shouted Bridget, 'my sowl to glory, but the tail of your cothamore's a-fire—you'll be burned. Don't you see the smoke that's out of it?'

"'Cross yourselves three times,' said Harry, widout stoppin', or even lookin' behind him, 'for, as the prophecy says –Fill the pot, Eddy –' They could hear no more, for Harry appeared to feel like a man that carried something a great deal hotter than he wished, as anyone might see by the liveliness of his motions, and the quare faces he was forced to make as he went along.

"'What the dickens is he carryin' in the skirts of his big coat?' asked Paddy.

"'My sowl to happiness, but maybe he has stole the pudden,' said Bridget, 'for it's known that many a sthrange thing he does.'

"They immediately examined the pot, but found that the pudden was there as safe as tuppence, an' this puzzled them the more, to think what it was he could be carryin' about wid him in the manner he did. But little they knew what he had done while they were sky-gazin'!

"Well, anyhow, the day passed and the dinner was ready, an' no doubt but a fine gatherin' there was to partake of it. The Prosbytarian ministher met the Methodist praicher – a divilish stretcher of an appetite he had, in throth – on their way to Jack Rafferty's, an' as he knew he could take the liberty, why he insisted on his dinin' wid him; for, afther all, begad, in thim times the clargy of all descriptions lived upon the best footin' among one another, not all as one as now – but no matther. Well, they had nearly finished their dinner, when Jack Rafferty himself axed Katty for the pudden; but, jist as he spoke, in it came as big as a mess-pot.

"'Gintlemen,' said he, 'I hope none of you will refuse tastin' a bit of Katty's pudden; I don't mane the dancin' one that tuck to its thravels today, but a good solid fellow that she med since.'

"'To be sure we won't,' replied the priest; 'so, Jack, put a thrifle on them three plates at your right hand, and send them over here to the clargy, an' maybe,' he said, laughin' – for he was a droll good-humoured man – 'maybe, Jack, we won't set you a proper example.'

"'Wid a heart an' a half, yer reverence an' gintlemen; in throth, it's not a bad example ever any of you set us at the likes, or ever will set us, I'll go bail. An' sure I only wish it was betther fare I had for you; but we're humble people, gintlemen, and so you can't expect to meet here what you would in higher places.'

"'Betther a male of herbs,' said the Methodist praicher, 'where pace is –.' He had time to go no farther, however; for much to his amazement, the priest and the ministher started up from the table jist as he was goin' to swallow the first spoonful of the pudden, and before you could say Jack Robinson, started away at a lively jig down the floor.

"At this moment a neighbour's son came runnin' in, an' tould them that the parson was comin' to see the new-married couple, an' wish them all happiness; an' the words were scarcely out of his mouth when he made his appearance. What to think he knew not, when he saw the ministher footing it away at the rate of a weddin'. He had very little time, however, to think; for, before he could sit down, up starts the Methodist praicher, and clappin' his two fists in his sides chimes in in great style along wid him.

"'Jack Rafferty,' says he – and, by the way, Jack was his tenant – 'what the dickens does all this mane?' says he; 'I'm amazed!'

"'The not a particle o' me can tell you,' says Jack; 'but will your reverence jist taste a morsel o' pudden, merely that the young couple may boast that you ait at their weddin'; for sure if *you* wouldn't, *who* would?'

"'Well,' says he, 'to gratify them I will; so just a morsel. But, Jack, this bates Bannagher,' says he again, puttin' the spoonful o' pudden into his mouth; 'has there been dhrink here?'

"'Oh, the divle a *spudh*,' says Jack, 'for although there's plinty in the house, faith, it appears the gintlemen wouldn't wait for it. Unless they tuck it elsewhere, I can make nothin' of this.'

"He had scarcely spoken, when the parson, who was an active man, cut a caper a yard high, an' before you could bless yourself, the three clargy were hard at work dancin', as if for a wager. Begad, it would be unpossible for me to tell you the state the whole meetin' was in when they seen this. Some were hoarse wid laughin'; some turned up their eyes wid wondher; many thought them mad, an' others thought they had turned up their little fingers a thrifle too often.

"'Be goxty, it's a burnin' shame,' said one, 'to see three black-mouth clargy in sich a state at this early hour!' 'Thundher an' ounze, what's over them at all?' says others; 'why, one would think they're bewitched. Holy Moses, look at the caper the Methodis cuts! An' as for the Recther, who would think he could handle his feet at such a rate! Be this an' be that, he cuts the buckle, and does the threblin' step aiquil to Paddy Horaghan, the dancin'-masther himself? An' see! Bad cess to the morsel of the parson that's not hard at *Peace upon a trancher*, an' it of a Sunday too! Whirroo, gintlemen, the fun's in yez afther all – whish! more power to yez!'

"The sorra's own fun they had, an' no wondher; but judge of what they felt, when all at once they saw ould Jack Rafferty himself bouncin' in among them, and footing it away like the best o' them. Bedad, no play could come up to it, an' nothin' could be heard but laughin', shouts of encouragement, and clappin' of hands like mad. Now the minute Jack Rafferty left the chair where he had been carvin' the pudden, ould Harry Connolly comes over and claps himself down in his place, in ordher to send it round, of coorse; an' he was scarcely sated, when who should make his appearance but Barney Hartigan, the piper. Barney, by the way, had been sent for early in the day, but bein' from home when the message for him went, he couldn't come any sooner.

"'Begorra,' said Barney, 'you're airly at the work, gintlemen! But what does this mane? But, divle may care, yez shan't want the music while there's a blast in the pipes, anyhow!' So sayin' he gave them *Jig Polthogue*, an' after that *Kiss My Lady*, in his best style.

"In the manetime the fun went on thick an' threefold, for it must be remimbered that Harry, the ould knave, was at the pudden; an' maybe he didn't sarve it about in double quick time too. The first he helped was the bride, and, before you could say chopstick, she was at it hard an' fast before the Methodist praicher, who gave a jolly spring before her that threw them into convulsions. Harry liked this, and made up his mind soon to find partners for the rest; so he accordianly sent the pudden about like lightnin'; an' to make a long story short, barrin' the piper an' himself, there wasn't a pair o' heels in the house but was as busy at the dancin' as if their lives depinded on it.

"'Barney,' says Harry, 'just taste a morsel o' this pudden; divle the such a bully of a pudden ever you ett; here, your sowl! Thry a snig of it – it's beautiful.'

"'To be sure I will,' says Barney. 'I'm not the boy to refuse a good thing; but, Harry, be quick, for you know my hands is engaged, an' it would be a thousand pities not to keep them in music, an' they so well inclined. Thank you, Harry; begad that is a famous pudden; but blood an' turnips, what's this for?'

"The word was scarcely out of his mouth when he bounced up, pipes an' all, an' dashed into the middle of the party. 'Hurroo, your sowls, let us make a night of it! The Ballyboulteen boys for ever! Go it, your reverence – turn your partner – heel an' toe, ministher. Good! Well done again – Whish! Hurroo! Here's for Ballyboulteen, an' the sky over it!'

"Bad luck to the sich a set ever was seen together in this world, or will again, I suppose. The worst, however, wasn't come yet, for jist as they were in the very heat an' fury of the dance, what do you think comes hoppin' in among them but another pudden, as nimble an' merry as the first! That was enough; they all had heard of – the ministhers among the rest – an' most o' them had seen the other pudden, and knew that there must be a fairy in it, sure enough. Well, as I said, in it comes to the thick o' them; but the very appearance of it was enough. Off the three clargy danced, and off the whole wedderiners danced afther them, everyone makin' the best of their way home; but not a sowl of them able to break out of the step, if they were to be hanged for it. Throth it wouldn't lave a laugh in you to see the parson dancin' down the road on his way home, and the ministher and Methodist praicher cuttin' the buckle as they went along in the opposite direction. To make short work of it, they all danced home at last, wid scarce a puff of wind in them; the bride and bridegroom danced away to bed; an' now, boys, come an' let us dance the *Horo Lheig* in the barn 'idout. But you see, boys, before we go, an' in ordher that I may make everything plain, I had as good tell you that Harry, in crossing the bridge of Ballyboulteen, a couple of miles below Squire Bragshaw's demense-wall, saw the pudden floatin' down the river – the truth is he was waitin' for it; but be this as it may, he took it out, for the wather had made it as clane as a new pin, and tuckin' it up in the tail of his big coat, contrived, as you all guess, I suppose, to change it while Paddy Scanlan an' the wife were examinin' the sky; an' for the other, he contrived to bewitch it in the same manner, by gettin' a fairy to go into it, for, indeed, it was purty well known that the same Harry was hand an' glove wid the *good people*. Others will tell you that it was half a pound of quicksilver he put into it; but that doesn't stand to raison. At any rate, boys, I have tould you the adventures of the Mad Pudden of Ballyboulteen; but I don't wish to tell you many other things about it that happened – *for fraid I'd tell a lie.*"

Morraha

❖

MORRAHA ROSE IN THE MORNING and washed his hands and face, and said his prayers, and ate his food; and he asked God to prosper the day for him. So he went down to the brink of the sea, and he saw a currach, short and green, coming towards

him; and in it there was but one youthful champion, and he was playing hurly from prow to stern of the currach. He had a hurl of gold and a ball of silver; and he stopped not till the currach was in on the shore; and he drew her up on the green grass, and put fastenings on her for a year and a day, whether he should be there all that time or should only be on land for an hour by the clock. And Morraha saluted the young man courteously; and the other saluted him in the same fashion, and asked him would he play a game of cards with him; and Morraha said that he had not the wherewithal; and the other answered that he was never without a candle or the making of it; and he put his hand in his pocket and drew out a table and two chairs and a pack of cards, and they sat down on the chairs and went to card-playing. The first game Morraha won, and the Slender Red Champion bade him make his claim; and he asked that the land above him should be filled with stock of sheep in the morning. It was well; and he played no second game, but home he went.

The next day Morraha went to the brink of the sea, and the young man came in the currach and asked him would he play cards; they played, and Morraha won. The young man bade him make his claim; and he asked that the land above should be filled with cattle in the morning. It was well; and he played no other game, but went home.

On the third morning Morraha went to the brink of the sea, and he saw the young man coming. He drew up his boat on the shore and asked him would he play cards. They played, and Morraha won the game; and the young man bade him give his claim. And he said he would have a castle and a wife, the finest and fairest in the world; and they were his. It was well; and the Red Champion went away.

On the fourth day his wife asked him how he had found her. And he told her. "And I am going out," said he, "to play again today."

"I forbid you to go again to him. If you have won so much, you will lose more; have no more to do with him."

But he went against her will, and he saw the currach coming; and the Red Champion was driving his balls from end to end of the currach; he had balls of silver and a hurl of gold, and he stopped not till he drew his boat on the shore, and made her fast for a year and a day. Morraha and he saluted each other; and he asked Morraha if he would play a game of cards, and they played, and he won. Morraha said to him, "Give your claim now."

Said he, "You will hear it too soon. I lay on you bonds of the art of the Druid, not to sleep two nights in one house, nor finish a second meal at the one table, till you bring me the sword of light and news of the death of Anshgayliacht."

He went home to his wife and sat down in a chair, and gave a groan, and the chair broke in pieces.

"That is the groan of the son of a king under spells," said his wife; "and you had better have taken my counsel than that the spells should be on you."

He told her he had to bring news of the death of Anshgayliacht and the sword of light to the Slender Red Champion.

"Go out," said she, "in the morning of the morrow, and take the bridle in the window, and shake it; and whatever beast, handsome or ugly, puts its head in it, take that one with you. Do not speak a word to her till she speaks to you; and take with you three pint bottles of ale and three sixpenny loaves, and do the thing she tells you; and when she runs to my father's land, on a height above the castle, she will shake herself, and the bells will ring, and my father will say, 'Brown Allree is in the land. And if the son of a king or queen is there, bring him to me on your shoulders; but if it is the son of a poor man, let him come no further.'"

He rose in the morning, and took the bridle that was in the window, and went out and shook it; and Brown Allree came and put her head in it. He took the three loaves and three bottles of ale, and went riding; and when he was riding she bent her head down to take hold of her feet with her mouth, in hopes he would speak in ignorance; but he spoke not a word during the time, and the mare at last spoke to him, and told him to dismount and give her her dinner. He gave her the sixpenny loaf toasted, and a bottle of ale to drink.

"Sit up now riding, and take good heed of yourself: there are three miles of fire I have to clear at a leap."

She cleared the three miles of fire at a leap, and asked if he were still riding, and he said he was. Then they went on, and she told him to dismount and give her a meal; and he did so, and gave her a sixpenny loaf and a bottle; she consumed them and said to him there were before them three miles of hill covered with steel thistles, and that she must clear it. She cleared the hill with a leap, and she asked him if he were still riding, and he said he was. They went on, and she went not far before she told him to give her a meal, and he gave her the bread and the bottleful. She went over three miles of sea with a leap, and she came then to the land of the King of France; she went up on a height above the castle, and she shook herself and neighed, and the bells rang; and the king said that it was Brown Allree was in the land.

"Go out," said he; "and if it is the son of a king or queen, carry him in on your shoulders; if it is not, leave him there."

They went out; and the stars of the son of a king were on his breast; they lifted him high on their shoulders and bore him in to the king. They passed the night cheerfully, playing and drinking, with sport and with diversion, till the whiteness of the day came upon the morrow morning.

Then the young king told the cause of his journey, and he asked the queen to give him counsel and good luck, and she told him everything he was to do.

"Go now," said she, "and take with you the best mare in the stable, and go to the door of Rough Niall of the Speckled Rock, and knock, and call on him to give you news of the death of Anshgayliacht and the sword of light: and let the horse's back be to the door, and apply the spurs, and away with you."

In the morning he did so, and he took the best horse from the stable and rode to the door of Niall, and turned the horse's back to the door, and demanded news of the death of Anshgayliacht and the sword of light; then he applied the spurs, and away with him. Niall followed him hard, and, as he was passing the gate, cut the horse in two. His wife was there with a dish of puddings and flesh, and she threw it in his eyes and blinded him, and said, "Fool! Whatever kind of man it is that's mocking you, isn't that a fine condition you have got your father's horse into?"

On the morning of the next day Morraha rose, and took another horse from the stable, and went again to the door of Niall, and knocked and demanded news of the death of Anshgayliacht and the sword of light, and applied the spurs to the horse and away with him. Niall followed, and as Morraha was passing, the gate cut the horse in two and took half the saddle with him; but his wife met him and threw flesh in his eyes and blinded him.

On the third day, Morraha went again to the door of Niall; and Niall followed him, and as he was passing the gate, cut away the saddle from under him and the clothes from his back. Then his wife said to Niall:

"The fool that's mocking you, is out yonder in the little currach, going home; and take good heed to yourself, and don't sleep one wink for three days."

For three days the little currach kept in sight, but then Niall's wife came to him and said:

"Sleep as much as you want now. He is gone."

He went to sleep, and there was heavy sleep on him, and Morraha went in and took hold of the sword that was on the bed at his head. And the sword thought to draw itself out of the hand of Morraha; but it failed. Then it gave a cry, and it wakened Niall, and Niall said it was a rude and rough thing to come into his house like that; and said Morraha to him:

"Leave your much talking, or I will cut the head off you. Tell me the news of the death of Anshgayliacht."

"Oh, you can have my head."

"But your head is no good to me; tell me the story."

"Oh," said Niall's wife, "you must get the story."

"Well," said Niall, "let us sit down together till I tell the story. I thought no one would ever get it; but now it will be heard by all."

The Story

When I was growing up, my mother taught me the language of the birds; and when I got married, I used to be listening to their conversation; and I would be laughing; and my wife would be asking me what was the reason of my laughing, but I did not like to tell her, as women are always asking questions. We went out walking one fine morning, and the birds were arguing with one another. One of them said to another:

"Why should you be comparing yourself with me, when there is not a king nor knight that does not come to look at my tree?"

"What advantage has your tree over mine, on which there are three rods of magic mastery growing?"

When I heard them arguing, and knew that the rods were there, I began to laugh.

"Oh," asked my wife, "why are you always laughing? I believe it is at myself you are jesting, and I'll walk with you no more."

"Oh, it is not about you I am laughing. It is because I understand the language of the birds."

Then I had to tell her what the birds were saying to one another; and she was greatly delighted, and she asked me to go home, and she gave orders to the cook to have breakfast ready at six o'clock in the morning. I did not know why she was going out early, and breakfast was ready in the morning at the hour she appointed. She asked me to go out walking. I went with her. She went to the tree, and asked me to cut a rod for her.

"Oh, I will not cut it. Are we not better without it?"

"I will not leave this until I get the rod, to see if there is any good in it."

I cut the rod and gave it to her. She turned from me and struck a blow on a stone, and changed it; and she struck a second blow on me, and made of me a black raven, and she went home and left me after her. I thought she would come back; she did not come, and I had to go into a tree till morning. In the morning, at six o'clock, there was a bellman out, proclaiming that everyone who killed a raven would get a fourpenny-bit. At last you could not find man or boy without a gun, nor, if you were to walk three miles, a raven that was not killed. I had to make a nest in the top of the parlour chimney, and hide myself all day till night came, and go out to pick up a bit to support me, till I spent a month. Here she is herself to say if it is a lie I am telling.

"It is not," said she.

Then I saw her out walking. I went up to her, and I thought she would turn me back to my own shape, and she struck me with the rod and made of me an old white horse, and she ordered me to be put to a cart with a man, to draw stones from morning till night. I was worse off then. She spread abroad a report that I had died suddenly in my bed, and prepared a coffin, and waked and buried me. Then she had no trouble. But when I got tired I began to kill everyone who came near me, and I used to go into the haggard every night and destroy the stacks of corn; and when a man came near me in the morning I would follow him till I broke his bones. Everyone got afraid of me. When she saw I was doing mischief she came to meet me, and I thought she would change me. And she did change me, and made a fox of me. When I saw she was doing me every sort of damage I went away from her. I knew there was a badger's hole in the garden, and I went there till night came, and I made great slaughter among the geese and ducks. There she is herself to say if I am telling a lie.

"Oh! You are telling nothing but the truth, only less than the truth."

When she had enough of my killing the fowl she came out into the garden, for she knew I was in the badger's hole. She came to me and made me a wolf. I had to be off, and go to an island, where no one at all would see me, and now and then I used to be killing sheep, for there were not many of them, and I was afraid of being seen and hunted; and so I passed a year, till a shepherd saw me among the sheep and a pursuit was made after me. And when the dogs came near me there was no place for me to escape to from them; but I recognised the sign of the king among the men, and I made for him, and the king cried out to stop the hounds. I took a leap upon the front of the king's saddle, and the woman behind cried out, "My king and my lord, kill him, or he will kill you!"

"Oh! He will not kill me. He knew me; he must be pardoned."

The king took me home with him, and gave orders I should be well cared for. I was so wise, when I got food, I would not eat one morsel until I got a knife and fork. The man told the king, and the king came to see if it was true, and I got a knife and fork, and I took the knife in one paw and the fork in the other, and I bowed to the king. The king gave orders to bring him drink, and it came; and the king filled a glass of wine and gave it to me.

I took hold of it in my paw and drank it, and thanked the king.

"On my honour," said he, "it is some king or other has lost him, when he came on the island; and I will keep him, as he is trained; and perhaps he will serve us yet."

And this is the sort of king he was – a king who had not a child living. Eight sons were born to him and three daughters, and they were stolen the same night they were born. No matter what guard was placed over them, the child would be gone in the morning. A twelfth child now came to the queen, and the king took me with him to watch the baby. The women were not satisfied with me.

"Oh," said the king, "what was all your watching ever good for? One that was born to me I have not; I will leave this one in the dog's care, and he will not let it go."

A coupling was put between me and the cradle, and when everyone went to sleep I was watching till the person woke who attended in the daytime; but I was there only two nights; when it was near the day, I saw a hand coming down through the chimney, and the hand was so big that it took round the child altogether, and thought to take him away. I caught hold of the hand above the wrist, and as I was fastened to the cradle, I did not let go my hold till I cut the hand from the wrist, and there was a howl from the person without. I laid the hand in the cradle with the child, and as I was tired I fell asleep; and when I awoke, I had neither child nor hand; and I began to howl, and the king heard me, and he cried out that something was wrong with me, and he sent servants to see what was the matter with me, and when the messenger came he saw me covered with blood, and he could not see the child; and he went to the king and told him the child was not to be got. The king came and saw the cradle coloured with the blood, and he cried out "where was the child gone?" and everyone said it was the dog had eaten it.

The king said: "It is not: loose him, and he will get the pursuit himself."

When I was loosed, I found the scent of the blood till I came to a door of the room in which the child was. I went back to the king and took hold of him, and went back again and began to tear at the door. The king followed me and asked for the key. The servant said it was in the room of the stranger woman. The king caused search to be made for her, and she was not to be found. "I will break the door," said the king, "as I can't get the key." The king broke the door, and I went in, and went to the trunk, and the king asked for a key to unlock it. He got no key, and he broke the lock. When he opened the trunk, the child and the hand were stretched side by side, and the child was asleep. The king took the hand and ordered a woman to come for the child, and he showed the hand to everyone in the house. But the stranger woman was gone, and she did not see the king – and here she is herself to say if I am telling lies of her.

"Oh, it's nothing but the truth you have!"

The king did not allow me to be tied any more. He said there was nothing so much to wonder at as that I cut the hand off, as I was tied.

The child was growing till he was a year old. He was beginning to walk, and no one cared for him more than I did. He was growing till he was three, and he was running out every minute; so the king ordered a silver chain to be put between me and the child, that he might not go away from me. I was out with him in the garden every day, and the king was as proud as the world of the child. He would be watching him everywhere we went, till the child grew so wise that he would loose the chain and get off. But one day that he loosed it I failed to find him; and I ran into the house and searched the house, but there was no getting him for me. The king cried to go out and find the child, that had got loose from the dog. They went searching for him, but could not find him. When they failed altogether to find him, there remained no more favour with the king towards me, and everyone disliked me, and I grew weak, for I did not get a morsel to eat half the time. When summer came, I said I would try and go home to my own country. I went away one fine morning, and I went swimming, and God helped me till I came home. I went into the garden, for I knew there was a place in the garden where I could hide myself, for fear my wife should see me. In the morning I saw her out walking, and the child with her, held by the hand. I pushed out to see the child, and as he was looking about him everywhere, he saw me and called out, "I see my shaggy papa. Oh!" said he; "Oh, my heart's love, my shaggy papa, come here till I see you!"

I was afraid the woman would see me, as she was asking the child where he saw me, and he said I was up in a tree; and the more the child called me, the more I hid myself. The woman took the child home with her, but I knew he would be up early in the morning.

I went to the parlour-window, and the child was within, and he playing. When he saw me he cried out, "Oh! My heart's love, come here till I see you, shaggy papa." I broke the window and went in, and he began to kiss me. I saw the rod in front of the chimney, and I jumped up at the rod and knocked it down. "Oh! My heart's love, no one would give me the pretty rod," said he. I hoped he would strike me with the rod, but he did not. When I saw the time was short I raised my paw, and I gave him a scratch below the knee. "Oh! You naughty, dirty, shaggy papa, you have hurt me so much, I'll give you a blow of the rod." He struck me a light blow, and so I came back to my own shape again. When he saw a man standing before him he gave a cry, and I took him up in my arms. The servants heard the child. A maid came in to see what was the matter with him. When she saw me she gave a cry out of her, and she said, "Oh, if the master isn't come to life again!"

Another came in, and said it was he really. When the mistress heard of it, she came to see with her own eyes, for she would not believe I was there; and when she saw me she said she'd drown herself. But I said to her, "If you yourself will keep the secret, no living man will ever get the story from me until I lose my head." Here she is herself to say if I am telling the truth. "Oh, it's nothing but truth you are telling."

When I saw I was in a man's shape, I said I would take the child back to his father and mother, as I knew the grief they were in after him. I got a ship, and took the child with me; and as I journeyed I came to land on an island, and I saw not a living soul on it, only a castle dark and gloomy. I went in to see was there anyone in it. There was no one but an old hag, tall and frightful, and she asked me, "What sort of person are you?"

I heard someone groaning in another room, and I said I was a doctor, and I asked her what ailed the person who was groaning.

"Oh," said she, "it is my son, whose hand has been bitten from his wrist by a dog."

I knew then that it was he who had taken the child from me, and I said I would cure him if I got a good reward.

"I have nothing; but there are eight young lads and three young women, as handsome as anyone ever laid eyes on, and if you cure him I will give you them."

"Tell me first in what place his hand was cut from him?"

"Oh, it was out in another country, twelve years ago."

"Show me the way, that I may see him."

She brought me into a room, so that I saw him, and his arm was swelled up to the shoulder. He asked me if I would cure him; and I said I would cure him if he would give me the reward his mother promised.

"Oh, I will give it; but cure me."

"Well, bring them out to me."

The hag brought them out of the room. I said I should burn the flesh that was on his arm. When I looked on him he was howling with pain. I said that I would not leave him in pain long. The wretch had only one eye in his forehead. I took a bar of iron, and put it in the fire till it was red, and I said to the hag, "He will be howling at first, but will fall asleep presently, and do not wake him till he has slept as much as he wants. I will close the door when I am going out." I took the bar with me, and I stood over him, and I turned it across through his eye as far as I could. He began to bellow, and tried to catch me, but I was out and away, having closed the door. The hag asked me, "Why is he bellowing?"

"Oh, he will be quiet presently, and will sleep for a good while, and I'll come again to have a look at him; but bring me out the young men and the young women."

I took them with me, and I said to her, "Tell me where you got them."

"My son brought them with him, and they are all the children of one king."

I was well satisfied, and I had no wish for delay to get myself free from the hag, so I took them on board the ship, and the child I had myself. I thought the king might leave me the child I nursed myself; but when I came to land, and all those young people with me, the king and queen were out walking. The king was very aged, and the queen aged likewise. When I came to converse with them, and the twelve with me, the king and queen began to cry. I asked, "Why are you crying?"

"It is for good cause I am crying. As many children as these I should have, and now I am withered, grey, at the end of my life, and I have not one at all."

I told him all I went through, and I gave him the child in his hand, and "These are your other children who were stolen from you, whom I am giving to you safe. They are gently reared."

When the king heard who they were he smothered them with kisses and drowned them with tears, and dried them with fine cloths silken and the hair of his own head, and so also did their mother, and great was his welcome for me, as it was I who found them all. The king said to me, "I will give you the last child, as it is you who have earned him best; but you must come to my court every year, and the child with you, and I will share with you my possessions."

"I have enough of my own, and after my death I will leave it to the child."

I spent a time, till my visit was over, and I told the king all the troubles I went through, only I said nothing about my wife. And now you have the story.

And now when you go home, and the Slender Red Champion asks you for news of the death of Anshgayliacht and for the sword of light, tell him the way in which his brother was killed, and say you have the sword; and he will ask the sword from you. Say you to him, "If I promised to bring it to you, I did not promise to bring it for you"; and then throw the sword into the air and it will come back to me.

* * *

He went home, and he told the story of the death of Anshgayliacht to the Slender Red Champion, "And here," said he, "is the sword." The Slender Red Champion asked for the sword; but he said: "If I promised to bring it to you, I did not promise to bring it for you"; and he threw it into the air and it returned to Blue Niall.

The Three Crowns

THERE WAS ONCE a king, some place or other, and he had three daughters. The two eldest were very proud and uncharitable, but the youngest was as good as they were bad. Well, three princes came to court them, and two of them were the moral of the two eldest ladies, and one was just as lovable as the youngest. They were all walking down to a lake one day that lay at the bottom of the lawn, just like the one at Castleboro', and they met a poor beggar. The King wouldn't give him anything, and the eldest princes wouldn't give him anything, nor their sweethearts; but the youngest daughter and her true love did give him something, and kind words along with it, and that was better nor all.

When they got to the edge of the lake, what did they find but the beautifulest boat you ever saw in your life; and says the eldest, "I'll take a sail in this fine boat"; and says the second eldest, "I'll take a sail in this fine boat"; and says the youngest, "I won't take a sail in that fine boat, for I'm afraid it's an enchanted one." But the others overpersuaded her to go in, and her father was just going in after her, when up sprung on the deck a little man only seven inches high, and he ordered him to stand back. Well, all the men put their hands to their soords; and if the same soords were only thraneens they weren't able to draw them, for all sthrenth was left their arms. Seven Inches loosened the silver chain that fastened the boat and pushed away; and after grinning at the four men, says he to them: "Bid your daughters and your brides farewell for awhile. That wouldn't have happened you three, only for your want of charity. You," says he to the youngest, "needn't fear; you'll recover your princess all in good time, and you and she will be as happy as the day is long. Bad people, if they were rolling stark naked in gold, would not be rich. Banacht lath!" Away they sailed, and the ladies stretched out their hands, but weren't able to say a word.

Well, they were crossin' the lake while a cat'd be lickin' her ear, and the poor men couldn't stir hand nor foot to follow them. They saw Seven Inches handing the three princesses out of the boat, and letting them down by a nice basket and winglas into a draw-well that was convenient, but king nor princes never saw an opening before in the same place. When the last lady was out of sight the men found the strength in their arms and legs again. Round the lake they ran, and never drew rein till they came to the well and windlass, and there was the silk rope rolled on the axle, and the nice white basket hanging to it. "Let me down," says the youngest prince; "I'll die or recover them again."

"No," says the second daughter's sweetheart, "I'm entitled to my turn before you."

"And," says the other, "I must get first turn, in right of my bride." So they gave way to him, and in he got into the basket, and down they let him. First they lost sight of him, and then, after winding off a hundred perches of the silk rope, it slackened, and they stopped turning. They waited two hours, and then they went to dinner, because there was no chuck made at the rope.

Guards were set till morning, and then down went the second prince, and, sure enough, the youngest of all got himself let down on the third day. He went down perches and perches, while it was as dark about him as if he was in a big pot with the cover on. At last he saw a glimmer far down, and in a short time he felt the ground. Out he came from the big lime-kiln, and lo and behold you, there was a wood and green fields, and a castle in a lawn, and a bright sky over all. "It's in Tir-na-n Oge I am," says he. "Let's see what sort of people are in the castle." On he walked across fields and lawn, and no one was there to keep him out or let him into the castle; but the big hall door was wide open. He went from one fine room to another that was finer, and at last he reached the handsomest of all, with a table in the middle; and such a dinner as was laid upon it! The prince was hungry enough, but he was too mannerly to go eat without being invited. So he sat by the fire, and he did not wait long till he heard steps, and in came Seven Inches and the youngest sister by the hand. Well, prince and princess flew into one another's arms, and says the little man, says he, "Why aren't you eating?"

"I think, sir," says he, "it was only good manners to wait to be asked."

"The other princes didn't think so," says he. "Each of them fell to without leave nor license, and only gave me the rough side o' his tongue when I told them they were making more free than welcome. Well, I don't think they feel much hunger now. There they are, good marvel instead of flesh and blood," says he, pointing to two statues, one in one corner and the other in the other corner of the room.

The prince was frightened, but he was afraid to say anything, and Seven Inches made him sit down to dinner between himself and his bride, and he'd be as happy as the day is long, only for the sight of the stone men in the corner. Well, that day went by, and when the next came, says Seven Inches to him, "Now, you'll have to set out that way," pointing to the sun, "and you'll find the second princess in a giant's castle this evening, when you'll be tired and hungry, and the eldest princess tomorrow evening; and you may as well bring them here with you. You need not ask leave of their masters; they're only housekeepers with the big fellows. I suppose, if they ever get home, they'll look on poor people as if they were flesh and blood like themselves."

Away went the prince, and bedad it's tired and hungry he was when he reached the first castle at sunset. Oh, wasn't the second princess glad to see him! And if she didn't give him a good supper it's a wonder. But she heard the giant at the gate, and she hid the prince in a closet. Well, when he came in, he snuffed, and he snuffed, an' says he, "Be (by) the life, I smell fresh mate."

"Oh," says the princess, "it's only the calf I got killed today." "Ay, ay," says he, "is supper ready?"

"It is," says she; and before he ruz from the table he hid three-quarters of the calf and a kag of wine.

"I think," says he, when all was done, "I smell fresh mate still."

"It's sleepy you are," says she; "go to bed."

"When will you marry me?" says the giant; "you're puttin' me off too long."

"St. Tibb's Eve," says she. "I wish I knew how far off that is," says he; and he fell asleep with his head in the dish.

Next day he went out after breakfast, and she sent the prince to the castle where the eldest sister was. The same thing happened there; but when the giant was snoring, the princess wakened up the prince, and they saddled two steeds in the stables, and magh go bragh (the field for ever) with them. But the horses' heels struck the stones outside the gate, and up got the giant, and after them he made. He roared, and he shouted, and the more he shouted the faster ran the horses; and just as the day was breaking he was only twenty perches behind. But the prince didn't leave the Castle of Seven Inches without being provided with something good. He reined in his steed, and flung a short, sharp knife over his shoulder, and up sprung a thick wood between the giant and themselves. They caught the wind that blew before them, and the wind that blew behind them did not catch them. At last they were near the castle where the other sister lived; and there she was, waiting for them under a high hedge, and a fine steed under her.

But the giant was now in sight, roaring like a hundred lions, and the other giant was out in a moment, and the chase kept on. For every two springs the horses gave the giants gave three, and at last they were only seventy perches off. Then the prince stopped again and flung the second skian behind him. Down went all the flat field, till there was a quarry between them a quarter of a mile deep, and the bottom filled with black water; and before the giants could get round it the prince and princesses were inside the domain of the great magician, where the high thorny hedge opened of itself to everyone that he chose to let in.

Well, to be sure, there was joy enough between the three sisters till the two eldest saw their lovers turned into stone. But while they were shedding tears for them Seven Inches came in and touched them with his rod. So they were flesh and blood and life once more, and there was great hugging and kissing, and all sat down to a nice breakfast, and Seven Inches sat at the head of the table.

When breakfast was over he took them into another room, where there was nothing but heaps of gold and silver and diamonds, and silks and satins; and on a table there was lying three sets of crowns: a gold crown was in a silver crown, and that was lying in a copper crown. He took up one set of crowns and gave it to the eldest princess; and another set, and gave it to the second princess; and another set, and gave it to the youngest princess of all; and says he, "Now you may all go to the bottom of the pit, and you have nothing to do but stir the basket, and the people that are watching above will draw you up, princesses first, princes after. But remember, ladies, you are to keep your crowns safe, and be married in them all the same day. If you be married separately, or if you be married without your crowns, a curse will follow – mind what I say."

So they took leave of him with great respect, and walked arm-in-arm to the bottom of the draw-well. There was a sky and a sun over them and a great high wall, and the bottom of the draw-well was inside the arch. The youngest pair went last, and says the princess to the prince, "I'm sure the two princes don't mean any good to you. Keep these crowns under your cloak, and if you are obliged to stay last, don't get into the basket, but put a big stone, or any heavy thing, inside, and see what will happen."

So when they were inside the dark cave they put in the eldest princess first, and she stirred the basket and up she went, but first she gave a little scream. Then the basket was let down again, and up went the second princess, and then up went the youngest; but first she put her arms round her prince's neck and kissed him, and cried a little. At last it came to the turn of the youngest prince, and well became him – instead of going into the basket he put in a big stone. He drew on one side and listened, and after the basket was drawn up about twenty perch down came itself and the stone like thunder, and the stone was made brishe of on the flags.

Well, my poor prince had nothing for it but to walk back to the castle; and through it and round it he walked, and the finest of eating and drinking he got, and a bed of bog-down to sleep on, and fine walks he took through gardens and lawns, but not a sight could he get, high or low, of Seven Inches. Well, I don't think any of us would be tired of this way of living for ever! Maybe we would. Anyhow, the prince got tired of it before a week, he was so lonesome for his true love; and at the end of a month he didn't know what to do with himself.

One morning he went into the treasure room and took notice of a beautiful snuff-box on the table that he didn't remember seeing there before. He took it in his hands and opened it, and out Seven Inches walked on the table. "I think, prince," says he, "you're getting a little tired of my castle?"

"Ah!" says the other, "if I had my princess here, and could see you now and then, I'd never see a dismal day."

"Well, you're long enough here now, and you're wanting there above. Keep your bride's crowns safe, and whenever you want my help open this snuff-box. Now take a walk down the garden, and come back when you're tired."

Well, the prince was going down a gravel walk with a quick-set hedge on each side and his eyes on the ground, and he thinking on one thing and another. At last he lifted his eyes, and there he was outside of a smith's bawn gate that he had often passed before, about a mile away from the palace of his betrothed princess. The clothes he had on him were as ragged as you please, but he had his crowns safe under his old cloak.

So the smith came out, and says he, "It's a shame for a strong big fellow like you to be on the sthra, and so much work to be done. Are you any good with hammer and tongs? Come in and bear a hand, and I'll give you diet and lodging and a few thirteens when you earn them."

"Never say't twice," says the prince; "I want nothing but to be employed." So he took the sledge and pounded away at the red-hot bar that the smith was turning on the anvil to make into a set of horse-shoes.

Well, they weren't long powdhering away, when a stronshuch (idler) of a tailor came in; and when the smith asked him what news he had, he got the handle of the bellows and began to blow to let out all he had heard for the last two days. There were so many questions and answers at first that, if I told them all, it would be bed-time before I'd be done. So here is the substance of the discourse; and before he got far into it the forge was half filled with women knitting stockings and men smoking.

Yous all heard how the two princesses were unwilling to be married till the youngest would be ready with her crowns and her sweetheart. But after the windlass loosened accidentally when they were pulling up her bridegroom that was to be, there was no more sign of a well or a rope or a windlass than there is on the palm of your hand. So the buckeens that were coortin' the eldest ladies wouldn't give peace nor ease to their lovers nor the King till they got consent to the marriage, and it was to take place this morning. Myself went down out of curiosity; and to be sure I was delighted with the grand dresses of the two brides and the three crowns on their heads – gold, silver, and copper – one inside the other. The youngest was standing by, mournful enough, in white, and all was ready. The two bridegrooms came walking in as proud and grand as you please, and up they were walking to the altar rails when, my dear, the boards opened two yards wide under their feet, and down they went among the dead men and the coffins in the vaults. Oh, such screeching as the ladies gave! And such running and racing and peeping down as there was; but the clerk soon opened the door of the vault, and up came the two heroes, and their fine clothes covered an inch thick with cobwebs and mould.

So the King said they should put off the marriage, "For," says he, "I see there is no use in thinking of it till my youngest gets her three crowns and is married along with the others. I'll give my youngest daughter for a wife to whoever brings three crowns to me like the others; and if he doesn't care to be married, some other one will, and I'll make his fortune."

"I wish," says the smith, "I could do it; but I was looking at the crowns after the princesses got home, and I don't think there's a black or a white smith on the face of the earth could imitate them."

"Faint heart never won fair lady," says the prince. "Go to the palace, and ask for a quarter of a pound of gold, a quarter of a pound of silver, and a quarter of a pound of copper. Get one crown for a pattern, and my head for a pledge, and I'll give you out the very things that are wanted in the morning."

"Ubbabow," says the smith, "are you in earnest?"

"Faith, I am so," says he. "Go! Worse than lose you can't."

To make a long story short, the smith got the quarter of a pound of gold, and the quarter of a pound of silver, and the quarter of a pound of copper, and gave them and the pattern crown to the prince. He shut the forge door at nightfall, and the neighbours all gathered in the bawn, and they heard him hammering, hammering, hammering, from that to daybreak, and every now and then he'd pitch out through the window bits of gold, silver, or copper; and the idlers scrambled for them, and cursed one another, and prayed for the good luck of the workman.

Well, just as the sun was thinking to rise he opened the door and brought the three crowns he got from his true love, and such shouting and huzzaing as there was! The smith asked him to go along with him to the palace, but he refused; so off set the smith, and the whole townland with him; and wasn't the King rejoiced when he saw the crowns! "Well," says he to the smith, "you're a married man, and what's to be done?"

"Faith, your majesty, I didn't make them crowns at all; it was a big shuler (vagrant) of a fellow that took employment with me yesterday."

"Well, daughter, will you marry the fellow that made these crowns?"

"Let me see them first, father." So when she examined them she knew them right well, and guessed it was her true love that had sent them. "I will marry the man that these crowns came from," says she.

"Well," said the King to the eldest of the two princes, "go up to the smith's forge, take my best coach, and bring home the bridegroom." He was very unwilling to do this, he was so proud, but he did not wish to refuse. When he came to the forge he saw the prince standing at the door, and beckoned him over to the coach. "Are you the fellow," says he, "that made them crowns?"

"Yes," says the other.

"Then," says he, "maybe you'd give yourself a brushing, and get into that coach; the King wants to see you. I pity the princess." The young prince got into the carriage, and while they were on the way he opened the snuff-box, and out walked Seven Inches, and stood on his thigh. "Well," says he, "what trouble is on you now?"

"Master," says the other, "please to let me back in my forge, and let this carriage be filled with paving-stones." No sooner said than done. The prince was sitting in his forge, and the horses wondered what was after happening to the carriage.

When they came to the palace yard the King himself opened the carriage door to pay respect to the new son-in-law. As soon as he turned the handle a shower of stones fell on his powdered wig and his silk coat, and down he fell under them. There was great fright, and some tittering, and the King, after he wiped the blood from his forehead, looked very cross at the eldest prince. "My liege," says he, "I'm very sorry for this accidence, but I'm not to blame. I saw the young smith get into the carriage, and we never stopped a minute since."

"It's uncivil you were to him. Go," says he to the other prince, "and bring the young prince here, and be polite."

"Never fear," says he.

But there's some people that couldn't be good-natured if they were to be made heirs of Damer's estate. Not a bit civiller was the new messenger than the old, and when the King opened the carriage door a second time it's a shower of mud that came down on him; and if he didn't fume and splutter and shake himself it's no matter. "There's no use," says he, "going on this way. The fox never got a better messenger than himself."

So he changed his clothes and washed himself, and out he set to the smith's forge. Maybe he wasn't polite to the young prince, and asked him to sit along with himself. The prince begged to be allowed to sit in the other carriage, and when they were half-way he opened his snuff-box. "Master," says he, "I'd wished to be dressed now according to my rank."

"You shall be that," says Seven Inches. "And now I'll bid you farewell. Continue as good and kind as you always were; love your wife, and that's all the advice I'll give you." So Seven Inches vanished; and when the carriage door was opened in the yard, out walks the prince, as fine as hands and pins could make him, and the first thing he did was to run over to his bride and embrace her very heartily.

Everyone had great joy but the two other princes. There was not much delay about the marriages that were all celebrated on the same day, and the youngest prince and princess were the happiest married couple you ever heard of in a story.

The Fate of Frank M'Kenna

❦

THERE LIVED a man named M'Kenna at the hip of one of the mountainous hills which divide the county of Tyrone from that of Monaghan. This M'Kenna had two sons, one of whom was in the habit of tracing hares of a Sunday whenever there happened to be a fall of snow. His father, it seems, had frequently remonstrated with him upon what he considered to be a violation of the Lord's day, as well as for his general neglect of mass. The young man, however, though otherwise harmless and inoffensive, was in this matter quite insensible to paternal reproof, and continued to trace whenever the avocations of labour would allow him.

It so happened that upon a Christmas morning, I think in the year 1814, there was a deep fall of snow, and young M'Kenna, instead of going to mass, got down his cock-stick – which is a staff much thicker and heavier at one end than at the other –and prepared to set out on his favourite amusement. His father, seeing this, reproved him seriously, and insisted that he should attend prayers. His enthusiasm for the sport, however, was stronger than his love of religion, and he refused to be guided by his father's advice. The old man during the altercation got warm; and on finding that the son obstinately scorned his authority, he knelt down and prayed that if the boy persisted in following his own will, he might never return from the mountains unless as a corpse. The imprecation, which was certainly as harsh as it was impious and senseless, might have startled many a mind from a purpose that was, to say the least of it, at variance with religion and the respect due to a father. It had no effect, however, upon the son, who is said to have replied, that whether he ever returned or not, he was determined on going; and go accordingly he did. He was not, however, alone, for it appears that three or four of the neighbouring young men accompanied him. Whether their sport was good or otherwise, is not to the purpose, neither am I able to say; but the story goes that towards the latter part of the day they started a larger and darker hare than any they had ever seen, and that she kept dodging on before them bit by bit, leading them to suppose that every succeeding cast of the cock-stick would bring her down. It was observed afterwards that she also led them into the recesses of the mountains, and that although they tried to turn her course homewards, they could not succeed in doing so. As evening advanced, the companions of M'Kenna began to feel the folly of pursuing her farther, and to perceive the danger of losing their way in the mountains should night or a snow-storm come upon them. They therefore proposed to give over the chase and return home; but M'Kenna would not hear of it.

"If you wish to go home, you may," said he; "as for me, I'll never leave the hills till I have her with me." They begged and entreated of him to desist and return, but all to no purpose: he appeared to be what the Scotch call *fey* – that is, to act as if he were moved by some impulse that leads to death, and from the influence of which a man cannot withdraw himself. At length, on finding him invincibly obstinate, they left him pursuing the hare directly into the heart of the mountains, and returned to their respective homes.

In the meantime one of the most terrible snow-storms ever remembered in that part of the country came on, and the consequence was, that the self-willed young man, who had equally trampled on the sanctities of religion and parental authority, was given over for lost. As soon as the tempest became still, the neighbours assembled in a body and proceeded to look for him. The snow, however, had fallen so heavily that not a single mark of a footstep could be seen. Nothing but one wide waste of white undulating hills met the eye wherever it turned, and of M'Kenna no trace whatever was visible or could be found. His father, now remembering the unnatural character of his imprecation, was nearly distracted; for although the body had not yet been found, still by everyone who witnessed the sudden rage of the storm and who knew the mountains, escape or survival was felt to be impossible. Every day for about a week large parties were out among the hill-ranges seeking him, but to no purpose. At length there came a thaw, and his body was found on a snow-wreath, lying in a supine posture within a circle which he had drawn around him with his cock-stick. His prayer-book lay opened upon his mouth, and his hat was pulled down so as to cover it and his face. It is unnecessary to say that the rumour of his death, and of the circumstances under which he left home, created a most extraordinary sensation in the country – a sensation that was the greater in proportion to the uncertainty occasioned by his not having been found either alive or dead. Some affirmed that he had crossed the mountains, and was seen in Monaghan; others, that he had been seen in Clones, in Emyvale, in Five-mile-town; but despite of all these agreeable reports, the melancholy truth was at length made clear by the appearance of the body as just stated.

Now, it so happened that the house nearest the spot where he lay was inhabited by a man named Daly, I think – but of the name I am not certain – who was a herd or care-taker to Dr. Porter, then Bishop of Clogher. The situation of this house was the most lonely and desolate-looking that could be imagined. It was at least two miles distant from any human habitation, being surrounded by one wide and dreary waste of dark moor. By this house lay the route of those who had found the corpse, and I believe the door of it was borrowed for the purpose of conveying it home. Be this as it may, the family witnessed the melancholy procession as it passed slowly through the mountains, and when the place and circumstances are all considered, we may admit that to ignorant and superstitious people, whose minds, even upon ordinary occasions, were strongly affected by such matters, it was a sight calculated to leave behind it a deep, if not a terrible impression. Time soon proved that it did so.

An incident is said to have occurred at the funeral in fine keeping with the wild spirit of the whole melancholy event. When the procession had advanced to a place called Mullaghtinny, a large dark-coloured hare, which was instantly recognised, by those who had been out with him on the hills, as the identical one that led him to his fate, is said to have crossed the roads about twenty yards or so before the coffin. The story goes, that a man struck it on the side with a stone, and that the blow, which would have killed any ordinary hare, not only did it no injury, but occasioned a sound to proceed from the body resembling the hollow one emitted by an empty barrel when struck.

In the meantime the interment took place, and the sensation began, like every other, to die away in the natural progress of time, when, behold, a report ran abroad like wild-fire that, to use the language of the people, "Frank M'Kenna was *appearing*!"

One night, about a fortnight after his funeral, the daughter of Daly, the herd, a girl about fourteen, while lying in bed saw what appeared to be the likeness of M'Kenna, who had been lost. She screamed out, and covering her head with the bed-clothes, told her father and mother that Frank M'Kenna was in the house. This alarming intelligence naturally produced great terror; still, Daly, who, notwithstanding his belief in such matters, possessed a good deal of moral courage, was cool enough to rise and examine the house, which consisted of only one apartment. This gave the daughter some courage, who, on finding that her father could not see him, ventured to look out, and she *then* could see nothing of him herself. She very soon fell asleep, and her father attributed what she saw to fear, or some accidental combination of shadows proceeding from the furniture, for it was a clear moonlight night. The light of the following day dispelled a great deal of their apprehensions, and comparatively little was thought of it until evening again advanced, when the fears of the daughter began to return. They appeared to be prophetic, for she said when night came that she knew he would appear again; and accordingly at the same hour he did so. This was repeated for several successive nights, until the girl, from the very hardihood of terror, began to become so far familiarised to the spectre as to venture to address it.

"In the name of God!" she asked, "what is troubling you, or why do you appear to me instead of to some of your own family or relations?"

The ghost's answer alone might settle the question involved in the authenticity of its appearance, being, as it was, an account of one of the most ludicrous missions that ever a spirit was despatched upon.

"I'm not allowed," said he, "to spake to any of my friends, for I parted wid them in anger; but I'm come to tell you that they are quarrelin' about my breeches – a new pair that I got made for Christmas day; an' as I was comin' up to thrace in the mountains, I thought the ould one 'ud do betther, an' of coorse I didn't put the new pair an me. My raison for appearin'," he added, "is, that you may tell my friends that none of them is to wear them – they must be given in charity."

This serious and solemn intimation from the ghost was duly communicated to the family, and it was found that the circumstances were exactly as it had represented them. This, of course, was considered as sufficient proof of the truth of its mission. Their conversations now became not only frequent, but quite friendly and familiar. The girl became a favourite with the spectre, and the spectre, on the other hand, soon lost all his terrors in her eyes. He told her that whilst his friends were bearing home his body, the handspikes or poles on which they carried him had cut his back, and *occasioned him great pain*! The cutting of the back also was known to be true, and strengthened, of course, the truth and authenticity of their dialogues. The whole neighbourhood was now in a commotion with this story of the apparition, and persons incited by curiosity began to visit the girl in order to satisfy themselves of the truth of what they had heard. Everything, however, was corroborated, and the child herself, without any symptoms of anxiety or terror, artlessly related her conversations with the spirit. Hitherto their interviews had been all nocturnal, but now that the ghost found his footing made good, he put a hardy face on, and ventured to appear by daylight. The girl also fell into states of syncope, and while the fits lasted, long conversations with him upon the subject of God, the blessed Virgin, and Heaven, took place between them. He was certainly an excellent moralist, and gave the best advice. Swearing, drunkenness, theft, and every evil propensity of our nature, were declaimed against with a degree of spectral eloquence quite surprising. Common fame had now a topic dear to her heart, and never was a ghost made more of by his best friends than she made of him. The whole country was in a tumult, and I well remember the crowds which flocked to the lonely little cabin in the mountains, now the scene of matters so interesting and important. Not a single day passed in which I should think from ten to twenty, thirty, or fifty persons, were not present at these singular interviews. Nothing else was talked of, thought of, and, as I can well testify, dreamt of. I would myself have gone to Daly's were it not for a confounded misgiving I had, that perhaps the ghost might take such a fancy of appearing to *me*, as he had taken to cultivate an intimacy with the girl; and it so happens, that when I see the face of an individual nailed down in the coffin – chilling and gloomy operation! – I experience no particular wish to look upon it again.

The spot where the body of M'Kenna was found is now marked by a little heap of stones, which has been collected since the melancholy event of his death. Every person who passes it throws a stone upon the heap; but why this old custom is practised, or what it means, I do not know, unless it be simply to mark the spot as a visible means of preserving the memory of the occurrence.

Daly's house, the scene of the supposed apparition, is now a shapeless ruin, which could scarcely be seen were it not for the green spot that once was a garden, and which now shines at a distance like an emerald, but with no agreeable or pleasing associations. It is a spot which no solitary schoolboy will ever visit, nor indeed would the unflinching believer in the popular nonsense of ghosts wish to pass it without a companion. It is, under any circumstances, a gloomy and barren place; but when looked upon in connection with what we have just recited, it is lonely, desolate, and awful.

The Beresford Ghost

❖

"THERE IS at Curraghmore, the seat of Lord Waterford, in Ireland, a manuscript account of the tale, such as it was originally received and implicitly believed in by the children and grandchildren of the lady to whom Lord Tyrone is supposed to have made the supernatural appearance after death. The account was written by Lady Betty Cobbe, the youngest daughter of Marcus, Earl of Tyrone, and granddaughter of Nicola S., Lady Beresford. She lived to a good old age, in full use of all her faculties, both of body and mind. I can myself remember her, for when a boy I passed through Bath on a journey with my mother, and we went to her house there, and had luncheon. She appeared to my juvenile imagination a very appropriate person to revise and transmit such a tale, and fully adapted to do ample justice to her subject-matter. It never has been doubted in the family that she received the full particulars in early life, and that

she heard the circumstances, such as they were believed to have occurred, from the nearest relatives of the two persons, the supposed actors in this mysterious interview, viz., from her own father, Lord Tyrone, who died in 1763, and from her aunt, Lady Riverston, who died in 1763 also.

"These two were both with their mother, Lady Beresford, on the day of her decease, and they, without assistance or witness, took off from their parent's wrist the black bandage which she had always worn on all occasions and times, even at Court, as some very old persons who lived well into the eighteenth century testified, having received their information from eyewitnesses of the fact. There was an oil painting of this lady in Tyrone House, Dublin, representing her with a black ribbon bound round her wrist. This portrait disappeared in an unaccountable manner. It used to hang in one of the drawing-rooms in that mansion, with other family pictures. When Henry, Marquis of Waterford, sold the old town residence of the family and its grounds to the Government as the site of the Education Board, he directed Mr. Watkins, a dealer in pictures, and a man of considerable knowledge in works of art and vertu, to collect the pictures, etc., etc., which were best adapted for removal to Curraghmore. Mr. Watkins especially picked out this portrait, not only as a good work of art, but as one which, from its associations, deserved particular care and notice. When, however, the lot arrived at Curraghmore and was unpacked, no such picture was found; and though Mr. Watkins took great pains and exerted himself to the utmost to trace what had become of it, to this day (nearly forty years), not a hint of its existence has been received or heard of.

"John le Poer, Lord Decies, was the eldest son of Richard, Earl of Tyrone, and of Lady Dorothy Annesley, daughter of Arthur, Earl of Anglesey. He was born 1665, succeeded his father 1690, and died 14th October, 1693. He became Lord Tyrone at his father's death, and is the 'ghost' of the story.

"Nicola Sophie Hamilton was the second and youngest daughter and co-heiress of Hugh, Lord Glenawley, who was also Baron Lunge in Sweden. Being a zealous Royalist, he had, together with his father, migrated to that country in 1643, and returned from it at the Restoration. He was of a good old family, and held considerable landed property in the county Tyrone, near Ballygawley. He died there in 1679. His eldest daughter and co-heiress, Arabella Susanna, married, in 1683, Sir John Macgill, of Gill Hall, in the county Down.

"Nicola S. (the second daughter) was born in 1666, and married Sir Tristram Beresford in 1687. Between that and 1693 two daughters were born, but no son to inherit the ample landed estates of his father, who most anxiously wished and hoped for an heir. It was under these circumstances, and at this period, that the manuscripts state that Lord Tyrone made his appearance after death; and all the versions of the story, without variation, attribute the same cause and reason, viz., a solemn promise mutually interchanged in early life between John le Poer, then Lord Decies, afterwards Lord Tyrone, and Nicola S. Hamilton, that whichever of the two died the first, should, if permitted, appear to the survivor for the object of declaring the approval or rejection by the Deity of the revealed religion as generally acknowledged: of which the departed one must be fully cognisant, but of which they both had in their youth entertained unfortunate doubts.

"In the month of October, 1693, Sir Tristram and Lady Beresford went on a visit to her sister, Lady Macgill, at Gill Hall, now the seat of Lord Clanwilliam, whose grandmother was eventually the heiress of Sir J. Macgill's property. One morning Sir Tristram rose early, leaving Lady Beresford asleep, and went out for a walk before breakfast. When his wife joined the table very late, her appearance and the embarrassment of her manner attracted general attention, especially that of her husband. He made anxious inquiries as to her health, and asked her apart what had occurred to her wrist, which was tied up with black ribbon tightly bound round it. She earnestly entreated him not to inquire more then, or thereafter, as to the cause of her wearing or continuing afterwards to wear that ribbon; 'for,' she added, 'you will never see me without it'. He replied, 'Since you urge it so vehemently, I promise you not to inquire more about it'.

"After completing her hurried breakfast she made anxious inquiries as to whether the post had yet arrived. It had not yet come in; and Sir Tristram asked: 'Why are you so particularly eager about letters today?' 'Because

I expect to hear of Lord Tyrone's death, which took place on Tuesday.' 'Well,' remarked Sir Tristram, 'I never should have put you down for a superstitious person; but I suppose that some idle dream has disturbed you.' Shortly after, the servant brought in the letters; one was sealed with black wax. 'It is as I expected,' she cries; 'he is dead.' The letter was from Lord Tyrone's steward to inform them that his master had died in Dublin, on Tuesday, 14th October, at 4 p.m. Sir Tristram endeavoured to console her, and begged her to restrain her grief, when she assured him that she felt relieved and easier now that she knew the actual fact. She added, 'I can now give you a most satisfactory piece of intelligence, viz., that I am with child, and that it will be a boy'. A son was born in the following July. Sir Tristram survived its birth little more than six years. After his death Lady Beresford continued to reside with her young family at his place in the county of Derry, and seldom went from home. She hardly mingled with any neighbours or friends, excepting with Mr. and Mrs. Jackson, of Coleraine. He was the principal personage in that town, and was, by his mother, a near relative of Sir Tristram. His wife was the daughter of Robert Gorges, LL.D. (a gentleman of good old English family, and possessed of a considerable estate in the county Meath), by Jane Loftus, daughter of Sir Adam Loftus, of Rathfarnham, and sister of Lord Lisburn. They had an only son, Richard Gorges, who was in the army, and became a general officer very early in life. With the Jacksons Lady Beresford maintained a constant communication and lived on the most intimate terms, while she seemed determined to eschew all other society and to remain in her chosen retirement.

"At the conclusion of three years thus passed, one luckless day 'Young Gorges' most vehemently professed his passion for her, and solicited her hand, urging his suit in a most passionate appeal, which was evidently not displeasing to the fair widow, and which, unfortunately for her, was successful. They were married in 1704. One son and two daughters were born to them, when his abandoned and dissolute conduct forced her to seek and to obtain a separation. After this had continued for four years, General Gorges pretended extreme penitence for his past misdeeds, and with the most solemn promises of amendment induced his wife to live with him again, and she became the mother of a second son. The day a month after her confinement happened to be her birthday, and having recovered and feeling herself equal to some exertion, she sent for her son, Sir Marcus Beresford, then twenty years old, and her married daughter, Lady Riverston. She also invited Dr. King, the Archbishop of Dublin (who was an intimate friend), and an old clergyman who had christened her, and who had always kept up a most kindly intercourse with her during her whole life, to make up a small party to celebrate the day.

"In the early part of it Lady Beresford was engaged in a kindly conversation with her old friend the clergyman, and in the course of it said: 'You know that I am forty-eight this day'. 'No, indeed,' he replied; 'you are only forty-seven, for your mother had a dispute with me once on the very subject of your age, and I in consequence sent and consulted the registry, and can most confidently assert that you are only forty-seven this day.' 'You have signed my death-warrant, then,' she cried; 'leave me, I pray, for I have not much longer to live, but have many things of grave importance to settle before I die. Send my son and my daughter to me immediately.' The clergyman did as he was bidden. He directed Sir Marcus and his sister to go instantly to their mother; and he sent to the archbishop and a few other friends to put them off from joining the birthday party.

"When her two children repaired to Lady Beresford, she thus addressed them: 'I have something of deep importance to communicate to you, my dear children, before I die. You are no strangers to the intimacy and the affection which subsisted in early life between Lord Tyrone and myself. We were educated together when young, under the same roof, in the pernicious principles of Deism. Our real friends afterwards took every opportunity to convince us of our error, but their arguments were insufficient to overpower and uproot our infidelity, though they had the effect of shaking our confidence in it, and thus leaving us wavering between the two opinions. In this perplexing state of doubt we made a solemn promise one to the other, that whichever died first should, if permitted, appear to the other for the purpose of declaring what religion was the one acceptable to the Almighty. One night, years after this interchange of promises, I was sleeping with your father at Gill Hall, when I suddenly awoke and discovered Lord Tyrone sitting visibly by the side of the bed. I screamed out, and vainly endeavoured to rouse

Sir Tristram. "Tell me," I said, "Lord Tyrone, why and wherefore are you here at this time of the night?" "Have you then forgotten our promise to each other, pledged in early life? I died on Tuesday, at four o'clock. I have been permitted thus to appear in order to assure you that the revealed religion is the true and only one by which we can be saved. I am also suffered to inform you that you are with child, and will produce a son, who will marry my heiress; that Sir Tristram will not live long, when you will marry again, and you will die from the effects of childbirth in your forty-seventh year." I begged from him some convincing sign or proof so that when the morning came I might rely upon it, and feel satisfied that his appearance had been real, and that it was not the phantom of my imagination. He caused the hangings of the bed to be drawn in an unusual way and impossible manner through an iron hook. I still was not satisfied, when he wrote his signature in my pocket-book. I wanted, however, more substantial proof of his visit, when he laid his hand, which was cold as marble, on my wrist; the sinews shrunk up, the nerves withered at the touch. "Now," he said, "let no mortal eye, while you live, ever see that wrist," and vanished. While I was conversing with him my thoughts were calm, but as soon as he disappeared I felt chilled with horror and dismay, a cold sweat came over me, and I again endeavoured but vainly to awaken Sir Tristram; a flood of tears came to my relief, and I fell asleep.

"'In the morning your father got up without disturbing me; he had not noticed anything extraordinary about me or the bed-hangings. When I did arise I found a long broom in the gallery outside the bedroom door, and with great difficulty I unhooded the curtain, fearing that the position of it might excite surprise and cause inquiry. I bound up my wrist with black ribbon before I went down to breakfast, where the agitation of my mind was too visible not to attract attention. Sir Tristram made many anxious inquiries as to my health, especially as to my sprained wrist, as he conceived mine to be. I begged him to drop all questions as to the bandage, even if I continued to adopt it for any length of time. He kindly promised me not to speak of it any more, and he kept his promise faithfully. You, my son, came into the world as predicted, and your father died six years after. I then determined to abandon society and its pleasures and not mingle again with the world, hoping to avoid the dreadful predictions as to my second marriage; but, alas! In the one family with which I held constant and friendly intercourse I met the man, whom I did not regard with perfect indifference. Though I struggled to conquer by every means the passion, I at length yielded to his solicitations, and in a fatal moment for my own peace I became his wife. In a few years his conduct fully justified my demand for a separation, and I fondly hoped to escape the fatal prophecy. Under the delusion that I had passed my forty-seventh birthday, I was prevailed upon to believe in his amendment, and to pardon him. I have, however, heard from undoubted authority that I am only forty-seven this day, and I know that I am about to die. I die, however, without the dread of death, fortified as I am by the sacred precepts of Christianity and upheld by its promises. When I am gone, I wish that you, my children, should unbind this black ribbon and alone behold my wrist before I am consigned to the grave.'

"She then requested to be left that she might lie down and compose herself, and her children quitted the apartment, having desired her attendant to watch her, and if any change came on to summon them to her bedside. In an hour the bell rang, and they hastened to the call, but all was over. The two children having ordered everyone to retire, knelt down by the side of the bed, when Lady Riverston unbound the black ribbon and found the wrist exactly as Lady Beresford had described it – every nerve withered, every sinew shrunk.

"Her friend, the Archbishop, had had her buried in the Cathedral of St. Patrick, in Dublin, in the Earl of Cork's tomb, where she now lies."

* * *

The writer now professes his disbelief in any spiritual presence, and explains his theory that Lady Beresford's anxiety about Lord Tyrone deluded her by a vivid dream, during which she hurt her wrist.

Of all ghost stories the Tyrone, or Beresford Ghost, has most variants. Following Monsieur Haureau, in the Journal des Savants, I have tracked the tale, the death compact, and the wound inflicted by the ghost on the hand, or wrist, or brow, of the seer, through Henry More, and Melanchthon, and a mediaeval sermon by Eudes de Shirton, to William of

Malmesbury, a range of 700 years. Mrs. Grant of Laggan has a rather recent case, and I have heard of another in the last ten years! Calmet has a case in 1625, the spectre leaves

The sable score of fingers four on a board of wood.
Now for a modern instance of a gang of ghosts with a purpose!

When I narrated the story which follows to an eminent moral philosopher, he remarked, at a given point, "Oh, the ghost spoke, did she?" and displayed scepticism. The evidence, however, left him, as it leaves me, at a standstill, not convinced, but agreeably perplexed. The ghosts here are truly old-fashioned.

My story is, and must probably remain, entirely devoid of proof, as far as any kind of ghostly influence is concerned. We find ghosts appearing, and imposing a certain course of action on a living witness, for definite purposes of their own. The course of action prescribed was undeniably pursued, and apparently the purpose of the ghosts was fulfilled, but what that purpose was their agent declines to state, and conjecture is hopelessly baffled.

The documents in the affair have been published by the Society for Psychical Research (Proceedings, vol. xi., p. 547), and are here used for reference. But I think the matter will be more intelligible if I narrate it exactly as it came under my own observation. The names of persons and places are all fictitious, and are the same as those used in the documents published by the S.P.R.

FLAME TREE PUBLISHING

In the same series:
MYTHS & LEGENDS

Chinese Myths • Japanese Myths
African Myths • Greek & Roman Myths
Indian Myths • Native American Myths
Polynesian Island Myths • Aztec Myths
Scottish Myths • Arthurian Myths
Egyptian Myths • Norse Myths
Celtic Myths • Myths of Babylon

Also available:
EPIC TALES DELUXE EDITIONS

African Myths & Tales
Chinese Myths & Tales
Japanese Myths & Tales
Greek Myths & Tales
Native American Myths & Tales
Celtic Myths & Tales
Norse Myths & Tales
Witches, Wizards, Seers & Healers Myths & Tales
Gods & Monsters Myths & Tales
Heroes & Heroines Myths & Tales

flametreepublishing.com
and all good bookstores